THE GRAY CONSPIRACY

The Gray Conspiracy

J. S. HUNSAKER

Sense of Wonder Press
JAMES A. ROCK & COMPANY, PUBLISHERS
FLORENCE • SOUTH CAROLINA

The Gray Conspiracy by J. S. Hunsaker

SENSE OF WONDER PRESS
is an imprint of JAMES A. ROCK & CO., PUBLISHERS

The Gray Conspiracy copyright ©2009 by J. S. Hunsaker

Special contents of this edition copyright ©2009
by James A. Rock & Co., Publishers

*Front Cover photo ©1996, 2009 by J. S. Hunsaker: Ain Ghazal statue
Photo taken by the author at the Smithsonian Arthur Sackler Gallery
Back Cover Photo: Australian aborigine cave painting, c. 3000 B.C.*

Address comments and inquiries to:

SENSE OF WONDER PRESS
James A. Rock & Company, Publishers
900 South Irby, #508
Florence, SC 29501

E-mail:
jrock@rockpublishing.com   lrock@rockpublishing.com
Internet URL: www.rockpublishing.com

Trade Paperback ISBN-13/EAN: 978-1-59663-574-6

Library of Congress Control Number: 2007930241

Printed in the United States of America

First Edition: 2009

For

my

father

I miss you
Dad

Acknowledgments

There are many individuals who I would like to thank whose influence helped contribute to this novel. First I would like to thank my former wife, Cheryl, for her continued patience during the often arduous writing and editing process. I would also like to thank my friends for their love and support, especially Greg & Sharon Petrecca for standing by me when I needed them most. Also, a special thanks to Danielle Perozich, who was gracious enough to edit the first rough draft of this novel. I would also like to thank Dr. Robert Dillingham of the Pathology Lab at the Winchester Medical Facility in Winchester, Virginia, for his kindness and generosity in opening his offices to me. Additionally, I would like to thank the owners, management, and staff of The Red Fox Inn, in Middleburg, VA, for their friendship and support, especially Juliette. Finally I would like to thank my father, for everything he taught me, his wisdom, his charity, nobility, kindness, and sacrifice.

Contents

Foreword xi

PROLOGUE
Of Blacks and Grays 1

CHAPTER ONE
Grove Haven, May 1983 9

CHAPTER TWO
Dr. Gottlieb 34

CHAPTER THREE
Providence, Rhode Island, November 2003 47

CHAPTER FOUR
The Origins of Species.. 56

CHAPTER FIVE
Mr. Black 80

CHAPTER SIX
Ain Ghazal 90

CHAPTER SEVEN
Mr. Black's Confession 115

CHAPTER EIGHT
Nasca 136

CHAPTER NINE
Mr. Black Continues 152

CHAPTER TEN
Gottlieb's Capture 170

CHAPTER ELEVEN
Surgery 185

CHAPTER 12
Sarah Dawson 201

CHAPTER THIRTEEN
The Chase 206

CHAPTER FOURTEEN
Caught 222

CHAPTER FIFTEEN
Divine Providence 247

CHAPTER SIXTEEN
Back to the Present 261

CHAPTER SEVENTEEN
The Men in Black 268

Epilogue 274

Afterword 276

Sources 281

Foreword

Just what exactly is *The Gray Conspiracy*? Put simply, it is the lie we live with every day of our lives. It is the face we put on when we go to church. It is the mask of things 'being normal', upon which we are so dependent. It is the farce that we, for fear of chaos, desperately cling to like a child's security blanket. Put another way, it is the continued willful suppression of public knowledge concerning The Grays or Greys. And just who, or what, are The Grays? The Grays, in short, are a species of Extra-Terrestrials who have born witness to and have literally altered the face and history of man himself.

That's a pretty outlandish statement, isn't it? Well, yes. It is. But fortunately or unfortunately depending upon your interpretation, it is an accurate one.

UFO's and their occupants, the Grays, have always captured my imagination. Though I have never seen or beared witness to anything remotely resembling an Extra Terrestrial being, I have always been fascinated by the tales of people who have. The stories of Barney and Betty Hill, Roswell, and Travis Walton are perhaps some of the most renown and most compelling examples of UFO lore. And if we choose to believe even one of these incidents, we must accept the consequences and enormous burdens that these incidents describe. And what 'enormous burdens' could I possibly be referring to?

First, in all three incidents, the witnesses described that there were no more than three aliens present. Further, in their descriptions of the crafts, none of them detailed any crew quarters or living areas. From these two facts we may conclude that the crafts were not interstellar vehicles but rather short range reconnaissance vessels. And what can we conclude from this? That there must in fact be either a larger craft that transported them here, a fleet larger vessels, or a base of operations somewhere in close proximity to the earth. Historical evidence supports the latter, and indeed, Travis Walton in his autobiographical tale *Fire in the Sky*, describes seeing several craft of various sizes in a "hangar like room."

In addition to seeing the Grays themselves which he describes as looking "disturbingly like a human fetus," Walton also describes seeing humans who had "striking good looks" and were "smooth skinned, blemishless, and shared a family resemblance, although they were not identical." Although there are many things about this experience that we can speculate about concerning humans amongst the Grays, if we choose to believe this story, we must conclude that either there are human beings working in cooperation with the Grays, these humans were a product of genetic engineering, which would make sense given their familial resemblance, or an even more terrifying thought, that these humans are amongst us now carrying out an agenda for which purpose we can only begin to fathom. Such are a few examples of the 'enormous burdens' of belief. In any case, Travis Walton and the Hills were not the first human beings to be abducted by these creatures, nor will they be the last. Careful examination of the historical record clearly bears witness to the transgressions of these alien beings upon humanity.

This is what The Gray Conspiracy attempts to offer: a theory that connects historical evidence into a viable and logical explanation of events, past, present, and future concerning these creatures and their reason for involving themselves with humanity. To this end, I have enlisted the help of several fictional characters to tell this story. But to be clear, the characters themselves do not exist, nor do they resemble any living persons. Their purpose is purely to explore the possibilities of truth that, I believe, can and does exist, and theorize the meaning and more importantly, the consequences of public realization of the Grays themselves.

Like Dan Brown's now infamous best seller, *The Da Vinci Code*, *The Gray Conspiracy* is a novel that is speculative in nature: it is a theory based on fact and told through fictional people and storyline. Unlike Dan Brown, however, I have included a Sources section to the text in support of my arguments. Anything and everything (hopefully) that I looked at, read, watched, heard, or linked with on the Internet while researching and writing this novel of sorts can be found there.

Finally, the debate is not whether aliens exist. Anyone with an open mind who takes the time to study the archaeological evidence can and will see empirically, that they do. The real debate, or answer to the argument, is that we do not want them to exist. Why? Because it would serve to undermine everything that we have been taught and have come to believe. It would subvert order, distort faith, and cast doubt on our very being.

—*J. S. Hunsaker,*
August 10, 2004

Time always reveals Truth,
but seldom is Truth revealed in Time.
—Peter Paul Reubens

Of Blacks and Grays

The Gray Conspiracy. I refer to it as such because it is so intricate and obscure that one really doesn't know who, in fact, is involved; except of course the architects of the conspiracy, *the Grays* themselves. I have never actually had the pleasure of meeting a Gray, though I am probably exaggerating when I refer to the possibility of an interpersonal relationship, exchange, or chance encounter with one as a "pleasure." For those of you who are not familiar with what a "Gray" or "Grey" is, it is quite simply for purposes of this discussion, an alien, an extraterrestrial, a sentient being from another world. A "little green man" only they happen to be gray.

The standard description of a Gray you can find in virtually hundreds of thousands of websites, magazines, books, and articles pertaining to the subject of UFO's. In brief, they are described as what we would call short, 4-5 feet tall at most, with light gray skin, completely hairless, very large oval shaped heads that appear slightly disproportionate to their bodies which are thin, gangly and almost appear stretched as though put through a taffy machine. Their fingers are long and spindly; some say they have four or six, it really isn't important though. The most distinguishing feature about the Grays is their eyes, which are very large, very penetrating, and very, very, black.

The Grays have been traveling throughout the stars and here on this planet long before the human race was even conceived, and not by chance, it is very likely that it is they who conceived us. Perhaps the most used and convincing argument against the presence of the Grays usually runs along the lines of "Well if they were here, why don't they take over?" or something akin to that. The answer to that question lies within the inability of humans

1

to think more fourth dimensionally. We are so concerned about the "here and now" and what is happening within our own meager lives that we are unable to see or grasp the big picture from a cosmological point of view. To whom is this not happening? If you can travel the speed of light you can be alive for the birth and death of not just the human species, but can witness the end of time. Truly the human race is not ready for intergalactic space travel, the visitation of other worlds, and the consequences of the realization of these ideas. No. The Grays are far more devious, clever, and infinitely more patient than we are. Why take by force what you can take and control simply with the power of space and time?

It is a common fact we humans are only able to use about ten percent of our brain mass, which means ninety percent is really nothing more than wasted space, or, probably put more precisely, space that has yet to be filled with either information, function, or even possibly, *abilities*. As someone with years experience in the medicinal field I can attest that indeed, one can literally take a spoon and delve out a large helping from the cranium of someone and that person would for the most part be unaffected. One can only imagine what percent the Grays use of their minds. Someone knows. I'm sure *they* do.

There is actually quite a bit one can theorize and probably be very accurate about concerning the Grays and their evolution with just a little bit of earth science (I feel it necessary to point out here the conceit to which we humans place ourselves at the center of the universe. "Earth science" as we call it, should more appropriately be named "natural science." "nature study" or simply, "geology").

In any case, regarding *the Grays,* and using natural laws to our advantage, there is quite a wealth of information we can infer just from their mere appearance concerning their evolution, people, and world. For one, there is not much sunlight on their planet. It is probably very cloudy and dark. We can deduce this for several reasons. The first is their pigmentation; the Grays (according to witnesses) are indeed Gray, a very light gray, almost a white and their skin can almost be seen through when up close. Indeed, if it were sunny, the Grays would not be Grays but would be "tans" or no earthly pun intended, "blacks." Another reason we can theorize that sunny days are not the norm on "Gray-World" we'll call it, is their eyes.

Their eyes are their most striking feature; and indeed it is their eyes that paralyze you to the soul when you look into them. More than anything else, it is the eyes that brings witnesses to tears, howls of fear, literal shock, and invokes visions so terrible that those who have been unfortunate enough to see them wake in the night screaming in terror. It is the eyes that when looking upon you seemingly know your innermost thoughts and secrets, and can read your soul as quickly as glancing at a newspaper headline. Ever watchful and seemingly all-knowing, their eyes are a force to be reckoned with.

Interestingly enough their eyes, at least for the purposes of our discussion, betray them. For what happens to our eyes when we move to a dark room? The answer, of course, is they dilate and our pupils become bigger and blacker. Given the size of the Grays' eyes, they must come from a very dark place. And dark places in nature are vicious, cruel, and without mercy or want of life. This probably is another reason they only come at night; if they came during the day, aside from being extremely obvious, they might have difficulty actually seeing due to the sheer brightness of the sun, and quite obviously might incur severe sunburn.

Since we are on the subject, it is very likely that the size of their heads also has something to do with light-deprivation (the Grays are known as I will in time reveal, to have somewhat larger heads than ours, at least in proportion to their bodies). This may be somewhat of an evolutionary throwback, or scar, if you will—in dark places when we can't see our attention span and awareness instantly goes up, which requires a heightening of the senses and as a result greater brain activity. It's possible that their brain casings may have swelled through evolution to accommodate extra sensory perceptions needed to navigate, habituate, and pro-create on their world.

Or, the other possibility, of course, is that their craniums have increased in size due to demand placed upon them as they have evolved through countless millennia. In any case, I think we can agree that when we are in the dark, either physically or mentally, concerning a subject, we are forced to use our minds, even here, even now, this "reasoning" on this page, of the Grays themselves. Imagine what the human race would be capable of, if we were forced by nature to continually use our minds to survive—every waking moment a concentrated and deliberate thought for existence. No laughing, no crying, none of the emotional amenities we take for granted; simply the will to succeed, dominate, and control one's fate without rest or reprieve. No, I imagine we would be very powerful indeed.

Which brings us to our next conclusion concerning the anatomy of the Grays—their speech, or lack thereof. The Grays do not communicate verbally in the same manner that we do. Oh, they speak, but not with their mouths, which are really nothing more than tiny slits, possibly also evolutionary scars, (it is not known if they can actually use them or not). The Grays speak with their minds; indeed when they talk you hear them inside your head, not necessarily in tangible words but in feelings, expressions, or as most have unfortunately experienced, *intentions*.

It is basically a form of "thought projection," if you will, which also illustrates our argument concerning the darkness of their world. How do you find someone if you can not see them in the dark? You must sense them, and then you must feel them. Shouting in the dark not only takes up too much energy, but would create chaos amidst hundreds or thousands of people. You would need to develop some way of speaking to a particular individual that would not interfere or cloud the conversation of others. Hence, you would need to learn to speak with your mind and not your mouth, which would be small, as it would be for the most part, unused.

There are other things we can infer from Gray-World's dimness. For one, the flora and fauna of the planet are probably extremely limited, at least in comparison to our Earth. For it is the sun which allows for the evolution of birds, beasts, trees, and flowers in myriad countless assortments, and the ever changing, continually evolving climate on our earth. Gray-World, in its, I imagine, dark dreariness is very different. Due to the lack or limited amount of sunlight their world receives, any life that manages to evolve would be precious. It has been suggested by some that the Grays are perhaps photosynthetic; meaning, they do not eat directly or consume food as we do, but like plants receive and convert their energy directly from the sun. This would make sense given we have established that their world is probably a very dark one and as such limited in the fauna that is so abundant here on earth (this would also corroborate another supposed though not widely renown fact about them—they have no anus or excretory organs). With very little sun there on Gray-World there must be very few plants, very few animals, and very few food chains which ecological life here on earth, and everywhere else in the universe with a system such as ours, it would make sense that the Grays convert their energy from sunlight.

I think the Grays, though very much ahead on the evolutionary scale than we are, are somewhat envious of us. They do not eat or enjoy the wonderful pleasures of eating. They do not run and frolic in the sun or surf. All of life's simple pleasures they must forego because of the manner in which they evolved. I think they are somewhat repulsed by us and yet at the same time curiously envious. It has been said or rumored that they are a species of liars; they are devious and manipulative. They are prudish, methodical, and deliberate; forced to, no doubt, by their environmental upbringing.

In many ways, I think that they are somewhat ashamed—to be so superior and evolved yet they are unable to enjoy even the simple pleasure of eating a ripe peach or nectarine in the summer sun. But then again they don't need to, and perhaps they don't want to. Perhaps they are disgusted and sickened by the very thought of it. But whatever the case, they seem to be interested in us and the DNA we carry, the building blocks of life. To them, at least it would for the meantime appear, that is what is most sacred; the genes which allows them a purpose of existence, and what is also very possible and what should concern our world leaders most—ours. For the earth is an ocean teeming with life, and our planet is a veritable if not an actual Petri-dish to the Grays.

I have never understood why scientists and anthropologists are so skeptical that the human race evolved without outside genetic manipulation or influence. Given time, Natural Selection allows for great changes in any given species, but Artificial Selection is more methodical and almost infinitely faster. As any archaeologist will tell you, the human race has been the fastest evolving species in the history of the planet earth. We therefore must ask ourselves, how is it possible for Natural Selection to account for this purely on its own? If it were we must presume that there must be or have been other species that evolved here that are as intelligent as we, but there were not. Among other things, Artificial Selection from Extra-Terrestrials seeks to explain "the missing link" theory as it is so often referred to. It also helps to explain why the fossil record reflects there were certain "stages" of evolution of the human species, just as there were "stages" or "models" with Henry Ford's first automobiles, and some of these early humanoids were coexisting together at the same time.

The argument against this is, it would be quite impossible for a species to directly manipulate our evolution because we evolved over a period of millions of years and it is very doubtful that a species could be so long-lived, which is a very accurate statement if it were not for Einstein's theory of relativity. As we know, and has been proven by planes circling the earth at great speeds, time slows down the faster you approach the speed of light. What I, by the events that I shall unfold, have come to know is this: if the Grays have been manipulating our gene pool since the dawn of our creation, it would be very feasible to repeatedly visit the earth over millions of years, especially if they are traveling throughout the galaxy at near-light speeds.

Time on earth would continue as normal and for the Grays a million years or more could pass by their next visit—and I am certain they are no dummies when it comes to "timing" their space travel and earthly visitations. Indeed, they *must* be if they have vehicles that can traverse vast distances of the cosmos in short periods. Indeed, I believe, the changes to our DNA they are implementing on a global scale are directly related to the advancement and manipulation of the human species. They are here. Now. As I write these words on this page.

Since we are on the subject of our place in the universe, it happens to lie exactly on one of the spiraling outer arms of what we refer to as the Milky-Way galaxy. It takes somewhere in the realm of a quarter of a billion years; 250 million years to completely circumnavigate the center of our galaxy and make one complete rotation. Since the earth's creation, our sun and the solar system have only made this journey less than twenty times. We are, for lack of a better word, *newbies,* and are outright insolent to believe and culturally support the idea that we haven't been visited by extra-terrestrials in the past. But, that is where we find ourselves; and here we are.

Fortunately though, our society has grown by leaps and bounds in the past fifty years in terms of cultural awareness of our place in the cosmos, and raising the evil specter that aliens *might* exist elsewhere. Much of that we have to thank to the entertainment industry, though I cringe sometimes when I hear of (I say *hear* of because I will not bring myself to see them knowing the truth) films such as *Men in Black,* especially when I know that the real Men in Black are not gallivanting around the Earth protecting it's citizens from malicious alien entities. No. The real Men in Black, or "M.I.B.".s," for short, are assassins. And they are not protecting the Earth from evil *E. T.*'s; they are protecting us from ourselves.

At least that is their rationale. If it were discovered, and more importantly made public, that the human race has been genetically manipulated by aliens for millennia, there would be mayhem. Religions would fall, world markets would crash, people would run riot everywhere on the Earth, raping, pillaging, murdering—that sort of thing. The Men in Black's job is quite simple—to hunt down, kill, and neatly dispose of anyone and any evidence that might be a threat to leaking or proving the existence of the Grays to the public. And as I have come to find out, *no one* is exempt or safe from their treachery. They are specially selected, trained, bred, and rooted in the philosophy that public knowledge of the Grays would be the death of our culture.

If this ever were to happen, of course, there would be some excitement to be sure; but the middle class, who drives the economy and pays the bills for our nation have bills of their own—and those bills won't go away simply because there is now a world with aliens in it. Mortgages would still need to be paid, children would still need to go to college, and people would still need to eat ... all the things which we normal citizens go about on a daily basis would endure, as they should. We would endure. We would go on.

I imagine at some point they will reveal the truth or, probably put more accurately, the truth will be revealed, and it is here in this dilemma that I find myself. I can only hope that I will succeed in my lifetime; but the forces that pursue me in this quest are great, and can not be easily bartered or reasoned with. I only hope that if I fail someone will succeed in my place, and I am comforted by the fact that it is inevitable. I have learned through difficult and sometimes miraculous experiences, as I will relate, that it is the very *nature* of truth to reveal itself.

But until such time, we are emerged in those values and in a world of deceit, murder, and treachery concerning the subject; the paranoia which surrounds us is very real. But I have come to believe that if it was staged properly, safely, appropriately, we would be all right. The human race *will* survive, whether, in fact, we have been created by the Grays or not.

Speaking of survival, I am quite an oddity, having had an encounter with one of the notorious *Men in Black,* and lived to tell about it. I guess in the end I really have no evidence, just my experience, and who in the hell really cares about *that.* I am, after all, only a psychiatrist, or rather, I was when this tale all began—assigned to a little hall, in a tiny ward, in St. Paul, Minnesota. I have often wondered since then what forum would be appropriate to inform the world and everyone in it that everything that we have come to believe in is a *lie.* From what angle should I approach this argument so as not to appear insane myself, or offend and rile those who would so easily become zealots in the name of religious righteousness?

I only know that this story must be told; it needs be told. I have kept silent and have been in hiding, living under assumed names and aliases for twenty years, six months, eighteen days, and ten hours, and throughout each of them have had to wonder whether or not I should have chosen to remain like you—ignorant of the possibilities and sequestered from the truth.

But where to begin? Where should I start this truly fantastic and terrible saga? Perhaps I should start by introducing myself, or rather, who I was, for my true identity was taken from me by the nefarious agents I have just mentioned, and was buried those many years ago. My name is Dr. Evan Stattler, and the tale I am about to unfold concerns someone who was my patient.

CHAPTER ONE

Grove Haven, May 1983

The first time I heard the name of Dr. Jacob Francis Gottlieb was in early May, 1983, at the Grove Haven Federal Mental Institution in St. Paul, Minnesota. It was my first 'real' job within the psychiatric profession. My wife, Kathryn, and I had moved to St. Paul a year after we both graduated from John's Hopkins in Baltimore. Her parents both lived outside the city, and we moved to St. Paul in the fall of 1980 so that we could be closer to them as both were in their early eighties, their health was failing, and her father had had a heart attack the year before.

We married in the spring of 1981 and at the time we both interned at St. Mary's Hospital in downtown St. Paul. Kate was the first to land a career position after our internship at Grove Haven in Internal Medicine, and served as the assistant to Dr. Jonathan Bailey, the Chief Medical Physician for the medicinal care of the patients in the facility. I was accepted six months later to the Department of Psychology and was assigned to assist one of the senior psychologists on the board, Howard Jacobs.

On July 30, 1982, Kathryn had given birth to our son, David Malcolm Stattler, and we were both in the throes of being new parents. With our new positions secured at Grove Haven, we were able to squirrel away some money and purchased a small rambler in the same neighborhood as Kate's parents. They were without question the happiest years of my life, each day bringing new and exciting possibilities and stability for our growing family. I wanted it to last forever, indeed, I thought it would. But the forces of nature and the universe abhor a vacuum; there must be change, there will always be change; it is the forces of change that are inevitable. It is change that makes us grow and evolve as a species in what I was to find was in more ways than one. It was during a staff meeting after the New Year that the name of Dr. Jacob Francis Gottlieb would become forever entwined with mine.

* * *

"Dr. Stattler, are you paying attention?"

I was jolted to my senses by the Facilities Coordinator, and Director, Frank Sikes. Kathryn sat opposite me across the boardroom table and had been sneaking her foot up the leg of my trousers.

"Yes," I said, "new arrivals. Who do we have?"

"Well if you start listening instead of thinking for a change Dr. Stattler I will tell you," said Frank.

I turned and glowered at Kathryn who smiled and suppressed a giggle under her breath.

"So," Frank continued. "We have four newcomers to Grove Haven this morning. The first, Billy Dean, is an autistic savant. Apparently his parents can no longer afford to care for him and have relinquished custody and care for him to the state. The state, at this time, doesn't have any room for him at St. Mary's and he has, for the meantime, been turned over to us."

I looked at Frank as he paced slowly around the boardroom table. His muscular six foot four frame was imposing and commanded respect. He was the youngest Facilities Coordinator ever to serve at Grove Haven. At 45 to rise to such a position, took not only brains and ambition, but know-how. He was very certain of himself, very forthright, and very conservative, and though he and I differed on whether I was ready to receive tenure on the staff and have patients of my own without supervision, I nonetheless begrudgingly respected him. This was a real contention for me, as Kate was assistant to the Chief Medical Examiner and would perform duties and operations without supervision. After nearly eighteen months working under Howard, I was still not able to receive and monitor patients of my own.

Frank continued, "Howard, I'd like you to take him and outline if you can what his needs and comforts are. Savants are meticulous when it comes to establishing and adhering to a routine and it's important that we understand and begin to establish just what his routine is. Although his chart has his medical file and evaluations, it says nothing about *who* he is. I'd like us to have that information in his file, as it is just as imperative to his well-being as knowing his blood type. If you could have something on my desk by Thursday, that'd be a big help, as we still don't know for certain whether Mr. Dean will be staying with us permanently or going back to St. Mary's. In any case, if he's not staying with us, I want to give St. Mary's more information about him than they gave us."

I looked at Howard Jacobs who sat to my right as Frank handed him the dossier on Billy Dean. Howard was in his late thirties and had been with the facility for over six years. As I had finished my first year three months ago I was coordinating with him and assisting him with mundane tasks for all the patients he received.

"Next up is James Grant," Frank continued. "Convicted on a triple homicide in April of last year, you might have heard about this one in the news. Killed two little girls and his neighbor with a meat cleaver. Been in and out of prison and juvenile homes since the age of nine. Seems his lawyer got him off on an insanity plea with a life sentence at a federal institution, that's us. John, I'd like you to take this one. This guy's priors has your, shall I say, 'finesse' written all over it."

I looked across the table at John Stimple, who sat next to Kate and whom I always suspected had a crush on her, despite the obvious fact that we were married. I was never worried about this though, as his physical characteristics and mannerisms were something less than to be desired. His black, beady eyes, squinting through what must have been half-inch thick lenses held together in a rigid black late fifties, early sixties style frame, looked up at Frank as he held the file out to him.

John was in his mid-forties and had been at Grove Haven since he was my age. He was the one who always received the complete psychopaths, serial killers, or other degenerates and this seemed to suit him as there were times either through his strange manners or disheveled appearance that made me think he should be one of his own patients and not a physician. He had never married, was somewhat of a loner, and had a very nervous, almost obsessive-compulsive personality which I guess is why he preferred to take on, and which I also might add was very good at, diagnosing dissociate and psychotic disorders. This was somewhat of an oxymoron, of course, as he seemed to be somewhat dissociate himself. He was always wearing dark gray trousers and short-sleeve oxford shirts, usually white, though he did on oc-casion wear blue, and these shirts were always flanked by a pocket protector filled with both pens and pencils. He was constantly shifting his position, chewing on a pencil, or fidgeting with strands of his hair that hung in long loose tangles above his ears, dangling precariously from under a shiny bald head.

He took the file on James Grant carefully from Frank's fingers, opened it, and held it less than six inches from his face, his eyes darting back and forth almost frantically, as though searching for something. He quickly flipped the pages of the file, seeming to devour their contents. Finally after a few minutes of this he spoke.

"I'll, I'll, I'll have something for you tomorrow," he stuttered as he set the file down squarely in front of him and then quite purposefully set his pencil, which like all his writing instruments bore the signs of him chewing on the end, neatly at the top of it.

"Take your time, Stimple. The world's not going to end tomorrow and Mr. Grant is going to be with us here at Grove Haven for a very long time," said Frank, quite obviously very bemused with the spectacle that John Stimple unceasingly provided. "Which reminds me folks, has anyone had a chance to look at your new DSM's?"

Frank looked around the room and everyone groaned and sighed audibly as though in discomfort.

"I know they're not your preferred choice of literature but the state board feels and I have to say that I agree that they would like to get away from labeling patients of the sort of Mr. Grant here as 'psychopaths.' They feel that this term casts a negative stereotype due to recent films and negative stigmatization in the media and the press and would therefore like us to phase out this vocabulary in favor of the term 'antisocial', and I'll be expecting you all to comply here. There is a new sub-heading in the DSM entitled 'Antisocial Personality Disorders.' Please read up on it."

Dr. Stimple began to flip through his new edition of the *DSM-IV* barely before Frank could finish.

"All right, third on our list for the day we have Melissa Oakencroft, convicted last year for drowning her infant son. She's been appealing the case but the decision to have her incarcerated for six years was upheld by a federal appeals court after testimony from her first husband. Apparently he came forward after learning of her current troubles. Seems when they were married they, too, lost a child under suspicious circumstances which, at the time, was blamed on SIDS, Sudden Infant Death Syndrome."

Frank walked around the table while thumbing through the cases he held in his hand. He stopped in front of the only female psychologist at the facility and continued.

"Joan, I'd like you to take this one. At the risk of sounding sexist but as the only person of female persuasion serving on our staff you may possess certain insights that the rest of us might not. See what you can learn from her and try to determine whether or not she can be rehabilitated. Though not widely recognized as a quote 'disorder', Post-partum-depression is very real and I believe that her case though tragic is not unheard of. Pay attention to this one people as I think we're going to be seeing more and more of these cases in the future. In any case, Mrs. Oakencroft is going to be with us here for at least six years and I want a concrete diagnosis, pathology, meds, and treatment outlined when her turn comes up to go before the board."

I looked at Joan Cartwright who took the file firmly from Frank. She was slightly older than Kate and me, late thirties, very conservative and calculatingly cautious. She dressed like a school librarian, dark business suits, nothing revealing, very proper, hair tied neatly in a bun and glasses that were wrapped around her head and held in place on her authoritative brow with a braided gold chain. When she would speak to anyone except Frank Sikes, it was always with an annoyed 'Humph' or a sigh, as though whatever it was you were asking of her was a pointless and inane question which any two-year old would know the answer to. When she would speak to you, she would do so almost glaring over her glasses which continually slid down her nose in what I could only describe as a dim glower.

She was nonetheless, for all her social inadequacies, quite attractive, though she certainly did her best to hide this fact from anyone she came into contact with. She had a husky, sultry voice, when it wasn't condescending, which was a rarity, and she had a unique somewhat disconcerting habit of molding all of her responses into questions. Kathryn and I had tentatively christened her, 'The Ice Maiden', due to her unflattering appearance and mannerisms.

There was, I suspected, something uniquely false or contrived in her deliberate conservatism. Ever since I met her on my first day at Grove Haven, I thought or suspected of her as being someone afraid of her own sexuality, as though she was a kettle on the back burner of the stove, and when the lid blew and the sexual tension was inevitably released it might very well rip the penis off whatever poor soul was with her. I would have volunteered for this ominous task if it weren't for Kathryn, but Joan didn't seem to be fond of me much anyway. Both Kate and I noticed and remarked about on several occasions that the only man in the building she seemed to take a liking to was Frank, and I wondered if this were genuine or just an example of feminine scheming to 'get a-head' in the workplace.

She was, however, very striking, had seemingly flawless straight dark hair, and judging by the bun which she systematically wore day after day it must have hung nearly to her waist when she let it down, a sight that no one at Grove Haven to my knowledge had of yet beheld. Like my Kathryn, she had shapely, voluptuous hips, almost Reubanesque, though not quite so voluminous.

She flipped through the file briefly and then put it in her satchel, which she carried with her even to the bathroom. "I'll get right on it," she said, while looking squarely at Frank. Kate and I both looked at each other and rolled our eyes as I knew that we were both thinking this statement had a double meaning that I'm sure Joan thought was known only to her, and as I mentioned, both Kate and I thought that she would, in fact, 'get right on it' if Frank ever gave her the opportunity.

"Who's next?" I said, trying to break the quiet tension that had enveloped the room after Joan's demure response. I was also hoping for an opportunity to get assigned a case myself without Howard having to scrutinize my every deduction and decision. I had a lot of respect for Howard; he was honest, forthright, and distinguished. I generally felt and indeed had witnessed that as a psychiatrist he had helped a great many people. However, he seemed to have no difficulty with constructive criticism. There were several times with past patients I had clearly disagreed with his 'classical' interpretation of psychology, which in a facility such as ours was usually akin to just taking notes and doping the patients up on dopamine or lithium based stabilizers.

I felt that he was holding me back, and that I was ready to be released from under his wing and establish myself at Grove Haven. I had spoken to Frank several times in the past six months but his response was always an immutable, 'You need more time.' From his point of view as Director, I understood, he needed to be certain that all acting psychologists under his jurisdiction were adequately prepared and trained, not only for reasons of liability but for reasons of safety as well. Some of the patients we received were notorious murderers—human killing machines who, if the proper precautions were not strictly adhered to, could lead to severe injury or even death. Just last year an orderly named Sampson who is regularly assigned with me had his arm broken in three places by one of John Stimple's patients.

But still, I thought that Frank was being overprotective in his role as Director. After all, he hired me with the intention of having me be a Psychologist on his staff, I'd done my time, and I was ready. Not just for any case, a big case; a case that I could wow him with, to show him my potential as a physician within this facility. I was hungry, and worst of all, Frank knew it.

Frank looked at me, almost reproachfully when I asked the question about who was next, as he, and everyone else in the room knew if not suspected my enthusiasm to be officially welcomed into the fold as one of them.

"Next, Dr. Stattler is something of an enigma. Name's Jacob Francis Gottlieb, apparently barely escaped from the Nazi death camp of Bergen-Belsen. He immigrated to this country when he was ten years old in 1939, attended Yale through a scholarship in 1947, and later became one of the foremost archaeologists of his time. He has PhD's in archaeology and anthropology and a Masters in astrology. It says from his chart here that he was one of the United States foremost investigative archaeologists and has conducted excavations in Malaysia, Africa, Jordan, and Peru. He was one of the first scientists to propose that several species of early Hominids were evolving and co-existed at the same time. His findings have been both decorated and published in National Geographic, and he speaks German, French, Latin, and Farsi, in addition to English of course."

"So why is he here?" asked John Stimple, chewing on the cap of his pen.

Frank Sikes hesitated a moment before responding.

"It says here that in late November of 1963 he was diagnosed with Paranoid-Disorganized Schizophrenia at the ripe age of thirty-four, after returning from an excavation near Nasca, Peru." Frank flipped through his chart as though looking for something and then continued. "He had probably been ill for some time and it went largely undiagnosed because of time spent in the field and his expertise. Symptoms include delusions of grandeur, having conversations with people who aren't there, auditory hallucinations, wild mood swings, and bizarre, erratic behavior. He's been in altogether eight Federal Institutions in the past twenty years, Grove Haven being the ninth."

"Why the need for a federal institution? Surely if he's only suffering from schizophrenia he should be in a state-sponsored hospital?" Joan asked from across the table.

"That's not all," said Frank, the confident intonation of his voice changed to a much more dour tone. "He killed several men, maimed them, cut open their faces, neck, behind the ear, and these weren't just ordinary citizens that he butchered, these guys were federal agents with the NSA. He was tried, convicted, and sentenced to life imprisonment to a federal institution in a closed military court in the same year that he was diagnosed. Due to the occupation of the victims and nature of the killings the court's transcript was sealed and labeled classified."

"The NS what?" Howard interrupted.

Joan sighed, rolled her eyes in her typical 'Don't you know anything' expression.

It was I, who answered, deciding to take the opportunity to one-up and upstage my mentor. "The N.S.A., Howard, was created under the Truman administration. I believe it's the National Security Agency."

"Kudos to Dr. Stattler for that brief lesson in United States history," said Frank wryly. "Now then, as for the good Dr. Gottlieb, Stimple, I'll be giving this one to you as well."

"That's not fair Frank," I blurted out, barely even aware that I had said it, as I sometimes had the unfortunate habit of thinking out loud. This was one of those times when I wished I hadn't.

Director Sikes looked at me reproachfully from under his glasses and continued as though I hadn't actually said it at all. "Now then, unless anyone has anything to add I think we're finished for today."

Silence.

"All right, we'll reconvene Thursday morning and I'll be expecting a brief behavior analysis and a synopsis of recommended medications including dosages from those with new patients."

The boardroom became filled with the sounds of chairs scooting, pencils and papers being rustled, bodies rising and scuffling from the table, and shoes clacking on the polished tile floor.

"Dr. Stattler, can I speak to you for just a minute?" said Frank in a tone that implied that his request wasn't in fact a question, but rather an imperative.

I glanced sidelong at Kate who returned my stare as if to say, "I told you so."

I sighed and sank back into my chair and organized my folio on the table while bracing for the impact from Director Sikes, which was sure to be a barrage of rhetoric questions that I needn't bother answering. Only once everyone had left the room, the door was closed, and we were alone did he speak.

"Dr. Stattler do you disapprove of the manner with which I operate this hospital?" There was the first. He continued as though knowing that I wouldn't or couldn't answer such a base and pointless question.

"The reason I'm asking is that it appears to me and most of the people on this staff that you do, especially when you make proclamations condemning my judgment in the middle of a meeting."

I decided to be bold and illustrate an error of the obvious. "I wasn't aware that you spoke for everyone in this facility Dr. Sikes," I said.

He grimaced at this and then his face relaxed, probably not surprised by my rebuttal. He then paced slowly around the table until he stood in back of me where I couldn't see him, like a sergeant-at-arms during roll call.

"When it comes to the care of the patients under my supervision," he paused, leaned over until his face was even with my ear and then continued almost in a whisper, "*I do.*" He continued to walk slowly around the table, arms behind his back, gradually waving up and down a patient's file that moved in sync with his footsteps, quite obviously deliberating what his next statement would be. "You may find this hard to believe, Dr. Stattler, but I genuinely like and respect your work."

"Then why can't I have patients of my own yet, without being under Howard's supervision?" I interrupted.

"For the same reason we're having this discussion," he retorted, raising his voice slightly, and simultaneously slamming the file he was carrying behind his back down on the table to force home the point. He paused, realized his error in becoming agitated, and then continued in a much more subdued tone. "You're not ready."

"That's bullshit Frank," I said blankly. "Last time I checked, I had a Ph.D. just like everyone else. I've been working under Howard now for nearly eighteen months. I just think that it's time that I am let in the fold."

I stared at him forcefully, not backing down from this assertion and I could read in his face that he was clearly giving this some thought. He was silent, considering my words for a few moments and then continued. "Perhaps," he said. "But not for Gottlieb. This guy's been in and out of nine institutions. Nine, Dr. Stattler. And do you know why?"

"Why?" I asked, somewhat defiantly.

Frank walked back towards his chair at the head of the table and answered while sitting down. "Though it doesn't say it in his file and I'm certainly not surprised to see that it doesn't, because no one wants to put pen to paper and admit it, but this guy's probably trouble. No one wants to have him. This guy has two doctorates, PhD's Evan, and a Masters. He was the foremost thinker in archaeology for his time, and as it also happens, is a convicted murderer for a double homicide with a history and pattern of psychological illness. That makes him incredibly intelligent, cunning, patient, and because he's patient that also makes him dangerous. This guy would dance circles around you, Evan, and I'm not ready or willing to see or let that happen."

I sighed out loud at this, seemingly resolved to my fate.

"However," he said, and I looked up from the table with a ray of hope as he continued. "While I don't think you're ready for patients of the caliber of James Grant or Dr. Jacob Francis Gottlieb, I do think you're ready to take some patients on your own. Why don't you take the autistic kid from Howard?"

I sighed again heavily and said warily, "All right." While I wasn't getting the case that I really wanted I guess I could at least for the meantime rejoice as at least I could tell that Frank was trying to meet me halfway.

Frank could visually tell that I was still distressed and continued, "What's the matter? I've done the best I can do here, Evan, you said you wanted your own cases, so I'm giving them to you. What's the problem?"

"I wanted the Gottlieb case, Frank. I wanted a case that would help define my career."

"And you'll get those cases, Evan. Patience," he said, somewhat beseechingly.

"It's the patients that I want," I said underhandedly, quite pleased with myself at this punning retort.

Director Sikes huffed, leaned back in his chair, and began to fidget with his thumbs, quite obviously deep in thought. We sat together for nearly a minute in silence until he spoke. "Perhaps if your schedule permits it, you can assist Mr. Stimple with our good friend the Doctor. I think it would do you some good to watch Stimple, learn what he does, how he interacts with the somewhat less than to be desired cases he has. You've been under Howard for long enough."

I stared back at him blank faced, quite surprised that my persistence had gotten me this far, not only to receive patients of my own, but to assist with such a unique individual as Dr. Gottlieb, and the other severe cases that Stimple was regularly assigned to was, I felt, a great honor indeed.

"Thank you, Frank," I said, half-stammering.

"It's not you I'm doing the favor for, Evan. Stimple's a little overburdened right now. Nearly half the cases that come in here now are all violent offenders, and I need someone who is familiar with and can assume some of his workload. In retrospect I should have had you working with him instead of Howard. Report to Dr. Stimple this afternoon. He'll be interviewing his new arrivals in the staging area, and unless there is anything else, I believe we're finished here."

"No, I don't think so," I said, barely able to contain my enthusiasm.

"Very good, then I will see you later this afternoon on the observation deck."

I nearly ran out of the boardroom and down the long, white corridor to the O.R. where Kathryn was working. She was scrubbing up in the wash room, no doubt preparing for a surgery of some sort. I knocked on the door, which was open, and entered the room.

"Whatcha got?" I asked, while pointing to her gloves, referring to the operation she was about to perform.

"Nothing much. Dr. Bailey wanted me to remove some skin tabs from a couple of patients."

"Eeew. Always a favorite," I said sarcastically.

"What's up?" she said, as I sauntered up to her, quite coolly, attempting to feign my excitement, crossed my arms and leaned against the sink and cast a grim and dour expression over my face.

"Oh, not much," I said. "Seems I won't be working with Howard anymore."

"I told you to cool it," she said. "You shouldn't be countering Director Sikes in the middle of a meeting."

"Oh, he was pretty rough," I said.

"So what'd he say to you anyway?"

"Seems I'll be working with Stimple."

"Uh-huh," she said, while rolling and snapping on sterilized, plastic gloves, obviously not listening to what I was saying. I smiled at her pathetic attempt to placate me in what she assumed was an overwhelmingly unpleasant discussion with Frank.

"*And* I'll be assuming some of his caseload."

This she heard and she stopped putting on her gloves and looked at me dumbfounded. "You're kidding?"

"Nope," I smiled almost wickedly at her and reveled in her disbelief.

"What did you say to him?" she asked incredulously.

"I just convinced him of what a superior physician I was, how his judgment was for shit, and that I was going to be assuming all high-profile cases that walked through our doors."

"Now I know you're joking," she said, and we both laughed at this obvious distortion of the truth.

"Well Evan, that's wonderful. But seriously, what did you say?"

"I'll tell you over dinner tonight, I gotta grab lunch and then meet Frank in the observation lounge. He wants me to observe Stimple interact with his patients. He should be interviewing Grant and Gottlieb sometime after two and I don't want to be late."

"Ok. See you at six," she said, and resumed putting on her gloves. "And don't be late! The sitter charges us an extra half-day if we are."

"All right, all right," I said, while nodding to pacify her and exiting the door to the infirmary.

I had to admit, though I never expected to enjoy being a parent, my heart was filled with a special pride and longing every time I saw my son. And in truth, I never believed what other parents told me, how, 'it would be different' when it was your own. But I had to admit, if not sometimes begrudgingly, that they were right. It *was* different when it was your own. How or why I did not know. In my defense and procrastination in becoming a parent, I would always remember with the utmost clarity, visions of screaming infants in public restaurants or supermarkets, while the parent, usually the mother, would be desperately trying to coddle and shush the poor, miserable, child, much to the chagrin of nearly everyone in the vicinity. I vividly remember, and in fact, believed after witnessing every single one of these inevitable spectacles that life provides, that I would never give up my personal freedoms and actually choose to raise a child. What then, I wonder, had changed my mind?

I left and went down to the employee lounge. Wolfing through lunch, my mind was filled with excitement! I was going to finally be released from the dull and seemingly lifeless cases that Howard inevitably received. Sometimes it absolutely amazed me that our primary purpose here as physicians was to try and help these people or at the very least make their lives a little bit easier and more manageable. Instead, most often, we pumped them up full of meds, gave them a pat on the back, and let their brains attempt to sort through the quagmire of thinking, usually with some neurosis. They were undoubtedly nine times out of ten reeling from all the medication they had received, and sometimes so much so that they became life-size statues. I was sure to see more of this with Stimple's patients, who were usually violent with aggravated tendencies.

I stuffed down what was left of my sandwich while on the way to the observation lounge, which was a large room shielded from an examination room with a one-way mirror, and there were tables and chairs enough so that several physicians could meet and discuss patients as they were brought in. Below the mirror was a panel with a microphone which could be used to speak to those in the exam-room. There were also several speakers which broadcast the conversation of those inside, and, if needed, an emergency lever which activated an alarm to summon several orderlies if things got out of hand. We used the room primarily for training purposes, such as I was about to experience with John and the two patients he had received today. I sat down in a chair and waited for Dr. Stimple and Frank Sikes.

After about ten minutes Dr. Stimple entered the room heading towards a table and two chairs in the center, carrying a clip-board, several folders, and wearing a white physician's frock. Behind him, judging by the age of the man carefully gripped between two orderlies was the figure of what I assumed to be James Grant, the triple homicide whom I heard about in this morning's staff meeting. Dr. Sikes entered through the door behind me and pulled up a chair next to me in front of the one-way window and gave me a nod of recognition. He then flipped the 'AUDIO ON' switch on the panel in front of us and the room became filled with the sounds of John Stimple's voice.

"Please be seated," he said, while pointing to the chair that stood opposite him on the pink tile floor of the observation room. James Grant looked around the room with a somewhat dazed and confused expression.

"Sit down," he repeated encouragingly. The man, restrained by ankle and wrist braces, hobbled over to the chair and tried to sit down without falling over himself. One of the orderlies came over from against the wall to assist him. The orderly, Sampson, held his arms and gently guided James Grant into the chair below.

"I don't think we'll need those for now, Sampson," said Stimple, quite obviously trying to establish himself to James Grant as an authority figure who could be trusted. Sampson unbuckled the leather ankle wraps and wrist restraints that held him and retreated to his former place against the back wall of the room.

"Now then," said Dr. Stimple in a gentle voice, which was somewhat disconcerting as it so drastically contrasted with his makeshift and disheveled appearance. "Why don't we get to know each other better? My name is Dr. Stimple, and I'll be responsible for your care during your stay with us."

James Grant said nothing and looked at him suspiciously while simultaneously leaning back away from Dr. Stimple in his chair. He then looked around the room and at the two orderlies who were standing against the back wall on either side of the door frame.

"Do you know where you are?" asked Dr. Stimple.

James Grant seemed to ignore the question and continued to look around the room and gazed at the mirror behind which we were sitting.

"What's that?" he asked while pointing to the mirrored glass.

"Why don't we start with why you're here? Do you know where you are?" asked Dr. Stimple again patiently, trying to change the subject and put his patient at ease.

Silence.

James Grant continued to look around the room and then back at the two orderlies standing at the far wall.

"Who are they?" he asked.

"Those men are here to help you, James. May I call you James?" asked Stimple, trying to open the lines of communication. James Grant looked at John Stimple squarely and then shot his gaze away quickly as though he had seen something that had offended him. Dr. Stimple, unperturbed by this behavior pressed on while fidgeting with his pencil. "James, I'm going to ask you a few questions and then I'm going to show you some pictures and ask you some questions about them, would that be all right?"

James Grant replied with a muffled, "Uh-huh," while staring down at his shoes.

"James, I don't know whether anyone has told you this before but it's very impolite not to look at someone when they're talking to you."

James Grant looked up at Dr. Stimple for a moment and then returned his gaze downward to the pink tile floor. I could sense that Dr. Stimple was becoming slightly irritated, as he stopped fidgeting and set his pencil at the top of the folder near the middle of the table.

"James, I'm here to help you. But it's hard for me to talk to you when you're staring at the floor. Do you think you can lift your head up and talk to me for a few minutes?" Dr. Stimple asked patiently.

"Don't wanna," came the impudent response.

"And why is that?" Stimple asked inquisitively.

Silence.

"James, why is that?" he repeated.

James Grant looked up from the floor and around the room, deliberately avoiding any eye contact with Dr. Stimple.

"James, if you don't talk to me those two men back there will have to put the restraints back on and take you back to your room. Now you don't want that to happen, and I'd like to learn a little bit more about you. Now, why don't you want to talk to me?" Stimple addressed him more sternly this time, his patience clearly beginning to wane.

"Because you're ugly," he sneered.

I couldn't help but suppress a chuckle and Dr. Sikes looked over at me disapprovingly. "Sorry," I said, and re-focused my attention to the two individuals in the examination room.

"I see," said Dr. Stimple unfazed. Undoubtedly, he had heard worse things in his adolescence to say nothing from his patients. "Well how about this, if you have trouble looking at me maybe then you can look at some pictures and tell me what you think they look like. Would that be all right?"

James Grant nodded his head while staring down at the table. Dr. Stimple reached into his attaché case and removed a notepad and a series of Rorschach inkblot drawings, still widely used within our field and even in the early eighties, as the cornerstone of a revealing interview technique. Dr. Stimple set the drawings on the folder in front of him and slipped one underneath James Grant's face, which was still downcast upon the wooden table.

"Now James, I'd like you to look at these pictures and tell me the first thing that pops into your head when you see them. Ok?"

James Grant nodded in silent assertion.

"All right, what does this picture look like to you?"

He studied the print for a moment and said, "Hornets."

John Stimple jotted some notes on his pad and said, "Very good," while handing him the next slide.

"A thunderstorm."

Dr. Stimple kept scribbling on his note pad and while pushing up his glasses which had begun to slide down his nose handed him the next picture.

"A snake," was the next response.

This proceeded for about five to ten minutes until they had gone through the stack of black-ink blot slides.

"Very good James," Dr. Stimple responded while simultaneously scribbling on his pad. "Now I'm going to show you some drawings that are similar but instead of being only black and white have several colors on them."

He then slid one of the drawings under the nose of James Grant who still had his head glued to the table. He stared at it for a few seconds and then began to grip his stomach while laughing hysterically. I looked at Frank who shrugged his shoulders as if to say, 'Beats me.'

Dr. Stimple seemed to be taken unawares by this and he asked, "James, do you see something funny?" James Grant continued to laugh out loud in response.

"James what do you see that's so humorous."

James Grant gradually came to his senses, finally looked up at Dr. Stimple and said while half-laughing, "It looks like you doc," as he erupted into another fit of pealing laughter and pounded the palm of his hand on the table while gripping his mid-section with the other.

I could not help but laugh out loud when I heard this and the observation lounge was briefly filled with the echoing laughter of Dr. Stimple's patient and my own.

"That's not funny," said Frank turning to me.

I looked at the sour expression of Dr. Stimple through the window and again began to chuckle. "Oh come on, use your imagination Frank," I said, while peering through the glass at the drawing on the table. "You see, that blank spot is his bald head; the circles are his glasses, and see that funny-shaped triangle—that's his hooked nose." I continued to laugh and even Frank began to chuckle under his breath once I pointed out the resemblance.

"All right, maybe it is a little," Frank admitted. "But don't tell anyone I said so or you'll get us both into trouble." And we both continued to snicker at poor John Stimple's expense.

Once the laughter had died down and James Grant returned to normal Dr. Stimple resumed the blot-tests.

"Hurricane," was the next response, "Tornado," the next, "Lightening storm," and so on. Dr. Stimple dug through his stack and handed him the next picture.

"I'm very concerned about the images you've described here James."

James Grant was silent at this and Dr. Stimple continued. "All of the things you've characterized here are violent forces of nature. Do you realize that, James?"

James Grant sat motionless, staring down at the table at the picture in front of him.

"Why do you think that is James?"

James Grant stretched his arms forward across the surface of the table, deliberating over Dr. Stimple's question.

"I don't know," he choked from under his breath.

"Well what do you think?" asked Stimple inquisitively.

"I don't know," he said again.

"Would you like to know what I think, James?"

No answer.

"I think that you're someone who has a history of violent behavior. I think that there is something empirically wrong with your thought processes. I think the violence you've contributed to is some sort of acting out, some sort of retribution or repetition from a past event, possibly from a disturbing incident in your childhood. I think you need treatment. I think you need help."

James Grant still sat motionless at the table, absorbing what Dr. Stimple had said to him. After about thirty-seconds of silence he looked up at Dr. Stimple for the second time and stared at him squarely in the face. He handed the colored inkblot drawing to him and said, "You didn't ask me what I see."

"What do you see James?" Dr. Stimple asked in a comforting tone.

"I see an ugly doctor," he said, and leaning forward, half-rising from his seat he continued. "I see an ugly doctor with a pencil in his neck."

Before anyone realized what was happening James Grant grabbed the pencil John Stimple had set down at the top of his note pad and thrust it forcefully into his jugular. Blood poured forth like a fountain onto the table between them as Stimple clasped his throat and collapsed on the floor making a horrible gurgling noise. James Grant turned to face the orderlies who were now sprinting from their positions against the wall and kicked Sampson square in the chest. He fell backward and skidded across the polished tile floor. I slammed my palm onto the emergency lever and pulled it. The alarm began to sound and it echoed throughout the room. James Grant looked up at the speaker which was blaring and then turned his attention to the other orderly who was heading toward him and they began to saunter around each other like boxers in a ring, each probing one another for an advantage.

"Come on big boy, come to Papa. I'll give your big, black ass a whippin' you won't soon forget," he said.

Frank raced to a small cabinet on the wall pulled out a syringe and began to fill it from a small vial that was located inside. "Come on," he said, as we both raced out the door to the interrogation room. By the time we reached the door two more orderlies had joined us. As we scrambled inside, James Grant was beginning to make short work of the orderly that stood opposite him in the middle of the room.

He was pounding his face with a barrage of fists, and I could see his head jerking back and forth from the blows.

"Take him," Frank commanded to the orderlies, and we all rushed forward and circled around the frenzied Grant. One of the orderlies lunged at him and as he moved to respond to the blow I circled around him, grabbed him in a headlock and pulled him down to the table. The other three orderlies wasted no time and held down and secured his arms as he thrashed about wildly.

"Hold on to him, this should only take a second," said Director Sikes, flicking the syringe to remove any excess air bubbles. I still had my grip around his head and I began to feel him biting my arm through my coat. I began to scream in pain as Frank plunged the needle into his arm and injected the contents. I felt Grant's body go limp beneath me, and my attention was diverted to Dr. Stimple, who began to paw at me, still bleeding and writhing in agony on the examination room floor.

I grabbed one of the orderlies and said practically yelling at him, "Go get Kathryn here, now!" and he dashed frantically down the corridor. I watched him run out of the room as fast as his rotund body would take him, and I was about to turn to Dr. Sikes when my attention was diverted by Dr. Stimple who was tugging on my pant-leg on the floor. I leaned over his face and began to examine the wound to his throat. The pencil appeared to have slid between several major arteries and must have at least slightly nicked one of them as blood seemed to be almost pouring from the wound. I stood up, took off my belt and leaned over him once more.

"This may hurt a bit," I said, and Dr. Stimple grimaced and nodded as though giving me approval to proceed. I pulled on the pencil and it came clear of his neck. Blood spattered my forehead and sprayed into my hair. There was no question about it, James Grant had struck home with his blow and if Kathryn didn't get here soon and I didn't act quickly Dr. Stimple might very well bleed to death on the examination room floor. I put my thumb over the wound.

"Sampson, give me your shirt!" I yelled.

Sampson, who had risen off the floor about a minute earlier, was still gripping his chest where James Grant had kicked him. Wasting no time, he tore off his white orderly's jacket, spraying its pearlescent buttons into the air and on to the floor, and one of them rolled right in front of me until it plopped over into a puddle of Dr. Stimple's blood, which was pooling and growing in size with every second next to my knee. Sampson continued to undress and handed me his white orderlies' shirt-jacket. I took it with my free hand and spun it like you would a wet-towel until it for the most part collected into a single long strand, and then carefully wrapped it around Stimple's neck. I slipped my belt under his head and passed the free end through the loop.

"Hold on," I said, as I tightened the makeshift bandage around his neck.

Not soon after Kathryn came through the door with two more orderlies who were pushing a gurney. They wheeled it over to our position by the desk and chairs that had been toppled over in the melee in the center of the room. Kathryn looked at me and then down at Stimple.

"Let's get him up," she said.

Dr. Sikes, Sampson, another orderly whom I didn't recognize and I, each took hold of one of Dr. Stimple's appendages and hoisted him up on the gurney. Kathryn leaned over John loosened my belt strap and with the end of her pencil peered under the rapidly reddening orderlies' coat. Dr. Stimple shook, and inhaled deeply in protest. She turned to Sampson and the other orderly.

"Get him down to ER stat, and have Dr. Bailey scrub and meet me in the OR. We'll examine your injuries after we get him stabilized."

The other orderly and Sampson rushed off pushing poor Dr. Stimple and I could hear the wheels of the gurney rustling over the alarm which was still blaring. I barely turned to face Dr. Sikes before he addressed me sternly.

"Get Howard, Joan, and Kathryn as soon as she's able and have every-one in a staff meeting in one hour." He then turned to the one orderly who was remaining.

"Shut that thing off will you," he said, while nodding his head toward the ceiling. "And get him out of here and in to isolation." I looked down at James Grant, as he said this, who was still lying motionless on the table. He then strode out of the room with an angered, irritated look, and I was not looking forward to facing the aftermath in the meeting.

By 6 PM, everyone had assembled into the boardroom. Kathryn was the last to join us and we all pretty much sat in mute silence until her arrival. When she finally emerged through the door, Director Sikes nearly pounced on her without even letting her sit down.

"How is he?" he inquired directly.

Kate didn't answer until she took her seat opposite me across the table. She looked tired, haggard, and was still wearing her blue surgical scrubs which bore the signs of Stimple's blood. She sighed audibly, and methodically removed her surgeon's mask which hung from her neck before answering.

"He's stable," she said.

At this nearly everyone simultaneously also sighed out loud, which in another situation might have been humorous. Kathryn waited for everyone to finish before continuing.

"Dr. Bailey is closing up as we speak, but he's lost a lot of blood, and it seems the pencil not only struck an artery but pierced through his trachea and some of his vocal cords. He may suffer some permanent damage to his larynx which means that his voice may be altered somewhat. There's no way to tell for sure, however, until he recovers."

Frank tossed the characteristic Mont-Blanc pen he always had with him to the table and it thudded softly on the stack of papers that he had in front of him.

"Great," he said sourly. "And how long for a complete recovery?"

"Difficult to say really, but if I had to guess I would say anywhere from three to six months."

"Three to six months!" Howard exclaimed, almost whining. "From a pencil?"

"There was a lot of internal damage Howard, and you're forgetting the fact that what you do here is chiefly speaking and interacting with your patients. Dr. Stimple can't do that successfully and may cause more damage until his vocal cords have completely healed. Dr. Bailey agrees with my assessment of the situation which is he's not going to be able to return to active duty for another three to six months."

"But what's going to happen with his patients?" Howard moaned.

Joan rolled her eyes and leaned back from the table in apparent disgust at Howard's behavior.

"You're going to take them," Director Sikes said sternly. "We're all going to take them, including me. Starting now I want all Class 3 offenders manacled when in close proximity with physicians. No exceptions. Joan, I'd like you to take the female cases and Class Ones that Stimple was working with. I will assume the Class Three's, Howard, you'll take the Two's and I'll see if we can't recruit some help from St. Mary's to help juggle your case loads."

Howard sighed audibly at this, seemingly resigned to his fate, and I couldn't help but suppress a smile with the thought that he might actually have to work around here instead of just holding the status quo for a change. My attention was diverted as Frank addressed me.

"As for you, Dr. Stattler, you'll be assisting me." He paused a moment, exhaled loudly while staring down the middle of the table, looking at no one. "I know none of you were expecting this, I'm sorry. But we have to deal with the situation at hand, and that means I'll need all of you at your best, and any vacation or leave time that you may have had scheduled until Stimple returns will have to be canceled. Lastly let us pray for John and a speedy recovery. Unless there's anything else we'll reconvene at 0-nine hundred to go over your new patient profiles. That's all until tomorrow."

The air became filled with the familiar rummaging and I looked across the table at Kathryn who still looked tired and haggard. The blue operation mask still dangled by the lower strings around her neck, and signs of the stress of the day showed under her eyes and in her tattered hair.

"I'll be with Dr. Bailey in post-op; you can meet me in the lobby. And don't be later than we already are!" she reminded me again. "The sitter."

"All right, all right," I repeated again. "I'll meet you downstairs."

"Dr. Stattler, a moment if you please."

I looked over at Frank who still had not risen from the table, and he once again held his pen and was thumping it up and down against his lips. I sank back down in my seat and looked at Kate as she was leaving and she gave me a subtle wink. Once the door closed Director Sikes spoke to me directly for the first time since the altercation in the examination room.

"I don't have to tell you what's at stake here, Dr. Stattler. When the state board hears about this fiasco, and it won't take long with Howard whining about his new case load, there's going to be hell to pay. In any case though, it has forced this ward into the position of needing good psychologists now, which means I can't afford to wait another four or six months for you to absorb all the procedures and everything here that I want you to. I am therefore promoting you, albeit reluctantly and against my better judgment, to full-staff status with your first priority being Dr. Gottlieb. I have my hands full here Evan, and as much as I hate to do it there's no one else that I can assign him to. It would seem that thanks to James Grant you got your wish after all," he said, while leaning forward and pushing the file down the table until it stopped short in front of me.

I could not help but suppress a relieved smile at this, which I made the mistake of letting Frank see. He then looked at me square in the eye and leaned forward in his chair asserting himself.

"I'm making a leap of faith here, Evan. A leap that I'm usually not inclined to make but in this case I don't seem to have any other alternative. Don't disappoint me," he said sternly.

He then gathered his things and rose to leave. Before he left the room he added as though to comfort me, "That was good work back there today. You saw what needed to be done, asked no questions, and you did it. Congratulations, Dr. Stattler, though I wish the circumstances were different."

He closed the door behind him and I sat there, alone, somewhat elated, somewhat nervous about the opening of the future that lay before me. I couldn't wait to tell Kate. She would be as thrilled as I was, but again, there was the thought that I had a severely disturbed mental patient to thank for my good fortune. I picked up the dossier on Gottlieb and stared at it, while slowly flipping through the contents, and decided to make a brief introduction to my new assignment while waiting for Kathryn. She would be in post-op with Dr. Bailey for at least another twenty minutes or so. I had some time to kill, and after all, after the harrowing events of the day, I could afford to be a little late.

I strolled down the corridor to the Class 3 wing and double-door mantrap. As I saw the letters, "WARD 3 SECURITY CHECKPOINT" I began to wonder what Howard was whining about at the meeting. As a general, unwritten rule, it was well known amongst all of us on the staff that Stimple usually only received Class 3 patients. Those fortunate enough to be staying here at Grove Haven were, once admitted, divided into three classes based on their behavior and history. The first, Class 1, required minimal supervision and medication. The third, requiring the most with added security measures to protect both Dr. and patient, with Class 2 somewhere in between. Howard's complaining of what was sure to amount to few, if any, new patients to care for only served to demonstrate publicly his laziness.

Only once Sampson had finished buzzing me through and the heavily-barred doors clanged behind me did I again look at Gottlieb's file. '9a', read the number of his cell, which we recorded after the patient names on the index tab of their folder. I slowly made my way down the corridor, my shoes echoing loudly off the bare-painted cement walls and pink tile floor. I had not been in this section of the building many times, and I counted audibly in my mind the holding cells to my left as I passed them. I slowed my pace as I passed number eight until I stood at the center of Gottlieb's cell. He was lying on his cot, his head towards the bars that separated us, bent over reading. He must have known I was standing there due to the sound of me walking down the corridor, but he did not seem to indicate this or acknowledge my presence. I cleared my throat attempting to garner his attention, but he merely turned the page of whatever it was that he was reading in response.

"Whatcha reading?" I asked inquisitively, slightly raising the intonation of my voice at the end of the question.

"Merchant of Venice," was the reply, and he did not move or stir when responding.

He appeared to be in his early to late fifties, was about five foot ten, and was dressed in the bright orange jumper required of all Class 3 patients. His hair was thinning slightly, and he had a wispy goatee, which seemed to sprout in large, dark, thick whiskers from his chin, and contrasted sharply from the silver-gray hair on his head.

"Shakespeare," I said. "That's not what I would have expected of you. I would have presumed something more along the lines of astrophysics or quantum mechanics."

"My books from the Phillip's haven't caught up with me yet, and your library is somewhat lacking in areas of my, shall I say, expertise."

"Do you like Shakespeare?" I asked, trying to keep the conversation going.

"Actually, I think he was an anti-Semitic, racist, son of a whore, his depictions of Jews invariably turn us into greedy, usurious, scheming, Christ-killers."

"I see ..." I said, not quite sure what to make of this, as I was somewhat taken aback by his matter-of-fact delivery. "So why are you reading one of his plays?"

He paused for a moment, reflecting before answering.

"Because despite their racial overtones they reflect what I would call universal truths. Truths that are sometimes exposed in interesting, if not unexpected, ways. It is the nature of truth, Doctor, to reveal itself. It, like the light, abhors darkness and always triumphs against seemingly unconquerable odds. Truth is to good what oblivion is to evil. Light and darkness. Good and evil. Truth above all, inspires, incites, and drives humanity."

"I've never heard it put quite that way," I said calmly.

"Tell me, Doctor, do you believe in truth that is worth killing for, worth *dying* for?"

"It would depend on what that truth was," I answered. "Do you?"

He smiled and then said, "I shall have my *bond*, Doctor. The truth shall set it free."

"And to what *bond* are you referring?"

He looked at me as though I had struck him physically; almost as though he were insulted by my question and he rose from the cot and slowly, deliberately walked toward me.

"Hath not a Jew hands, organs, dimensions, senses, affections, passions; fed with the same food, hurt with the same weapons, subject to the same disease, healed by the same means," he said as he strode toward me, raising his voice with each footstep and sentence until with the last he was screaming and his voice echoed off the walls down the corridor. "If you prick us, do we not bleed? If you tickle us, do we not laugh? If you poison us, do we not die? And if you wrong us, shall we not REVENGE?"

Drops of spittle flew from his lips as he said this last word, and his black, beady eyes glared and darted at me intensively through the bars that separated us, which he had clasped so firmly between his hands that the veins along his knuckles looked as though they would burst from his skin. My first impulse was to back away, but I knew it was important that I establish control and not give in to his ranting. He eyed me suspiciously up and down, starting at my feet until again rising to my face. After a few moments his face relaxed and he broke into a smile.

"You show promise, Doctor," he said, while staring fixedly at me.

Clearly he was attempting to test and intimidate me. I said nothing and simply looked back at him expectantly.

"You know, I once saw a performance while on holiday in New York, 1957," he said, and he held up the play which was still in clasped in his hand. "The man who was playing Shylock, the rich, *evil* Jew, and antagonist in the story had this ingenious way to make himself more loathsome and repulsive to the audience by *hissing* his lines with what I can only describe as a 'malicious glee.' *Sssssssooo*, Doctor, do you consider yourself a *Chrissssstian?*" he asked, while glaring at me excitedly. I could not help but chuckle as he said this last word, evidently imitating the character he was describing.

"My wife is," I said. "But I am not. I think that religion serves man, not God, and closes many minds that might otherwise be open."

"*Yesssss*," he hissed again. His speech returned to normal and he backed away from the bars as he continued. "You do show promise, Doctor, perhaps we might eventually even become friends."

I smiled when he said this and he returned the gesture with a wide, broad, grin which exposed the whites of his teeth. I laughed out loud at this and decided to take the opportunity to formally introduce myself.

"I've been assigned to you, Dr. Gottlieb, my name is ..." and he interrupted me mid-sentence before I could continue.

"Dr. Evan Stattler, yes, I know. I've been expecting you."

CHAPTER TWO

Dr. Gottlieb

"Expecting me, how?" I asked.

"Sampson told me while bringing my dinner this evening of the trouble this afternoon in the examination room. It would seem that Mr. Grant is probably in for a heavy dosage of electroshock therapy."

"It's very possible that might be on his agenda," I said wryly.

Dr. Gottlieb smiled, almost wickedly at me from behind the bars and said nothing.

"I wouldn't know though," I continued. "It seems that Director Sikes will be assuming most of Dr. Stimple's caseload until he's fit to return."

"Not a very attractive man is he? He looks like a sewer rat I once saw as a child in the camps," he said, no doubt referring to his internment at Bergen-Belsen.

"Charisma is not one of his finer attributes, no."

"They'd get to be as big as dogs you know, feasting on the bodies of the dead. They were strewn everywhere, and it was not unusual to wake up in the mornings and cast those who had died in the night in a pit. One of my earliest and clearest memories is that of a rat gnawing on the naked arm of a bald and rotting babe in the muck of the gutter."

"Is there a point to this, Doctor?" I said, trying to sound sympathetic, but at the same time I did not see any relevance of continuing the conversation in that vein.

"No. It's just a story from my childhood. That's all you psychiatrists want to hear isn't it, stories from my childhood so you can make your little deductions, your pet theories about the reasons and why's of my existence and behavior."

"I'm not here to make an examination of you now, Doctor. Truthfully I just had some time to kill before I left for the evening and thought I would introduce myself."

"Interesting expression, that. *Time to kill.* I guess Mr. Grant felt it was his 'Time to kill' today. Can't say I blame him, really. Dr. Stimple is quite obsequious and loathsome."

"Maybe," I said. "But he is very good at what he does."

"And that is?" he asked inquisitively.

"Work with patients like you."

"And what are patients *like me*?" he said bitterly.

"You've been diagnosed with schizophrenia, Doctor. Your very presence here is a result of that fact. You show the characteristics of disturbed perceptions, inappropriate emotions, actions, and behavior."

"And what are *appropriate* emotions, actions, and behavior, Dr. Stattler? Do you consider yourself to be the model for which these abstract things are to be held accountable, scrutinized, and measured up to? Sometimes you people who call yourselves 'Doctors' both amaze and disgust me, and incidentally, since you brought up the subject, the reason I'm here is not what you think. It's not what's in that file you hold in your hand."

"Then what is it?" I asked coolly, placating him and encouraging him to go on.

He then looked about his cell nervously, as though someone or something was listening, and he continued in a whisper through the cage between us. "It is what I discovered, what I *know* to be the *truth* that we discussed earlier."

"... delusions of persecution or grandeur," I continued, interrupting him.

He turned from me and sat down once again on his cot against the wall with an audible sigh, clearly dejected and apparently disgusted by my observation.

"You know, Doctor, if what you know is so important, why didn't these nefarious forces that put you here simply have you executed? Be a lot simpler, wouldn't it? And less expensive too. Do you know what it costs the government per day to keep you here? I don't know right off hand but I'm sure it's not cheap."

He rose up off his bed once again and strode towards the bars that separated us glaring at me with what I could only describe looked like an intense hatred.

"Don't patronize me, Doctor, with what you think are clever little musings or witticisms. Do you think I don't know what it is you're thinking? I've been held captive in Federal Institutions for over twenty years now, observed by some of the finest minds in the field of psychology, and none of them would have me in their facilities for scarce more than a year or two. So if you think that a young upstart such as yourself can engage and coerce me into betrayal of my own beliefs and what I know to be the truth by appealing to what you think is common sense, think again. I have seemingly all the time in the world, Doctor, so if you have any respect for me as a person or patient, you'll think twice before rubbing my nose in what you *think* is the obvious."

I was taken aback by the severity and intensity of his response, and though I hated to admit it, when I heard this I thought for a moment that Frank may have been right.

"I'm sorry," I said. "I didn't mean to insult your intelligence."

"That's better," he said, his voice returning to normal. "Now we can be friends again."

I was somewhat relieved to hear him say this, and I was glad that I decided to apologize for offending him. Clearly, though delusional, somewhat paranoid, and certainly suffering from wild mood swings, he was very extremely cognizant of his surroundings and what was being said to him. I could only assume that what separated him from most schizophrenics, who were usually from lower socioeconomic levels or homeless street-people, was the broad extent of his education, which was rare.

"You don't strike me Doctor as the type of person who makes friends easily," I said, somewhat bemused.

"I don't," he said abruptly.

"And why do you think that is?"

He looked at me then thoughtfully, was about to respond but caught himself and smiled, waving a finger at me.

"There you go again, Doctor, attempting to draw out my secrets! You physicians never give up do you? It's never enough to go about your business, smile, and hold the status quo."

"Depends on who your physician is," I countered. "I can name a few who have their residency here who would be happy to do just that with you."

"So what do you want with me then, Dr. Stattler? Hmmmm? What is it you think you can find by delving into the confines of my brain, hmm? Or perhaps you're just seeking to make a name for yourself. You are rather young, aren't you? You can't have been practicing long."

Clearly he was quite amused with himself at this, and he was also demonstratively clever, smiling at me, egging me on to see just how I would respond to what we both knew was probably the truth. I decided that honesty would serve me best, and perhaps also help me to gain his trust. It seemed he valued friendship, as he quite probably hadn't had someone to truly confide with in a very long time.

"Perhaps a little of both," I said. "But also perhaps because I just want to help you."

He audibly huffed at this and then returned to sit down on his cot, and I decided to continue to press the matter.

"You seem to have a lot of mistrust of people, especially those in positions of authority. Do you know why?" I asked.

"Of course I know *why*," he snapped bitterly.

"Would you like to tell me?"

"I can't," he said.

"You can not, or you will not," I asked, somewhat rhetorically.

"I can't because I won't," he retorted back. He stopped before continuing in a more subdued tone. "If you genuinely mean to help me, I can not. It would destroy you."

"Don't you think that I should be the judge of that?" I asked.

He eyed me suspiciously and didn't respond.

"How about this, you tell me only what you feel comfortable telling me, and we'll start at the beginning. That way, you can control how far we go, and I won't be in any danger unless you make the decision. It would be in *your* power," I said, trying to placate him. "Does that sound fair to you?"

He still said nothing, and I decided to try another more simple approach.

"Doctor, I'm going to be honest with you. Although I will be assisting Dr. Sikes with the rest of Dr. Stimple's patients, at present, you're the only one to whom I've been assigned, and I'll confess, you're the first in an 'official' capacity. Director Sikes is going to ask me about you and if I have nothing to tell him it's not going to look very good for me. Why not just tell me about the first bad experience you had that comes to mind? Surely there's no harm in that?"

He was still silent, but I could tell by his expression that he was beginning to break, so I decided to press on.

"If I go back to Frank with nothing it's likely that he'll assign someone else to you who is more closed minded, someone probably who is more *Chrisssstian*, as well," I hissed as he had before when imitating the character Shylock, and then continued. "Someone who might merely, 'hold the status quo', as you so eloquently put it. If that is, of course, what you *really* want, then fine, tell me nothing."

I could see I had him and I was beginning to enjoy what had become a match of will and intellect between us. It was a game of chess of sorts, and I had just put his King into check, and called his bluff.

"All right, Doctor. You have finally wooed my conscience with your plea for understanding from your superiors, but don't expect any from me, after all, you know what they say, 'Be careful what you wish for …'" he stopped and then continued, almost hissing in the manner that he had before. "…'you may get it.'"

I decided to accept his invitation, and unfolded a chair that we periodically left along the wall of the corridor opposite the cells for interviewing patients and sat down. When I finally stopped shuffling my things and he could see that I was comfortable and attentive he began.

"The first time I tasted the horror and torment that now lies within my soul was when I was taken with my mother from the Jewish ghetto on the train to Bergen-Belsen. We were stuffed in the car, all of our possessions that we could carry littered the floor, so there was no room to sit down, and we were forced to stand the entire fourteen hour journey in the German winter of 1939. As the train approached the camp, the air, which was stifling in the box-car began to change, and took on a faint odor of damp smoke. I remember, as I stood there next to the window sill of the wagon, a fine silt of ash began to collect upon the bars, as we chugged slowly into the station. At the time I was only nine years old, and had no idea that the fires in the incinerator that burned with an eerie glow, day and night were feeding off the tallow of human flesh. When we arrived there was of course the customary greeting for all Jews, faggots, and other degenerates waiting for us. Other prisoners, whom I came to know as the Capos, entered the car speaking all manner of European or other languages."

"Capos?" I asked, uncertain and unfamiliar with the term.

"The Capos, Doctor, were the worst of us, the Jews and other prisoners I mean, sometimes worse than the SS themselves. The Capos were prisoners who were favored, and hand selected by the SS. They were often far more cruel and sadistic than their masters. They would often beat to death a slow worker or the elderly for the sheer pleasure of it. They would rape both men and women, and would steal food and rations from the poor and dying, if for nothing else, to justify their behavior at a later time. The Capos were chosen chiefly because of the viciousness of character, and they became 'wardens' overseeing the rest of us. If you did not comply with the Capos in charge of your barracks, the punishment was torture, or death, and of course the officers and SS would only look on at such activities with a detached amusement, sometimes gambling to see who would die first."

"I'm sorry, I wasn't aware that prisoners fought against each other."

"It's not your fault Doctor; most people whom I have encountered believe that the holocaust was merely the Jewish lamb led to the slaughter. It is not something that is commonly known or recognized that some Jews in order to save themselves were amongst the wolves, and in truth, it is not something that we survivors wish to remember about ourselves, as some of us were Capos."

"I understand," I said.

"But, to return to the subject at hand, once we reached the station the Capos instructed us to leave our things on the floor of the car and form a line while exiting the train. Unbeknownst to me, but suspected by my mother, our fate was to be decided by officers of the dreaded SS, once we exited the car, as to whether we would be dispatched to the showers and then fuel the fires, or whether we would spend the last of our days in hollow and empty despair at the labor camp.

"As our line began to shorten, and the gap between the Officer in charge of our queue and us began to narrow, I could see him clearly for the first time and I began to marvel at his candidness, eccentricity, and efficiency. His method was deliberate and simple, he merely looked each person up and down, would sometimes grip them by the shoulder to determine their stoutness, and when having come to a decision would merely with the tip of his right index finger gesture either to his right or to his left. He was for all intents and purposes indifferent to the awe-inspiring gloom and suffering of those around him, and he sized up his human commodities as though selecting a piece of meat from the butcher, or sorting through old clothes deciding which he would keep and which he would throw away or burn. In another setting his detached mannerism and cool demeanor might have been for lack of a better word, 'inspirational.'"

"*Inspirational?*" I asked incredulously, somewhat surprised and almost offended that such an astute observation would come from the mouth of someone who had witnessed such atrocities.

"Yes, Doctor," he said, casually. "Had this been a film this man would have no doubt been nominated for an academy award. But it wasn't a film. It was very real, and I was in the middle of it." He stopped then, stared forward at the wall in front of him as though remembering, and he continued in a voice scarcely above a whisper. "Sometimes I dream of him, the one I call *the man. Mr. Black*. Sometimes I still awake in the night, sweating, my number rapidly approaching until Fate and time bring us together, and I look into his face to hopefully catch some glimmer of humanity or compassion, but I can never see anything beyond the blackness of his eyes. Coal black. Black as night, and soulless and empty as time forgotten. They stare into me with a malevolent, annoyed, disregard, and seem to be able to decipher all my hopes and thoughts and dreams, and as he waves his long, skinny, pallid, gray finger, I awake screaming."

I stared at him, as he seemed to lose himself within the dream, until he finally looked over at me and smiled.

"What happened?" I said.

"Well, obviously I am here, and was not gassed to death, my body with a death grip clinging naked to some stranger."

"Well, yes, I gathered that."

"My mother and I were separated, though we both survived the showers she did not survive the camp. A Capos named Helmut, who was in charge of the barracks to which I was assigned saw to that, well, more or less."

"What do you mean?"

"Each Capos was assigned to a particular barracks. Each barracks had 6 eight foot beds made of wood with three tiers and slept 8 to 9 persons per tier, and housed up to 144, sometimes up to 160 persons. At daybreak, we were fed, if we were to be fed at all, and we were separated into work details. Some of the prisoners would lay train track, some would build walls around the camp, some would move boulders around all day, some would assist the Capos in the incinerators, and the younger, healthier boys such as myself, would sometimes assist the women in the laundry.

"It was on one such day that I was fortunate enough to be working with my mother, when the Capos Helmut came looking for me. He said he had a job for me, and if I hurried back to the barracks there was bread waiting for me. As I turned to leave I heard him say to my mother, "*Er ist ein süssliches Kind, so schön, und sanft.*" Though I did not understand what he meant by that then, I really didn't care. It had been two weeks, and I had scarce had a few stale *brötchen* mother had been kind enough to smuggle to me in the laundry, and the real pangs of hunger were beginning to set in. How I longed then and *now* for *eine echte Thüringer mit starker senf und semmel*," he said, while closing his eyes dreamily, and he held the bars of the cage separating us languidly, almost lovingly between his hands as though he were tasting whatever it was he was imagining.

"Pardon my asking Doctor, but, I was not under the impression that you were under similar conditions here."

"Well …," he said. "Conditions perhaps not, the food, perhaps yes. Have you ever *really* tasted your 'American' food, as if that were possible? Hmmm? Everything in this country of yours is so bland and processed that it barely has any flavor at all. American bread, American cheese, American mustard, the ever popular American Spam, even your American beer, none of your culture's food has any flavor whatsoever, and I cringe daily at the thought of ingesting any of it. Not that I have much choice in the matter anymore. I once asked a Frenchman if America had contributed anything to world cuisine and the only thing that came to mind was pancakes. With food like this," he said gesturing towards his tray which Sampson had brought him earlier that evening and for the most part was untouched, "I might as well be back in that camp. At least there once in awhile I would have, albeit stale, *real* bread, not this mushy doughy-white substance, you Americans *refer* to as bread," he stopped and held up the standard piece of Wonder-type bread for me to see, which accompanied dinner that was on his tray, and threw it back as though it offended him.

I said nothing at this gesture and he returned to his cot and sat a few moments before reminiscing again.

"How I long for the taste of beer," He said. "*Real* beer. I remember during my tenure at Bergen-Belsen, once in awhile, if I was fortunate, I would find a few swallows left in *Pfand flasche* outside the officers' mess."

"Pfand flasche?" I asked.

"Ah yes," he said, and seemed to be searching for the translation. "Deposit bottles? Does that sound right?"

"You mean recyclables?" I asked.

"Hmmm, no. Well, yes, and no. You see, in Germany, unlike in this country, where you commingle and melt down your glassware, if you do it at all, they actually re-use their bottles for water, sodas, beer, and you pay a deposit on them, or *ein Pfand*. Pfand-flasche are thicker than are American bottles, nearly half a centimeter or a quarter of your inches thick, and they are made to be extremely durable, due to the reason that they clatter against each other on the filling line or in the large crates which you purchase them in," he said, somewhat excited at describing the difference in cultures. His excitement and smile faded as he continued. "Yes. It was, in fact, due to a Pfand-flasche that my mother was killed."

I looked at him, searching for some sign of emotion in this, but he seemed dispassionate about the incident, as though it were only trivial.

"You know, it's funny, Doctor. Even though at first I was overwhelmed and overjoyed to become a citizen of this country, as it was my salvation from the camp, over time I have always in some way felt a prisoner by it. I realized as I became an adult and traveled the world and visited ancient places that my heritage and what I consider myself to be is still a German-born Jew. I never hear my native tongue anymore, only in my dreams, and I have come to understand that America's ignorance of other cultures and other languages makes it and its people disrespected, and a laughing stock in the eyes of the rest of the world," he said reflectively, and then continued. "But I digress ..."

His face then soured abruptly. "When I left the washroom that day, my mother knew what he meant to do. She knew what Helmut meant when he said that I was sweet little child. She *knew* that he meant to have me, she *knew* what was going to happen, and I waved to her as I went out the door with him, and I saw her weeping in the middle of the wash room."

After this admission Dr. Gottlieb began to slide down the bars separating us, and he began to sob as he slowly slid to the floor.

I looked at him and tried to suppress the well that I felt filling up inside me. Subjectively, I did not know for certain if what he was relating to me was the truth, or, if, in fact, it was one of his delusions. But if it was a delusion, the emotion he clearly felt was etched on his face in lines of helplessness and misery, and I admitted to myself then that if I did not believe what he was saying was true, I wanted to.

After he composed himself he continued, without emotion.

"That night as I lay there in my bunk, suffering through the pains I had experienced, I wanted to crawl into a ball and disappear from the world. I wanted to 'run the wire' which was a phrase used by the prisoners to describe the most popular method of suicide—running into the electric, barbed-wire fences that surrounded the compound. As I lay there, contemplating just how I would destroy myself, I saw my mother with an object in her right hand enter the barracks. She looked to me, and saw that I was watching, and put her finger to her lips. My heart raced and began to pound, and I thought for sure that at any instant it would wake the man lying next to me. She looked round the room for Helmut's place, the only single bed in the room with a mattress, and slowly crept up towards him. I watched her as she moved silently, deftly around the beds, and tried to take notice if anyone had seen her, but in so far as I could tell, everyone was so exhausted from the day's labors that they would not have heard her if she came in clamoring with a trumpet or a drum.

"When she finally reached Helmut, who had passed out from drinking with the officers, I could see what she held in her hand. It was a broken Pfand-flasche, a broken bottle of *Häake Beck*. I stared at her, as the moonlight cascaded in through the window where she stood. She looked like Artemisia's *Judith*, and standing there, with Carravagian tintilism in the moonlight, her drab prison garb became Judith's bright blue dress, her thin, bald, and bony frame became a strong, matronly, figure, and her facial expression changed from one of anxious fear to cool deliberation. Barely pausing before striking, she put her hand over his mouth and sliced at his neck and jugular with the broken end of the bottle. I heard him begin to struggle, but the blood poured from his neck too fast, and as he was already inebriated, his attempts at stopping her were moot at best. I looked around the room but could not discern if anyone had awoken or noticed, and by the time I looked back to where she was standing next to the now lifeless Helmut, she was gone."

"What happened?" I asked, trying to do my best to sound clinical and objective, without emotion.

"She was apprehended of course. Either by the blood on her clothes and hands or by other would-be Capos in her or my barracks who had seen what had happened and identified her. Under the watchful eyes of the SS, the other Capos took her to the common yard once she had been discovered. In a special ceremony the following afternoon, they tied her naked to a large wooden pole in the center of the yard, and took turns raping her with beer bottles in front of all the prisoners. When they were finished they flogged her, shouting insults until the flesh began to tear from her body, at first in little rivulets, and finally in large swaths across her chest and breasts. When she finally stopped breathing they doused her in gasoline and set her aflame. It was the last time the flogging pole would be used. It became obsolete in that afternoon, under the dark, December sky."

I didn't know what to say, and again, I didn't know if what he was telling me was real. I looked at down at my watch and realized that over an hour had passed since I had come up here and Kathryn was probably going to be furious with me.

"Oh shit!" I said out loud without thinking. "I'm sorry."

"Nothing for you to be sorry about, Doctor, these things happen in times of war. Man confronts his own worst enemy—himself."

I laughed somewhat distractedly and said, "No you don't understand, I'd better get downstairs. Kathryn has undoubtedly been waiting for me for some time in the lobby and we're already running late for the sitter."

"Kathryn in the infirmary? Is that your wife?" he asked curiously.

"Yes," I said, aware that I had surrendered a piece of personal information and I probably shouldn't have.

"And you have a child too?"

"Yes," I answered. "His name is David."

"Funny," he said, apparently deep in reflection. "For some reason I developed the impression that you were not meant to be a parent."

I stared at him, perplexed, wondering what he meant by this. I was about to respond when he reminded me of my already tardy situation.

"Well don't let me keep you; I'm sure that we'll have plenty of time to get to know each other better, Dr. Stattler."

"I'm sure we will," I said, being careful not to volunteer anything.

I began to turn to leave when he approached the bars more closely and he gripped them between his two palms.

"Dr. Stattler," he said. "Do you trust me?"

I was unsure of how to answer this question, so I decided that as he seemed to respect honesty I answered truthfully.

"I don't know whether I do or don't. I can tell you, as a rule, as a physician it's important for me not to, and to remain objective concerning your treatment."

"Objective, or subjective, Doctor?"

"Maybe a little of both," I admitted, trying to see at what he was getting at.

"It's important that you trust me, Doctor. How do you presume to help me if you won't believe what it is I'm saying? How as a physician can you possibly provide treatment for me, if you automatically and habitually, as the psychiatric profession is prone to doing, do not believe what it is your patient tells you."

I decided to placate him as I was now running late and knew that I was in for a severe hen-pecking from Kate.

"I trust you," I said.

He extended his hand through the bars that held him in a gesture suggesting that he wanted me to take it and physically profess what it is I had just verbally committed to. I stood there for a few seconds and blankly stared at it, wondering just what I should do.

"Go on, Doctor. I won't bite. At least not you, though I might think twice about that sewer-rat Stimple," he said encouragingly.

I thought about the day's events and I knew that he knew this was foremost on my mind, as well as the new directive from Director Sikes. It was a test. He was testing me to see if I would betray Frank's ruling and my principles and embrace him. I decided that honesty had for the most part served me well so far and I answered him.

"Director Sikes made it clear in a meeting this evening that there is to be no unsupervised physical contact between physicians and Class 3 patients," I said, and trying to turn the tables on him continued. "Surely, you wouldn't want me to jeopardize my position and the relationship that we have just established by betraying that."

He thought about this for a moment, and smiling withdrew his hand.

"Of course not, Doctor," he said. "It was only my intention to show friendship."

"I'm sure it was," I said. "But my instructions in this matter are very clear, especially after what happened this afternoon. I'm sure you respect that." I could read in his face that he did, and I was glad that I chose the path that I did, and it did not result in any bruised feelings on his part.

"Until tomorrow then," he said, and he stepped backward, further into his cell.

"Until tomorrow," I repeated, and turned down the hall, back to the security checkpoint, when I heard him, reciting the lines of the poor, miserable, Jew, Shylock, from the MERCHANT OF VENICE, echoing down the corridor.

"For sufferance is the badge of all our tribe. You call me misbeliever, cut-throat-dog, and spat upon my Jewish gabardine, and all for use of that which is mine own ... You that did void your rheum upon my beard and foot me as you spurn a stranger cursed ..."

"Goodnight, Doctor," I bellowed sternly down the hall, my voice and tone indicating that I was not going to be impressed or coerced into guilt by his performance.

His reading was stopped by a brief pause and then I heard his voice once more.

"See you tomorrow, Dr. Stattler," and he continued with his soliloquy. "To buy his favor, I extend this friendship. If he will take it, so. If not, adieu."

I shook my head at this, pondering what possessed a man of such a keen and seemingly noble intellect to destroy his reputation and his life by murder. If it wasn't an antisocial personality disorder or paranoid schizophrenia, then what was it? I knew from experience and training that it was always better to study the roots or specific symptoms of the paranoid delusions themselves rather than to summarize someone in Gottlieb's condition with a diagnostic label. Labels always had the tendency to create pre-conceptions that could alter and bias interpretations, and I did not want to follow in the mistakes with which I so often disagreed with treatment Howard usually specified for his patients. Yet, at the same time, I was unsure as to how far I should go the other way.

One thing was certain though, clearly I needed to do something that others hadn't in their interactions with Gottlieb, and I felt that I was on the right track. We had established a rapport, which was hard to do with a patient of his caliber, and was certainly something I had never seen Howard do. It partially wasn't his fault though, he was from the 'old school' which for the most part depended on labels which, in my opinion, only served to stigmatize patients, and relied chiefly on drugs for treatment of their psychological disorders, rather than physically and personally interacting with a patient and determining the roots, or cause, of the illness.

In any case, I needed to make a decision on a method of treatment and stand by it, and the only way to do that was find out exactly *why* Gottlieb chose to kill those men, and determine how the events that he began to unfold to me led to his current disorder.

I stopped at the gate which separated Class 3 patients from the rest of the facility, and had Sampson buzz me once more through the man-trap.

CHAPTER THREE

Providence, Rhode Island
November 2003

Providence. I always liked the sound of it, even when I was a youth. Its name somehow even promises better times, financial fulfillment, and for me and most of all, it has an air of 'security' about it that I can never seem to let go, even, ironically, when it has let me go. The first time I came to Providence I was 19, and in med-school at John's Hopkins in Baltimore. On long weekends and holidays my long time friend Jeff and I would come up to visit a friend of mine, Jonah, who lived here while attending Rhode Island School of Design, which was located near Brown University in old-town now referred to as "College Hill" (the newer down-town area is at the base of College Hill across the River Providence.) The Old Town is beautiful, especially in autumn. Nearly every building has a brass plaque stating some historical significance that supposedly happened some time on some date, somewhere. Thayer Street especially.

It reminds me almost of the pictures one envisions when they think of Nantucket, a quaint, colonial, northern town near the sea. As it was a college town the nightlife was bustling too; there were parties everywhere, every weekend, and when Jeff and I would come up the three of us would spend our nights drinking and usually end up rolling bowling balls down the bus tunnels at 3am on College Hill to the great delight of our drunken cohorts and onlookers.

Now I just usually end up drinking, no, escaping, and passing out, sometimes on the floor at eight-thirty. There are times when the whole building

could for all intents and purposes just burn right up around me and consume me whole, scatter my ashes to the wind, and I wouldn't feel a thing
and be the better man for it.

The building where I live sits next door to a pizza parlor, the best in
town really, where I work, right at the corner of Wickenden and Hope streets.
It's a small little hovel with no place to sit-down really, except a counter, but
it's always busy, even when I was here on holiday weekends, as a customer
over thirty years ago. As a hobby I have always enjoyed wine, cooking, and
preparing fantastic meals.

Indeed, in my youth here I said that I would someday learn the secret of
Fillini's fantastic pizza. I never dreamed that at 52, I would be here prepping
it, serving it to all the drunk, stoned, or other fucked up college kids who
come in at 1 a.m. I was one of them once. Once. In many ways I still am.

My apartment sits on top of an old appliance store, which at one time
was a federal-style bank. It was, in fact, where my friend lived when I came
up to visit all those years ago. He and his roommates had painted it in
primary colors, bright blue, red, and yellow on the baseboards, door frames,
fixtures, even the light-switch plate covers. At the time it looked like a big
romper room for adults. They made their own furniture from books and
models they had seen in class at RISD, and painted it, in turn, to match the
room. There is not much left of it now. At some point I guess the land-lord
had a tizzy and painted everything white again, though when cleaning or
moving something I am sometimes able to see a peek at some remnant or
speck of paint he missed, and I will spend the rest of the day reminiscing in
my wine. But I digress … I did not choose it solely due to sentimental
reasons, though I admit it may have played a small role. I chose it because of
the view. It has big glass windows that face north, east, and west—the only
ways in which you could approach the building, and there is a large fence
that separates Highway 6 to the south. It helped provide the "air of security"
I needed. I thought I would be safe here. Safe from *them*. No. Safe from *him*.
I thought at 50, even if I wished to tell my story to someone, anyone, who
would listen to the ramblings of a washed up, drunken old man who ekes
out his existence in hiding, cleaning and spraying out garbage bins, and
making pizza? Who would ever guess or even imagine that I hold a doctorate in psychology and once was a practicing physician? At this point in my
life, hopefully no one. Just who, exactly, would care to know?

I thought I was, now, exactly what *the man*, for I do not know his *real*
name, wanted me to become—tired, worn out, and nearly useless and most

important: a shell of a man that no one would pay attention or give credence to, and when they find me dead, drowned in my own vomit, no one would care about either.

I thought that I was done running. I have ran nearly half my life—moving from town to town, place to place, living under an assumed name, employing myself with false social security numbers on odd jobs so *he* couldn't track me. I have run with all my possessions in a bundle under my arm from *the man* for what in one week will be twenty years, six months and eighteen days. I thought that I had escaped, and was finally free. I thought that Providence, would at last, save me from the man and myself. I have been here five years without incident. But, this morning when I went downstairs to Fillini's when I saw the all-to-familiar-look on, Pauli, the owner's face, I knew the man had come. He looked at me with saddened eyes and started to apologize and I put my hand on his shoulder to re-assure him and told him,

"It's Ok. It's not your fault. It's mine."

"Who *is* he?" he asked.

And as I looked at him with his troubled and sorrowful expression I told him the truth which had been for over twenty years simmering quietly on the back burner of my mind—

"He is no one," I answered.

He handed me an envelope, which out of courtesy I did not open in his presence. I folded my apron, handed it to him, smiled, and shook his hand.

"You've always been good to me Pauli," I said.

"Five years, Evan. Five years. Where am I going to find anyone else like you?"

"You won't," I said smugly.

Fighting back his tears and wiping his face he said, "Get outta here!"

I made my way downtown along the canal that divides College Hill from the downtown and gazed up at the building which had been the model for *The Daily Planet* in the Superman comics, and just below it I noticed a billboard advertising the final chapter for *The Matrix*. I thought how poignant for the two to be juxtaposed. It was almost as if the two were beckoning to me, longing to draw out and expose the truth, as if, even if I had the power to expose it, would I now?

"What would Clark Kent do?" I asked myself as I leaned on the bridge and kicked a stone in the river. I then began to berate myself and thought about things that I have ignored for a long time, 'You are no *Superman* and no *hero*. You are nothing. And the truth that you would reveal would cause anarchy and cost the lives of thousands, even if you could reveal it, which you can't, and even if you had evidence, which you don't.' And I began to once again remind myself what exactly *the truth* was—aside from actually producing an alien corpse or an alien themselves no network producer would run *any* story confirming the existence of *The Grays.*

And the chip. The sacred chip, which thousands, tens of thousands, even perhaps hundreds of thousands and maybe more carry and don't know it. The chip that tells all and tells nothing. I gave up my life for the chip. Some gave up more, I thought. Dr. Gottlieb gave up his freedom. I wondered if he were still alive, somehow, somewhere, rotting away forgotten in some federal institution with no one to talk to or listen, or worse as I found out, believe him. At least I still had my freedom.

No wonder then that I am banished as what I have come to know as the *Under Government* would have me so, and in so doing pull the wool over the eyes of the entire human race. As indeed, most of the human race would rather live in a world without extra-terrestrials. Most people if given a choice would *choose* to have the truth about *The Grays* existence hidden from them; much like many would *choose* to live in The Wachowski Brothers' *Matrix.* I marveled at the irony and wondered if the directors might somehow know the *Undergov's* greatest conspiracy, and if in some way they were making an allegory between the fantasy and the reality.

I made my way across the river into the downtown area. It was still only ten o'clock a.m. None of the bars or restaurants would be open yet, and for the first time in a long time I had all the time in the world. I thought that I was safe this time; I was very careful and Pauli, the owner of Fillini's was very obliging. I insisted on being paid cash and *only* cash. I paid the rent in cash. I paid for bus fare in cash. I had no automobile, no bank accounts. No papers. No nothing. I was living on the fringes and as far as I knew there was nothing that they could trace or find me with, and I wondered what had given me away this time. Why was *he* still hounding me after all these years? What threat did I pose to the passive existence of humanity now, forgotten as I had become—as *he* wanted me to become. It was an answer that truthfully I did not want to begin to fathom.

I decided to break down and have a cigarette. I have made it somewhat of a tradition when I am found out and vanquished from the loving arms of a city and place of hiding. It is my one reprieve and vice from times past. I have not had a cigarette in five years and exactly twenty-two days. That was the day when I left New Orleans—what a wonderful city that is. The French

Quarter with all its honeysuckle and jasmine seems to always smell of spring and overgrowth. The warm winter nights and damp nourishing morns— how I missed them now, in this cold, dreary, and frozen place.

I walked past *The Daily Planet* and made my way, slowly, ambling across the square past the Omni Hotel into town. I spotted Phillip's Discount Drug store and went inside. Kools. They're what my father smoked, though I was too young to remember. My mother told me that sometimes she would go into his study and there would be a thin layer of ash all over his desk, which was organized by chaotic method. My father never believed in aliens, though oddly enough science fiction was his favorite subject. That was the *lawyer* in him. He could never break the boundary where fiction sometimes becomes a reality, and as he believed and would always say, "There must always be evidence … And there is none!" Much like the law I guess that depends on what, exactly, one is referring to, and most importantly what one is including as evidence. How many cases, I wonder, were decided adversely for this reason? How many innocent men have been sent to prison, and how many guilty men have been set free, because evidence for one reason or another was not admitted into the courtroom?

Strangely though, he had literally thousands of paperback books and what were then dime novels of every science fiction work ever published it seemed. When he died my mother must have sent three truckloads of books to the Salvation Army. I suppose he knows the answer now. I wanted to tell him before he died. I wanted to let him know that I was alive. I tried to several times but the consequences to him and my mother would be too great, and in the end I was not given the chance to let him know I was alive or even to say that I loved him. No, he was set in his ways, like many of us are, and not going to change his rationale or way of thinking. It was his world, his pattern, his routine that I would disrupt with such thoughts. He was content to live out a lie, so long as it was not disruptive, knowing full well that it was, in fact, a lie, and yet intent on believing in it anyway. For someone who was not a believer in religion his pattern of thinking was very religious. I thought that way once too about many things. Once.

I paid the clerk and removed one of the many fifties that Pauli had so thoughtfully tucked in my envelope.

"Where to now?" I asked the clerk, who was gathering his things. I asked the question more for me than for him, as if he really had an answer for me.

"Home," he said. "My shift is over," as a young blonde headed creature came behind the counter carrying her drawer.

I walked outside. It was beginning to rain and I could hear the city starting to come to life and the unmistakable grinding sound of water spraying out of tire treads on wet asphalt. "Where to now?" I asked myself again, not even really noticing that I was speaking. The rain drizzled down my face and I kept walking, oblivious of where I was going or where I was headed to, absent mindedly puffing away at the cigarette between my lips. Maybe I should just retreat to Montana and live out in the woods somewhere like the Uni-bomber, I thought. Or maybe Europe ... but that requires a passport and, depending on the country visas, which are quite an impossibility, and if caught with a forgery, a lengthy stay in federal prison, where *he* would surely find me, and as for even finding someone who could fashion a reputable fake passport I hadn't the slightest idea where to begin. Perhaps I could somehow book passage on a freighter and then quietly disappear once we've reached our destination. I have always wanted to see Mykonos and the Greek Isles. After we were to be married Kathryn and I had discussed going there for our honeymoon.

I remember seeing pictures of Santorini. It is rumored to be the location of the lost city of Atlantis, destroyed by the ancient volcano. How I would love to lose myself among those white and aqua buildings and clear blue sea! It seemed like a dream worth dying for—to live out the rest of my days among the quiet sands and pebble beaches of the Mediterranean, maybe working as a cook somewhere in a Travatoria.

I had to stop and think awhile. There were some things that I needed to sort out: How much money I had. What cities I haven't been to. Where I could go.

Where I could find someone who wouldn't mind quietly employing me, paying me cash with no questions asked. The last was the hardest. I thought about New York but somehow among eight million people *he* managed to find me there too. What I find most aggravating about the whole thing is that it's not enough that I have been beaten, that I have given up all hope and evidence of exposing the Grays and their agents ... it's the relentless pursuit by the M.I.B.'s, or more specifically, *the man* to keep me on the run, to keep me afraid and undermine all hope of a normal life and security.

Better to just kill me or lock me up like Dr. Gottlieb if I was a threat. But this, this 'hounding' of my person was nothing but pure malice. It was disdainful.

It was evil. How long must I wait for peace? How long must this cruel farce go on?

And how long will it continue? Will I be seventy years old, poor, homeless, destitute, still running, and scrubbing dishes to survive? They have taken everything from me that I ever could have wanted, my career, my wife, my home, my child, and at times it seems my very soul and will to go on. Do I regret the choices I have made? Yes. And no. Is it Pride that damns me so? I did not know.

I looked down at my watch. Water had beaded up on the face and I wiped it away with my handkerchief, which had become thoroughly soaked as it had been sticking out of my coat pocket. It read 11:03 a.m. Magiano's should be open by now, I thought. I felt that I should visit my favorite bar one last time before I left Providence. In the past as soon as I had known that I had been discovered, I always left town immediately as I did not want *him* to find me and carry out his threat. But as the cold November rain came down and spattered my face and dripped on to my clothes I did not care anymore, and what better time than now, at eleven in the morning to dull the senses with some scotch whiskey and sort through those questions in my head that I so desperately needed to answer.

I walked the long hike up Friendship Street until I came to the familiar glass doors with the heavy custom made Baldwin-Brass handles.

"Good morning, Mickey," I said as I shook off my coat and hung it on the rack next to the door.

"Morning Evan. You're here awful early?" the barman replied, who I have come to know through many hazy nights sitting alone in this place. "What brings you in this time of day, I usually expect you after five or so?"

"I suppose you could say I was *induced* to be here," I said. "Johnnie Black neat with a Guinness chaser."

"Black, eh?" he said. "Drinking the good stuff ... special occasion?"

"You could say that," I answered, smiling slightly under my breath, trying for him not to notice ... I wasn't in the mood for a conversation in which I was going to have to tell Mickey that he was going to be losing one of his best customers. I sat down on my usual stool at the end in the corner with my back to the door.

"Black it is ..." he said, and smiling added, "No pun intended," as he set down the Guinness and then the whiskey.

"You're a trip Mickey, have you always been so verbally crafty?" I asked while lifting the scotch to my lips. I let it slowly trickle down my throat and I could feel it begin to warm my insides and it helped me to ignore the dampness of my clothes.

"A '93 English Major." he replied.

"Why didn't you ever do anything with it?" I asked.

"You know," he said. "People are always asking me that and my answer is that if I did I wouldn't be here to serve you clowns now would I?"

"You have a point," I said, nodding my head in agreement.

"Besides," he went on. "There's no money in it … what could I do with it anyway, teach high school, maybe, go on to get a Masters and earn thirty-five a year teaching at some community college … I earn nearly twice that here working 4 days a week, what would be the point? Unless I wrote a novel or something …"

"You have a point," I repeated while finishing my whiskey. I pulled out the pack of Kools from my shirt pocket and began to light one.

"Those things will kill you. When'd you pick that up?"

I looked at my watch. "'Bout ten minutes ago," I said smiling. "And yes, I know they'll kill you. I'm a doctor," I slipped. "Well, at least I used to be," I continued softly, talking more to myself than him.

"Johnnie Black, smoking cigarettes … something's up …" he said in what seemed to be a combination of both a question and a statement while kindly refilling my whiskey without even offering.

Truly the art of being a bartender is not only knowing and taking care of your regulars but in carefully crafting your words into what can be interpreted both as a question *and* a statement thus granting the opportunity to those in the conversation to either feel comfortable continuing or letting the subject rest without offending the other party. Yes, I liked Mickey, who was an exceptional bartender indeed. I was going to miss him. It's hard to find the right bar in the right place that has the *right* people. You could have the greatest cocktail lounge in the world serving every drink imaginable in the busiest spot in town with hot young women all wanting some frequenting the place six ways to Sunday, but if you don't have the staff, then you really don't have shit.

"All right, I'll bite," I said. "Do you believe in aliens, Mickey?" I asked with what I knew to be a sly smile on my face.

"Aliens!?" he answered sounding shocked and befuddled. "Course I do … Tony's got a couple washing dishes in the back."

I laughed. "No, not that kind," I said, lifting the scotch to my mouth.

"You mean those short-little-guys with the huge heads and big eyes?"

"The very same."

"Well it's like this," he went on. "I can't imagine that all these people are

supposedly seeing the same thing and it's all some great big coincidence ...
I mean where'd the idea and the icon come from anyway ... my daughter's
even got an 'Alien' lunch box with a picture of one of them on it. Thirty
years ago you never saw such things. Is it some fad, I don't know ... what I
do know is that there's something, somewhere, somebody ain't telling us."

I was about to answer when I heard the front door open. I heard the
unmistakable sound of what I knew to be black, patent leather shoes squeak-
ing on the ceramic tile floor from the rain. It was a sound that I had heard
before, and remembered with the utmost clarity, even though I had done
my best to forget it by hiding it in the back corner of my mind. Before I
could turn to look and see who it was I heard the voice. The voice I had not
heard in over twenty years.

"Dr. Stattler," it said. "How nice to see you again."

And I knew he had at last found me. It was *him*. It was the Man in
Black.

CHAPTER FOUR

The Origins of Species

"Would it be all right if I asked *you* a question, Doctor?" he asked, his voice and tone seemed to musingly smile at me from behind the pages of a book he was reading and which concealed his face.

After yesterday's unusual first encounter with him I couldn't help but wonder what he meant by this and what possible deranged, sordid, or probing question he might have. Clearly he was extremely intelligent, and I knew I was dealing with a mind that while greatly disturbed and stratified, was still human. Clearly he *needed* something, perhaps the sense of companionship, which having been incarcerated for over twenty years and being constantly moved about to institution after institution would quite predictably become a void in his life. As we had seemed to develop a rapport I decided to let him build on this.

"Sure," I said, standing in front of his cell, his chart in my hand.

"Before we begin with this 'interview' of sorts you seem to be intent on conducting, I was wondering if I might ask a few questions of you?"

"And that reason would be?" I asked, trying to peer at the root of his interest.

"There you go again, you Doctors, you *psychiatrists*, who think yourselves *soooo* smart, trying to lure me and pick and push and prod and hack your way into the confines of my brain in the dim and vague hopes of attempting to understand my moods and behaviors! For what purpose, I wonder? So that you can help others with the same *condition?*" He was lying on his cot with his back against the wall, his face immersed behind the fold of a book, which he had not looked up from since I arrived, his voice speaking in a detached interest, as though he did not believe he had any 'condition' at all, and it was all he could to do tolerate my inquiry.

He went on, "Isn't enough that you have me here, and locked away for all eternity so that I may not spread my madness and mayhem, my *chaos* elsewhere? Or perhaps are you afraid to answer some of *my* questions, lest they may distract you from your purpose? Hmmm? Might that be it then?"

"It would seem that for whatever reason, you have succeeded in that," I said coolly, trying to let him know that I was aware of the cognitive game he was playing.

This seemed to garner his attention as he finally diverted his attention from the book he was reading and smiled at me in a mischievous manner.

"Excellent," he said, and once again returned his attention to the book he was reading, but continued speaking to me in a straight forth and deliberate manner. "In order to begin, you must understand that we are dealing with both the universes of the infinitely large and infinitely small. It is curious that in this great interstellar order of ours that both exist so precisely and cooperatively."

"I'm not sure I understand," I said, trying to grasp his meaning.

"Have you ever heard of the term, 'Ten minutes to midnight', Dr Stattler?"

When I attempted to answer, he did not look up from his book, which he held even with his face.

"Before I answer, I'm curious. How did you know it was me coming down the hall and standing here? You have only just looked up from your reading," I asked.

"Who else would be coming to visit, surely not Santa Claus, I've been a very naughty boy," he said, looking back to his book.

"It might have been Sampson bringing your lunch," I said, offering a possible explanation for his insight, knowing that it was wrong, but wanting to keep the conversation going.

"That's true, although Sampson has already brought me my lunch as you can see," he said, while motioning with his arm to the tray on the night table next to him. "And Sampson is much heavier than you, Doctor, and those hideous white orderlies shoes he is forced to wear don't make the same 'clack' that yours do when he comes down the hall," he said, still involved with what he was reading. I looked at the title, 'William Shakespeare's MACBETH', it read, in large black letters.

"Shakespeare again, Doctor, at this pace you'll go through all his plays in, how would Shakespeare put it? A 'fortnight' maybe," I said, trying to be witty.

"As I told you before, Doctor, they contain many truths. Truths that are in need of revealing." He shut his book with the one hand that was holding it and looked up at me for the first time. "Good afternoon, Doctor, and how are we today?" he asked, while grinning somewhat mischievously.

"I am fine," I said. "How are you?"

"I would like to answer, but I believe it was I who first posed a question to you," he stared at me expectantly and then continued. "'Ten minutes to midnight?'"

"Ah, yes," I said, remembering what he had first asked me when I came down the hall. "No, I haven't heard of it." His expectant face suddenly became sullen, as though I had insulted him with my answer. I decided to press on to find the root at what he was getting at. "Should I have?"

He glared at me disappointedly, "It was one of my greatest donations to the field of anthropology! It was the thesis for my first doctorate, in anthropology, at Yale in the spring of 1958. It was later adopted by every anthropologist and archaeologist the world over," he said, making a sweeping gesture with his hand to accentuate this. "Every student taking Anthropology 101 knows about that!" he said, trying to jog my memory.

"I took Biology and Geology," I said, hoping not to further offend him with my ignorance.

He heaved a large sigh and then began to speak, as though teaching his theory to a two-year old. "Well, at least you took Geology, though it is helpful, I can see we are indeed going to have to start at the beginning," he said. "No pun intended. You are at least familiar with the theory of 'The Big Bang'?"

"I'm not *that* far gone Doctor." I said ruefully.

"Good," he said. "I wouldn't want you to waste my time." He glared at me, did not wait for me to respond, rose off his cot, and while pacing about his cell, his hands behind his back, still gripping *Macbeth*, began to talk to the ceiling as though on a lectern. "Now then, we know from fossil evidence that the earth is approximately five to six billion years old. We also know that 'The Big Bang' occurred somewhere in the realm of say, fifteen billion years ago, give or take a few billion years. If we were to map out, as it were, the extent of these fifteen billion years to a single year in a 'Cosmic Calendar' of sorts, midnight January 1st would be the explosion or epicenter of 'The Big Bang.' The present, now, as we sit here would be at the very end of December 31st. So modern human beings, *Homo sapiens,* existence in the universe would roughly span only ten minutes out of the fifteen-billion year -year."

"I'm not sure I quite follow you," I said, trying to grasp more of what he was saying.

"Each month in the 'Cosmic Calendar' is 1.25 billion years, each day 40 million years, each minute 30,000 years, and each second 500 years. It wasn't until the month of May that the Milky Way galaxy formed; September, what we call the sun, and the earth. The apes that would evolve into man did not appear until 10:30pm on December 31st. Fire was not discovered until 11:46pm. Modern mankind did not take his first steps until 11:50pm on December 31st, hence the term, 'Ten minutes to midnight.' At 11:59 and twenty seconds, man began to domesticate plants and animals. At 11:59 and thirty five seconds, agricultural communities evolved into the first cities.

"We humans have existed so recently on the 'Cosmic Calendar' that our entire history, all our memories, every person that we have ever known to exist occupies only the last few seconds, in the last minute, of December 31st. Thus we can now see the immense duality of the universe; the very large, and the very small. And which do you think we are, Dr. Stattler?" He stopped pacing and stared at me, clearly awaiting a response.

"That's great and very informative," I said with somewhat of a detached tone. "But what does that have to do with why you're here?"

"I told you we were starting at the beginning, Doctor. In order to understand all I will tell you, it is important that you understand this. It is the root of my discoveries, my travels, everything that I ever did, every dig I supervised, every fossil I examined, every piece of research I ever formulated comes down to this simple truth concerning mankind and his existence in the universe. It is important that you understand it," he said, and looked at me expectantly.

"All right," I said, and decided that it was probably best from a clinical perspective to let the patient proceed in his own manner in order to better perform a dynamic formulation of the case material. As I had been standing there the whole time listening to him I decided that if we were going to continue I was going to need to sit down. I unfolded the chair that leaned against the wall across from his cell and once I was properly seated he continued.

"A promising student of mine once told me that there are more stars in the cosmos than there are grains of sand, on every beach, and every desert of the planet Earth. Tell me, Doctor, you seem to be asking most of the questions and quite tactfully avoiding mine, let me see if I can now poke and prod an answer out of you. How does that make you feel?" he asked, somewhat indignantly.

I thought for a moment before replying, "Small."

"*Yesssss ...*" he hissed, again repeating and reminding me of his performance of the Jew, Shylock, the evening prior. "It makes one question the point of it all." He backed away from the bars that separated us and began to speak loudly, and full of vigor. "Tomorrow, and tomorrow, and tomorrow, creeps in this petty pace from day to day, to the last syllable of recorded time; and all our yesterdays have lighted fools the way to a dusty death. Out, out, brief candle! Life's but a walking shadow, a poor player, that struts and frets his hour upon the stage, and then is heard no more. It is a tale told by an idiot, full of sound and fury, signifying nothing."

I waited a moment after he had finished performing his soliloquy before responding. "Very appropriate," I said.

"I thought you might think so."

"Tell me, Doctor Gottlieb, do you have all of Shakespeare's works memorized?"

"No, of course not, only the ones that contains truths which I covet. Truths that contain wonders both subtle and gross, and yet at the same time terrors to freeze the soul." He stopped a moment, reflecting on something before continuing. "Interesting phrase in that stanza though, 'recorded time', as though Shakespeare was suggesting that time itself were recorded, every moment, every month, every minute and every hour in the 'Cosmic Calendar' were planned; mapped out, as it were, since the very beginning, and everything that we have ever done, and everything that we will ever do, has already happened. I have always wondered if that were true. What if everything happened in that brief moment when the atom containing everything in the universe exploded, and unleashed its contents to what would be the heavens, and our lives were just a brief flicker in that instant, occupying not even the smallest fraction of a second on a great cosmic clock, which slowly ticks in a pace and manner that we can never fully understand, into what we call eternity. But perhaps from a different perspective in reality, the tiniest portion of an instant."

I studied him as he spoke, seemingly oblivious to my presence, as there were times when it appeared he didn't even notice my being there at all. It seemed as though he were, in fact, performing one of Shakespeare's dramas, and as the spotlight was in his face, he had no idea or presumably did not even care as to whether there was an audience listening. He, like an actor playing the part, just went on, consumed by some inner force that I could only begin to imagine. As I sat there in that chair across from him, watching him, animated by some compulsion that was driving him on, the realization came to me that his psyche was also something that I could only begin to comprehend and understand.

He continued, "Now that we established the nature of the very large and infinitely gross forces at work in universe, let us now turn our attention to the universe of the infinitely small. Take, for example this piece of hard and stale cake that this institution and the kind and benevolent state that while keeping me incarcerated, refers to as my dessert."

I couldn't help but suppress a snicker at his clever sarcasm.

"It was that same promising student I just spoke of who once argued on one of my final exams that if you *truly* wish to make a chocolate cake from scratch, you must first invent the universe." He leaned over from his cot to the edge of his night table on which laid his as yet untouched lunch tray. He opened the sealed bag in which his plastic eating utensils were kept and began to slice down the middle of the cake. "Suppose, Doctor, that we cut this cake in half, in half again, and so on and so forth, how many cuts would you think it would take until we arrived at the division of an individual atom?" He then turned and looked at me through the cage between us, raising his left eyebrow just a tad to no doubt establish control of the conversation and demonstrate his intellect.

"I have no idea," I said placidly, trying not to placate him.

He turned his attention back towards the now mangled cake which he had cut through and through until it lay in a pile dried crumbs. "The answer is, about ninety successive cuts, but this plastic knife is too dull, as that benevolent state that I so recently spoke of, of course, would not want me to injure myself or others ..." He paused and stared at me through the bars again, as if to imply that I might be 'the others' he spoke of. He then continued, "... but, besides that of course the cake is, as I mentioned earlier, too dry and stale, and an atom, which was once the size of the universe before the 'Big-Bang', is too small to see with the naked eye. But it *can* be done."

I sighed, crossed my legs, trying to get comfortable as it didn't take long sitting in that metal fold out chair to develop muscle fatigue, especially in the rear-end.

He read my expression and interrupted himself. "He was right of course, and you might have heard of him. His name was Carl Sagan."

"Interesting," I said, though I'm sure it did not appear as though I was interested.

"I assure you, Doctor, I'm not trying to bore you with this dissertation of cosmic and atomic discussion, and if you have some patience with your patient, I assure you their meanings will become very clear soon. Now, as you may or may not remember from your Biology and Chemistry, a typical atom is surrounded by a cloud of electrons, much like the earth is surrounded by a cloud of atmosphere. Electrons are negatively charged, and it is they who help determine the chemical and physical properties of the atom—say the cast iron bars that separate us, or if this were indeed glass instead of plastic," and he held up his juice cup to illustrate.

"The transparency of the solid is made between silicon and oxygen. But *deep* inside the atom is the nucleus, composed of positively charged protons, and neutrally charged neutrons, as the name suggests.

"One hundred thousand atoms placed end to end would be no longer than the tip of my index finger, and the nucleus of these atoms would be a hundred thousand times smaller still. Despite this, most of the mass of an atom is in the nucleus, again, much like most of the mass of the earth lies on the surface; the electron cloud surrounding atoms is as light and airy in relation to the atoms mass as the earth's atmosphere is. There are some ninety-two chemically distinct naturally occurring atoms found on earth, and as you are well aware these are referred to as the chemical elements. Everything we see and know is made of these ninety-two atoms arranged in often amazing and harmonious orders.

"The fact that atoms are composed of only three kinds of elementary particles, protons, neutrons, and electrons, is a relatively recent discovery in human history, especially when you stop to consider the *ten minutes* of our insect-like existence. It is these three units that when arranged in different patterns, make essentially, everything. When we decided to cut this cake down beyond a single atom we confront an infinity of the very small, as I have attempted to illustrate. When we imagine the enormity of the heavens, the hundreds of billions of galaxies each containing hundreds of billions of stars like our own, the seemingly unending lengths and depths of space and time, we are confronted with the infinity of the very large. These infinities are the most awesome and astounding truths in the universe—they represent for what to us is a never-ending expanse that goes in both directions of the human condition, forever.

"Let us now imagine a parallel between these two extremes. Let us imagine that our entire solar system is an atom, in someone else's massive and incomprehensibly enormous universe, and the sun is the nucleus of that atom, and the planets, the negatively charged electrons orbiting it. Our solar system binds with others to what we call galaxies and what someone else from a different and much larger perspective may simply call a cluster of cells. These many clusters of 'cells' of hundreds of billions of galaxies in our universe may form functional 'organs' in another, all working in unison together to some purpose we can not even begin to fathom or imagine. What then, I wonder, would that make us, Dr. Stattler?

"The point of all this rhetoric, Doctor, is that it is through the infinitely small, that the infinitely large is changed and manipulated, forever. It is through the infinitely small, our cells and our DNA, and the genes we carry that mankind has evolved to the state in which it now has. And for the first time in history, mankind is on the threshold of successfully unraveling the Deoxyribo-Nucleic-Acid, the key to understanding the human genetic composition, and how it was created. And what's worse still, how it can be, and I believe has been, *manipulated* over the course of hundreds of thousands, if not millions of our years."

"I'm not sure I understand where you're going with this, Doctor."

He sighed as though exasperated and continued.

"Let us take another example from my lunch tray, shall we?" He said, and leaned over and plucked a strawberry from the dessert plate next to the now mangled cake. "Take this strawberry for instance. Evolution and the preservation of the species works in either one of two ways, by *Artificial* selection, such as our friend the strawberry here, or *Natural* selection. Both of which, are always manipulated by *external* forces. This strawberry exists because we, humans, have selected it to exist. We like the way it looks, we like the way it tastes. We encourage the reproduction of like-traits of strawberries, and destroy or discourage aberrations and mutations. Virtually everything we humans consume survives because we have imposed *Artificial* selection among them. *Natural* selection works in much the same way as artificial, with the exception that there is no cerebral force at work behind which mutations of species survive. As you know from your Darwin, in each and every species during the reproductive cycle, there occasionally occurs a genetic mutation or error of the reproduction of the genetic code. If this error does not benefit the species, it does not survive and the abnormality does not pass on to future generations. If, however, the mutation does benefit the organism in question, and is beneficial, the traits hold true and pass on to the next generation of species."

"I'm sorry, Doctor." I interrupted. "But I still don't see how this biology lesson applies to extra-terrestrials."

He thought on this for a moment and continued.

"You're right. I do digress, however, as you shall soon see, it was necessary to first explain these simple truths of nature to you. Now, as we have already discussed how infinitely large or small the universe is, depending upon your perspective, there stands to reason some simple *unexplainable* facts using current scientific models and theories, concerning mankind's existence and rise to dominance over the other species of the earth. Specifically, though, these seemingly '*inexplicable*' phenomena lie directly in the *time* it took for man to evolve. You see, Doctor, it is in the universe of the infinitely small, the internal universe within each and every one of us, that evolution and history dictates we *have* changed, and yet, it is from the universe of the infinitely large that came the forces which brought about these changes."

"I'm not sure I follow you." I said.

"Haven't you ever wondered, Doctor ..." he stopped, interrupting himself. "No, I guess you haven't if you've never heard of the 'Cosmic Calendar' or 'Ten minutes to midnight ...'" he stopped again and then abruptly continued. "In any case Doctor, don't you find it unusual that we humans have only been around for a few minutes before midnight on December 31st, whereas the dinosaurs made their first appearance somewhere around December 22nd? They made their debut in what is called *The Permian Period* as small reptiles, and then later grew into the giant beasts we know of today in the late *Triassic*.

"In any case, for nearly 300 million years they never evolved beyond the ability to hunt in groups, and possibly communicate with one another, until some great cataclysm took place somewhere around midnight on December 30th. Three hundred million years they were here, Dr. Stattler, three hundred million years, over a week on the Cosmic Calendar, and we humans have evolved and come as far as we have in the span of only five to six million years, ten minutes on that same calendar? As any archaeologist will tell you Doctor, no other species in the four billion year history of the planet Earth evolved as fast, as quickly, or has come as far as we have, despite being given more than ample time and opportunity. Doesn't it seem as though that's a trifle hard to believe? If Natural selection alone was indeed responsible for human development, surely a prior species would have come about that was at least intelligent as we, don't you think? Doesn't that strike you as *odd* Dr. Stattler? Doesn't that strike you as *suspect*?"

"Suspect to what?" I asked.

He paused before responding, eyeing me warily to see if I had detected the answer to what it is he was trying to say.

"What do you think?" he said.

"I don't know, you tell me, that's why we're here isn't it?"

He paced about his cell slowly, clearly deliberating on how he was about to deliver the answer to the question I had asked.

"Suspect, Dr. Stattler, to the one thing no other archaeologist or anthropologist other than myself, dared ask, Dr. Stattler. The one thing that no reputable scientist would put a claim to lest it damage his name or reputation. It is suspect, Dr. Stattler, to *Artificial Selection,* or to put it more bluntly, *intervention.*"

"Intervention?" I said. "From what?"

"Not from what, Dr. Stattler, but from *whom.*"

I wasn't sure where he was going with this, if this was genuinely one of his theories or part of his delusion, or both. However, I had to admit, that if this was a paranoid delusion it was by far the most logical and well thought out one I had ever encountered, and because he was apparently speaking of events that happened millions of years ago when mankind did not even exist there was no feasible way to counter or disprove it.

"The answer, Doctor, lies in time itself. Which do you think works faster, Artificial Selection, or Natural Selection?" He asked, amusedly.

"I have the feeling you're about to tell me."

"To answer, let us return one last time to another example of the top notch cuisine of this venerable institution. Take this carrot for instance." He said, while sifting through the vegetable medley on his uneaten plate. "Do you know precisely why carrots are orange?"

"Because God made them so?" I chided, knowing full well his dislike of religion. I could tell he was repressing a smile at this as he continued.

"No, Doctor. But you are right in assuming that *Intelligent Design* made them that way. For you see, up until the eighteenth century, there were no orange carrots. There were carrots of just about every other color, black, white, red, but the carrots that we all love and cherish today did not exist, nor would they exist possibly ever, if the Dutch had not imposed *Artificial Selection* among them. You see, the ruling class at the time were French, whose colors were, you guessed it, orange. For whatever reason or political agenda, the scientists of the day had the purpose of mind to create an orange carrot to impress upon the French aristocracy. By cross fertilizing several different species of European varieties of carrots with African, eventually they were able to produce the wonderful vegetable that we have today. I trust that now you are beginning to see the answer to the great riddle. Nature when left on its own in four and a half billion years did not produce an orange carrot, nor is it likely that it ever would, but within only a few generations of Artificial Selection the Dutch were able to accelerate the creation of the orange carrot."

He smiled smugly before continuing. "Who is to say that man isn't the only species to unravel the secrets and manipulate genetic code? As we have discussed, the universe is a very, very, large place, Doctor, perhaps too large for us and our closed and often impermeable minds—minds that for whatever reason insist on adhering and believing the fact that neighbors amongst the stars are inconceivable. In some ways it is amazing that we have evolved at all, but then again, we wouldn't have, certainly not as fast as we did, and certainly not without *their* help anyway."

A feeling of dread began to wash over me as the possible answer as to what he was suggesting became clear.

"And who are *they*?" I asked.

He looked around the confines of his cell frantically, as though someone were listening, and once he had composed himself, continued, staring at me steadfastly through the bars in a whisper. "*Them*. The Ones. The deceivers. The beings that come and take us in the night. The Ones who made us, and can read our souls and minds, our thoughts and secrets."

"I don't understand," I said.

"The Ones responsible for *us*, Doctor," he whispered again. "The Ones who created and shaped mankind itself. *They*, Dr. Stattler, are what I have come to call *The Grays*."

"I'm assuming you found evidence of this in your excavations around the globe," I said, my voice implying doubt concerning his story.

"Naturally," he said, his voice returning to normal. He looked around the room while holding the bars that separated us in his hands. "Or I wouldn't be here."

"Is that why you think you are here?" I asked, and went on. "According to our records you murdered two men. Two federal agents and tore their faces open. Do you remember that?"

I was unprepared for the severity of his next response, and I felt as though I would nearly fall out of my chair from the sheer force of his voice as he ran to the bars and attempted to rattle the cage between us.

"THEY CAME INTO MY HOME!" he shouted. "TO KILL ME!"

I composed and steadied myself before responding, "And you're sure you're not concocting this story to justify those killings?"

"I HAVE NEVER LIED TO YOU DR. STATTLER, AND I NEVER WILL," he shouted again. He stepped back from the bars and flopped on his cot, seemingly dejected at my objectiveness. "You sound like Stimple when you talk like that. If you're going to talk like that I'd just assume you not talk at all."

I was starting to get irritated and decided to lay the facts straight out to him. "Let's switch places for a minute here Doc, I'm on your side of the bars and you're on mine. Your chart says your patient is a homicidal paranoid-schizophrenic, his behavior is erratic, extremely temperamental, and you're doing your best to treat your patient and understand why he is ill."

"Then listen to what your patient has to say before making judgments," he interrupted me.

"All right, fair enough," I said, and crossed my legs to get more comfortable.

Once he could see that I was comfortable and properly situated he continued.

"The first time I was exposed to evidence of their existence was June, 1950, in Swartkrans, South Africa. It was the summer of my junior year at Yale. At the time, the field of archaeology was much divided amongst several camps and evolutionary theories concerning the differences and similarities between the australopithecines and that of Homo-*habilis*. The primary argument being, specifically, as to whether habilis was descended from *afarensis*, *africanus*. In so far as I know, whether it was either, both of them, or neither of them, are still matters of debate and conjecture. It has been some time since I have made any investigations or contributions to the field, as I'm sure you'll understand."

Dr. Gottlieb paused and winked at me as he said this before continuing. "It is possible that none of the known australopithecines is our ancestor, not that it really matters anyway, knowing what I now know. However, for the purposes of our discussion, it is and was even in 1950, generally accepted that *Homo erectus*, the line from which we come, was descended from *Homo habilis* (or, at least, some of the fossils often assigned to *habilis*), but the relationship between *erectus*, *sapiens* and the Neanderthals is still unclear, at least to those who are unwilling to *really* see what it is they are looking at; to put all the myriads of pieces in to place. Sadly though, I don't really think any one wants to, or at very least, risk their credibility and career by doing so."

He paced about his cell, his hands behind his back, deep in thought until he once again sat down on his cot, and ran his fingers through the graying, wispy, stubble that pocked his head. I studied him, trying to find some clue that might indicate some method to his madness. Though I had to admit to myself, I did not believe that schizophrenia in his condition was present. Clearly his mood swings were irrational, and he was prone to psychotic, indignant behavior. Indeed, I was glad the bars separated us on more than occasion since I met him. But I couldn't help but feel that the schizophrenia was a label that had been misdiagnosed in his case. I trusted my instincts, as they usually had proven true, and what they told me as I watched him that he was suppressing nothing less than a fierce, primal rage.

The way he methodically paced around his cell, premeditated his responses, and manipulated the conversation suggested some sort of calculated pretense. I suspected there was an event in his past he had not yet revealed that had led him on to what would become a downward spiral of wrath and murder, and of course, his incarceration.

"Suffice as to say though, Doctor, the tedious details of human evolution do not really concern us here, only the reasons for my excursion to Africa. As I had stated previously, it was the summer of my junior year at Yale, and one of my professors, a Dr. Fourie was conducting a dig in Swartkrans. It was just the opportunity I was looking for, and it was due to this trip and another in the spring that I would later write my thesis for my first Ph.D., *The Simultaneous Evolution of Species*—the gist of which, of course, we now take for granted, that multiple species of humans were co-existing together, and amongst themselves and nature, battling for supremacy. This was especially true with the more modern humans, *Homo sapiens* and *Neanderthals*; however, it was my assertion that this was additionally true among some of the australopithecines.

"It was one such *australopithecine* which turned out to be the object of the excavation. Dr. Fourie had, on a previous excursion to South Africa, found several bone fragments in a lake bed in Swartkrans. He felt he was getting close to a major discovery, but had to return to Yale before he could complete his work due to a recent political upheaval in the region. Once things had simmered down and the mass tribal warfare had been replaced with a despot who was, for the meantime, favorable to the United States, he had decided to return the following year with a research team composed of two students, who would receive academic credit in exchange for time spent in the field. I was one of the two who would accompany him on the dig.

"Within two weeks we found more fragments, and finally after nearly a month of scouring the dry lake bed, we hit pay-dirt, to which now Dr. Fourie is credited—the discovery of what would be later termed *Australopithecus robustus*, formerly known as *Paranthropus crassidens*. To give you some background information, *robustus* had a body similar to that of *africanus*, but with a larger and more robust skull and teeth. Best estimates indicate that it existed somewhere between one and a half to two million years ago. It was the find of a lifetime, the most complete skull of *robustus* ever found, and once it was discovered and confirmed Dr. Fourie wasted no time in making his announcement to the world. He took a gas jeep with my counterpart to the town of Krugersdorp, the closest settlement, to contact the university.

"While they were gone I was entrusted to remove excess debris so that we could eventually free the skull from the lakebed. This took several hours of tedious, boring labor, not the highlight of archaeology to be sure. It was while I was clearing away the excess dirt and dust from the skull that I happened upon something quite unexpected. There appeared to be a large fossilized lump behind the lower jaw of the skeleton. I decided to see if I could remove it as it did not seem to be directly attached to the skull itself. Although I thought I was chiseling delicately enough to remove the fragment, I wasn't paying attention to the stratification of the surrounding layers of rock, and with what I thought was only a light tap from my Jackson Trowel, I accidentally split the fragment.

"I remember loathing myself then, for my carelessness and stupidity, when something odd caught my eye. A glimmer, from *inside* the fossil. I began to brush off the surface area, heavily at first, excited about what I might find, but being careful not to damage whatever was inside. Once the surrounding dirt and dust were clear, I grasped it with a pair of tweezers and lifted it from its resting place of nearly two million years. It was perfectly spherical, about the size of a pea, and had a dull metallic gray color to it. It had no abrasions, no rust, nor any damage that I could see or detect after no doubt witnessing the elements and erosion of millennia. Though I did not know it then, I was holding within my grasp the evidence which would become my greatest achievement—and my greatest failure."

"What did you think it was?" I asked.

"I had no idea. But the one thing I was certain about was that it didn't belong there, inside the head of some crude form of man and ape. It was a foreign object of some kind, and did not mysteriously appear there. The one thing I was also certain of was that I would not reveal it's presence to Dr. Fourie or the other student, whose name I have since forgot. Dr. Fourie would have his day, and would be accredited this discovery without revealing mine. I decided to save it for some future purpose which in time I had almost forgotten, and it remained in a glass vial in my desk drawer for nearly nine years before I was reminded of it again."

"Why nine years, specifically?" I asked, studying him intently, searching for any clues that might reveal more purpose other than his own machinations.

"I was in school, Doctor, writing my second thesis which I have already described to you when we met this morning, pursuing my second Doctorate, and when I wasn't in the classroom I was teaching undergraduate courses. I was also assisting others with research in the field, either for academic credit, or to build experience. It was on one such endeavor in the summer of 1959 that I was again reminded of the mysterious and often nefarious forces which surrounded and consumed us, since the very inception of our origins.

"My reputation was beginning to build in the university with the publication and subsequent acceptance of my first thesis regarding the co-existence of early and modern hominids. If I had to guess as to the nature of this reputation, it was probably of someone who was willing to take chances, make their case and take a stance, who ignored the 'camps' as it were of current methodology, preferring investigation to conjecture. It had gained me notoriety and a great deal of respect from many of the senior professors with tenure. It also allowed me to take advantage and be a part of excavations not normally offered to the student body or faculty.

"It was shortly after I had received my doctorate in archaeology and my Masters in anthropology that I was approached by Louis Leakey, an alumnus of Yale, who was conducting a dig at the Olduvai Gorge in Tanzania the following spring. He said he had heard of my work in Africa previously through an old colleague turned professor, Dr. Fourie, who spoke very highly of me, and he was wondering if I would accompany he and his wife, Mary, to the excavation site. As his wife was getting up there in years, she was no longer able to handle some of the more mundane and physical labor involved in excavation, and he said he needed someone who was bright, with fresh ideas, and most importantly, a strong back.

He originally discovered the site in 1931 and instantly understood its immense value to the fields of anthropology and archaeology. He was quick to recognize that the geological forces which created the Gorge, known as *faulting,* exposed geological beds near the surface. In turn, Olduvai's active volcanoes would cause rapid sedimentation of bone and other early human artifacts that might otherwise be lost to scavengers or erosion.

"Due to the war, he was forced to leave the area in 1936, and only returned sporadically for lack of funding. In 1952, he petitioned the School of Archaeology for a grant to continue the excavations, and after being driven through the grindstone of academia bureaucracy, his request was finally approved in 1958. I was thrilled at the prospect, and since it had been nine years since in the field or to Africa, I found it hard to refuse. We were to leave for Tanzania the second week of May, 1959, as it was the onset of the rainy season, which was perfect for me as it gave me the fall and winter semesters to finish the last of my academic credits, get my affairs in order for the trip, and complete what was to be my second great thesis *10 Minutes to Midnight—the Momentary Existence of Man.*

"And, I had to admit, I liked Dr. Leakey. He was bold, straightforward, confidant, and best of all, had an affinity for *real* German beer. Before we left in the spring we would often go over the surveys he and his wife had already made and plan for possible excavation sites over a few glasses of Deutschland's finest. And once we arrived in Tanzania, he made it a point to have shipped every month to the dig site, in addition to the essentials, at least two to three cases of Andech's, a small monastery/brewery, located on the outskirts of town of Herrsching, in Bavaria. We would chill them in the shallows of the river Olduvai, and enjoy them after a hard days work under the shade of the giant Baobab trees that littered the landscape, keeping out of the sometimes blistering Tanzanian sun."

"Sounds tranquil," I said, studying him as he reflected inward, lying on his cot, his eyes closed, somewhere in that far off place devoid of time and captivity. My comment seemed to jeer him back to his cell, and his tone changed from one of sheer longing to one of passive discipline.

"I learned during my brief stay that the Baobab was referred to as *the upside down tree* in the local tongue, and the sometimes thousand year old trunks were hollowed out to serve as reservoirs to collect the rain. Although May through September was what was referred to as *the rainy season,* from what I could tell it was only because it rained at all, completely unlike parts of India, where the term *rainy season* meant you would be wearing a raincoat for several months at a time. Not so with the arid climate of Tanzania. When it did rain the storm clouds would roll in off the prairie until they would build into a dense and violent deluge, usually lasting no more than an hour. Flash floods were common, and what were dry, desolate, and empty ravines would turn into torrent, turbulent rivers that would literally wash away time.

"It was precisely for this reason that Louis chose the excavation when he did. Much of the sediments that covered the unfound remains of early humans could be removed in the span of an afternoon with one brief storm. The downside, of course, would be that any fossils near the surface might be washed away completely. However, he felt this was worth the risk, and he said it was also cooler than the dry season, although I found no comfort in his consolation of this. The days were nearly unbearable and full of toil, and were for the most part spent setting out site grids, steel ranging rods, and diagramming section plans. When we weren't preparing for a dig, we were excavating large swaths of earth and debris with a mattock head and pick ax. With the exception of the gorge and some of the foothills, the surrounding land was mostly flat, and dry, and spattered with occasional brush and grasses.

"Long ago when man first walked these lands, it was a lush and dense forest, filled with tropical fruit and fauna. If there ever was such a place, it was the 'Eden' of man's beginnings. It was where he took his first steps. It was where man started on the path of what he would become today. Now it was empty, arid, and nearly barren of life save a few grasses and the occasional sheanut or baobab tree. I had never physically worked so hard in my life, and at the time was seriously entertaining the idea of changing careers to Astrology, where labor would be confined to cool air-conditioning or under the calm of a clear evening sky.

"Finally, one afternoon after a brief rain storm, we found what we were looking for. Just peeking out of the soil Louis found what appeared to be small, fossilized metacarpals, probably from a child. Further excavation revealed two definite cranial fragments of a child, somewhere between the ages of six and nine, and then finally a lower jaw. I had never seen Louis so excited, as the bones appeared to be that of a *Homo Habilis*, and he and I were both giddy as schoolboys.

"But my joy in sharing in his discovery soon changed dramatically. As I was gathering the samples in an empty Andech's crate to return to base camp, I heard him call out from the rock basin behind me.

"'Gottlieb, what do you make of this?'" he asked.

"I set down the crate and lumbered over to where he was standing beneath me. He had a pair of forceps held up for me to see, and clutched between the ends he had what I secretly hoped I would never find again. My heart froze at the discovery, for it confirmed what I suspected those many years ago and tried to forget, and my mind began to race out of both excitement and fear.

"'Where did you find that?'" I said to him, nearly shouting. "'Give it to me!'" and he it pulled it towards him instinctively, clearly seeing that I wanted it.

"'It was buried in some debris near the jawbone,'" he said. "'What is it?'" he asked again, looking at it and securing his prize.

"'You don't want to know,'" I said, and I picked up the crate to return to camp.

"Did you tell him what you suspected?" I asked, intrigued by his story.

"No, I never did tell him," he said, looking into my eyes. "In the end he decided that he did not want to know. That night as we sat in mute silence, sipping our Andech's beside the fire, his wife finally off to bed he asked pointedly, "'What is this thing, Gottlieb? You've seen it before. What are you hiding?'"

"'I don't know for sure,'" I said. "'Only a suspicion that has now been confirmed. But if proven true, a suspicion that could change the world as we know it, and would destroy the lives of many, you included, should you choose to reveal it.'"

"'What do you intend to do?'" he asked.

"'I'm not sure,'" I said. "'But I do know that I can act only as my conscience dictates.'"

"'Then take it,'" he said, and he held out his hand with the metallic pea-sized ball that I had come to know resting blissfully in the middle of his palm. "'And God be with you, for you go where I cannot, and never mention to anyone that you found it with me. At my age and at this stage of my career, if what you say is true, I have far too much to lose, and very little to gain.'"

"I plucked it, carefully then from the center of his palm and put it inside my shirt pocket. Though he suspected what I was implying and must have had some idea about the unworldly nature of the artifact, he never asked again what it was. Possibly because he knew what the consequences were, possibly because he did not want to know what the truth contained.

"As I sat there by the fire, looking at Louis, who returned my gaze, I was certain that what I had discovered nine years ago had been no accident. I knew that somehow or another these 'chips', these unearthly relics, were somehow calling to me, beckoning my very future, and dangling it before me like a prize. I knew what I had to do. I had to find as much evidence as possible to support my theory of what I suspected was interference—direct interference from another species in the evolution of ours.

"I had to find another chip in a more modern human, either an archaic or modern *Homo sapiens* to both establish and finish the pattern. I had to construct a geological timeline to measure their interference. I had to find other evidence, paintings, sculptures, and drawings, anything that might serve to prove their existence.

"I also knew I could not stay on the dig much longer, as because of the chip, things had changed between Louis and me. It was sort of like sleeping with someone for the first time, whose relationship had always been a strictly platonic one, and because of either a mistake or fate, things had changed irrevocably, and would never be the same again. There was an eerie silence between him and me after that day, and the chip which he found beside the lower jaw of that child in the fossilized mud would never be discussed between us again."

"What happened?" I asked, as he had paused for a few moments.

"What happened then?" he repeated my question. "I stayed through the end of the rainy season, until he could find someone else to replace me, and I came back to Yale in the fall of 1959. I eagerly began to set about conducting research and either supervising or participating on any excavation I could find to prove my theory, a theory that if proven true, would change the world and humanity forever."

"And what exactly was your theory, Doctor?"

He looked at me with a somewhat detached expression, composing himself before responding.

"It's quite simple really. You see Doctor, although I was certainly not aware of it at the time, my experiences at Bergen-Belsen were preparing me for something greater, for lack of a better word, something far more sinister and deviously contemplated. Something that would put the detached efficiency of the Nazi mind to shame. Something that was, truly, for lack of a better expression, and I hope that you'll pardon the pun, 'out of this world.' You see, in concentration camps, every prisoner had a number," and he lifted up his forearm and held it out in front of me, while rolling back the orange jumper he was wearing so I could read the tattoo still clearly etched in black and legible on his skin.

"Having seen first hand and bared personal witness to the keen proficiency with which the Germans were nearly able to complete their answer to 'The Jewish Question', I was beginning to form questions of my own, and my experience there gave me, I think, a truly unique perspective into the phenomenon that I was now determined to expose. You see, Doctor, somewhere, in that camp, either in the Captain's office, or in his desk, or on a shelf somewhere, there was a ledger, a ledger that was the Rosetta stone in translating prisoner numbers to names, and somewhere in that ledger was a listing for prisoner," and he read the number off his forearm still extended almost malevolently in front of me. "... Prisoner 276584, as Jacob Francis Gottlieb, a Jew, age 9."

After making his point he carefully rolled back his sleeve, returned to his cot against the wall and sat down with a careful deliberateness before continuing.

"Ironically, Doctor, the greatest mistake of the Germans and the one that exposed their atrocities at Nuremberg was this tenacity for precise record keeping. Ledgers like the one in Bergen-Belsen and evidence they collected was used against them in their trial, as is also the case, Doctor, with our little friends here."

"What do you mean?" I asked apprehensively.

"These artifacts that I had discovered were the very evidence not only of the existence of extra-terrestrial beings, but of their direct intervention in the course of our evolution. Somewhere in the cabins of one of their vessels or more likely in a computer there is also a ledger of sorts. Perhaps a database, that is probably capable of tracking every single one of these devices, each of which, like my prisoner number, is unique and probably transmits a different signal, and this database records the effects of their 'intervention,' through time. I would also theorize that these artifacts also serve as a means for reacquiring certain individuals, individuals who might carry DNA pertinent to whatever it is they hope to accomplish, and to that end they probably also serve as a tracking device of some sort."

He then stared at me intently, and the tone of his voice changed from one that sounded of reasonable speculation to one of dire seriousness.

"When I was in that line and I saw that Captain sorting through the herd of Jews with the tip of his finger, either to the showers or to the camp, it was not *evil* I saw in his eyes, Doctor. It was merely indifference. These creatures who are taking us, experimenting on us, and perhaps in many cases killing us, Doctor, also do not view their actions as *evil* or 'crimes against humanity.' They do not view their actions as crimes at all.

"You see, like the Germans, and as you said yourself, like we do in artificial selection with plants and animals, they are simply sorting through the human gene pool, allowing whatever genes and DNA they find more favorable to survive, and probably replicating those traits as latent genes, as well as adding DNA strands of their own, which to truly answer the 'Ten minute' question, Doctor, is why we evolved from primates so quickly."

I sat there listening, silently horrified at the possibilities of what he was implying, and for the first time truly began to doubt whether this was a paranoid delusion. What if what he were saying were true? What if all of human kind had been the subject of some great experiment from a race which had probably existed before the dinosaurs, and very possibly created man himself? But still, there were questions, questions I did not understand.

"But why take us at all? Why change us? And to what end, to what purpose does it serve?" I asked.

"I do not know!" he snapped bitterly. "I do not even pretend to know the full reasoning behind their logic. What I do know, Doctor, is that the two chips I had helped to unearth were found in skeletons that were at significant points in the evolutionary timeline. Changes, if you will, occurred in these fossils that were not seen in previous skeletons, cranium size, height, brain capacity, et cetera. The other thing that I also knew was I certainly couldn't have been the only one who had found these artifacts. Other archaeologists in the field must have come across them at one time or another, and they either took no note of their meaning and significance, *or*, they suspected what they were, and chose to reveal nothing. One thing was certain though, no one was talking."

"Who would?" I asked, attempting to illustrate the obvious, while offering an alternative explanation, more for my sanity at the moment than his. "And besides, it was all still a theory, you had no concrete evidence. After all, what is easier to believe, anyway? That some strange metal object found in close proximity to a human ancestor is an alien artifact designed to monitor, track, and aid in the abduction and evolution of the human species, or just some strange lump of metal?"

"Are you patronizing me again, Doctor? Your voice has the unique and condescending sound of Stimple," he said.

"I'm not attempting to patronize you, Doctor, I'm just attempting to illustrate that maybe there might be some other explanation than the one you've concocted."

"As you'll soon see, Doctor, I didn't 'concoct' anything," he said, while

"Thrice the brinded cat hath mewed," he said. "Thrice, and once the hedge-pig whined! Harpier cries, 'tis time!' 'tis time!' Round about the cauldron go, in the poisoned entrails throw!" and with that he began to toss invisible objects into the imperceptible cauldron he was circling.

"Toad, that under cold stone days and nights has thirty-one swelt' red venom sleeping got, boil thou first in the charmed pot! Double, double, toil and trouble; fire burn and cauldron bubble. Fillet of a fenny snake, in the cauldron boil and bake! Eye of newt and toe of frog, wool of bat and tongue of dog, adder's fork and blind-worm's sting, lizard's leg and howlet's wing! For a charm of powerful trouble, like a hell-broth, boil and bubble! Double, double, toil, and trouble; fire burn and cauldron bubble," he repeated, and without stopping his eerie monologue continued. "Scale of dragon, tooth of wolf, witch's mummy, maw and gulf, of the ravin'd salt-sea-shark, root of hemlock digged in the dark! Liver of a blaspheming Jew!" at this he stopped abruptly, and glared with fury at the two of us watching him and his macabre dancing. His eyes glared at as us as though on fire and were consumed with rage and hatred. It soon became clear as to why he stopped at that last ingredient.

After a few seconds his face changed suddenly, as though he had just come out of a trance, and he smiled at Director Sikes and me. Chuckling to himself, he waved his hand as though I had chided him and said quite calmly, "Come now, Doctor, *aliens*, you say?" He then began to giggle, which turned to a cackle, and then a knowing, loud, maniacal laughter, that penetrated everything as it echoed furiously down the cement corridor and off the walls of the cell block, until he resumed, screaming in his witches voice, "Tis True! Tis True!"

CHAPTER FIVE

Mr. Black

"I see you're smoking again," he said as he sauntered up to me, quite obviously taking his time, enjoying and reveling in the moment.

Ours was a game of cat and mouse, of which I was playing the mouse for over twenty years, ever eluding a mysterious and seemingly omnipotent black cat, and now he was predictably gloating over his trophy. I sat motionless with my back still turned to him.

"And that you've become a hopeless alcoholic," he added, almost stuttering the last word as if to mock me, as he leaned into the bar next to me right into my ear. "For someone who's a physician you should know better."

"I'm not a physician anymore thanks to you," I said.

"There you go again assessing blame Dr. Stattler. What makes you think or even *believe* that I was acting on my own intentions? You know as well as I do the myriad of forces at play in this great conspiracy of ours …"

"Maybe it's because you seem to take such pleasure in it," I replied sneeringly.

"While I'll admit there is certain tenacity with which I enjoy my work …"

"Work?" I blurted out. "You murder innocent people."

"Now, now, Dr. Stattler, there's no need to make a scene," he then parted his trench coat so that I could see his gun holstered at his side. "And what is *innocence* truly, after all. It is nothing more than blind luck, being at the wrong place at the right time … you should be more reverent Dr. Stattler. After all, I never killed you," he said smiling.

"What kept you from it," I said. "*Orders?*"

"If you must know Dr. Stattler I was *dis*obeying orders when I made the decision to let you live. The powers that be," he said looking around as

80

though they were listening, "thought you should suffer for your insolence or at the very least share the same fate as our mutual friend Dr. Gottlieb. You see, Dr. Stattler, for personal reasons I thought you may yet prove useful. And you will."

"Gottlieb didn't do anything except seek the truth. It disgusts me that you would imprison and incarcerate an innocent and harmless old man. I have nothing but hatred and contempt for you and whoever or whatever your 'bosses' are," I spat back at him.

"Yes, yes … but you must understand that he was quite a young man and full of ideals when I took him, and if I might add, you should be more grateful. If it were not for him, you and I would never have met. But, returning to Dr. Gottlieb that was a busy week for me, if I do recall. I had, after all, just assassinated the President," he said smiling at me looking as though he was trying to suppress a giggle.

I merely rolled my eyes in disgust.

"Actually, Dr. Stattler, it's concerning those forces that I am here today. In short I have a proposal for you …"

"Fuck off," I interrupted, perhaps too loudly as my words echoed off the tile in the empty restaurant to the glancing stares of the wait-staff.

"… one I don't think you should ignore. Join me at a table?" He motioned with his left arm toward one of the many empty booths lining the wall of the cocktail area.

It was at this moment that Mickey decided he had remained in the shadows of this conversation long enough and sauntered over. Throwing a bar rag over his shoulder he asked, "This guy giving you trouble Evan?"

The Man in Black, or, "Mr. Black" as I shall from now refer to him, did not hesitate to answer for me.

"Mickey Fiorentino why don't you bring us two coffees to that table over there," he said, motioning to a table in the corner.

I couldn't help but smile at Mr. Black's charm, black, as it was, and it caught

Mickey unawares as he had quite obviously never met the man who was speaking to him. I gave him a subtle nod to let him know that I was alright.

"Be right over," he said with a somewhat diffident and defiant tone, as if to say, 'If we weren't in my place of employment I would kick the living shit out of you and rub my feces all over your face.'

Mr. Black motioned to me again without saying a word with his hand to the table in the corner. I got up off my stool without looking at him, walked across the bar and slid into the right side of the booth. It was made of soft, black leather, which had become almost like a chamois with years of use. It was ensconced in dark brown oak with brass railings trim, and a large brass coat hanger on each corner that connected one booth to another all along the west wall. It was on the coat hanger closest to him that Mr. Black took off his trench coat and hung it. He then removed his gun from its holster and set it on the table. It was stainless steel, very large, looked to be a 10 millimeter with a small laser scope at the top and what appeared to be a 3-inch silencer screwed onto the end.

"No need to be frightened Dr. Stattler, I assure you, it's just it's hard to sit comfortably with that thing butting into my hip."

"I'll try to bear that in mind," I said, glancing at him and then the gun. "In the meantime do you think perhaps you could move it to the back corner of the table where it's not quite so obvious?"

"Quite right, quite right," he said sliding the gun across the table to his left deftly with one hand. "Besides, we wouldn't have room for our coffee," he said, motioning towards Mickey, who was approaching with a tray. He proceeded to set down two heavy mugs filled to the brim and a small silver pot between us with a saucer of cream and a sugar caddie. In doing so, I noticed him glance at the gun on the back left corner of the table. When he was finished he asked in an authoritative voice, "I'm not going to have any trouble with you two am I?" while looking not at me, but directly at Mr. Black.

Mr. Black did not even so much as flinch or even look at Mickey. Reaching for his coffee and spooning sugar into his mug he said, "Mickey Fiorentino. Born 9-15-71. Divorced, April of 2000. One daughter Anja, Born 6-30-94. Social Security Number 228-37-4032. Drives a 98 Mustang convertible, blue, Rhode Island license plate XJF-572. Lives at 228 Thayer St, Apartment B, eats Cheerios for breakfast and is sometimes prone, while his daughter is staying with her mother, to dancing in his underwear to the Village People."

This was the manner in which Mr. Black established control of a situation. However he got his information, he used it and only revealed it when the time was called for it. He was patient, methodical, and ruthless no doubt as The Grays had taught and trained him to be. He had, no doubt before our encounter today, followed me for weeks, even months possibly. Followed my habits, followed who I regularly talked to, this bar and Mickey among them, so that when a confrontation inevitably boiled down he was absolutely prepared to seize and take control. By dropping this personal information, which virtually anyone with half a mind could find out if they bothered to do even a minor bit of investigative work, he was *really* saying without saying, "I know who you are. I know where I can find you. I know who the ones you love are, and I can hurt them. And if you even *think* of fucking with me, I'll destroy you." It demonstrated *because* he took the time to know these things, he was willing, capable and could *do* these things. And in that moment I couldn't help but wonder what terrible things he had said to poor Pauli. Truly knowledge *is* power.

I empathetically looked up at Mickey as he stood there with the tray dangling at his side an ashen gray. "I'll, I'll be behind the bar if you need me Evan," he stuttered.

"Thank you, Mr. Fiorentino. When I need you, rest assured, you *will* know it," answered Mr. Black, who still hadn't turned to face or even look at the six foot two hundred twenty pound bar-man whose ego he had just turned to a pile of fermenting jelly.

"I see you haven't changed," I said, studying him face-to face for the first time. Indeed, in the twenty plus years since last I saw him, he seemed to have aged no more than five or ten years at most. His face was a bit more hard-lined and he had a few wisps of gray hair here and there poking out of his mane of coal black, but for a man who had to be at least approaching seventy he looked like he was maybe in his late forties. I continued, "... even still wearing the same sunglasses even though it's raining outside." I looked him up and down so he could see. "... Even still wearing the same suit," which was black with a white shirt and black tie.

"Yes, well, the good thing about black, Dr. Stattler, is that it never goes out of style," which he said in answer to my statement but by the tone of his voice suggested a hidden, deeper meaning.

"What do you want?" I asked, seeing no purpose in beating around the bush. He had been controlling the conversation with everyone since he walked in the door and I thought it was my turn to try and call the shots. After all, he was here for something. He *wanted* something.

"You, Dr. Stattler," he said without moving or flinching.

"It would seem you already have me, *Mr. Black*, or whatever your real name is ..."

He interrupted, "Mr. Black will suffice. That is what your predecessor called me; in fact it was his ..."

I interrupted him before he could continue, feeling slightly ballsy from the two glasses of scotch I had had in a quarter of an hour. "But whatever

the case I'm not going to continue this conversation unless I can see just
who it is I am talking to!"

With this he sighed begrudgingly, somewhat displeased from what I
could gather, but after a brief second relented and removed his sunglasses,
folded them neatly and put them in the inside pocket of his suit jacket.
"Better?" he asked, somewhat annoyed.

"Quite," I said steadfastly, admiring my little victory of the moment. I
looked into his eyes for the first time. His eyes were jet black, and though
you wouldn't know it at first glance, the pupils were somewhat larger than
normal, and it wasn't just the darkness of the room due to the rain outside.
He seemed to have little or no iris whatsoever, no color. It was as though he
had been recently to an ophthalmologist and had them dilated for purposes
of an examination.

"Yes, I know," he said, seeming to know my thoughts. "One of the
many genetic *enhancements* of my creators, hence the need for these," he
said gently patting the sunglasses now ensconced in his suit pocket. "The
more modern agents have more *normal* looking eyes. As I was one of the
first prototypes, I lacked certain, how should I put it, *amenities*." He said
this last word while almost *hissing* the 's,' and I couldn't help but wonder
whether he felt some animosity about this.

"What do they do?" I asked.

"I can see objects, people, and the entire world around me with perfect
clarity in almost complete darkness. A gift you see, from my benefactors."

"I guess this helps to make you a more efficient killer," I said.

"Peace-keeper, Dr. Stattler. Peace-keeper," he said in a monotone drone
which made me question whether or not if he believed what he was actually
saying. "You and I both know what the forces at work here are."

"You'll forgive me if I question your motivations."

"Still full of tenacity I see, Dr. Stattler. I was hoping you would be."

"Well, you'll have to forgive me again," I said with bitterness. "I lost my
job this morning."

"Lost your job, lost your job," he said mockingly. "I freed you from that
dismal existence of scrubbing pots and grease-traps and you act as though
I've committed a travesty. May I?" He gestured toward the pack of Kools
which were still in my hand, and took one without my answering. He then
removed a stainless steel *Zippo* from his coat pocket and lit it. "Besides," he
exhaled. "I had to do something to get your attention. I had to let you know
I was here."

"I think I could have figured that out on my own. I was a psychologist you know. I do have *some* understanding of the workings of human behavior."

"So you like to think," he replied knowingly, suggesting that there was some truth to the contrary which he was hesitant to reveal. "And tell me then, though I know it's been a long time since you were forced to use that brain of yours, instead of plugging away at drudgery work and inundating your skull with whiskey … .frankly I'm surprised how you've managed to survive."

"You didn't make it easy," I said.

"Of course not, but you see that's my job. Did you know that the security guard who stumbled upon the *Watergate* scandal was *never* able to find work again for the *rest* of his life?"

"You?" I asked, in a befuddled tone.

"Naturally, though that assignment, I regret to say, was not from my superiors directly. It was more so, how shall we say, a 'favor' to the G.O.P."

"Lovely. I'm sure I could be sickened for days listening to the crimes you've committed in the name of 'freedom' … I won't even ask about the Kennedy's," I said.

"Now that *was* an assignment, a regrettable, but necessary one …" he stammered and sipped his coffee.

I rolled my eyes in disgust and disbelief.

He then continued, observing my agitation with the subject.

"You see, it wasn't the mob, or Castro, or suffice it to say Oswald, who couldn't hit the side of a barn with a baseball bat in broad daylight. It was quite simple, really. Jack Kennedy was ambitious. *Too* ambitious as it turned out. It was his ambition, more than anything else, which killed him. It was his plan to be the first man, the first leader of a nation in the history of the planet earth to reveal the existence of what you call *the Grays*. It was part of his *space agenda*. Even more so it was his belief that the Soviet Union, Castro, and Communism itself would have no choice but to crumble before the United States at such a revelation. It was a convenient way of perpetuating him as one of the greatest men in world history and at the same time ridding himself of all his enemies in one fell swoop.

"As the 'official' first contact would have been with the United States, the U.S. and its leaders would have virtual world dominion over public opinion. What nation would dare stand against one whose allies have the technology to breach the vast distances between the stars? When Mr. Kennedy broached the subject with them, the Grays delayed, placated, and eventually capitulated and agreed that the announcement would take place at the end of his second term, if elected, which of course there was little doubt. As you are well aware, he never finished out the length of his first. It was for this reason that my superiors decided all evidence and information concerning the Grays existence would be kept from all future presidents unless humanity was on the verge of self-destruction. Nuclear war, for example."

"Why?"

"Because we could not allow one man and his ambition to dictate to who are literally the fathers of humanity their purpose. To say nothing of the fact that the revealing of their existence would put an end to their gallivanting around the earth at night and kidnapping its citizens for purposes of their experiments. Experiments that have taken *generations* and *millions* of years to produce results. How could the United Nations and the countries of the world at large look the other way while their governments were sanctioning the theft and molesting of their peoples? There would be revolts. Riots. Anarchy. Governments would fall. The world as we knew it would end, because the Grays, quite frankly, are not willing to put a halt to these goals or achievements. They have been here for several million years, there was too much involved, too many resources at stake.

"It was therefore decided that myself and three of my men would make an example of this 'Mr. Kennedy.' This was not the random assassination of a president by a lone gunman, or even a group of well organized conspirators. It was a message to the present and future leaders of the world who were in the *know* to make them aware of exactly *who* and *what* was in charge." After this diatribe, he leaned back in the booth and comfortably sipped his coffee calmly, as if he had only just revealed that John Kennedy was only a flagrant womanizer.

I felt ill.

"I think I'm going to be sick," I said. I paused and thought a moment. "Let me guess, the head shot ... that was you?"

"Naturally. How did you guess?" he smiled and seemed surprised, almost *proud* that I discovered this truth without any further help from him.

"It had your signature," I said dourly.

"But we digress, Dr. Stattler, of the purpose in my coming here today."

"And what is, exactly, the purpose of your coming here today? Somehow I don't think you're selling Girl Scout Cookies," I said. "So what exactly are you selling?"

"I'm here to give you a second chance, Dr. Stattler. A second chance at redemption. A second chance at what you wanted most. A second chance at the truth."

"And what exactly does that mean?" I asked nervously.

"You see, Dr. Stattler, I am getting old. Too old to pursue you or my other assignments much longer. I am growing tired, Dr. Stattler."

"Well that's good," I said. "Because I'm tired of running from you."

"I don't think you quite understand, Dr. Stattler. My days as peace-keeper are numbered, not because of age or health but because of desire, because of the will ..."

"Peace-keeper?" I interrupted him, having heard him use it a second time now.

"Yes, I much prefer that term," he said. "It gives me comfort in my old age ... that I have somehow in some way done *some* good for humanity."

"'I suppose you can legitimize and justify murder or just about anything can't you, Mr. Black? All in the name of salvation and saving us from ourselves. I pity you." I said it out of courtesy, but what I really felt was a more loathsome disgust. I leaned back into my side of the booth, my arms outstretched against the table, trying to put as much distance between myself and him as possible, like I was dangling something that smelled of pure foulness from the tips of my fingers and holding it away from my person as far my arms could reach.

He looked at me reproachfully, his black eyes unwavering, full and solid as piece of polished coal.

"Suffice as to say, Dr. Stattler, I did not come here today for your pity. You see I like you Dr. Stattler, in fact you're the closest thing I have to a *true* friend in this world. I find there to be something uniquely competitive in this game of ours; who can outsmart and outthink, and outrun the other the longest."

"I'm so thrilled to hear you say that," I said bleeding sarcasm. "Which reminds me, how did you find me this time?"

"I'd been following you for some time now. Following your habits, places you go, people you see."

"I'd gathered that," I interrupted.

"Actually it was quite by chance that I found you this time Dr. Stattler. I had nearly given up hope and succumbed to defeat. I was at the end of my tether when I was going through some old *Amtrak* rail records and found that you had purchased several round-trip train tickets from Baltimore to

Providence in the early seventies ... I thought it worth a look. I figured you had been there before, you knew the area, the landscape, the town, the people. Anyway, it took me about two months to case all the restaurants and places of odd jobs before I happened upon you at your last place of employ. Quite a dive really, what drove you there anyway?"

"Best pizza in town," I said confident and smiling, feeling somewhat more relaxed.

"Well, I'm glad to hear that you've been eating well," he said with a smirk.

"Is that an attempt at humor?" I leaned forward and asked inquisitively, "You'll have to forgive me because I just didn't think that was possible from a *creature* like you." I hissed this word half joking and half full of menace at the same time. I was taunting him. I remembered what he told me long ago and I threw it back in his face.

"You will find, Dr. Stattler, that although I may be pieced together from a host of genetic components in a laboratory, I'm not as devoid of human compassion and dignity as you may think."

"I think many things of you, Mr. Black, and none of them would seem to indicate that you have compassion."

He smiled at this, leaning back in the booth, puffing on his cigarette. He studied me quizzically, his eyes slowly looking me up and down as though he was examining goods for purchase. He paused a moment before speaking, quite obviously carefully considering what his next words would be.

"You're a smart man, Dr. Stattler. A smart man indeed. You have kept me intrigued since the very beginning over twenty years ago when you were willing to sacrifice the well-being of your wife and child to preserve an ideal."

I responded hastily, partially out of anger, partially out of regret. "I did what I did because I was young and cocky. I was naïve. I believed in righteousness and the inherent good in our society. I was wrong. You taught me that, and it was a very bitter lesson to learn."

"So tell me then, Dr. Stattler, how will the game finally end? What *reason* do I have in coming here today?" he said ruefully.

"I was hoping that you would tell me, though if I were forced to guess I would venture to say that you *needed* something from me. Something you can't get from anyone else, or that no one else will give you."

"You are a smart man indeed. And tell me then, what is it exactly that I *need* from you?" He pronounced and accentuated *need* to egg me on, to mock me on some benign level only the two of us could understand.

I sat quietly for a moment and relaxed my arms, which were still stiff-ened from our earlier conversation. I looked at him and his eyes widened and blackened even further in some sort of expectant expression. If I had to describe it, it was almost a malignant joy, and he was smiling excitedly.

I thought about it for a moment and then finally said, "You need my help."

"Excellent, Dr. Stattler, truly excellent," he then paused before continu-ing, his face returning to normal. "Yes. It's true," he admitted finally, after stopping only a moment to tap the ash off his cigarette. "I need your help."

CHAPTER SIX

Ain Ghazal

"What, in the Jesus-fuck was that!?" Frank said, as he threw his clipboard loaded with patient charts onto the boardroom table making a loud "whack" as it smacked the surface of the table.

"I can only surmise that he doesn't like you Frank," I said, somewhat amused at his distress. "He was quite placid before you arrived."

Director Sikes looked at me sternly and with an audible "Humph" sank and spun into his chair at the head of the boardroom table. I sat down at my usual spot across from where Kathryn would be sitting at the opposite end, even though it was only the two of us in the room, and put my things on the table.

"What have you got for me, Doctor?" he said, almost pleadingly, as if he needed some good news to brighten his day.

"I'm not sure yet," I said, trying to bring to mind all that I had witnessed and observed concerning Gottlieb's behavior.

"What do you mean 'you're not sure yet,'" Frank said, imitating my voice pattern and mannerisms. Clearly this was not what he wanted to hear and he was letting me know it. "You've spent part of yesterday evening and most of this afternoon with him. You must have sort of initial assessment at least."

"An assessment, yes," I responded quickly. "But a judgment, no."

"Well, then give me your assessment," he replied shrewdly.

"You're not going to like it," I said, trying to prepare him for what I was about to tell him. "I'm not so sure he's schizophrenic."

"What do you mean you're not sure he's schizophrenic?" he added almost angrily. "Was that display back there not enough for you?"

90

"Clearly he's delusional, yes, but I think he was acting out for some reason because of you. He heard you buzzed through the man-trap and knew it was probably a physician based on the sound of your shoes."

"The sound of my shoes?" he said, disbelievingly.

"Yes. In one of our conversations he mentioned that Sampson's white shoes, which he feels are hideous, don't make the same 'clack', I think was the word he used, that ours do. Therefore, he knew it was someone in a position of authority, which he seems to have difficulty with. I was able to pry out of him last night that this probably stems from an SS prison guard at the camp he was detained at. He has a keen awareness and attention to detail. The scene he was reading from *Macbeth*, and in particular the last ingredient he threw in his make-believe pot, 'liver of a blaspheming Jew' suggests that what he was telling me before you arrived could be considered unholy or an untruth, specifically because it came from the mouth of a Jew, himself."

"What was he discussing?" Frank said, for the moment appearing intrigued and taken with my report.

"From what I gather so far, he seems to feel that he is part of a conspiracy, a conspiracy that involves aliens, and possibly members of our government. He mentioned there were 'others', others who might kill because of information he had."

"Sounds like a paranoid-delusion to me," Frank said, as if contesting my earlier statement concerning his schizophrenia.

"It is, and it isn't," I said, countering his quick condemnation. "For one, the people within his 'delusion,'" I said, italicizing in the air the word to make clear my point, "really existed. He mentioned a Dr. Louis Leakey and his wife. I checked and he did discover some fossils he mentioned. Some of his story checks out."

"Fossils?" he said, questioningly, obviously not aware as to the depth of our conversation.

"He feels there is evidence that the aliens I previously spoke of influenced human evolution. He apparently lightly touched on this in his *Ten Minutes to Midnight* thesis, which apparently is now literature in every archaeology or anthropology 101. He seemed offended when I didn't know what it was."

"I know it, I've heard of it. I took Anthropology while at Princeton," he said, and he leaned back in his chair, immersed in thought, while thumping a pencil to his lips. "You don't believe him?"

"Of course not, there are so many variables, but, my instinct tells me he's holding something back. Something he's either afraid of or doesn't want to mention."

Frank continued to thump the pencil at his lips, contemplating what I had said. "Your assessment is good, Doctor. Very detailed, informative, and brief, just the way I like it. Keep at it with him and let me know what you find. He seems to be taken with you for some reason and I'd like you to build on that relationship. It would seem he trusts you. If we're going to solve the mystery of his being here, we're going to need that; I also need to know why Phillips dumped him on us so quickly and without some sort of notice. If you have no other questions that will be all."

I gathered that I had been dismissed, and I collected my things and headed for the door. Although I had seen Frank curt before, I couldn't help but wonder why he had discharged me so quickly. I was about to leave when he said something over his shoulder as I approached the door.

"And Doctor, I'm relying on you, don't forget that."

I merely nodded without responding and left the meeting room. I wondered what he meant by this last statement. Although I was working under Howard, I had evaluated and monitored other patients before. Why was Gottlieb so important? What did Frank mean when he referred to the John Phillips Institution for the mentally insane 'dumping' him on us. Clearly there was some information that I was not privy to. And why add the psychological burden that he was 'depending on me.'

It made no sense, or was at the very least, as Dr. Gottlieb himself would put it, 'suspect.' I put aside these thoughts as I came to the infirmary, and watched Kathryn in the doorway over a patient. She was drawing some blood from one of Joan's patients, the new arrival, Melissa Oakencroft who had drowned her infant son. It was standard practice at Grove Haven to screen all new patients for communicable diseases, such as hepatitis and other illnesses which might run rampant if unchecked.

"Hey honey," she said while removing the syringe from Melissa's arm. She looked tired and haggard. "Be down in about ten minutes."

"I'll be in the lobby," I said. She was beautiful, and there were times such as these that would creep up on me where her hair would be hanging in tangles or she would strike some unflattering pose and I would feel she was all the more beautiful for it. Shakespeare had it right when he said, 'And yet, by heaven, I think my love as rare, as any belied with false compare.' I had not thought of Shakespeare since my days as an undergrad, and I realized that it was the Doctor who making me see things *because* of Shakespeare in a different light. He was right, of course, there were truths buried beneath his plays, and his sonnets. Truths that the Doctor seemed to be simultaneously experiencing.

I did not see him again until the following afternoon. I spent the morning helping Kate in the infirmary dispense medication because one of the nurses had called out sick. When I came to his cell he was on his cot, reading again. He did not look up when I stopped at the entrance.

"You aren't serving your interests when you act out like that," I said trying to draw his attention. "Especially in front of Dr. Sikes."

He was silent for a moment before responding. "Maybe I wasn't serving *my* interests, Dr. Stattler, maybe I was serving yours," he said, not looking up from his book.

"You know, that's very clever and cute, but I don't buy it. You're too smart for that, quit playing games."

"Well, if it's a game I'm playing at, Dr. Stattler; to be sure it's a deadly one. Besides," he continued. "I add a little excitement to your lives and all you do is complain. Where's your sense of adventure, Dr. Stattler? You get to go home at the end of the day, have dinner with your wife over a nice bottle of wine, plan your next vacation, all the little banalities you take for granted, and in time forget, whereas I, it would seem, have the rest of my existence merely to contemplate only the thought of them. You should be more thankful," he said, looking up at me for the first time, lifting up the corner of his book to smile at me. It was Shakespeare's *HAMLET*.

"Your readings are becoming more and more philosophical and tragic, Doctor. If I didn't know better, I would say you were in some manner manipulating our discourse. I would say you were plotting something, as if your performance was well rehearsed," I said, folding out the chair and seating myself in front of him. "Care to tell me why?"

He snapped his book shut and came towards the bars and said as though he were beseeching pity from me, "Why, look you now, how unworthy a thing you make of me! You would play upon me, you would seem to know my stops, and you would pluck out the heart of my mystery. You would sound me from my lowest note to the top of my compass; and there is much music, excellent voice, in this little organ, yet you can not make it speak. Do you think I am easier to be played on than a pipe?!"

I couldn't help but smile at his ingenuity for reciting that particular stanza.

"Your timing and intonation is excellent, Doctor, you should have considered a career in theater instead of archaeology. It might not have brought you to such a foul end."

"Yes, the play is *the thing*. But in the theater, once the curtain goes up, the play is over. The drama is done, you get in your vehicle with your lovely wife and you drive home. But in archaeology, and geology, *the thing* is *the play*, the play of the slow forces of time, sediments, erosion, all meticulously working in unison for some greater purpose, to reveal *something* to us, but to what end? Hmmm? If for nothing else, it is to reveal truth, truth in the forces of nature, truth in the history of mankind, truth in the consistency of the inner workings of the universe, and of course, truth in what these forces reveal. It is these complex forces of truth, more than anything, that mankind in his quest for knowledge strives to perfect and emulate. It is the answer to the age old question, 'why are we here?'"

I thought that I would be clever in countering him, of bringing this overly philosophical conversation back to reality. "And why are we here, Doctor?" I said, holding up my hands, gesturing to the cell-block around us.

He gazed at me steadily then without blinking and while smiling said, "Because of the truth, Doctor."

I looked at him dourly. "Now, Doctor, I know that you'd like to believe that, perhaps you even do believe it. But it doesn't answer the question as to why you're in that cell, now."

"Truth isn't what you *believe*, Dr. Stattler, anyone can believe anything, it doesn't make it true. Truth is what you *know*. If you know an event transpired, you know it to be true."

"All right, how do you know then, that what you told me yesterday is true?"

"Because someone else did, too. As I told you yesterday, in the fall of 1960 I received a letter from someone who would provide me with vital information. Information that changed the course of my investigation."

"Go on." I said, staring into his eyes. They were dancing and almost whimsical and appeared as though they could barely contain themselves in the confines of his skull. They expressed a delighted and curious eagerness that had not been seen before or since.

"The first time I met Dr. Rasp was in the spring of 1954 at Yale."

"I thought you said you met someone in the fall of 1960?"

"Patience, Doctor. For someone who is supposed to be *listening* you seem to do a great deal of talking. Now where was I?" he said, leaning back against the brick wall of his cell, appearing distracted.

"1954." I said.

"Ah yes, as I was saying, the first time I met the man I came to know as Dr. Rasp was in early spring at Yale in 1954. He was visiting from Princeton and was teaching a seminar on Egyptology."

"So you knew him from before?"

"Only vaguely, as a student would a teacher. Though I was a fully accredited professor by then, in my spare time I found myself going to other teacher's lectures to see if they might reveal any clues or connections to what would ultimately be my life's purpose."

"Which was?"

"Verifiable and unequivocal proof, Doctor. Proof of *their* existence. Proof that *they* have been here. Proof that man has seen them before recorded history was ever even conceived. Proof of what they *looked* like."

"Little green men?" I asked, trying to sound as objective as I could.

He seemed unperturbed and continued, closing his eyes and concentrating, seemingly in deep thought. He then responded slowly, drawing out the intonations of a little rhyme, "The ones who haunt my days and nights. The ones who come when you turn out the lights. The ones who seek to control our days, the ones whom I've come to call *the Grays*." He flicked open his eyes and peered at me, looking for something, I know not what.

"What did you expect to find?" I asked.

"Some other means of evidence that I could draw upon than what I already had."

"But you said that you already had two of these things, these chips ..." I was about to continue when he interrupted me.

"By themselves they were meaningless, Doctor. Just two gray metallic balls found in the aged bones of long dead mutant breeds of men and women. I needed to put a face on these beings, Doctor. I needed something to show the world what these creatures looked like. And, if my theory was correct, and I was able to find the evidence I was looking for, I would change the very face and history of mankind itself—for I believed that it was *they* in fact, who created us ... that they were continuing still, to alter us, making us evolve faster, swifter, and in different directions than natural selection could and can account for. It was my belief that someone, somewhere, in some part of the globe must have seen these creatures. They must have seen and recorded their likeness in a cave wall, or edifice, or perhaps created a figurine of some kind, an extra-terrestrial *Venus of Willendorf*, if you will.

"And did you find anything?"

"Of course, Doctor, lest I wouldn't be here, now would I? And besides, do you honestly believe that a visitation, or more precisely put, repeated encounters with what were quite obviously alien beings would go unrecorded in the annuls of human history? HAH!" he said, shouting this last word, which echoed and resonated down the cell block. He then sat up straight and approached the bars, grabbed hold of one in each hand and poked his face through as far as he was able. He glared at me maniacally, and his face had a broad and what I could only describe as 'shit-eating' grin, like the cat that had stolen the canary. Clearly he was trying to rattle and test my nerve, but I wasn't going to give in. It was too important that I remain objective and focused.

"What did you find?" I asked coolly, letting him know that I was unfazed of his behavior.

"But there's just so much to tell," he said, once again imitating the witch's voice from *MACBETH*. "About the statues of *Ain Ghazal* ... "He chuckled and continued to cackle over his whimsical little rhyme. He then straightened and stepped away from the bars and continued, his voice returning to normal.

"Tell me Doctor, what do you think you would do, if you actually saw an alien for the first time, hmmmm? Faint? Vomit? Scream? *Go Insane?*" he asked, carefully accentuating this last possibility.

"I don't know," I said, wondering about the possibility for the first time myself. "I suppose I would have to be confronted by the situation to really answer that."

He studied me intently, eyeing me through the cage between us.

"I was," He said, smiling wickedly at me, as if to say, 'Gotcha.' He waited a moment before continuing. "Pity. Though your answer is nothing less than I expected, I was hoping for something more *tangible*, something I could amuse myself with the thought of during my stay here, but ..." he paused before continuing. "The truth serves you well, Doctor." He smiled at me mischievously, drawn and inspired by some greater purpose that I could only hope to endeavor to understand.

"You were saying about this, Dr. Rasp?" I asked, looking down at my notes to remember the name.

"Quite right, quite right, Doctor, we do digress and time grows short."

I looked at him, wondering what he meant by this. He was to be incarcerated for the rest of his life. What reason did he have to worry about *time*? He was going no where. He had all the time in the world, and I was perplexed by his attention to it. This was, unfortunately, not the last time I would hear this phrase.

"As I was saying, the first time I saw Dr. Rasp he was giving a guest lecture on the Egyptian dynasty of Tuthmosis the third. He was a crotchety old man, who with his flowing white hair looked a bit like Samuel Clemmons in the white-southern gentile suit he was wearing. He carried with him a black, silver topped cane which he periodically leaned on for support and would now and again use as a pointer to illustrate some topic concerning the artifacts that he was discussing on the slide screen behind him. His voice was throaty, like a man who had smoked too many cigars or cigarettes, and he would periodically cough and hack into a handkerchief which he kept in his coat pocket. Despite this the tone of his voice was deep and resonant and held your attention … that is, until he started coughing again.

"So you two were colleagues together?"

"No," he paused. "Well, only in a sense. As I said, he was a guest lecturer visiting from Princeton; I didn't know him and never spoke to him at all, other than maybe asking a few questions during his seminar."

"But you did come to know him?"

"Yes," he said smiling, but his voice then changed to an almost regretful tone. "Yes," he repeated. "You see, Doctor, it was Dr. Rasp who sought me out."

"What do you mean?"

"The fliers I had distributed, Doctor. It was he that responded to them."

"How?"

"As I said, it was a cold November morning, six years later in 1960. I had been up late the night before studying photographs of some aboriginal cave sites that Dr. Wilkes had just brought back from Australia. There were several photos in particular that fascinated me for some reason, which Dr. Wilkes had labeled on the backs and in his notes as being of "The Death cave." The locals and his guide, who was a native, apparently called it this. It had painted on its walls thin short, white, figures, with large, black eyes, twisted in various menacing like poses. I couldn't quite put my finger on it, but there was something about them that stirred and fascinated me, and for hours the night before I poured over them with a magnifying glass, making notes and sketches as to the possible real proportions and dimensions of these strange and eerie creatures.

I fell asleep sometime in the wee hours, draped over my desk, my face mashed against my notebook. And so it was I was awakened by a knock at 8 a.m. on my door. Unshaven and disheveled, pushing my papers and photographs about, I arose and opened it, but there was no one there, only a small parcel. I opened it and found many of the fliers and photographs that I had distributed. Only a single note on parchment paper gave a clue as to their meaning. It read:

'You are in danger. Post no more of these messages. Come to Princeton Library tonight. 10pm. Anthropology. Come alone.'

"What did you do?"

"I wasted no time in preparing. As soon as I was able to arrange for a T.A. to take over my lectures for the day, I gathered a bundle of essentials and made the long familiar trip to Princeton. In the car I remember speculating to myself, *'who would take down my posters and why?'* For awhile I actually became angry, incensed that some one would deliberately hamper and seek to conceal my research. There *must* have been other professors, archaeologists, anthropologists, *someone* other than myself who knew or at the very least suspected what I knew, or should I say, at that time, *believed* to be true."

"What did you expect to find?"

"All I was interested in was the sharing of evidence, the gathering of empirical facts. After all, like the devices I found, as I told you earlier, in and of themselves they were nothing, but placed within the context of a greater whole, their significance takes on monumental importance. Still, I had to find the solution, and whoever it was that sent me that parcel had some of the answers I was looking for. They had to. They must. Why bother to spend the time and energy, to say nothing of the risk of exposure, to reveal them to me?"

"So then you believed you were in danger? And that by drawing anyone else into your research you would be endangering them as well?"

He chuckled at this and then continued.

"Frankly, you amaze me, Doctor. After everything I've described to you, you're *finally* figuring that out?"

"Go on," I said wearily.

"It was intriguing, and I was devoured by curiosity to find out who would go through such lengths to contact me and why. I arrived at Princeton that afternoon and checked into a local hotel, had dinner in one of the student union buildings, and once again poured over the photographs that

Dr. Wilkes had loaned me for study, trying to distract myself from the im-
minent rendezvous that awaited me. Based on the size of the figures in the
drawings on the 'death cave' wall, in comparison with other drawings of
what appeared to clearly be human beings, I estimated the strange figures to
stand four, no more than five feet tall.

"In addition, I noted that their heads, though oddly shaped, seemed
disproportionate to their size, and whoever the artist or artisans were who
drew them, they seemed chiefly concerned with their eyes, which took up
most of their face, again, disproportional to what we know as human. I
started to sketch drawings of them in various poses, and before I knew it, it
was almost ten o'clock."

"What did they look like?" I asked, lured and intrigued by his descriptions.

He shrugged at this and said, "Give me just a moment."

He then leaned over and pulled a notebook from under his bed and
began to sketch, at first slowly, and then frantically. After several minutes of
this he finally seemed satisfied with his drawing.

"It's a bit crude, but it will give you an idea," he said, and tore the page
from his spiral notebook and handed it to me through the cage between us.

I studied it for a moment before saying anything. Its head was large and
ovular, completely hairless. There was virtually no nose, and the mouth was
barely noticeable. The bodily proportion suggested that it was shorter than
a human, probably no more than four to five tall at most. The eyes were its
most striking feature, they were extremely, large. If I had to guess I would
say they were at least four times the size of a normal human, and though I
could see quite plainly that they did not, when looking at them they seemed
to take up most of the creatures face. They had no pupil, or iris, and they
were very, very, black, black as the depths of space itself, and had an eerie,
menacing-like stare, that even through the crude sketch on the notepad
penetrated me.

"Comments, Doctor?" he said somewhat amused.

"I'm not sure," I said. "I've never known what an alien looked like."

"Now you do," he said sharply, his voice full of cold certainty.

I paused before responding, an eerie chill filled my bones.

"What made you so sure that what were depicted in the caves were
aliens, why not ghosts, or demons, or something more terrestrial?"

"Instinct, Doctor."

"Instinct?" I asked, not sure of the relevance.

"You may find this difficult to believe, Doctor, but instinct has led me all of my life, in my career decisions, to my escape from Nazi Germany, even here, today.

You see, I have always been under the conclusion that everything happens for a *reason*, and it is for this *reason*, that I have devoted my life to following my instinct. As horrible as it may seem, Hitler happened for a *reason*. Pearl Harbor happened for a *reason*. All things that we consider bad and all things that we deem good happen for a *reason*. There is a *reason* why *all* things happen. There is a *reason* I am here behind these bars today. There is a *reason* why I've met you, Doctor."

"I see," I said, trying to remain objective to this monologue, and although I could see where he was going with his logic, I wasn't so sure I believed this rationale. My tone must have betrayed my thoughts, as he interrupted me as if to try and further convince me of his rhetoric.

"Now, mind you, Doctor, I didn't say that we always know what the *reason* is, just that there is one, some force behind all of it, behind space, nature, and time."

"So then you do believe in God?"

"I never said I didn't believe in God, Doctor. I said or at the very least strongly implied that I don't believe in *religion*. Religion serves man and his petty wants and political needs and agendas. It does not serve God's. But, we digress, Doctor."

"Yes, you were saying about Dr. Rasp."

"I left for the library at once. Once I arrived I walked slowly through the enormous aisles, marveling at the sheer volume of information that was collected there. It must have rivaled even the *Great Library of Alexandria* in its day. I sat down at a table near the anthropology section and waited for I knew not what. At about ten-fifteen I heard a thin, wiry, wispy voice behind me whispering.

* * *

"'I recognize you now, *Gottlieb*,'" it said, speaking my name with a somewhat defiant and disrespectful tone.

I turned to face him, but he was standing in the shadow of the window and I couldn't tell who it was, though I knew I had heard the voice before.

"'I remember you from the lecture I gave six years ago at Yale. You grilled me during the lecture about some eerie sightings during the reign of the Tuthmosis,'" he said, and then continued, reading from a book. "'In the year twenty-two of the third month of the winter, a circle of fire appeared in the sky. After some days it became more numerous and shone with the brightness of the sun, extending to the very limits of the heavens. Royal records of Tuthmosis the third, 1480 B.C."'

He closed the book from which he was reading shut and it made a loud "whump" in the darkness.

"'Dr. Rasp,'" I said, recognizing the scratchy voice finally. He then hobbled forward on his cane, stepping into the light so I could see him.

"'Dr. Gottlieb,'" he said. "'What are you doing here?'"

"'I might ask you the same question,'" I said.

"'Give up your quest, Doctor,'" he said. "'You won't find anything, and if you do, you'll be sorry that you did.'"

"'How do you know what I'm looking for?'" I asked.

"'Because you foolishly advertised it all over this campus,'" he said, choking on his last words and stomping his cane on to the floor to further emphasize his anger.

He then hobbled over towards two chairs next to the wall and motioned for me to sit down. After he was settled he turned and continued to whisper, his face lined and cracked with age.

"'You must stop what you're doing, or someone else will. I am here to warn you.'"

"'And from whom are you speaking,'" I said.

"'From *experience*, Doctor. There was a time I was like you; idealistic, thinking you can change the world with knowledge of *them*, knowledge of the truth! But the *truth*, Doctor, in this case just doesn't want or need to be found.'"

"'Time always reveals truth,'" I said.

"'But seldom is truth revealed in time,'" he retorted.

"'You see, I found, long ago, what you are looking for.'"

He reached into his pocket and removed a 35millimeter film canister and handed it to me. I opened it and it contained three of the small, gray, sphere-like objects, similar to the ones I had already unearthed.

"'I found some myself,'" I said.

"'Where?'" he asked.

"'At the Olduvai Gorge and Swartkrans.'"

He simply nodded and continued.

"'I have had those in my possession for nearly thirty years, Doctor, and frankly I'm happy to be rid of them. They've brought nothing but trouble. If you have some yourself than *they* know you know, or at the very least suspect. Suspicion is, however, for them, not motive enough to kill.'"

"'Who are *they,* exactly?'" I asked.

"'I advise you strongly to abandon this self-imposed mission of yours, Doctor, to undermine the fabric of our society. They won't let you, and to answer your question, *they* are the agents in our government who are working closely with them, the aliens.'"

I remember my jaw dropped.

"Don't look so surprised, Gottlieb," he whispered half-hacking. "Governments of many nations or at least individuals within them have been in cahoots with the aliens since recorded history began."

"How do you know this?"

"For a time, as I said, I was like you, driven to expose them. But something irrevocably changed my mind."

"And what was that?'" I asked intrigued.

"'Jericho,'" he said.

"'Jericho?'" I asked, trying to contain my eagerness at attaining new information.

"'Jericho,'" he repeated with a deep sigh while staring into nothing. The lines within his face cracked and his voice stress patterns changed abruptly, as he was clearly remembering some horrific event from his past. Once he recovered himself he continued. "'As you well know, Doctor, Jericho is one of the oldest human settlements if not the oldest on the planet. As I had discovered several of these strange gray spheres in previous expeditions to Giza, Morocco, and Baghdad to name a few, I wanted to test a hypothesis: What if these strange objects were evidence of extra-terrestrial influence? For what reason and *why* had it never occurred to anyone else before hand, and if it did, why not seek to answer it? I believed if there was a definitive answer it would be found at some of the world's oldest settlements: Jericho, Nahal Oren, Ain Ghazal, and Catalhoyuk. In 1935 I managed to get myself assigned to an expedition to Jericho led by Carl Garstang. After several weeks of intense digging we eventually found some PPNB pits dating to circa 6700-6500 B.C. with quantities of plaster pieces.'"

* * *

"PPNB? I not familiar with this term, Doctor." I said.

Dr. Gottlieb looked at me quizzically for a moment, almost indignantly, and I could tell from his expression that he was somewhat perturbed at my interrupting his story with Dr. Rasp. He straightened, bringing himself back to the present and answered politely.

"My apologies, Doctor Stattler. I shouldn't have expected you to know.

PPNB refers to *Pre Pottery Neolithic*, meaning the stage in human history where pottery had not yet been discovered but was on the verge of being discovered, which was roughly 7500-5500 B.C. Though it is not my wish to bore you with the finer details this classification structure has been further broken down into *Early, Middle,* and *Late* whose classifications are EPPNB, MPPNB, and so forth, with each span covering five hundred to a thousand years. By 5500 B.C. what was called the Yarmoukian Pottery Neolithic began and it was at this point that the Neolithic age started to draw to a close, introducing the *Chalcolithic* or *Copper Stone Age* which spanned from 5500-3000 B.C."

"Sounds intensely boring and complicated to learn," I said.

"Initially perhaps, but no more so than psychology," he said winking at me. "Now where were we?"

"Dr. Rasp. Jericho. Pre Pottery Neolithic," I said reminding him.

"Yes, yes. Quite right," he continued.

* * *

"'What types of pieces were they?'" I asked, knowing full well it must have been something of significant importance or we wouldn't be having this discussion.

"'Unfortunately, what fragments there were they were poorly preserved, which limited the possibility of a thorough stylistic analysis. What we did find seemed to be limestone plaster pieces painted with red and cream stripes. Some fragments bore the imprints of reeds around which they were molded but most contained a core of hard, crumbly, marl. There were, however, two pieces we found that gave me cause for concern, and which were clearly the most well preserved in the collection, at least that we had thus far excavated and weren't destroyed.'"

"'Destroyed?'" I asked and wondered out loud curiously.

"'I'll get to that soon enough, Doctor.'"

I sat still, and tried to contain my questions, burdening to me as they were. I knew that it was best to let Dr. Rasp continue and not further interrupt him.

"'The first piece was of a fragment of a foot with *six* not five toes, and the other was that of a large, flat head, completely oversized at least for any *human* representation. It had a small, upturned nose with prominent nostrils, a long labial canal, and a curious puckered lip-less mouth. It was the eyes, however, that were the most dominating and riveting detail. They were, again, larger than a human's, disproportionate to the skull, and they were represented by two large, glossy shells inserted below the brows, imitating the shiny texture of the cornea.'"

Dr. Rasp paused for a moment and cleared his throat before continuing. I interrupted him before he had the opportunity.

"'What were you thinking? Did you believe this was the face of an extra-terrestrial? The face of a *god* to whoever framed it?'"

"'I did not know,'" he said dourly. "'But I suspected. Carl was jubilant and excited at the find, and as soon as he was able and they were secure he drove into town to the university to carbon date them. He obviously did not share my suspicions on the matter; no reputable archaeologist would, not that I would ever disclose my thoughts on the subject to him anyway. No. He like everyone else assumed them to be depictions of Gods, Ancestors, or Ghosts, and ever since I started studying archaeology it always struck as me strange how desperately man clings to these notions like a security blanket or crutch,'" he said, tapping his silver topped cane on the floor for emphasis. "'No. But to answer your question Doctor Gottlieb I did not *then* know, but I suspected *afterwards*.'"

"'Afterwards?'" I asked, curiously eager.

"'That evening after Dr. Garstang had taken some of the pieces in for analysis, I lay awake in my tent, unable to sleep, wondering at the myriad of possibilities and mysteries that the plaster head might reveal. How old was it? *Could,* in fact, what I believed to be a possibility of visitation from another species be *real?* After all, there were over four-hundred-billion stars in our galaxy alone,. At least *one* of them must contain life, and who's to say that extra-terrestrials *hadn't* been here before? The site we were surveying was at least six- to eight-thousand-years-old, if not older. There was no recorded history. Just how would one depict a meeting of such cosmic significance? Perhaps they might create a likeness of what they saw. In any case, I was not able to wonder long.'"

"'What do you mean?'" I asked with trepidation.

"'When I heard the first scream I bolted upright and extinguished my lantern. I then heard the firing of weapons and the unsheathing of swords accompanied by horrid screams of the word, 'Kafer!' *Infidel* in Arabic.'"

Dr. Rasp leaned forward in his chair on his cane and grimaced and winced before continuing.

"'I did not stay to witness the massacre. I ran. I fled into the dark desert night like the coward I am. I was fortunate, I guess. It was a new moon, and the night was dark with only the light of the stars to guide me and protect

me from the whizzing bullets firing from their guns. The screams and torments of dying men and women filled the air behind me, and I was, and still
am, overcome by shame and grief that I did not stay to try and defend them.
Once I stopped running blindly in the dark I stopped to rest on an edifice.
I could still hear screams and gunfire echoing off the walls of the canyon in
the distance, and then, all was silent. I remember sitting there, alone in the
dark in misery and shame; berating myself for not having stayed, but what
could I have done? My mind was filled with remorse, fury, and my anger
was beginning to erupt. I was about to turn back and face my aggressors
when I heard a loud explosion followed by what sounded like large layers of
rock crashing into each other and collapsing.

"'When I finally summoned the courage to return at daybreak, I was
unprepared for the grizzly scene that greeted me. The entire rest of the excavation team was murdered, some disemboweled, and some were beheaded,
execution-style. And what was worse, the entire site was destroyed. We had
only opened one cache of the statuary, who knows what mysteries and priceless works of art were destroyed! It was a terrible loss, and though I mourned
the loss of my colleagues and companions, I felt the pain of losing everything I had hoped to achieve in coming there. Inscribed on the rock face
next to what was left of the entrance of the pits where the fragments were
found, were the words written in blood in Arabic 'This is what happens to
infidels.'"

I decided to wait a few moments before responding and let him compose himself.

"'Who were they?'" I asked.

"'Does it matter?'" he said wearily. "'Investigations were made but at
that time in that part of the world these types of events were common.
Murder for mayhem, murder for money, murder for pleasure, they were all
equally rampant and unchecked.'"

"'But that's not what you suspected?'" I said more than asked.

"'No,'" he said regretfully. "'After the incident I spoke with some members of nearby villages. It would seem that despite assurances from the Palestinian government of free-passage, we were indeed trespassing; that the site
was considered a holy … no, that's not the right word.'"

He stopped and stammered a bit, clearly searching his mind for the
correct means to describe his vivid account.

"It was considered, a *sacred* place by some of the locals,'" he continued.
"'And that the murders were more than likely the work of the *Mujahedin*,

those who fight the *jihad*, and deliver the souls of the *Kafer*, the non-believer to *Allah* for judgment. In the eyes of many we had defiled the sanctity of their lands by our excavation, and we received little or no pity for what had happened. At least that was the distinct impression left to me, but I have always since suspected *what if it was something deeper?* I found it odd that whoever this band of brutes were that they would be so well equipped, that they seemed to know *exactly* who and what they were looking for. And what's more, *Mujahedin* were typically nomadic peoples, they would place no more claim on an ancient excavation site than they would a transistor radio, it meant nothing to them!

"'Then the thought occurred to me, what if whoever killed our research team somehow *knew* of the importance of what it was we found? What if somehow the reason that we were to be killed was not necessarily that we disturbed one of their sacred places, but more so because *what* it was that we found? What if these men, these murderers, *Mujahedin* or not, were sent to destroy it, because they suspected what it was that we *might* find? It always struck me as odd that the night the discovery was revealed to the government of Palestine was the same night that a merciless band of mercenaries was conveniently dispatched from somewhere to kill us and destroy the dig site. Of the original team of thirteen men and women, two of whom were Palestinian, only Carl and I survived.

"'After that, I didn't see much point in further investigating my suspicions. It was getting too dangerous, and the potential for those individuals in power who could be involved was doing nothing but growing. It was enough that I had lived, and had to live the rest of my life with the shame of my cowardice. My cowardice for not staying there and defending my team, my cowardice for not voicing to others in the field what I had suspected, my cowardice for remaining silent all these years, and my cowardice for imploring you not to pursue this matter any further. I therefore decided to devote myself entirely to one study, one that was safer and posed less of a threat to my existence, and those around me, one that could give me the satisfaction of discovering some mystery, though obviously one with less prominence, Egyptology.'"

"'What do you mean, shame?' I said. "'There was nothing you could have done. They would have killed you and they would have killed Dr. Garstang as well. And how do you know for certain that it was members of the Palestinian government that ordered the execution of you and your research team?'"

"'I don't,'" he countered somewhat forcefully. "'And I don't want to. And neither should you. It is enough that they and most of the artifacts were destroyed.'"

I leaned back in my chair, biting my lip, wanting to argue and debate the subject with him but I didn't. I could tell that he could see I was not convinced of his story, that the truth behind his suspicions of a foreign government's assassination plot lacked evidence. But then again, I asked myself, so did my theory, our theory, as well, and if he were right, then there was no telling what other evidence was out there.

"'I can see I haven't convinced you of the severity of the forces with which you are dealing,'" he said calmly.

"'No, you haven't,'" I said after careful consideration. "'It's not that I don't believe your story, I do, for I have heard of the tragedy that befell the Jericho site, though obviously not from this perspective. It's just that ...'"

"'You would rather find out for yourself,'" he said, interrupting me. "'I can see I haven't fazed you, Dr. Gottlieb. Indeed, you are probably now more than ever determined to expose the lie under which we all exist and in the back of our minds quietly maintain.'"

"'Perhaps,'" I whispered, nodding in agreement with him.

"'Then you should go. Perhaps you will succeed where I failed; perhaps you will find the truth that you are looking for. I only hope for your sake you find it and reveal it before it destroys and consumes you.'"

"'What do you mean, go? Go where? You said the Jericho site was destroyed, that whoever it was dynamited the entire excavation.'"

"'You're a smart man, Doctor; you know there are other localities we were considering that had yielded preliminary finds and data for lost *Meso* and *Neolithic* civilizations. Jericho was only the first and most obvious among them. Its biblical ties and references made it a natural choice for study. But if these creatures, these *beings* are real, than they must have been visiting many cultures the world over. After all, if they have the technology to get here, than it's safe to assume they wouldn't confine their activities to one area or locale. If they can travel between the stars in a fair amount of time than circumnavigating the globe might and probably does take only seconds!'"

He then paused and started to cough his characteristic 'hack' into the familiar handkerchief he kept in his pocket. After coughing for quite some time he rose and leaned on his cane. I stood up, to help him and he shooed me away angrily as he would a fly.

"'You're a wise man, Doctor Gottlieb. You will know what to do. Pray you do it before it's too late,'" he said, limping forward on his cane, his back to me, still clutching the book in his hand from which he had read earlier that evening.

I watched him, scuttling slowly down the tall aisle of shelves, filled with seeming endless books upon books, of every size and volume imaginable. As he neared the end of the aisle, he lifted his white hat in the air, turned the corner, and vanished. I never saw him again."

* * *

"What did you do next?"

"Research of course. I canceled my classes for the following semester and delved into anything that I could get my hands on that held even the remotest possibility of containing clues as to an undiscovered Neolithic civilization."

"Why *Neolithic*, what makes the Neolithic period so special? Why not Paleolithic or something during the Bronze Age?"

"An excellent question, Doctor Stattler, one which I shall do my best to answer. For one, the Paleolithic Age can go back to four hundred thousand years B.C. Any evidence of extra-terrestrial contact would have long since been destroyed by the forces of nature or erosion. The only reason some cave paintings survive is because they were sheltered partially from these forces, and secondly man did not even begin to live in and form cities until at least the late Mesolithic. Clearly, Doctor, your knowledge of the anthro-sciences is somewhat lacking. But, to answer your question, the Neolithic period is the first time where we began to see with greater frequency religious shrines, figurines, the first appearance of crude forms of pottery, mural paintings. It is the period in human history where man is taking an interest in himself and his world; he isn't just hunting or fishing anymore. He is cultivating wheat, barley, and grain, living and dwelling in early cities. His mind was more open than perhaps ours is today, but that is essentially because he was ignorant of science and the scientific method.

"Because of this, if he did, in fact, have repeated encounters with extra-terrestrials, he would not know in essence, what they *really* were. He would probably assume they were from across the desert, or beyond the mountains, or over the seas, or whatever natural barrier or obstacle that was then deemed 'insurmountable.' It would never even *occur* to him to believe they were from beyond the stars or another planet. Why? Because this was a plane that simply did not exist to him. The stars were merely pinholes in the curtain of night that changed with the seasons and at times moved with a purpose. But, the good thing about this is, it makes him very likely to record an encounter with these beings for the simple fact that he did not have the social pressures which we do today."

"Social pressures?" I asked, not clearly understanding what he meant by this.

"Yes, Doctor. Pressures which might cause one to *judge*. Prejudice, Doctor, can be a terrible thing. If someone told you that they had seen an actual *alien*, well, you might just think that they were *insane*," he smiled and cackled giddily when he said this, clearly marveling at his own ingenuity.

I decided to change the subject and get back to the discussion at hand. "So what did you do next?"

He sighed audibly, apparently growing tedious of our discussion.

"I did what any good archaeologist would do. I petitioned the university for a grant to excavate the ruins of ÇATALHÖYÜK, a Neolithic site first discovered in Turkey in the 1950's. The site was rapidly becoming famous internationally due to the large size and apparent dense occupation of the settlement, as well as the spectacular wall paintings and other art that was uncovered inside the houses. The race was on, you see, and I was determined to win it."

"Race?"

"Yes. As I mentioned, due to it's enormous potential there were many archaeologists in the field who wanted to get the first look at it, though not for the reasons necessarily that I wanted to. I hand selected a team of students and assistants to accompany me, complied with all the necessary paperwork and answered request after request from the Turkish embassy. But, as you may or may not be aware, the arduous process by which universities review and approve requests of this kind can take months or even years. As it was, I discovered that I was beaten to the prize by James Mellart, when I read his *Excavations at Çatal Hüyük, first preliminary report,* in the 1961 edition of *Anatolian Studies*. I was shattered; months of meticulous and monotonous preparation and paper shuffling for nothing. I was longing for the chance to practice my Farsi and to be out in the field again, heading a team of my own where I wouldn't have to listen to the pedantic dispositions and pathetic pet theories of crotchety old men who were so aged and blinded that they couldn't see the truth of man's of existence if it jumped up and bit them.

"I grew withdrawn and depressed, and even began to do research in the growing UFO cult that was making headlines due to new revelations about Roswell and the supposed abduction of Barney and Betty Hill that year. If for nothing else, the drawings these supposed witnesses were producing at the very least confirmed what I already knew, what these supposed beings looked like.

"I began to wonder if what I was searching for was really hopeless and beyond my reach. I was beginning to lose all hope. Practically everything that was out in the media or in print concerning *the Grays,* though they were not then referred to as such, was hype and ridiculous philosophical banter meant to stigmatize and humiliate those foolish enough to voice it. In some instances they justifiably deserved it. In one particular case, though, I have to give credit for being the first in the field of archaeology to be brave enough to risk public outcry and disdain. It was a man named Eric von Danikin, who in his thesis and book titled thereafter, *Chariots of the Gods,* wrote concerning these beings. Actually, I should thank him really, for it was his travels that eventually led me to Nasca, and the wondrous discoveries that I would make there, even if his theories were ludicrously wrong."

"Nasca?" I asked. "I've never heard of it."

"I'm not surprised. It's not as well known as say, *The Roswell Incident.*"

"What is it?"

"Nasca, or more precisely *Cahuachi,* is an ancient city in the desert of Peru more than two thousand years old. It is the city where it is believed the people that existed there drew, or rather constructed the famous lines."

"What famous lines?"

"The Nasca lines, vast and sometimes miles long, were drawn, or rather created, on the floor of the desert plateau by these ancient peoples. Lines depicting shapes, trapezoids, polygons, and even animals—but the kicker is, they are so large, they can only be seen from above. They were not even discovered until the late 1920's when commercial aircraft began to fly over the region for the first time."

"So why was this guy, this von Danikin so misguided in his attempts to explain their existence."

"*Misguided,*" he said. "What an excellent word choice. You see, it was his contention that it was extra terrestrials who made the lines; that they were made by visiting craft, or UFO's—sort of like an intergalactic airport, and that the numerous enlarged craniums of skulls that were found were the result of intergalactic interbreeding. Ridiculous as it sounds, I had at least admired his enthusiasm for the idea."

"Why is it ridiculous? You implied in your discussion that you made some great discoveries there, discoveries that would supposedly aid you to prove the existence of these beings. And what's this about strange skulls?"

He sighed in apparent frustration before continuing.

"Honestly, Doctor, you do exacerbate me sometimes. As for the skulls I'll get to them later. I never said or even remotely suggested that the lines were created *by* extra terrestrials; what I came to discover is that they were made *for* extra terrestrials. Who else could see the lines? Not even their creators! We know from pottery samples discovered at various grave sites that the designs on the porcelain faces of the ceramics matched those of the designs and lines on the desert floor. They were clearly made by the same people, but the question always remained, why? Why take the time to draw immense pictures and drawings on the desert floor? Hmmm? For the 'gods' to see, perhaps? It was an interesting question, and for some reason I felt drawn to it. I put all thoughts of *Çatal Hüyük* out of my mind and began to make inquiries into this strange and eerie discovery."

"What did you find?"

"It was largely through, or rather due to, the work of Maria Reiche, a German anthropologist that the lines were even discovered and eventually preserved and declared as a world cultural heritage site by the United Nations Educational, Scientific and Cultural Organization. Like me, she fled Nazi Germany and reached Peru by chance in 1932 after answering an ad posted by the German consul in Cusco, who was looking for a German tutor for his sons. It was there that she became fascinated with Inca culture. She then published a book in 1939 titled *"Secret of the Pampa"*, and in 1946 convinced an American anthropologist, Paul Kosok to launch an in-depth investigation to study the lines.

"She was the first to survey the valley, and would hike around with her canteen, drawing kit, and later her broom and rake, trying to unravel the origins, characteristics and purpose of the petroglyphs. Eventually, she came to the conclusion that the lines were a gigantic astronomical calendar and she was convinced that it matched the "intihuatana" — the solar observatories of the Incas. She was a tough old bird, and would take to wandering hours, even days on the plateau. She first came to be known to the local villagers at Nasca as the 'crazy gringa', then later as their Guardian Angel. I knew as soon as I read it that Nasca was where I was meant to go. I contacted her immediately, and I could tell that although she had an enormous distaste for Germany and was, like I, scarred by the Second World War, she was happy to speak her mother tongue again. It was agreed that I would come in the spring and help her survey and assist a Doctor Giuseppe Orefici, Director of the Nasca Project in excavating the ruins and grave sites at Cahuachi."

"But what does all this have to do with *Ain Ghazal* and statues in Jordan?"

"I was wondering when you would get around to asking me that, Doctor. Just before I was to leave in the second week of March, 1962, it would seem that Fate would interfere once more. I received a call from a former student, now a professor, Doctor Ibin Hammas at the newly created University of Jordan. Apparently during the construction of a new highway near Amman, a cache containing many statues was unearthed by a bulldozer. He said judging from the initial radio carbon estimates the pieces they discovered were more than eight-thousand years old—an undiscovered and undisturbed Neolithic site. Mindful of the fate of the similar statues found at Jericho and because he had enormous faith in me while at Yale as a student, he had convinced or at least implored the Jordanian government for me to head the excavation. This was with a joint American-Jordanian team with cooperation from the Smithsonian's Analytical Conservation Laboratory, headed by Carol Grissom."

"Obviously you went," I said.

"I *had* to. It was an enormous opportunity, and I knew that Nasca would have to wait until the following year, or at the very least the fall, and though I hated to put it off until later, I knew that I had to. My *instinct*, though it was calling me to Nasca, was now beckoning me with utter abandon to *Ain Ghazal*. I wasted no time, and though it was difficult to get in touch with her as I knew she was out in the middle of a Peruvian plateau, studying her lines, I finally managed to get into contact with Maria. I let her know that I would be delayed, by how long I could not say, but that I would get a message to her as soon as I had an idea of my itinerary and how long the safe removal of the statues would take. I left for Amman at once."

I had to admit, I was becoming more and more intrigued by his story, not because it was, truly, a fascinating tale, but that it thus far rang *true*. You see, I had checked out these discoveries, excavations, and people that he mentioned, and most of them thus far were a matter of public record, and it was beginning to dawn on me then that I was going to have to make a choice in what I revealed concerning Gottlieb's strange tale and what I would put in his profile to Frank.

"And?" I asked.

He had paused for moment, his face crinkled and the lines drawn, clearly in intense deliberation.

"I was not prepared for what awaited me. Though I knew the find was a priceless treasure that peered into the murky depths of antiquity, I never believed or even suspected," he paused. "Well, maybe I suspected, but I did not for once dare to believe that what I would find would be the *face of the enemy.*"

"What do you mean, *'face of the enemy'*?"

He looked away, distracted before responding.

"Apparently I arrived none too soon. The bulldozer had damaged many of the pieces when it broke into the statuary, and great debate began as to how the rest of the statues would be removed. After a preliminary analysis of the site it was determined there were a total of 2 caches, containing at least fifteen and probably no more than thirty statues. It was Ms. Grissom's idea to remove the caches in huge blocks, dirt, earth, and all, and return them to their laboratory in the United States to study in order to come up with a strategy for their removal. I was hesitant, as I was mistrustful of an institution so closely tied with the United States Government. Who knew how long the statues would linger there, or whether or not they would be 'accidentally' destroyed as Dr. Rasp had described of those at Jericho? I remembered what Dr. Rasp had said, 'trust no one', and despite alluring candor and openness on the part of Ms. Grissom, I resolved to stick to the advice that Dr. Rasp had given. Until the fate of the statues could be decided, I insisted that Dr. Hammas take me to the University of Jordan's archaeology lab so I could make a thorough examination of those statues that were freed from the earth and make a determination on what should become of them based on my analysis."

"And?" I asked with trepidation.

"It was everything I had ever hoped and feared, an overwhelming experience that I don't know if I can accurately describe or relate in a manner that would convey the intensity of emotion I experienced when I first saw them."

He leaned back against the wall of his cell, closed his eyes, and pinched and massaged his nose. His voice was growing tense and he seemed to be anxious.

"They were large, compared with contemporaneous Neolithic, minuscule human clay or stone figurines found at this and other sites. At thirty-five to one-hundred centimeters high, the statues could literally have been termed *monumental.* Their thickness was about five to ten centimeters, basically flat, although pieces and remnants that were found suggested that others that may be embedded in dirt caches may have been thicker. It appeared as though they were balanced to stand up, and had a flat, stable base. Genitalia, for some reason, had been systematically omitted, on the all the pieces in the lab, and all the others I suspected. The head was over emphasized, much larger, and in disproportion to the human body. It represented about one-fifth the total size of the statues. The neck was also, longer, oversized, and disproportionate. They had a high forehead, well over half the size of the head. The mouth and base of the nose were the same size, the nose being conspicuously short and upturned, exhibiting long, thin nostrils. The minuscule mouth had no lips," he paused, sighing anxiously before continuing. "Lastly, they had an arresting, almost *piercing* glance as if they knew or could read your thoughts. The eyes ... the eyes were disproportionately large, twice the size of the base of the nose and many times that of the mouth. They were set far apart, the globes bulging slightly, surrounded by a deep oval ridge, containing two large, inset pupils that looked out with a fixed, striking stare. As they gazed back at me, penetrating my soul to its innermost depths, I knew why my instinct drove me here; I knew what it was that I was seeing, and that the artisans of nine-thousand years ago did too, and they had captured it with the utmost precision and accuracy in these statues. Lying on the table before me was not some arbitrary Neolithic discovery, it was one of *them.* It was the *Grays.* It was in that defining moment where I began to know all that was lost and discovered at the same time, and the weight of this discovery began to set upon me, that I was reminded of my *HAMLET.* 'Whether it is nobler in the mind to suffer the slings and arrows of outrageous fortune, or to take arms against a sea of troubles, and by opposing, end them. To die, to sleep, to sleep, perchance to dream—'"

He had a distant, far off look in his eyes as he said these words, and I couldn't help but wonder at the faint and dusty images that he was seeing. I stared at him marveling at his simplistic candor until he seemed to return to the present.

"Let us make a pact now, Doctor," he said. "Let us dream together, you and I, and let us see what dreams may come. You will dream of what *will* be, and I will dream that our two are one. You see Doctor, 'To be, or *not* to be, that *is* the question.'"

CHAPTER SEVEN

Mr. Black's Confession

I looked at him incredulously. I was beginning to seethe and was about to come to a boil and explode. "You want *me* to help *you?* After all you've done to me, the threats, the lies and the deceit? The murder? You locked my wife away and took my son to God knows where ..." I realized my voice was beginning to carry and I settled down to avoid a further scene. We were no longer the only table in the bar and the lunch crowd was starting to file in.

"Are you finished?" he asked smugly, and with what I could only describe as a slightly irritated expression while putting his sunglasses back on, no doubt so he wouldn't draw attention due to his eyes. He waited for me to calm down a little more before continuing. "What I'm offering you, Dr. Stattler, you can not even begin to fathom or imagine. It is what you've always wanted, what you've dreamed of, lying there on the floor in that hole you call an apartment, in yesterday's clothes next to a pile of your own vomit. It is what you've spent your entire life running from and at the same time, unbeknownst to you, at least consciously, in pursuit of."

"What do you mean?" I asked cautiously.

"I think we both know what we're talking about here Dr. Stattler—the revelation of *them.* The ones who have eluded you for so long. The beings of Zeta-Riticuli. The deceivers. The ones who come and take people in the night. The fathers and creators of mankind itself. What I'm talking about here, Dr. Stattler, is the revelation of the Grays and their presence and influence. Now. Here. On this planet you call Earth."

"Why would you help me do such a thing? You have spent your entire existence in defense of these creatures and protecting the lie that shields them."

"That shields you, Dr. Stattler. That shields *you.*"

"How can I trust you and know that you are telling the truth? How can I possibly believe you are willing to betray what you've spent your entire life preserving? And besides, even if I did believe you which I'm not sure that I do, I don't have any proof or even a leg to stand on. You said it yourself all those years ago, short of an alien corpse who am I really going to convince, even if I had the chip?"

"Ah, the blessed chip," he said, sighing, and then went on. "Times have changed, Dr. Stattler. I'm surprised that living on the fringe you haven't noticed this simple truth. Look around you, in this very bar where we are sitting ... nearly every race you can put a finger to on this earth is represented here having lunch today," he paused. "Twenty years ago did you ever see such diversity? Did you ever see such a mingling of the races?"

I looked around and it was true. There were Asians, Africans, African-Americans, Indians, even Mickey, and the Italian.

"... every race but one," he added smiling sarcastically. "But you'll have to forgive them as they don't eat the way we do." He smiled, leaned back and took another cigarette which he removed from the pack of Kools that I laid in the center of the table and continued. "As a matter of fact, they don't eat at all."

"What the hell does that have to do with anything?" I asked.

He lit his cigarette, slowly taking a drag and seeming to savor the menthol within his lungs as if it were one of the last he would ever smoke.

"The world is becoming whole, Dr. Stattler; barriers are breaking down, even now, as we speak. The European Union has been created; currencies, fences, obstacles, and racism are slowly being eradicated in favor of single unified global power and economy. You are slowly becoming one people, one power, one global nation. It is inevitable. We have seen in our time third world countries become modernized, technologically advanced, and able to feed their populations. Disease is being combated and beaten. It is the first time in history that human beings have fully decoded the DNA strand and possess the ability to copy themselves. The Internet has been created and is opening the doors to information that for decades, even centuries, have been lost to the modern every day man. And as we both know, Dr. Stattler," he took another drag from his cigarette before continuing. "It is *information* and new ideas that drives mankind and brings us here today. It is information and the *sharing* of information that begets knowledge and knowledge begets *power.*"

I listened quietly as he spoke, absorbing what he said. I thought for a few long moments and reflected. And it was true. The world was changing, all around us, every day, every second like an unrelenting tide that will not ebb.

"What does that have to do with the Grays?" I asked. "What does it have to do with proving their existence?"

"What it has to *do* with proving their existence, Dr. Stattler, is that those nations and peoples who are not open to new ideas and ways of thinking will find themselves on the way side technologically, economically, even physically. The time is right. I have seen it," he said.

"What do you mean you have *seen* it?"

"I can't answer that."

"Can't or won't?" I asked, my irritation growing.

"Won't, Dr. Stattler. It has to do with that *shield* that you so vehemently spoke of. The shield that protects you humans from yourselves."

"Bullshit! You started this, you finish it. You tell me everything, everything leading up to our initial encounter twenty years ago and everything after, or I won't even consider helping you. I have nothing to lose. You on the other hand, for whatever reason, appear to need me for something, and since thanks to you I lost my job and place of residence *yet again* it would seem I have plenty of time to spare … if you're here to kill me as you once said you would if you actually caught me, get it over with, because I quite frankly really don't give a shit," I said smugly, leaning back, feigning a relaxed pose to accentuate my point.

He frowned at this. "I'll agree to your terms, but with conditions."

"And what might those be?" I asked defiantly, as I could see he was willing to relent to my ultimatum.

"These will be things that you do not necessarily want to hear, Dr. Stattler. These will be things that will anger, infuriate you. These will be things that will likewise bring you to the depths of human misery, which even you have not yet seen. These will be things that will unsettle you and I know not what you will do when you hear them. These will be things that could destroy your very sanity. These are things which could consume you, as they consumed Dr. Gottlieb."

He stopped eyeing me beneath his sunglasses, waiting for me to respond but I did not. I stared at him coldly, back through my own reflection in his shades, hopefully penetrating his gaze.

"I must ask that you hear these things with an open mind. I must ask that despite the hardships you may bear in hearing them that you must not jump to conclusions. I must ask that you hear and absorb these things calmly," he continued. "And when I am finished you will make an objective decision considering my request and all that I have said and told you here today."

I'm not sure whether it was the booze or whether it truly was, as I said, that I didn't give a shit, which was true I didn't ... but what was not true that I didn't tell him was that I was scared. I was frightened. But to my great surprise I nodded my head in bewildered agreement, not really sure if I wanted to accept his offer or not. I knew from experience the dangers that lay ahead and in accepting I was committing myself to a possible path that I was uncertain I wanted to take. I had started to walk down it once, unable to finish, and it ruined and destroyed everything and everyone that I have ever loved or cared for.

"Go ahead," I stammered quietly, barely audible even to myself.

"Those you would call the Grays are from a star system known to some, through their carelessness I might add, not my own, as Zeta Riticuli. At least that's what human beings have christened it. I regret that I am unable to pronounce or describe what they call it. They have been traveling the cosmos and visiting and meddling in other worlds affairs longer than even Dr. Gottlieb cared to dream or imagine. The first time they came to this edge of the galaxy where upon our earth is adrift in space was some five to six million years ago. It was while surveying this primitive and barbaric world that they discovered a group of indigenous primates. It was decided during this survey, for reasons known only to them, that they would 'help' this species in attaining enlightenment. It was shortly after that other vessels were dispatched to study and further along this process. A 'base camp' of sorts was established and samples were taken, tagged, altered genetically by the Grays and then returned to the group to pro-create and spread their new DNA to the rest of the species."

"How were they altered?" I asked.

"The Grays added strands of their DNA to the primates. This was a necessary task in order to *speed* up the process by which man would eventually evolve. I'm sure that in your discussions with Dr. Gottlieb he enlightened you concerning these processes, how it was impossible for human beings to evolve from apes in trees to the people you see around you in this restaurant today in only a six million years *without* direct intervention. The dinosaurs after all inhabited the earth for *hundreds* of millions of years, an entire week on Gottlieb's famous calendar."

"You mean Gottlieb was right, it was both nature *and* the Grays which helped shape our evolution?" I asked somewhat puzzled.

"Yes, and I will clarify that shortly. Adding the DNA was a critical task as each pair sequence needed to be mapped precisely to the other so that they would not produce genetic aberrations and at the same time prepare and allow contingencies for the next genetic seeding cycle. As the two species were initially so different this could only be done through gene sequencing until the desired DNA strand could be altered and not reject the new material. This was a time consuming process, but not one that the Grays weren't familiar with or hadn't accomplished before with great success on different worlds. The first example of their efforts that bore fruit was what we would refer to today as *Sahelanthropus tchadensis*, the first bi-pedal human ancestor."

"Incredible … but how did they accomplish this … this process took tens sometimes hundreds of thousands of years to perfect? Surely no species in the universe has such longevity …"

"You forget your Einstein, Dr. Stattler. If you can travel the speed of light, it would be possible to witness the very birth of the human species, as well as their death, and further, to witness the end of time. Though he was correct that the speed of light is the highest maximum speed possible within the universe, he was somewhat disillusioned as to his discussions in the ability to travel faster."

"What are you saying?"

"What I'm saying, Dr. Stattler, is that the Grays visited the Earth in the initial stages of human evolution only frequently enough to guide their evolutionary progress with specific genetic material and enhancements which would allow for newer developments within the species and consequently higher brain functioning. It was neither necessary nor practical for them to remain behind while the initial genetic changes they implanted took effect amongst the group."

"So they would leave and periodically return once they felt the subjects were ready for the next installation," I said, taking grasp of the situation.

"Exactly, and because time slows down the closer you come to traveling the speed of light, they were free to return home or complete other errands within the cosmos and come back to Earth only once the estimated next stage of development had been reached, which of course they could, with a fair amount of accuracy, predict based on their speed, time, distance, and how long they had been traveling. Here on earth time continued as normal, but for the Grays it would grind virtually to a halt."

"So they were able to use the forces of nature to their benefit …" I said, more talking to myself than to him.

"Eventually one species change led to another and with each subsequent alteration the hosts could absorb more of the Gray's DNA. Just a point of note Doctor, the changes we are talking about are miniscule, careful inspection of the average human DNA molecule reveals that it is still ninety-six percent identical to a chimpanzee. I have to admit sometimes I loathe looking in the mirror, not for anything I have done, mind you, but because all I see staring back me is the face some barbaric primate."

A chill passed through me when he said this, and the psychologist in me longed to hear more of his personal details that had for so long eluded me, and I that I could only guess at or muse upon. Before I could respond he continued.

"There were setbacks, however, at times there were unforeseen environmental or climatic changes that would wipe out entire groups and consequently years of research. It was then decided because of these setbacks that they would start experimenting with several groups at the same time, thus insuring survival of at least one which should in theory prove to be the most dominant form. Paleoanthropology today defines these as the *australopithecines* and then later the genus *homo*. This is also why several species would co-exist at the same time, such as Neanderthals and early Homo Sapiens.

"Each successive transition led to a higher brain casing which directly translated into higher brain functioning and abilities. The first Sahelanthropus tchadensis had an average bran size of about 350 cc. Modern humans today have an average brain size of about 1350 cc. As for the Grays, they have an average brain size of just over 3000 cc, which grants them abilities and resources you can not even begin to imagine. For them, when they have interactions with us, it is as though they are interacting with an animal that can barely comprehend or even understand them. Perhaps a good analogy might be when you are communicating with a dog or other domesticated animal, or perhaps attempting to explain rocket science to a cave man."

"This would explain what I have heard of their warm bedside manner," I said thinking out loud. "Where were they conducting their experiments during this time … you mentioned a base of operations, surely this base would be destroyed by nature in the lapses of tens or hundreds of thousands of years between their visitations?"

"Very good Dr. Stattler, but you're missing something. Nature *abhors* a vacuum," he said.

"You mean it was in space," I said putting the pieces together, "and in between the DNA seedings, during the time it took to spread the new genetic material throughout the species, the Grays could simply decompress the facility until their return ... all their instruments, data, and failed 'test' subjects could remain virtually intact without even a layer of dust ... even over the span of a hundred-thousand years."

Mr. Black grimly nodded an assent of my hypothesis.

"Was it in orbit?" I asked, wondering how the Grays could keep such a structure from the wandering eyes of telescopes and space enthusiasts.

"*Is* in orbit Dr. Stattler," he said with an assured smugness.

"But that's impossible, surely *someone* would have seen it by now, you can't simply hide a space station around our planet ... even if it had some cloaking technology there would still be some sort of distortion."

"What is the one and only spatial body in the earth's system that does not rotate on its axis but has the same side always facing the earth?"

I thought for a moment.

"The moon," I said half-guessing.

"The moon," he repeated. "The base of operations lies in a crater on the dark side of the moon that never faces the earth. This base, though initially constructed to house only one craft and the necessary accouterments of their experiments, now holds nearly twenty dozen, and is about the size of a small city. I feel it necessary to point out the obvious; the average citizen does not have access to this type of information. In order for private citizens to actually *see* the base of operations, they would, for all intents and purposes, have to build something akin to a Saturn Rocket and orbit the moon themselves— a tremendous burden that even those with the financial ability, know-how, and belief would chafe at.

"After all, the only outlet of information of what, exactly, is on the other side of the moon has been through our government or agencies thereof. Do you honestly expect they would reveal this information to the general public? James Lovell on board the command module of Apollo 8 was one of the first to publicly admit this over the airwaves with the statement, 'PLEASE BE INFORMED THAT THERE IS A SANTA CLAUS.' The officials at both NASA, the CIA, the NSA, as well as others in our organization felt it would be suspicious to cover or block their transmission once Apollo 8 emerged from the dark side of the moon, so it was agreed for Lovell to reveal a statement which could both confirm the existence of the Grays and yet at the same time be unobtrusive. Though he did not know of its location, or to put it more precisely, *where, exactly, he was*, it was Travis Walton who was the first human being to describe and, more importantly report in his abduction account, one of the hangars of the lunar station in his story, *Fire in the Sky*.

"I read it … I was surprised you *didn't* kill him," I said.

"A *very* sloppy job on the part of the Grays, and it was not one that I enjoyed cleaning. I assure you had this incident occurred in the fifties or sixties when McCarthyism was rife, paranoia of Communists was everywhere, and the *information* we spoke of was not quite so available, Mr. Walton would never have published his book nor would he be alive today."

"I'm not quite sure I follow … .what led you to spare him?"

"Mr. Walton was fortunate enough to be living in a time where members of the press were no longer willing to turn a blind eye to the criminal actions of members of the United States government, or even the president himself. Times had changed. These were not the days of Kennedy where a president and, more specifically, his transgressions would go unreported. Ironically, it was the downfall of Nixon and the aftermath that *really* saved Mr. Walton. The fact he had six eyewitnesses to corroborate his story, who not only saw the vessel, summoned the media, and passed polygraphs, didn't jeopardize his well-being either or the credibility of his tale. It was too high-profile a case. Too dangerous. It had the potential of undermining just what it was we were attempting to preserve. Harming Mr. Walton and his compatriots would have generated inquiries we would rather not have asked."

"Is that why he was taken so long, for five days?" I asked.

"In most *Initial Contact*, or *IC* abduction cases as we call them, the subject is taken and their DNA is extracted for further study and future re-implantation with new genetic material. Then the chip is placed within the body in a location that is not prone to injury or investigation such as behind the jaw, or the lymph-nodes among other places, so that the subject may be located and reacquired at some point in the future. This is not unlike the "tagging" of endangered species. *IC's* normally take anywhere from 2-4 hours and are usually completed within the visiting craft. *RC's* or *Return Contacts* require the subject be taken back to lunar base for application of the new genetic material.

"Because Mr. Walton's case, although an *Initial Contact*, had immediately drawn such publicity and rancor it was necessary for the agents in our association to arrive at a decision concerning what was to be done with him. This caused quite a stir and a debate of the very purpose of our organization.

There were many, including myself, who felt that he should be sacrificed and the witnesses brought up on charges for murder. This became the initial plan but was thwarted when the witnesses agreed to and later passed polygraph examinations with flying colors. As you know this process took several days and it was necessary to hold Mr. Walton until the results of the polygraph were concluded, thus he was taken to the operations center on the moon for safekeeping. After the test results were broadcast on the police scanner it was decided after many days of debate that a "hands-off" approach would be taken towards his case, and he was returned to the earth's surface *without* the chip. We couldn't afford an investigation into this matter which might release a *Watergate* of extra-terrestrial information to the public."

I sat in a bewildered awe. So much was as I thought, and yet so much wasn't. It was hard for me to really believe Mr. Black and what he was saying. It was like I had opened Pandora's Box and knowledge that had been forbidden or lost was now pouring forth like a tidal wave, unstoppable ... .impenetrable, and unwavering, and I began to wonder when it would begin to consume me, and drown me within its depths. How much was yet unspoken? How many people have suffered and died for this knowledge? And worse still, what was yet to come? It was in that moment I couldn't help wondering whether I should have opened it at all.

"Were you scared?" I asked. "Of the truth getting out?"

"Fear is unknown to me Dr. Stattler," he said with a grim straight face.

"I'm sorry; I didn't mean to insult you."

"No apology is necessary Dr. Stattler ... I was, however, *concerned*," he accentuated this last word. "The arguments in Mr. Walton's case were among the most belabored and cumbersome in the history of our organization, especially in terms of making a decision as to what was to be done with a witness."

"It's interesting to hear the story *between* the lines. I wonder if he knows," I said, pondering whether or not Travis Walton knew just how close he had come to never waking from that fateful night where he was stunned by a 'tremendously bright blue-green ray' shot from the bottom of the Grays' craft in the Arizona Apache-Sitgreaves National Forest.

"He suspects," said Mr. Black, pushing his glasses back up his brow which were beginning to slide down his nose. "But to clarify the issue even further, it wasn't Walton specifically that the Grays were interested in anyway, and their blunder was that they grossly underestimated how many people were in the truck."

"What do you mean?"

"The *Initial Contact* while helpful to their genetic program, usually only serves as a means for subjugating an entire family and then as time passes and they pro-create, groups of families and individuals who unbeknownst to them have pro-created and spread the new DNA tags to their offspring. It is the offspring that the Grays are most chiefly interested in."

"Why?"

"The Grays prefer to study and work with children over adults, although it is adults who are initially required to begin DNA seeding procedures. The process by which *Initial Contacts* are taken and chosen directly coincides with their age and ability to have children. You may have noticed in the many abduction reports that litter the Internet on the subject of UFO's, there are nearly none that are or have been written by adults over fifty. This is for the simple reason that human adults over fifty are unlikely to procreate and if they do, as any physician would tell you, there is a greater risk of genetic abnormalities, which defeats the purposes of the Grays' interest. This, therefore, makes them unlikely candidates for abduction and genetic study, and subsequently is why they are not taken."

"Why do they prefer children, other than perhaps their inability to resist or harm them?"

"There are many reasons that the Grays prefer to take and work with children over adults. However, as children are not independent enough to travel alone on their own in a manner in which they can be safely acquired without detection, in order to contact and detain them for study it is necessary to first tag the adults who either have children already or are in a position to have children later. The latter being the preferential of the two as it obviously allows for greater study and manipulation of the genetic code. You see, children do not possess the inherent fear of the unknown that adults do. Their minds are more open, fresh, if you will, and they do not understand prejudice. Haven't you ever noticed that in every legitimate 'haunting' of earthbound spirits or ghosts there are always children involved? The mind of a child is uncorrupted, and as such is more able and willing to accept and, in some cases, see things that adult humans either can not or do not necessarily wish to. To put it plainly Doctor, the adult human mind is blinded by the lies it has through the years come to believe.

But to continue, secondly, and more importantly at least from a research perspective, children offer the Grays a longer window of opportunity to study the effects of DNA alteration over time. In a thirty year adult you may only have thirty to forty years of observational opportunity, and that's assuming, of course, that re-acquisition of the subject is possible, which in many and most cases isn't. In many, many cases, adults who experience an *Initial Contact* situation are never reacquired, either because they never again venture into a borderline area where they can be abducted without notice, or because they have not conceived children and are no longer considerable for study. It is therefore for this reason that the Grays abduct multiple persons in borderline areas on multiple continents on a nightly basis."

"What is a *borderline* area?" I asked, curiously.

"Yes. A borderline area or neutral zone is an area definitively outside major human settlements where the population is sparse and therefore more accessible to Gray incursions. For obvious reasons, the Grays would never touchdown to acquire a subject in the middle of a city, the panic and chaos which they would create would serve to undermine their purpose. In the initial armistice talks, which I will discuss later, senior members of the United States government and the Grays defined what specifically these *borderline* areas were and what their perimeters were that defined them. Of course, over time, as society grows and the population expands these areas become subject to change, and defining these areas and relaying this information to the Grays is one of the missions of our office."

"But, to return the discussion at hand, the third reason that the Grays prefer children is, as you indicated, more of a practical nature—children require less security. The chances of a child overpowering and injuring a Gray even though they are somewhat smaller and more frail than humans is minimal, especially since their minds are much more susceptible to influence than the average adult. There is also a distinct correlation between *IC's* taken at a younger age vs. older ones in the ability to reacquire the subject. *Initial Contacts* when taken at an early age always tend to feel that 'something is missing' in their lives. As they mature they are therefore more willing to venture out into the world and attempt to find these consuming and often abstract objects of their mind, to 'find themselves' whatever it is they think that may be. Thus, they are often more well-traveled than those subjects taken in later adulthood. As a consequence they share a greater probability of traveling into borderline areas where they can be reacquired for further study and genetic implantation.

"Eventually, these alterations roll on to the next generation over and over and over again, the changes are very subtle, but yet acting quickly enough that differences and pairings between generations can be measured by the

Grays with great exactitude. For example, haven't you noticed that more and more humans are being born without their wisdom teeth, or that they never grow and reach full maturity at all? This was *unheard* of ten to twenty years ago, yet you take this change for granted and do not attribute it to outside or *alien* influence, but you should. In nature and natural selection for a change like this to occur, it would take thousands or hundreds of thousands of years to make such a small but radical change in the physique and structure of a native species. This is just but one small example of their influence, Dr. Stattler, one of which that seems so insignificant and banal that it is easily ignored, and not even discussed. It quite simply does not even occur to humanity in their self-obsessed arrogance, that a species wide change like this to transpire would be impossible without outside influence."

"How is it done?" I asked, my mind racing. "How are these procedures performed?"

"Each time a person is taken they are inserted with an implant which transmits their location, their DNA profile, and the specified changes to their genes, which allows the Grays to track and maintain, in essence, a whole network of people who have been abducted and through procreation are unconsciously changing the human species."

"Incredible."

"Finally, to return to our discussion concerning Gray preference for using children as test subjects, children, unlike adults, require less memory auditing."

"Memory auditing?"

"Yes. When an adult is taken on an *Initial Contact* mission, before they are returned, the Grays, for obvious reasons, attempt to erase the conscious memories of the event from the short-term memory, and block them from becoming new, permanent long-term memories. While they have perfected this technique with a strong degree of reliability, these memories sometimes have a greater chance of resurfacing in an adult nervous system. Because the brain is more developed in adults there is greater development of neural networks and synaptic pathways which may contain residual mental images of the events. Also there is the fact that when an adult vs. a child is taken there is, in nearly every case, the accompaniment of primate impulses—fear, fight, or flight, which can often re-trigger memory consolidation, the conversion from short to long term memory. It is because of these instinctual impulses that there is a greater chance the events the person is experiencing may be 'photographed', if you will, in other areas of the brain. They may be consolidated into a *secondary memory*.

"A short term memory, as you know from your previous experience in the field of psychology, is easy to erase as they have not yet been formed. The information has not yet been stored and created as memory engrams, which of course is a single circuit in the brain that corresponds to a single memory. By artificially stimulating the *hippocampus*, the area of the brain responsible for converting short term memories to new long term memories, the Grays are able to induce a neural fatigue, which coupled with the shock and trauma of the experience of being abducted by aliens from another world, they are usually with a fair amount of success able to block the events from the memory of the poor wretch they seized and abducted.

"Now as you are well aware, Doctor, while it is possible to artificially stimulate areas of the brain to block new memories from forming, the sub-conscious memory records everything, and can not be altered. It is too deep within the human psyche, and it is for this reason that while the subject may not remember anything that happened to them, the events still may be re-lived, as you experienced with Dr. Gottlieb under hypnosis. Or they may be released during the sorting and shuffling of the unconscious indicated by Rapid Eye Movement during the dreaming cycle."

"Jesus ..." I said. "It just gets better and better doesn't it? But you still haven't told me why you're here ... and what you spoke of earlier, how you have *seen* these events between us come to unfold." I said, trying to draw more out of him. I was propping the lid of the box up even further and leaning back I prepared myself for what vicious and unsettling truths that might pour from his lips.

He stared at me through his glasses for a few moments before respond-ing, as if thinking or planning just how it was he was going to answer. He then finally spoke and asked, "Have you ever experienced *deja-vu* Dr. Stattler?"

"Of course I have, who hasn't?" I asked.

"Do you know exactly what it means?" he retorted.

"I have a feeling you're going to tell me."

"*Deja-vu*, Dr. Stattler, is an unusual side-effect we humans feel that is related to *second sight*. As you know, *deja-vu* is the feeling that you have done something before, whereas *second sight* is the ability to see something before it happens. They are both related and in fact share the same dormant gene, which was of course implanted from the Grays. *Deja-vu* is the beginning of true awareness of the behavior of the universe; the beginnings of the human brain to comprehend the true *universal order*, which is that everything in the universe no longer exists, that it has *already* happened. There is essentially no difference between the past and the future."

"I'm not sure I follow?" I said, trying to grasp what exactly Mr. Black was attempting to explain.

"You may find this hard to believe, Dr. Stattler, but every particle of matter created when the universe exploded from a single atom fifteen billion years ago has already been destroyed by a simultaneous universal collapse. Every living thing, every planet, every solar system, every nebula, every star, every grain of sand on every beach in the cosmos was created and destroyed, like a firecracker, in one instant."

"I'm sorry, I don't understand," I said.

He sighed as though having to explain himself to a two-year-old but continued. "Imagine you were standing *outside* of the universe and the space it was to occupy when 'the big bang' occurred. Time on the outside of the universe takes place at a different speed than within. On the inside of the universe, where we are, there are certain rules of nature which we have come to know are immutable. For example, if you were to see a gun or fireworks display go off, you first see the flash and then hear the report ... this is because light travels faster than sound and the further away you move from the epicenter of the explosion the *longer* it takes for you to hear it.

"Ok, I'm with you so far ..." I said, trying to comprehend what exactly he was saying.

"The same physical laws that are present here on earth are present inside the universe as well. Take the stars for example. In many cases the light that you are seeing may have taken hundreds of millions of years to reach your retina even while traveling three hundred thousand kilometers per second. By the time that light reaches your eyes the star from which it emanated could have long since been extinguished, having collapsed upon itself. This is why *time seems to slow down* the closer you approach the speed of light; it is because you are on the threshold of what the Grays call *universal time*, the true "present" time in the cosmos—the time *outside* the universe. In short, the universe itself and everything within it behaves in this same manner— but *only* to the *inside* observer. To the observer outside the universe, it was created and destroyed in the same instant. All the events you know, your history, and your future, everything that happened and will happen *inside* the universe transpired in less than a flicker of an instant on the *outside*, where time is measured differently. It is thought that the outside of the universe is the fourth dimension. The reason you sometimes experience *deja-vu* is because you *have* done that event before. The reason those with *second sight* can see into the future is because *it has already happened.* The future is not a set of unwritten variables that play themselves out randomly; it is simply a set of events which from *your* perspective in time you have not yet seen unfold—but to the observer *outside* the universe, you, your planet, your star, even this very galaxy no longer exists. This is why it is not possible to travel the *true* speed of light … you can approach it, you can come *infinitely* close down to the smallest fraction of a second, but it is impossible to enter."

"I thought you said Einstein was wrong, that he was 'disillusioned' in the ability to travel faster …" I added, quick to point out his error, somehow hoping that there was and would be a flaw in his explanations.

"It is, and it isn't," he said, taking another cigarette and tapping the end upon the table before lighting it. "The beings of Zeta-Riticuli have developed a system of artificially created wormholes which are marked and triggered by beacons at a fixed point in space. Each beacon is mapped to a specific star-system within the galaxy and they mesh in a large intersecting grid," and he illustrated this physically by crossing his hands and intersecting his fingers as he continued. "Thus allowing them to jump from system to system while traveling as close to the speed of light as possible.

"The only downside to the beacons is that they sometimes must be manually deposited and secured in a specific spot relative to the star of each solar system. Sending a probe containing the beacon isn't always possible because they need to be anchored to a specific point in orbit relative to the star in order to harness enough gravity from the star and create the wormhole. If it is placed slightly out of alignment, the geometric, nuclear, and atomic forces needed to activate it will be out of sync and it will not function."

"I'm not sure I follow …"

"Let's say we wanted to journey to Alpha Centauri, the closest star system to the Earth. Assuming we could travel light speed or as close as we could get, it would take us approximately 4 years to get there. Once there we would plant a beacon and create a wormhole or *conduit* to the next closest beacon …"

"And all other ships could follow without having to make the trip in the same amount of time … sort of like laying cable …" I finished his sentence as I was beginning to comprehend what exactly he was trying to say. It began to make sense and I continued. "And because they are traveling virtually at the speed of light, time slows down for them, but everywhere else in the universe it continues as normal."

"Precisely. And at this point in our history the Grays have amassed a network of beacons, which span nearly a quarter of the Milky Way Galaxy, some hundred billion stars. Ironically it was while 'laying cable' as you so eloquently put it that the Grays discovered you, well, primates here five million years ago."

"What does this have to do with *deja-vu* and *second sight?*"

"Quite right, my apologies Dr. Stattler, we digress," he said looking at his watch. "And time grows short."

"As I have stated earlier, the Grays have discovered and theorized for what in our time would be several million years that the birth and the subsequent death of the universe occurred nearly instantaneously. Everything we know, everything we are, everything that has been born or *will* be born—died in that instant.

Every asteroid, every star, every sun, every galaxy, every wormhole, every anomaly, every grain of dust and everything within the contents of the universe itself that either *has* been created or has not *yet* been created has already perished—in present universal time. The speed of light, time, sound, all are immutable and are continuously operating but only within the contents of the universe; the cosmos itself behaves and obeys these laws—but again, only in it's interior. To an observer in *true universal time* the big bang was no more than a flicker of an instant. A brief experiment, who knows really."

I sat looking at the table in mute silence, my head swooning, trying to make sense out of what Mr. Black was telling me; and the more I thought about it, the more it made sense. It wiped out all coincidence; nothing was ever, truly, random; and at the same time it seemed to me to give purpose and *reason* for the unexplained. *Nothing* was left to chance, and the scythe with which Fate reaped the future from us seemed to have a precise and eerie order about it—it had purpose, it had order. I would never be able to look at life the same way again; in the back of my mind I would always be second guessing myself. Indeed, I had opened the box, and there was no shutting the lid.

"But, to bring us back to the discussion, the second sight, *deja-vu*, are the realization in humans of the true universal time. The reason you think you have already done something before, or can *see* what can happen before it does,"

"… is because we already *have*." I finished his sentence for him.

I paused and waited a few moments, smoking my cigarette and reflecting on the cosmic truths that have been laid out for me. I remembered wanting to go into work early this morning so that I could get my prep work out of the way and leave early this afternoon. It all seemed so trivial now, as if my life were pointless and held no meaning in the great cosmic scheme.

"And if that's true," I said slowly, realizing what was at stake and looking at him. "Then free will does not exist, and neither does our concept of the future."

"Yes," he interrupted. "Don't you now see the importance of establishing *control*, Dr. Stattler? Don't you *now* see why this knowledge could destroy everything human beings have struggled to achieve? Don't you now realize just what is at stake?"

"If everything I have ever done has already happened, what is the point in continuing?" I asked, talking more to myself than him.

"Yes."

"Then there is no difference between good or evil … the just are not rewarded, the wicked are not punished …" I stopped and then continued. "There is no God."

"There is only indifference," he said, summarizing my revelation. "Religion, Dr. Stattler, is yet another means of *control*. Don't you see? To them we are no more than foolish idolaters. To the Grays there *is* no such thing as 'Good' or 'Evil.' The universe does not care whether we humans live or die. Countless civilizations are extinguished and destroyed everyday since the dawn of what *we* call Creation."

"I can't believe that … I won't," I said, feeling everything I have clung to, to help me survive the last twenty years slowly slip away; my passion, my morality, my forgiveness—my sanity.

"You must, or we will fail, Dr. Stattler."

"I don't know if I can," I said bitterly.

He paused a moment, reflecting on this and then spoke. "You should have more faith in yourself, Dr. Stattler," he said as if reading my mind. "I do."

"And why is that?"

"Because you haven't yet forced me to kill you,"

"Is that another attempt at humor?"

"Forgive me, Dr. Stattler; it is not something which I get to experiment with often in my line of work. Actually, I'll let you in on another little secret, Dr. Stattler ..." he continued. "That day twenty years ago when I had my gun drawn ready to kill you, I experienced something ..."

"*The second sight?*" I said, half-asking, half-joking really.

He continued as though I hadn't spoken. "I had killed 237 people to defend what I believed was preservation of the human race prior to that fateful evening, and *none* of them ever invoked that experience. When I said I thought I saw something I did see something in my mind. I saw you, though you had aged. I saw the way you are dressed, us having this discussion, at this table, in this bar, here and *now* and I *knew* it was necessary ... no, I knew it was *imperative* that I let you live, but I didn't know the full extent of it. I didn't know the *reason* behind it. I didn't know *why*—that is why I eventually became so obsessed with you. I *knew* somehow, that your participation in these events was *supposed* to continue and, at the time, your leaving me with no choice but to kill you, I admit, did leave me feeling a little unsettled. Lucky for you the universe and fate would play themselves out so precisely.

"Lucky for us both, perhaps." I said.

"But, as you can see, the universal constant I have just spoken of holds true. There is no denying it, for here we are."

"What do you think caused it?" I asked.

"In addition to my vision, the kind citizens of Zeta Riticuli enhanced us with other abilities as well, the *second sight* among them. Because the Grays are so advanced evolutionarily speaking they possess abilities we do not; abilities such as the second sight which can see the future. Abilities, that in some cases, they have *already* shared with us; abilities that we will develop because of *them*. Before installing the next genetic phase of human evolution, which is of course continual, everything on this planet is evolving as we speak. However it is the rate at which humans are evolving and *their influence* that concerns us here. Specifically, before the next installment on the Grays genetic hierarchy is implemented, a group is selected and tested to determine whether the species has reached the level of attainment necessary to accept the new material. In answer to your question I am the last of what is known only to some as the Groom Lake 6."

"Groom Lake," I said interrupting him. "You're referring to the Area 51 facility?"

"Very good Dr. Stattler, the common citizen is usually not familiar with its name by location."

"I've had plenty of time to do my homework ... and if I'm not mistaken that facility wasn't constructed until the mid-fifties ..." I said.

"1954, actually. Though there were other functions that the Area 51 complex served, the ultimate purpose was to test machinery and military vehicles, which possessed at the time new technology. New technology shared by the Grays with members of your government ..."

"Technology shared in exchange ..." I stammered, unintentionally interrupting him.

"Exchanged," he said, cutting me off. "For virtual dominion over the skies of the United States ... for the permission and ability to seize and take any citizen they wished to aid in their research and 'evolution' of our species, which really was a token if not empty gesture. After all, they are the fathers of humanity and have been abducting souls since before mankind even had the ability or brain to record time. The United States had no choice but to accept; what was the government going to do, say 'No'? They had been altering our existence, history, and even our evolution itself. It was agreed for obvious purposes that these abductions would take place only in sparsely populated areas of the country to minimize the risk and avoid detection of their presence as much as possible, and of course the revelation of this agreement between our two species."

"When was this agreement reached?" I asked. "How long in United States history has the government been aware of their existence?"

"December the 2nd, 1934 was the day of the first 'official' armistice of sorts between the Grays and the government of the United States during the tenure of Franklin Roosevelt. It was under his administration that *first contact* was made and the exchange I previously spoke of proposed and agreed to, with stipulations that I have, of course, already mentioned, lest they might draw attention to themselves and their activities."

"What caused it, what was the catalyst?" I asked.

"Commercial Air Flight and the development of the United States Air Force, Dr. Stattler. It was the first time in the history of mankind that we were able to take to the skies and fly to other continents with any regularity. Pilots began to see aircraft, which they could not explain. Eventually these sightings led to chases, games of cat and mouse in the clouds, and finally, a meeting in the Arizona desert."

"So Roswell wasn't the first official exchange between the Grays and members of our government?" I asked and then added. "How could it be ... you've got to be at least sixty-five years old?"

"Seventy, actually. Next week is my birthday, November the 7th, 1935," he said, and then continued. "The incident at Roswell was a tragedy and giant setback for the Truman administration ... it opened the doors from what was once only a select few who knew about the Gray's existence and influence to all the President's senior staff and top military officials. The subject *had* to be contained; there were too many variables and lives at stake. An organization needed to be formed to oversee and work covertly with the aliens. It was due to the Roswell incident that President Truman and the National Security Council issued a revised version of the National Security Council Intelligence Directive (NSCID) No. 9 on October 24th, 1952, which resulted in the formation of National Security Agency on November 4th, 1952."

"Is that your 'official' employer?"

"I have no official employer ... agents such as myself simply do not, for all intents and purposes, exist, not even on paper ... at least in an 'official' capacity," he said, exhaling his cigarette.

"What happened at Roswell, exactly?" I asked.

"An inexperienced pilot is what happened, Dr. Stattler. If the Grays have one weakness, and they don't have many, it is their over-confidence. They consider themselves to be beneath nothing or no one. They are God-less, Fearless, 'Masters of the Universe', as it were, that need not justify their actions and are without regret ... and in some ways they are quite justified in this analysis of themselves ..." he paused then continued. "And in some ways they are not."

"What do you mean?"

"The Grays, though clever and meticulous, still make mistakes ... perhaps that is the only *human* flaw they possess, though I do not necessarily think it human but more so a universal truth that nothing is perfect ... there are no 'perfect' spheres, there is no absolute square of PI. But, to return to the point, they do not make mistakes often, perhaps once in a few millennia."

"Great," I said with a hint of sarcasm.

He leaned back, smiled, and then chuckled. "Relax Doctor, that was another attempt at humor ... How am I doing?"

"It needs work," I said.

"Actually, I'm exaggerating a little ... you see before you evidence of their mistakes," he said, opening his arms to accentuate himself.

"You?" I asked. "How's that?"

"I am a mistake for several reasons Doctor. The first of course is obvious, this discussion, why we are here today."

I interrupted him, "... which you still haven't explained to me."

"Patience Doctor," he said with a wisp of a smile. "It is imperative for reasons you don't know yet, but will shortly, that these events be explained in a specific order."

"My apologies please continue."

"The second reason is less obvious and I wouldn't expect you to know. As I told you twenty years ago but never finished, I was a creation in a lab—I have no 'real parents.' I am a synthesis of DNA collected by the Grays from multiple hosts with over a decade of research and development. Initially, there were six of us and our purpose was two-fold. The first, we were test subjects, prototypes for the next *phase* in human development; we possessed genetic enhancements, the eyes, the ability to use more of our brain capacity and of course, as we have already discussed, *the second sight*, all of which were to aid us in our second purpose."

"Which was?" I asked.

"The second purpose of our creation was, as you will see now, all too familiar. As we had no parents we had no identities, we could neither be traced nor found except by what you have come to know as the notorious 'chip' in our heads.

We were to act as the intermediaries between senior officials of the United States Government and the Grays themselves. It was their intention to form an 'elite' squad of sorts; to serve as the basis for protecting humanity and preserving its culture against the truth of the Grays among us, which for reasons you now understand would destroy it. In essence, Dr. Stattler, our purpose was planned from the first day of our very inception in a vial on the lunar surface. We were to be the first," he paused, while tapping his cigarette methodically on the rim of the ashtray in the center of the table before continuing, "of the 'Men in Black.'"

CHAPTER EIGHT

Nasca

Frank was true to his word. During that morning's staff meeting he added to my case load four new arrivals, all violent convicted felons with rap sheets indicating violent and anti-social behavior all the way back to adolescence. All of them were in their late twenties or early thirties, all of them Class 3 patients, all of them considered extremely violent and all of them male. Dr. Stimple's favorites. I decided as they would be receiving their immunizations in the infirmary in the morning and then later getting assigned their cells and uniform numbers with Sampson and his crew until early afternoon, that I should take advantage of the time I had and spend it with Dr. Gottlieb. There were many questions that remained unanswered, and though I knew in time he would answer them, I began to wonder for not the first time whether or not I wanted to hear them.

Yesterday evening after dinner I decided to make use of the new public library constructed in downtown St. Paul to do some research and see if, in fact, it revealed any information concerning the lines of Nasca, and this woman he mentioned who seemed to be spearheading the project, Maria Reiche. Much to my dismay and not to my surprise, I did in fact find a reference to the book he mentioned that she wrote, *Secret of the Pampa*. Though I was not able to find the book itself, it was mentioned in a National Geographic periodical that was written about her and her struggle to secure the lines of Nasca as a world cultural heritage site by the United Nations. In any case I was becoming increasingly distressed, as the past two times I had looked to punch a hole in Gottlieb's story it for all intents and purposes checked out.

When I arrived at his cell he was reading, as usual. I immediately peered in and scanned the title of the book so that I might brace myself for what appeared to be carefully orchestrated revolutions into his psyche and his past. This time, it was Shakespeare's *King Lear*.

He did not look up from his reading as I unfolded the chair leaning against the wall, and sat down, nor did I expect him to. We seemed to have developed a routine, he and I, and as I felt he was more comfortable with this I didn't see any reason to attempt to change it. I knew, and it went without saying, that he was extremely intelligent and would reveal the secrets he carried in time. I just had to be patient, of the patient, and permit him to believe it was he who was in fact in control, that it was he who was leading me in this discussion, that it was he who was pulling the strings, and that in the end when all this was over and said and done allow him to think I would be helpless to do anything else other than believe him. That was my plan at least, but there was one contingency which I found to be slightly unnerving and knew I was unprepared for—what if it in fact, this premise failed, and I did?

I sat there for a few moments waiting for him to acknowledge my presence but he still seemed to ignore me, not purposefully or out of malice, I thought but more so because he was simply entranced with what it was he was reading. I cleared my throat to garner his attention, and he looked up suddenly as though I had jolted him from a deep sleep.

"Sorry, Doctor, I was engrossed in one of Lear's speeches."

"It's all right," I said, smiling to console him as he seemed a little distraught or embarrassed at the thought of making me feel ignored.

"Ready for today's lesson?" he asked with an over-exaggerated seriousness with which I could not help but surrender a subtle snicker to.

"Of course," I said placidly. "But I'm afraid you have me at a slight disadvantage."

"And what's that?" he asked, looking at me clearly intrigued by my quite calm and docile revelation.

"Where as the rest of the works you have thus far chosen were required reading as undergraduate, I regret, and am embarrassed to say, I have never read or ever seen a production of *King Lear*."

"Pish-posh, Doctor," he said, waving his hand in the air as though dismissing the foolish idea of a naïve child. "I'll walk you through it. It has all the great Shakespearean themes and motifs … madness, justice, betrayal, murder, and most importantly, authority vs. *chaossssss*," he said, once again hissing the s's of this last word. "Actually, you have no reason to be embarrassed Doctor," he went on. "Bradley began his famous lectures on *King*

Lear by asking why this work, repeatedly described as Shakespeare's greatest, was 'the least popular of the famous four', why for a century and a half it was never played in its original form, and why so many readers have shared a kind of distaste for a work whose greatness seems undeniable. In his answer, he concurs with what he takes to be the opinion of the common reader, pronouncing *Lear* 'Shakespeare's greatest achievement, but *not* his best play.' As for myself, I would emphasize reading it more than seeing it, as I have attended many stagings and invariably regretted being there. Directors and actors are continually defeated by this play, and it is my belief that we ought to keep reading *Lear*, and avoid its staged travesties.

"In any case, I absolve you Doctor, and shall therefore proceed both cautiously and clearly in what I have to tell you. Without wasting too much of your time with a synopsis concerning the plot and the characters, I will merely say that before he goes mad, Lear's consciousness is beyond being readily understood. His lack of self-knowledge, blended with his awesome authority makes him unknowable by us, the reader. For *Lear*, indeed, starts all the trouble, and is a tragedy unto himself and others, as is illustrated when he says, 'When we are born, we cry that we are come to this great stage of fools.' This is not to say, however, that *Lear* is solely responsible for the terrible outcome of the drama and the chaos that ensues. There are wicked characters of course, and rough justice is deservingly visited upon them; his ungrateful and uncaring whoring daughters and the bastard of Gloucester, Edmund, to name a few.

"But there is no satisfaction for us in this slaughter of the wicked. They are too barbaric to be tolerated, and their deaths therefore meaningless. *Lear* in his downfall proves himself to be the universal image of the destructiveness of paternal love at its most ineffectual, implacably persuaded of its own benignity, totally devoid of self-knowledge, and careening onward until it brings down the person it loves best, and we are left to wonder what will become of the world that at the end has been created."

After this, he rose up off his cot and pulled a chair from his desk and sat opposite me. "Now then," he said. "Refresh my memory. Where did we leave off yesterday?"

I smiled at his uncanny ability to change and flip to one topic or another with absolute precision and candor. Though I knew he was eager to discuss again the events of *Ain Ghazal* and *Nasca*, I also knew from experience with him now that we would again visit the depths of melancholy and despair of *King Lear*.

"You were telling me about the statues."

"Ah, yes, yes," he said. "Truly a unique and enormous find to say the least, though I can't help but wonder if they shall ever be completely unearthed."

"What do you mean; they weren't destroyed as those at Jericho were?" I asked.

"Well, no. Possibly. I don't know. I don't what became of them. The last I heard the whole block of earth containing the rest of the sculptures was removed from Jordan and sent to the Smithsonian's Analytical Conservation Laboratory, against my better judgment and wishes I should add, but I didn't really see much choice. They were too old, too fragile, and though I loathed trusting a sponsored institution of the United States government, in the end I capitulated to Dr. Hammas and the Jordanian government's wishes. After all, though I was head of the expedition they weren't my statues, they weren't found in my country, and the choice was really not up to me; it was what the best chance was of preserving the integrity of the find. The fact of the matter was the preservation technology that was available in Jordan did not, nor could not, hold a candle to the well-financed laboratory of the Smithsonian Institution.

"For years I made inquiries to the senior conservator, but heard nothing except that they had not yet settled on a strategy to safely unearth them from the blocks of earth in which they had been shipped. They're probably still there, trapped in dirt and dust and time, and I have to admit I have grown doubtful that the world will ever see them, and if it does, if they will be placed in the context which I had found them, for there were other mysteries too."

"Such as?"

"The inhabitants of Ain Ghazal who created these statues were from a Neolithic society over nine thousand years old. At that time, the plaster that the statues themselves were made of could not have easily been manufactured or engineered, which requires the heating of powdered limestone to nearly *nine hundred* degrees, a process not possible without the evolution of ceramics and proper kilns."

"How is that possible?" I asked.

"I don't know," he responded with a hidden smile. "You tell me. We're not likely to find any undiscovered texts that would prove useful in resolving such conjectures. For these statues were formed a good *three thousand* years before the advent of writing, Doctor."

"So they're still there, at the Smithsonian?"

"In so far as I know. However, it was agreed by Dr. Hammas and insisted upon by myself that once restoration was completed they would be returned to Jordan's department of antiquities. In any case, from the statues that were found free of the blocks of earth I examined, I was convinced that what was discovered was genuine. Though I did not voice this to the others, Dr. Hammas or Dr. Grissom, I knew what I saw was a Pre-Pottery Neolithic reproduction of a being from another world who had visited this one. I stayed on an extra few weeks as Director of the excavation to analyze and photograph the statues in great detail, and once I was satisfied and able to wash my hands of the whole endeavor I contacted Maria, and headed off to the Peruvian desert of Nasca, where I knew something larger and of even greater import was waiting for me."

"Tell me about the lines. How they were constructed, I mean. Although I've done a little research it proved inconclusive in so far as how the lines themselves were drawn."

"Checking up on me again, Doctor?" he asked with a somewhat mocking tone.

"Maybe," I said flatly.

"You can't hide the truth from me, you see, I know it all too well. But, to answer your question the lines were made by revealing the sand of the desert itself. Approximately five hundred thousand years ago, a great deluge or flood washed down from the Andes mountains loose rock, iron ore, and other deposits into the desert valley. As was demonstrated by some local schoolchildren during my stay, the lines were drawn by marking out a specific distance between two sighting poles tied together by pieces of rope or hemp. By removing all the deep brown rocks that were brought down from the mountains along the line, you expose the bright, white sand of the desert floor. Thus, the lines were created."

"Why were they created?"

"There are many theories and conjectures concerning who constructed the lines and what their purpose was. Maria Reiche felt, and in so far as I know still feels, that the lines, like Stonehenge, were part of some great archaeological calendar, aligned with the solstices and with specific lines related to specific months or seasons."

"You don't agree?"

"Of course not, though I didn't tell her nor would I presume to dictate to the 'Madam of the Lines' what I suspected was true. At the time I was

visiting her during the late spring and early summer of 1963, she was resid-
ing in a little makeshift cottage owned by a Ms. Evelyn Tugwood, I believe,
who was the owner of the San Pablo Hacienda, located near many of the
more complex drawings. Maria approached the lines from more of a math-
ematical perspective. A mathematician herself, she was thoroughly convinced
of the calendar theory, and our conversations over dinner would inevitably
turn to something she found or a clue she unearthed in some theorem or
another which she hoped to prove or disprove. She was fiercely independent, and I felt that though my being there was comforting for a time, she
truly longed to be alone with her lines. She would spend the whole day,
sometimes with broom and dustpan, cleaning up the smaller bits of rubble
and rock that the wind, though it blew seldom, caused to cover pieces and
fragments of the lines. She would also trace the shapes on a sketchpad and
draw, frantically at times, the figures that covered the desert floor.

"She assumed her destiny as champion and researcher of the Nasca figures, which no university was studying. Reiche accepted solitude and the
incomprehension of the locals as part of her life. Before she built a small
museum, which she maintained with contributions from visitors and institutions overseas, the local peasants, feeling sorry for the strange, solitary
German, left fruit at the door of her tent. I felt then and still feel bad for the
poor creature, and during my stay made sure to secure better provisions
than I'm sure she was used to. She was fiercely proud, and though I knew
she appreciated these small comforts, she never once thanked me for them,
and I did not expect her to. Germans are by nature a proud people, more
than I have encountered in other cultures, at least in a manner that suggests
independent stoicism.

"As her book gradually began to draw attention to the Nasca figures,
theories much like my own began to crop up, though theories such as Erik
van Daniken's did not have the benefit of my experience. Some said the
drawings must have been made by or for extra-terrestrials, because due to
their dimensions and location they can only be clearly seen from far up in
the sky. Such theories infuriated Maria, because they reflected a preconcep-
tion as to the scientific capacity of the ancient inhabitants of Peru, which
she held in high esteem after unraveling what she thought were mathemati-
cal relations between the figures and the constellations.

"Needless to say, I did not dare voice my concerns to her, and while she
was off during the day cleaning or investigating or calculating some meaning of the lines, I would wander by myself in some the small foot hills so that

I could see, sketch, and view them from a more aerial perspective. It was on one such afternoon that I was joined by her friend and archaeologist, Julio Tello, from the University of San Marcos. Maria had previously worked for him as a translator, and impressed by her tenacity and interest, he included her in an archaeological dig in Paracas on the Peruvian coast, geographically similar and relatively near the valley of Nasca. I think she felt bad for leaving me on my own during the day and she wanted me to have some company, and I was glad for it. Though my investigations and suspicions were thus far proving to be well founded, I loathed myself for not being able to discuss them with her, as I knew it would do nothing but incur her wrath and would also more than likely end what I otherwise felt was the beginning of a true friendship.

"In any case, it was on this afternoon that Julio and I were walking among the foothills that he made a suggestion to me which led to a discovery of astounding significance. We were following one of the longer trapezoidal formations that stretched from the valley floor to the base of the foothills. You must understand that although the primary focus of Nasca, and I believe rightly so, are the figures represented on the desert plateau, the hummingbird, the dog, the orca, and the spider, it is really the colossal amount of straight lines and trapezoid formations that are mind boggling. And what is truly even more staggering is that the lines of Nasca represent one-one hundredth of one percent of all the geoglyphs on the coast of Peru. These people were busy. But busy for what? And busy for whom? And why?"

"How do you know that Reiche was wrong, and why was she so defensive against an extra-terrestrial explanation? What made you so sure you were right and it was, as you say, these *Grays* that were the source of the artists devotion?"

"Maria Reiche led a determined effort to discredit theories of extraterrestrial visitors. The strategy of this attack was to argue that the Nasca Indians constructed the Lines relatively recently—some time between 300 BC and AD 800. In support of this possibility, many scientists have put forward ingenious ideas on how the geoglyphs could theoretically have been designed from the ground. To be honest I was really astonished at how rational, educated men could come up with some of the most irrational, ridiculous inventions, and the enormity, or should I say *ignormity* of the human condition.

"For example, a Dr. Alan Alford advanced the idea that Negroid Slaves of the Tihuanaco Culture constructed the lines, and that after a revolution

the Negroid population destroyed some of the figures. This was his explanation for some of the overdrawn zigzag-formations. Another archaeologist by
the name of Frederico Kauffmann-Doig claimed that the Nasca Lines were
magic lines from the cat cult in Chavin de Huantar. Perhaps one of the most
hysterical was the *loom* theory advanced by Professor Henri Stierlin, which
describes the Nasca-Indians using the line-system as a loom. In the Paracas-
culture cloth was made of textiles which were made of only one string, but
the Indians didn't have wheels and looms, so they organized hundreds of
men who held the string. Their position was defined by the lines.

"I have to admit the more and more I heard these ridiculous treatises
the more and more I had to admit at least to some degree that I agreed with
Maria in her stiff resolution to aliens. The only thing holding me back from
the veracity with which Maria attacked any notion of extra-terrestrial influence, however, was what I had previously found at Swartkrans, the Olduvai
Gorge, and Ain Ghazal, as well as a clever little euphemism one of my undergraduate professors once told me."

"Which was?"

"'Sometimes you just have to bow to the absurd.' In any case, the most
important evidence is that which attempts to link the Lines definitively to
the Nascan culture—neither of the two key pieces of evidence survives close
scrutiny."

"How so?"

"The first piece of evidence is a series of radiocarbon dates that Dr. Tello
and I conducted, based on ceramic and wood remains which were left at the
Lines by the Nascan people. Many, including Maria, claimed this proved
the Nascans constructed the Lines. Though Julio and I did not discuss this
with her, we felt this was quite to the contrary, as the dating of these materials tells us only that the Nascans lived in the area of the Nasca Lines. Since
the Lines themselves cannot be radiocarbon dated, the possibility remains
that they already existed when the Nascan culture emerged.

"The second piece of evidence is the alleged resemblance of the Nasca
geoglyphs to certain features found on Nascan pottery. This is an important
issue because it potentially offers proof that the Nascans either designed the
images or at least viewed them from the air. In any case there was, despite
our radio-carbon efforts, a great deal of mystery which still surrounded the
lines, and it was not these but our later discoveries at Nasca and the grave
sites of Cahuachi that proved most beneficial in advancing my theories concerning *Gray* involvement."

"The skulls?" I asked with trepidation.

"*Yessssss*," he hissed. "The skullsss."

"What was so unusual about them and why?"

"As I was saying, one afternoon while we were studying one of the trapezoidal formations on the far east of the pampas Dr. Tello suggested I come with him the next day to the dig site he and his team from the University of San Marcos were excavating in Cahuachi. Apparently they had found some rather unique finds and he felt they might have some pertinence in connection with the Nasca lines."

"Why did he not speak to Maria Reiche about this?"

"Because, like me, he felt that the lines were something more than a possible stellar calendar. There were too many of them, the drawings too vast, and we still hadn't answered the question as to how could they be drawn unless they could be seen from the air. It was an interesting predicament, and though he had suggested it was possible the ancient peoples who built these lines might have constructed some sort of balloon, there was no evidence either on the plateau or in his excavations at Cahuachi thus far that indicated any probability of this. In any case, I accepted his invitation and accompanied him the following afternoon."

"What was Cahuachi?"

"Molded from the desert itself, the pyramids and plazas of the lost Nasca city were the site of ceremony and ritual. It was a city of priests who were guardians of Nasca culture and religion. On the other side of the pampa lay the big, urban settlement of Ventilla. Between Ventilla and Cahuachi the Nasca people created their lines etched in the dry, stony desert."

"What happened there? And why was it deserted?"

"From what we could make out, sometime between 300 and 350 A.D. there were two natural disasters. A great, very powerful flood—we found the evidence in all the excavations—and an earthquake, an earthquake which split the temples in two. We also found dead bodies under the fallen walls, perfectly preserved by the arid desert air. It appears that's when the Nasca religion seemed to lose its power, at least some of the 'gods' as it were, or the ceremonial center itself lost power and the place was abandoned. But before they left, since everything was ceremonial, ritual, and everything had religious significance for the Nasca, they completely sealed all the monuments.

"When we examined the higher levels of the excavation pit we could see a crust of clay has been deliberately applied on top of a man-made layer.

They left behind a sacred place, called a 'Huaca.' Absolutely everything where we were standing had been *deliberately* covered by the Nasca themselves. By the time the Inca empire rose to dominate the Andes during what was the western world's Middle Ages, the Nasca and their *culture* had been long since forgotten, swept clean by the wrath of time. It was not until the people of the 20th-century sent planes into the sky above the pampa that the Nasca and the spectacular wonders they created in the desert were rediscovered."

"But what does this have to do with the strange skulls mentioned?"

"Very good, I was just getting to that, Doctor. The skulls were of a rather unusual and strange shape I had only seen once before in Nubia, and of course, by representation in the *statues of Ain Ghazal* and the aboriginal cave drawings."

As he said this I finally began to realize where he was going with this discussion, and I was filled with an overwhelming chill.

"The skulls were elongated, disproportionate—stretched as it were, deliberately, and in many cases it appeared they were from people sacrificed once they reached a certain stage of adulthood."

"How do you know it was done deliberately and not the result of some errant birth defect or accident or nutrition deficiency?"

"There were too many of them, over ninety percent of the loose skulls we found were like this, and to answer your question, we found burial evidence that the Nasca wrapped the heads of their new-born with bands made of leather or wood. As a result, the still malleable skull grew upwards into extraordinary, elongated, disproportionate shapes. There was another, puzzling discovery. Many of the skulls had circular holes cut into the foreheads. Many had ropes tied between them."

"But why would they do this?"

"We gathered information on about 350 individual skulls and mummies. As with every population, we found examples of diseases: anemia, malnutrition; illnesses which affect children and infectious diseases, but based on the statistics we had gathered about this people, statistics based on the age at the time of death, we can say that their life expectancy was around 37 or 38 years. That's comparable to Europeans at the turn of the nineteenth century when life expectancy was only 42 years. We should remember there were 2,000 years separating them. It is also important to remember that 2,000 years ago the dry and barren desert plateau would seem like an oasis. There was a river valley with fields, plenty of food to eat, no evidence of warfare. The people were fairly short with long black hair, probably muscular from working very hard, and we have evidence from the skeletal materials, particularly the teeth, that they were very healthy people. And from those same skeletons we see no evidence of trauma or warfare, except of course, in those skulls that were sacrificed."

"Why were they sacrificed?" I asked, but before it was out of my mouth I knew the answer. I knew where he was going. I knew what the answer was.

"Have you ever heard the saying 'Imitation is the highest form of flattery'? We must assume that the Nasca believed an elongated disproportionate human head was beautiful, and the act of sacrificing these individuals had meaning, lest why go through the trouble? Think of the iron will and purpose this takes, Doctor, to produce a child and deliberately torture and manipulate its body to a form your culture, for whatever reason, holds in high regard. To raise it, know it, identify with it, come to love it, rear it to adulthood, and then to wantonly murder it, butcher it, hang it on a rope, and display it to the 'gods.' Why go through all the trouble Doctor? Based on the age of the skulls, they were at least eighteen to twenty years old when they were sacrificed. These people were specifically chosen and bred and manipulated since birth to impress upon and be fodder for the gods. We can only assume being chosen for this duty was interpreted as a great honor in their culture. Why? Because we found no *normal* skulls that had been treated in the same manner—as nothing less than trophies."

Dr. Gottlieb then casually leaned back in his chair and began to pick his teeth with his finger nail, his foot resting on one of the bars between us.

"Incidentally, I'm sure I needn't tell you this but since we're on the subject, I had with me the drawings and sketches I made, both from the photographs of the caves of Australia, France, Spain and the statues in Jordan. I then made sketches and photographed many of the skulls we found. What I discovered, not surprisingly, was that the disproportion in all three cases matched in proportion to themselves down to a rate of error of plus or minus one hundred cubic centimeters.

"There could be no doubt now. Here you had, on three completely separate and distinct continents spanning back over one hundred thousand years, evidence of a people *not human*. And perhaps it even went further, if, in fact, it were true that the strange gray metallic devices Dr. Rasp and I had separately unearthed in early hominids and australopithecines were from these same beings. How far did it go, could it go? Perhaps, I feared, back to the beginning. Back to our creation! Back to the dawn of man itself!"

"But you didn't stop there, did you?" I asked.

"No," he said. "I believed there was more to find at Nasca, and I believed the key was in the lines. Although the skulls provided insights I had not dared dream or imagine were possible, I knew the secret was in the lines somewhere. Now that I had established, and believed concretely, that these beings were witnessing and meddling in the affairs and culture of humanity the world over for thousands of years, I felt it necessary to tie them to Nasca. The skulls were a convincing argument, but they weren't enough, as I had heard of, though never seen first hand, similar reports of discoveries in Nubia. I needed to tie the lines with the skulls together; I needed to find something out there in the desert sand which would help me do this.

"Once I did, I knew that I would have finally gathered enough evidence to make a petition for a hearing at Yale's Department of Archaeology. I had slides of literally nearly a hundred early Renaissance paintings depicting UFO's in their contents, one in particular, *The Madonna and St. Giovanni,* actually suggests upon close inspection that the infant Jesus at her side is the result of extra-terrestrial influence. Some fifteenth century tapestries also depict UFO's in hovering relationships with the Madonna, and with frescoes of a monastery in Kosovo, cave paintings made by the first *homo sapiens,* the aboriginal cave paintings of Australia, the strange metallic implants found in the bones of fossils, and of course the *Ain Ghazal* statues as well as everything I had thus far discovered at Nasca, I knew I was close.

"Each and every one of these artifacts and evidence was compelling, but by themselves were scarce more than perhaps a hypnotic suggestion by the author. It is only when putting them all together that we could see the picture the pieces of the puzzle constructed. I felt confident that my search was almost over. All I needed was something to tie the skulls of Nasca together with the drawings on the desert floor to concretely establish the presence of the *Grays,* and together with the help of Dr. Julio Tello, I eventually found it."

"What did you find?"

"While Maria worked busily on the ground measuring, drawing, and recording the lines of Nasca, Dr. Tello and I decided the pictures were best and meant to be seen from the air—this after all, was the premise on which I was proceeding, as it stood to reason that the drawings were made for the beings *from* the air. To this end I was able to convince Julio to petition the university of San Marcos for the use of one of their two Cessna's which the archaeology department occasionally had use of to ferry students and supplies to various excavation sites throughout the region.

"After several months of waiting and waiting for the paper shuffle to end, we were finally granted our request for the use of their 1949 Model 120 twin engine Cessna. Battered and scraped and scarred by years of abuse in the harsh desert climate, it was not the prettiest or most comfortable plane to behold, or navigate, but I didn't care. My only concern was to see the lines of Nasca from the perspective and forum in which it seems they were meant to be observed."

"I can't even imagine," I said in wonder.

"No, you can't. Please don't take that the wrong way Doctor, I meant it as a literal not figurative suggestion. As we only had use of the aircraft for three days, Dr. Tello and I agreed it would be prudent to cover and photograph as much of the area as possible within our time frame, and to this endeavor we framed a schedule of sorts which for the most part we stuck to. The lines were at first almost too numerous to count and record, however, they seemed to be broken up into three distinct groups: wavy lines and spirals, trapezoids, and then animals. Although I had no proof to substantiate this theory, I reasoned that the age of the lines ascended or rather descended in this order—the more simple lines constructed first and the more complex animal drawings later. Some of the lines stretched as long as six miles, perfectly straight and without an aberration.

"We also recorded some 300 geoglyphs, most of them trapezoids and triangles. The geometric figures spanned across the entire 85 square mile Pampa. Among the figures we recorded, and to which Nasca is now most famous, there were many birds. We recorded fifteen different kinds, although I have heard from recent reports and what few archaeological texts I can get my hands on pertaining to the subject that now eighteen different types have been found. We also were able to photograph from the air a spider, a monkey, a fish, a dog, and various strange assorted plants. It was on the last day of our use of the Cessna that I found at last the concrete connection between the skulls and lines."

"What did you find?" I asked with trepidation.

Dr. Gottlieb smiled at me whimsically; clearly I was enthralling him with my rapt attention to his story.

"What I found, Doctor, changed my life. There on the desert floor hiding just above and to the right of the tail of the dog was a treasure worth its weight in gold, what I called and christened *The Gray-Man*. It was much more difficult to make out than many of the others. Because of its location at the South east end of the pampas, it was exposed to more wind and therefore more of the dark stones which had initially been removed to create it slowly crept back over time. I remember shouting excitedly at Julio, 'Over it again, over it again!', but he clearly did not see it, and it was not until I pointed out some of the edges that he was able to grasp the shape. Care to ask what it looked like, Doctor?"

"I have the feeling you're going to tell me whether I ask or not."

Dr. Gottlieb smiled and continued.

"It was easy to see why we missed it before. Whereas I was looking for something that was on the scale of the other drawings and lines as, which I said, were sometimes miles long, this in comparison was at most only thirty to thirty-two meters in length. The figure had his hand extended as though waving to somebody, and not coincidentally had a very large, disproportionate head, accompanied by two large, disproportionate eyes. It was the figure of a being that I knew the Nasca had now undoubtedly seen. It was clear to me then that it was this being and its influence the Nasca had integrated into their culture and religion. It was this *creature* they came to know that was not of this earth. It was here, over two-thousand years ago, inscribed on the Peruvian desert floor for all to see—all to see who *could* that is, and since humanity *could not* until the last fifty years, we are left with only one solution to the paradox."

"Which is?"

"That perhaps, humanity is nothing more than an experiment to these beings. That these creatures *have,* in fact, been taking us for millennia. That is why the ancient peoples of Nasca drew their picture in the Peruvian sands, that is also why they mutilated, tortured and sacrificed themselves. They *knew* these creatures were periodically abducting them, and *incorporated* these abductions into their culture and religion, by deliberately manipulating their children's bodies, and then sacrificing them to the 'gods of the sky', probably on the presumption that if they honored and sacrificed some, then others might not be taken. That is why the Australian aborigines traced their likenesses in the 'death cave.' That is why the ancient people of Jordan cast their semblance into plaster statues, and that is why I knew I had to tell the world."

"What did you do?"

"I wasted no time. The next afternoon I took a jeep to the town of Nasca and had a telegraph sent to Yale that I would be returning shortly, and I wished to convene all the senior archaeological staff for a discussion that would change the world as we knew it."

"Did you ever tell Maria what you found or suspected during your time there?"

"Of course not. As I said, it would have destroyed our friendship, and though the truth was burning inside me, bursting to get out, I knew that I could not let it. I had to keep the discovery of *The Gray-Man*, and everything else I had discovered at Nasca, a secret. I therefore made preparations with due haste, and on November 28, 1963, six days after President John F. Kennedy was assassinated, I boarded a plane in Lima, and headed for home. Like the rest of the nation I was distraught and full of grief. Although there were things about America that disgusted and still repulse me, at the time I identified with her culture and considered myself to be among a privileged few in the world. And the news of Kennedy's death brought to my return to the United States what I strongly felt was a bad and terrible omen.

"As I was being driven home in a cab on the evening of the twenty-ninth, the city lights passing and streaking before my eyes, I remember contemplating oblivion. This president had pushed the world to the brink of nuclear war, and in a show of unbridled and unexpected diplomacy somehow avoided it. I wondered then what would happen when existence of *the Grays* was revealed. Would the earth destroy itself with this news? What might my place in history be? Would I serve to be the destroyer, liberator, or court fool? I did not know, and as I slowly and wearily trod up the steps to my home, my thoughts, once bursting with the excitement of a discovery beyond comprehension, were filled with horror, sickness, and grief, and I did not know whether I was up to the challenge I had once set for myself."

"So you didn't tell them?" I said half-asking, half-knowing the answer. "You never told anyone?"

"No," he said. "I didn't. It's kind of funny actually. Just last year I received a letter from Maria telling me about the current progress at Nasca and some of the new discoveries that were being made. It seems some man by the name of Eduardo Herran 'discovered' what he called *The Astronaut* in the spring of 1982. For nearly twenty years what was truly *my* discovery on the plains of Nasca was silenced from the world, and here was this cretin taking the credit for it. Bah!"

"I suppose it doesn't really matter anyway. For you see, Doctor, I don't remember. I don't remember anything after that night I returned home until I woke up in a room at St. Elizabeth's in Baltimore. I vaguely remember striking a man in my house with my rock hammer, but I don't remember killing him. I guess I must have though, I'm here aren't I? They say I killed two of them, but I can't remember any of it. You see, Doctor, like *Lear*, my mind and I have descended into chaos, and I fear that there is no returning from the void to which I am consigned.

"You tell me, Doctor, what you think will happen when this 'experiment' of the Grays becomes self-aware? What will happen, Doctor, when humanity discovers where it truly came from? What will happen in the throes that ensue? *Chaaaoooossss,* Doctor. *Chaaaoooosssss.* And what do we do with chaos, Doctor? Hmmm? We keep it locked away so the world can't see, bound and gagged by INFAMY!" he said, shouting this last word in a feral rage until it clamored down the cell block and silenced all other voices.

He then stood up out of the chair in front of me and stared blankly at me, and though I never, as I said, read the play, I knew it was the voice of *Lear* that would next be issued from his lips.

"Howl! Howl! Howl! Howl!" he screamed at the top of his lungs at me as he stood there, his eyes on fire and full of lamenting fury. "Had I your tongues and eyes I'd use them that heaven's vault should crack!"

CHAPTER NINE

Mr. Black Continues

"Interesting …" I said. "And perfectly logical, to be without an identity that could be traced now matter how hard an investigator might look is a remarkable idea. Without emotional ties or a trail of relatives or loved ones it makes you a more formidable opponent, one that can not be easily co-erced."

"Precisely, Doctor," he leaned back smugly as he said this.

"So there were originally six of you?"

"Yes. We were all from the same base pairs of DNA, not clones of each other but more like brothers and sisters, or fraternal twins would probably be the best analogy. We were 'born', or however you wish to describe the process, nearly one year after the first peace accord with Roosevelt."

"This may sound strange," I said, "but did you grow up knowing the purpose for which you had been created?"

"The first fourteen years of our lives the six of us were raised by the Grays at the lunar station. It was they who guided our education in genetics, cosmic theory, space and time travel."

"I bet the field trips must have been something out of this world," I said. "No pun intended."

He smiled at this and then said, "Did you know that for the first fifteen years of my life I never saw a *natural* shade of green, at least, not in person? It's an awful thing for a human being, such as I am, to be deprived of green. No trees, no grass to run on, no bright leaves in the spring. Confined to a static, sanitary environment …, and even then the first real shade of green I saw was desert brush. It was hardly green at all, more like a wispy, dried out, beige-ish-mauve with a slight tint to it."

I looked at him, trying to gauge what exactly he was trying to tell me and responded, "It must have been hard for you."

"In retrospect, it was terrible really ... which reminds me, Doctor, while we're here there's something I was hoping to get your professional opinion on as someone with a degree in human behavior ... is it common for human beings to *hate* their adolescence?" he asked with an imploring fascination.

I smiled and said reassuringly, "Believe it or not Mr. Black, quite." A silence passed between us then and I looked at him and wondered how he had managed to survive being raised by creatures who had created him in a glass tube; beings who probably showed no emotions and were devoid of compassion and all traces of anything human. It must have been extremely difficult to *never* have been nurtured, loved, or cared for, and yet it was *normal* for him. He did not know anything else, at least personally.

He did not know what truly having a mother and father was. He never had father-son fishing trips; he never had father-son anything. He never knew otherwise, at least not until he began to interact humans other than his siblings, and in many cases these were human beings, fathers, mothers, and children, who he was probably sent to kill. How could one retain their sanity?

Maybe it was like a sort of *vengeance* for him. Maybe he was killing and was able to go on killing because it became personal. Those souls he was extinguishing represented what he did not, and would never, have. He was truly remarkable indeed. We might have even been friends in another life, had the universe chosen to play out our roles in our finite existence differently. What I thought was completely bizarre and totally unexpected was that I was actually *enjoying* his company! Our relationship to one another was changing the more truths he revealed, with every word he spoke.

I looked at him then in that moment and thought, despite all he had done to me, the loss of my career, my wife, my son, I did pity him. While I'll admit the first time I met him, and every day of my life thereafter, I believed he would be the last human being in existence I could feel empathy for, there was no mistaking it; for the first time in over twenty years I felt like I could help someone, and maybe somehow, if I had the courage, to find some way to redeem him.

"So you were saying?" I said, breaking the silence.

"Ah yes, my apologies Dr. Stattler, I was lost in thought for a moment. Something about the color green always distracts me."

"Maybe it's envy," I said, half-joking half-serious.

"Maybe it is," he said, as though in agreement.

I looked around the bar, which was emptying out now. It was three o'clock and the lunch crowd for the most part had dispersed and we were alone again except for a few stragglers at the bar, sitting alone, no doubt drowning themselves in martinis in the early afternoon. I would be right up there with them, having finished nearly half a bottle of Johnnie Black by now if Mr. Black hadn't happened along.

"You said that the Groom Lake base served multiple functions, in addition to the testing of aircraft and military vehicles," I said, changing the subject.

"Yes. It also served as the base of operations for our training and the training of all new recruits to our association. The training center is located a quarter of a mile beneath the complex and only several members of the military, instructors, trainees, and the Grays themselves know how it can be reached, once inside. During our six year tenure we were to learn the skills of martial arts, marksmanship, cryptology, cryptanalysis, electronic intelligence, surveillance, operations security, and signals intelligence to name a few, in addition to, of course, skills which would make us more adept at the art of assassination," he grinned morosely as he said this last word. "As we were the first it was also our duty to develop a regimen for future recruits ..."

I interrupted him, "Excuse me but, recruits? I'm just a little confused, how do you sign up for this job."

"You don't Dr. Stattler. You are either created for the job as I was, or you are taken."

"Taken?"

"Before you're old enough to know any better ... taken to the lunar surface, taken and raised by *them*, such as I."

When he said this I felt a chill stir through my body as though I had come in contact with a ghost; it ran up my spine and the room itself seemed to me to be twenty degrees colder in that instant, though I knew that wasn't possible, yet I didn't know why.

"Go on ..." I said, mustering the courage to hear what I knew would be unsettling yet compelled by my intrigue.

"As I was saying, as we were the first of what was to be many it was necessary to develop a regimen of sorts to outline any potential difficulties we experienced so that the next group in turn would not experience these barriers. After our sixth year at what has become an institution in the areas of surveillance and research we were ready to take on minor clandestine missions which included, among other things, spying, gathering intelligence, and planting monitoring devices in homes and offices of abductees who were suspected to have taken photographs of the Grays spacecraft, or who were on the Bureau's list for reading 'forbidden books' or who might otherwise be a threat. As we grew more experienced these expanded into broader, greater, roles that would shape human history. Kennedy was one of our first major assignments and it would set the standard for which the 'Men in Black' were to operate."

I stared at him in his pressed black suit, starched white shirt and black silk tie as he poured himself more coffee from the miniature pot next to his cup. He took two sugars from the caddie, emptied them completely, and meticulously folded them and put them neatly next to the others he had folded on the plate containing the creamer. He took his spoon and stirred the coffee five times, tapped the spoon on the edge of the cup, and rested it under the handle of his cup on the saucer.

I could tell by looking at him that his life was rooted in order; there was a routine that must be followed, every day, rhythmically, like the pounding and resounding beat of a drum in a funeral procession. I wondered what would happen when that order was gone, his purpose for being. What fury would be unleashed? It was as though his very presence was speaking to me, and seemed to offer a glimpse of the future; of days gone by that have been forever silenced. And forever after when I would picture in my mind what I thought Fate would look like, it always had his face. And as I studied him I began to wonder what set him off, why we were here, what else he wasn't telling me, and what was yet to come.

He cleared his throat. "It's funny actually … the 'Men in Black.' We never called ourselves by that name; it's only what urban legend called us. I don't know exactly when it infiltrated our official language."

"What do you call yourselves then?" I asked.

"We only have numbers. To be given a name would be to become human, as unfortunately I am in danger of becoming myself."

"What do you mean?" I asked.

"As I indicated to you earlier, next week is my seventieth birthday, Dr. Stattler. For my seventieth birthday celebration, it has been decided by powers other than me that my presence in our organization as an acting field agent is no longer necessary. I have become too old, Dr. Stattler, and as such it is the opinion of those forces of whom we speak that I have outlived my usefulness for primary missions and agendas. Though I would still be recognized and consulted on various *peacekeeping* missions my primary purpose and duties are over … I am going to be—how should I put it—retired."

"Well that's a good thing isn't it?" I said.

"Have you ever realized your true reason for existence?" he asked, the intonation of his voice reflecting hostility.

"I'm not sure I understand the question," I said with bitterness, letting him know of my disapproval of being spoken to as a child.

"All my life, Dr. Stattler, I have been involved in something greater than any of you plebeian citizens could begin to fathom. I have assassinated world leaders, mothers, children, even infants to protect you from yourselves—to save humanity from the destruction which would ensue should the truth concerning my makers be unveiled. And for this dedication to duty, honor, and sacrifice of my soul, if I have one, I am being made to live within the lie I helped create. I am to be 'put out to pasture' as it were, given a home in the area of my choosing, funds to draw off of for the rest of my existence, so that I can become one of *you* people, Dr Stattler. I am to spend the rest of my days painting my white-picket fence, working in my garden and mowing my lawn, to go grocery shopping amidst the throngs of the fat and uneducated and blind masses too dimwitted to ever grasp or even wish to know the knowledge I contain. I am to live as one of you and among you, merely waiting for time to push this body to a point of complete disrepair. For everything that I have sacrificed, the seventy years of my life, service, my very existence given to humanity, and those that created me, I am to be consigned to exile within it; alone for the rest of my days, forever silenced, entombed within my own 'Kingdom of the Damned.'"

"Is that why you're here?" I asked. "Is that why you want to expose them?"

"I will do many things, Dr. Stattler. But never will I allow myself to be used and betrayed, not even by my creators, not even if He did exist, and it was 'God' himself. I would rather strangle and throttle the necks of ten thousand cooing infants than live out the rest of my life in silence waiting for death. To create me, raise me, give me purpose, and train me to kill in essence what I am to trying to protect, and then to dispatch me, dispose of me like some used prophylactic. It is an abomination. It is an insult."

"Well what did you expect? Did you honestly believe that you would still be gallivanting around the globe performing covert operations on your walker? Beating people to death with your cane?" I asked.

"I always imagined, that is I *believed* that somehow I would be killed as an agent in the field ... defending a greater good and purpose other than my own." he said.

I thought for a moment.

"Maybe you still will," I replied. "There's still time."

"For you, maybe, Dr. Stattler. Maybe for you."

I looked at him steadily, my gaze fixed upon his glasses, behind which concealed the truth. The eyes truly are windows to the soul and I was disappointed that I could not see them now, hoping for some, if any, insight into what his plans really were.

"There's still something you haven't told me that I must know."

"I was wondering when you'd get around to asking, Doctor, and in truth though I knew for certain that it was to come up in our 'discussion' of sorts, I was secretly hoping that it wouldn't."

"Why is that, are you afraid to tell me?"

"I fear nothing."

"Then tell me what happened to wife and child; tell me what became of my Kathryn!" I said, my voice beginning to betray feelings that I would not or could not let myself feel for years. "Tell me what happened to my son!"

He looked at me, thought for a moment and then responded. "Does it really make a difference, Dr. Stattler, to know what became of their fate? Can you bend back the forces of time and change the choices you made? Change what you did or what became of them? And even if you could save them, would you do the same thing all over, if you were given a second chance?"

"I don't know," I said shaking. "I just don't know."

"Free will is an amusing concept, Dr. Stattler, and it amazes me to think that so many humans actually believe in it." He leaned forward, gripping the table with his hands as he spoke. "You made the choices you did for a *reason*, Dr. Stattler, the reason being, of course, that you *already* did. And you would do it again, you're doing it now, and you *have* done it again. Your fate and humanity's have already been decided a long, long time ago, you only need to *experience* it."

"Cut the analytical, universal-bullshit, and tell me what happened to them," I said, my frustration rising at his avoidance.

"And if I do, you'll agree to my terms, you'll agree to help me?" he asked quite bemused with himself.

"No promises and no deals," I said resolutely.

He sighed, somewhat exasperated. "Why must you always make every-thing so difficult? I could have disposed of you in any number of ways any number of times. Why must you be so damned stubborn?" he asked, quite obviously vexed at my behavior.

I thought for a moment and said, "Because it's what you appear to covet."

He leaned back from the table, relaxing his arms in a thoughtful pose and said, "Perhaps."

"Tell me what became of them," I said. "What happened to my wife and son!?"

"I was given two choices regarding Katherine, Doctor, and neither of them was very appealing."

"Which were?"

"One choice was to kill Katherine then and there in front of your eyes, and to dispose of her body so it could never be found. My preferred method is to sever the corpse into nine pieces; these usually consist of the arms, each leg cut in two, the head, and then the torso cut in half below the rib cage. I then encase them within cement molds I carry in my trunk, and scatter them within several places in the nearest, largest body of water. You see, a body is much easier to transport and much more difficult to identify when it is cut into more manageable parts that are deposited over several loca-tions."

"You know, it wasn't so much the gritty details I was after, and you're forgetting that I was there … sounds like something reminiscent of what happened to Jimmy Hoffa."

"*That*, actually, wasn't me … but our network sources told me he shared a similar fate and is somewhere beneath the East River."

"Is there any honey-pot you *don't* have your hand in?" I said with a hint of sarcasm.

"Our business, as I explained before, Dr. Stattler, is that of *informa-tion.*"

"So what *information* can you tell me about my wife?" I said, redirecting the conversation.

He leaned back into the booth, a resolute and grim expression on his face. "All right I'll tell you," he said. "Kathryn Stattler was taken to the Groom Lake facility where she was to be interrogated and questioned con-cerning her participation in the acquisition of the chip from Dr. Gottlieb."

"Go on," I said nervously, loathing hearing but needing to know.

"After an initial interview of sorts, she was later taken to the lunar station for further," he paused a moment and then continued, "*analysis* by the Grays."

"*Analysis* being experimentation and torture."

Mr. Black nodded silently.

"Not so much torture, really, but you're right about experimentation. She served as a test subject for one of the next phases of human evolution and from what I'm told her eggs proved most valuable."

"Yes, well, again it wasn't so much the gritty details I was after."

"Let me remind you that you wanted to hear the truth, Dr. Stattler. Don't lay your anger or blame on me if the truth is not something you want to hear."

"All right, go on."

"Shortly thereafter she became hysterical. I was informed in a report that she could not stop screaming and had to be continually sedated. Finally, one afternoon when she was conscious and left unattended in her holding cell, she hung herself with her shoestrings."

I put my hands on the table, put my face into them and wept silently. It was as I had feared, though it made my heart ache to actually hear that my suspicions had not been unfounded, and that my poor Katherine had spent her last hours among beings from another world. Beings that had invaded her privacy, prodded her genitals, and taken DNA and human egg cells to further continue whatever evil and immoral purpose they had planned.

They *had* to be stopped; they *must* be exposed. But how? I did not see any hope. Even if we knew of any other intelligence within the galaxy how could we contact them without the Grays detecting it, and of course just who or *what* would come to our aid, and who's to say that we would be any better off? When Mr. Black first told me of their presence and activities I imagined they had some higher purpose, totally unfathomable, that it in some way we could not even conceive was in our best interest. But now I knew for certain, now after knowing for sure what had happened to her, I began to think otherwise.

I wondered how creatures so advanced could behave with virtual impunity toward beings that clearly possessed consciousness and intelligence without some sort of ethical standard. No wonder then that our world leaders simply acquiesced to their demands, if they made any, what choice did they have? Say 'no'? What would be the point? And if they could profit by technology that could, if called upon, defeat their enemies here on earth, so much the better. Why not? After all, according to Mr. Black and *Gray* science, we were all dead anyway. I could see my future slipping away before me, already written, a smattering of notes on a page, and the only duty left before me was to merely play what is left of my song—a single note in the vast and seemingly infinite cosmic fugue.

I don't know how long I laid there with my head in my hands, weeping silently, despairingly. We were nothing more than lab rats in a giant maze to them, and in my case the cheese that was being dangled so elusively in front of me that I could smell but never seem to come close to touching was evidence of their existence.

"Handkerchief?"

I looked up. Mr. Black sat motionless with his arm extended. In his hand he held white, pressed, cotton linen. In my grief I did not even notice him retrieving it from his pocket.

"Thank you," I said taking it and wiping my nose.

"You're welcome," he replied without either interest or sympathy.

"I'm sorry. I should have," I stopped a moment then continued. "I thought, well, I did know or at least suspect that I would never see or hear from her again, and that she might very well be chopped into little bits as you eloquently described and strewn about somewhere at the bottom of a riverbed. In some ways I am relieved."

"And why is that?" he asked somewhat perplexed.

"Because she isn't *still* alive, suffering the torments of her captors, the rape of her mind, her body ..." I paused a second reflecting. "Her soul."

"I understand," he said. "And you're right. Believe me Doctor, when I say that I have seen some of the unfortunate and unprecedented side effects of DNA insertion gone badly. I can tell you this, she didn't suffer long."

"At least there is that. What did they do with her body?"

"You know I've always wondered why human beings place such a great deal of personal emphasis on the comfort of the dead."

"What do you mean?"

"Well I've never understood it really, not just in this case, but socially. You've created this whole business and economy of plush, silk-lined caskets costing a year's wages to some and then what do you do, put it in the ground to rot."

"It's silly, you're right," I agreed.

"It makes no sense," he said lighting a cigarette.

"Human beings often do things that make no sense. I guess the Grays never do," I mused. "It must have been difficult for you, to grow up in the environment you did, only to be released to your own kind to find them passionate, illogical creatures. What do the Grays do?

"About what?" he asked curiously.

"About death."

"Oh, that," he said. "They do not die often, not as often as humans anyway, though when they do their bodies are ejected or set adrift in space. The philosophy being that fragments of their DNA could help to seed others of their kind on other worlds that are either in the process of evolving or even not yet created. It was your Carl Sagan who said, 'all life in the cosmos is based on star-stuff.' It is how life began on earth several billion years ago, is it not? Fragments of carbon from an exploded star set adrift in space. The Grays simply take this universal truth to the next level."

"Sort of like the reason we humans have children," I said.

"I've never heard it described as such, but, yes, I suppose that analogy could be used in this case," he replied, quite obviously perplexed and musing over this statement.

"What did you mean when you said 'they do not die often'? How long is their life span?"

"The Grays have developed a system of cloning and replicating their organs. To this end over time when their bodies begin to break down they simply reproduce the afflicted part of their anatomy that is failing. Since it is a virtual copy of the original there is no tissue rejection. But in answer to your original inquiry, the typical Gray life span, if properly maintained, can range close to several thousand earth-years, though by that time the only original part left of their bodies would be the brain and brain-stem. Walking or even moving in earth-type gravity is extremely difficult and painful due to what you would refer to as severe advanced arthritis of their spinal cord and surrounding tissue. For this reason most of the elder Grays that remain here in the earth's solar system prefer to remain on the lunar surface in areas with only the moon's natural gravity. Most modules and hangars on the lunar surface have artificial gravity or dampeners in the floor that create an earth-type environment."

"Jesus ..." I said, thinking out loud.

"Has nothing to do with it," he replied smugly. "Though there was a time when his actions did play a significant role in the Grays' presence here on earth. In fact, there are many figures and events in human history that have transpired quite unbeknownst to the good citizens of earth due to the influence of the Grays."

I looked at him somewhat appalled, my eyes rolled up into my forehead, as if to say, 'is nothing sacred?' "You've got to be kidding?" I said blank faced.

"Where's your sense of adventure, Dr. Stattler? Here's a chance for you to use that genetically-enhanced primate brain of yours! How humanity can embrace *religion* as controlling man's destiny is not only obscenely barbaric but ludicrous!"

"Not that I'm in total disagreement, but what do you mean?" I interrupted.

"Well, take for example man's knowledge of the stars. We know there are over four-hundred billion stars in the Milky Way galaxy. Now, there are several different types of stars: white-dwarf, red-giants, and your average yellow stars like the sun. Now the number of suns like our own that are neither too hot, too cold, too young or too old, and contain the possibility of supporting life over several billion years in the galaxy, is somewhere in the range of seventy-five to a hundred billion. But let's take a conservative estimate, let's just say fifty billion. Now, of those fifty-billion, again being conservative, let's say only ten percent, or five billion, contain planets like your solar system. And of those planets, again being conservative, let's say ten percent contain life, or some five hundred million. Of those five hundred million, again being conservative, let's say that only one percent has life that has evolved in much the same manner as we have. That leaves somewhere in the range of five million resident intelligent species in the Milky Way Galaxy. Now if we multiply this number by the actual number of galaxies, which your current science holds to be somewhere in the range of a few hundred billion, but Gray science has actually determined to be closer to seven hundred billion …"

"Wait just a moment," I interrupted. "Seven hundred billion? That's impossible. Scientists have clearly established there are only several hundred billion galaxies."

"Not impossible, Dr. Stattler. And quite frankly, I'm surprised at you. You should know from your days at John's Hopkins that not everything in the universe you can see with the naked eye."

"I'm not sure I understand," I said, trying to grapple with his meaning.

"Should I spell it out for you?" he asked, as though he were not speaking to me but to himself. "No, that's too easy! But I will give you a clue. The answer is here, all around us, everywhere."

I looked at him somewhat flabbergasted.

He sighed and continued. "What is the most common element in the universe, Dr. Stattler?"

I thought about it for a moment, trying desperately to recall my basic chemistry. Undoubtedly, the scotch was still clouding my brain a bit. "Hydrogen?" I asked uncertainly, though I knew it was the right answer.

"Hydrogen," he repeated calmly and then continued. "Think of the universe as one big hydrogen atom, and as a side note it is not coincidental that it is the most common element. But to continue, the ratio in the element hydrogen, as you know, is one to one. One proton for one electron. For every action, there is an equal and opposite reaction. The universe itself maintains and obeys these laws. Thus, for every galaxy you *can* see ..."

I interrupted him. "There is one you can't."

"For every positively charged galaxy ..."

"There is a negative one," I interrupted him again. "You're talking about *dark matter.*"

"Excellent, Dr. Stattler, though it took you long enough. Yes. That is essentially what dark matter is. Your scientists have been attempting to explain it for years, when all along the answer was right in front of them. Sometimes I wonder if humans aren't still thinking with primate impulses and if Gray interference has helped at all. Which reminds me, to continue with our discussion concerning the possible number of other species in the universe. If there were *only* a hundred billion galaxies, the approximate number of inhabited worlds that contain intelligent life lies somewhere in the realm of five times ten to the seventeenth power. In any case, there's a lot of zeros at the end of that five. Now, don't you think it would be a little bit conceited to assume that God, if there is one, chose your planet of the over hundreds of trillions of inhabited worlds in the cosmos to deposit his only son? Don't you think it more likely that a neighboring species, one of those possible five million in our galactic neighborhood just might have interfered in man's history, culture, evolution, and genetics? And this was just with conservative numbers. Actual numbers may be and in fact are closer to three-hundred-million intelligent species in our galaxy alone, but you didn't hear that from me. I wouldn't want to shatter too many illusions on our first date."

He smiled smugly at this revelation and I could tell he was enjoying and reveling in tearing apart illusions, illusions that man for some reason, despite knowing and having proven in the last twenty years all of what Mr. Black had revealed, desperately clung to. Why did we? Why, despite knowing these numbers and possibilities exist, despite knowing the feasibility of religion couldn't possibly be true, did we still cling to its throes like a child's security blanket? It made no sense. No wonder then, that our world leaders were hesitant to reveal knowledge of the Grays. We were still in our infancy; and we needed the security of false beliefs and religion, which was truly nothing more than an elevated sense of idolatry to make sense of the world. Despite all we have gained through science, it has been for the most part unable to penetrate the core of society, and I realized for the first time then that we were at the very most next to nothing.

"How many others?" I asked.

"Hmm?" he said, and looked at me questioningly.

"How many other religious figures have been influenced? In what other ways have the Grays contributed to our history?"

"Oh, that," he said. "Well, Jesus, of course, Buddha, Mohammed, a philosopher during the Ming Dynasty called IL Jong, a priest named Umatep during the reign of Tuthmosis in 1480 BC Egypt, several Incan rulers and spiritual figures whose names I can't pronounce ..."

"All right, all right, I get the idea." I looked at him steadily, my eyes fixed on his which I could barely see through his glasses from the sunlight streaming in through the front windows behind him. He shifted and seemed a little uncomfortable. Clearly he did not like this silence, this waiting; he was still hiding something—something he desperately did not wish to share.

"You still haven't told me what happened to my son, David Malcolm. Tell me what happened to my boy," I said.

"You must believe me when I tell you the choice was not mine. There was nothing I could do."

"Tell me what happened, now, or this conversation is over."

He sighed and looked at me, and if I didn't know better I would have thought his expression was that of sincere apology; something I never assumed he was capable of.

"Your son, like your wife, was taken to the lunar station and then to the Area 51 complex. There he was raised by the Grays under the same regimen as I was. He was trained, disciplined, and in time, introduced to the workings of our organization," he paused, and then continued slowly, resigning himself to the truth he had kept hidden from me for over twenty years. "He is now a peace-keeper, Dr. Stattler, or as you so euphemistically referred to earlier, an 'agent of evil.' His full designation is one-five-zero-nine."

Before I could even think about my actions, where we were, who was watching, or worse still, what he might do, I lunged across the table and grabbed him by the tie and pulled him toward me. I leaned forward so his face was even with mine and said, "You corn-hole-fucker, you turned my son, my baby boy into a God-damned assassin?? You *knew*, you *knew* all this time, and you never told me???"

He stared at me directly, looked down at my hand and then back again. I suddenly realized where I was and looked around the restaurant bar. As it was near four o'clock the happy hour crowd was beginning to file in and we were attracting some stares. Mickey looked at me from across the counter and I knew by his look that I could not continue this manner of discussion. I released him and he leaned back into the soft leather of the restaurant booth, straightening his tie and preening himself like a cat.

"If we weren't in this restaurant right now I would *kill* you," I said menacingly. "I'll be damned if I'm going to help you now, you fucking freak. You'll pay for what you've done."

He chuckled under his breath. "It would be a hard thing to kill *me*, Dr. Stattler. My body has an enhanced immune system and repairs itself faster, for one, and secondly, you don't even own a weapon."

"What makes you so sure?" I asked.

"At least not a *registered* one, anyway," he said with a smirk. "And third, even if you did, you'd have to shoot me in the skull or several times in the same place ..." he said, knocking on his left shoulder which sounded as though he were knocking on a hard-cover book, thus revealing the Kevlar bullet proof vest beneath his clothes. "... Which is unlikely as I doubt you're that good of a marksman," he finished, grinning at me with a malicious glee, as if to say, 'I told you so.'

"Besides," he said almost mockingly. "You *have* to help me. You have no choice."

"I don't *have* to do anything, and don't feed me that 'you already have' bullshit," I replied defiantly, looking away from him towards the bar to emphasize my disgust.

"Well you have," he said matter-of-factly. "And you must help me ... that is, if you want to save *him*," he said with a suggestive intonation, which bordered on something akin to blackmail.

I looked at him. "What do you mean?" I said.

"*Think* about it, Dr. Stattler. Just *think* a moment. If you expose the truth, if you expose the Grays' presence and the conspiracy to hide it, the nefarious Men in Black, the 'agents of evil', as you call them will no longer be necessary. They will become obsolete, outdated. Their purpose to protect the truth and humanity from it will no longer be required. The days of your son's employment within our organization would be over, and he will need a parent, someone to help guide him back into society. He will need something he has never known, Dr. Stattler. Something the Grays are incapable of demonstrating. He will need someone to love him."

I looked at him incredulously, my face glowering, and it suddenly began to dawn on me. "You knew," I said in sudden realization. "You knew all those years ago, you had the vision, you had *sight*, you *saw* what would happen. *That's* why you spared me ... and you let them have my son, because you *knew* there would be no other reason I would help you. You *repulse* me. I can't believe there's anything *human* about you at all," I said with disgust spitting off the edge of my lips. "You're pathetic, and truly are a monster, in every sense of the word."

"You're very intuitive, Dr. Stattler, but I'm not quite *that* clever. It was not until I came to Providence that I knew you were here and that the inevitable confrontation between us would happen at last. The sight does not allow me to understand the *circumstances* with which the universe will unfold, but only glimpses of the future itself ... sort of like the pieces of a jigsaw puzzle, but you don't know exactly what the picture of the puzzle is. This was something I had to figure out in time. No, that night I spared you I only knew I must. I had killed a president, two congressmen, families, women and children without any of them, ever, producing the vision I experienced that evening. I knew it was important; I *knew* that if I were meant to kill you I would feel no more compassion than when I blew Jack Kennedy's skull all over the pavement.

"No, this was something different. Something *else* was at work, and I knew from my upbringing and abilities that you were *meant* to live, that I was *meant* to spare you, and our future on this planet together would be inextricably linked, even until our death."

"You seem to know a great deal about everything ... have you seen your and my death as well? You seem to know pretty much everything else," I said, almost mocking him.

He looked down at his watch. "Time grows short, Dr. Stattler."

An eerie silence crept between us then, amidst the clinking of glassware and social chatter among the bar, and I couldn't help but wonder what he meant by this. Talking to him was like peeling an onion; every layer of truth he revealed, once I heard it, made me begin to well up inside and want to cover my eyes from the pain, and I wondered if at the heart, once all the layers were gone, there would be nothing remaining but emptiness and oblivion.

I began to wonder what my real role in this universe was. What *was* I *meant* to do? What *was* my purpose, anyhow? I thought of my son, my David Malcolm, now a killer with no name, no existence, no family, only a number with which to identify him from his colleagues. What *was* I to do? I still had the chance, to turn and walk away, to prove to Mr. Black once and for all I was *not* under his power, that I *did* have a choice, and that free will *does* exist. But in doing so, I realized I would jeopardize my soul and if God did somehow, somewhere, despite all of what Mr. Black said, exist, than I *must* help him, especially having failed to do so before. I must help *them*. I realized quite despairingly I *had* to help my son and Mr. Black, not necessarily because the will of the universe told me so, but more so because my conscience did. I looked at him then, pleadingly, as if he were my executioner, waiting for some further response to help guide me in the path I had reluctantly chosen.

"There is much yet still to tell, Dr. Stattler. There are things you must know; things you must be aware of, things you must have."

"Such as?" I asked, seemingly resolved to my fate.

He reached into his pocket and pulled out what looked like a thirty-five millimeter film canister and set it in the middle of the table.

"This is a chip like the one Dr. Gottlieb was implanted with, like the one you possessed all those years ago. Every agent has one implanted at birth behind their jaw, just below the ear by the facial nerve and parotid gland. This chip was mine. I had it removed two weeks ago in San Diego by a surgeon with whom I have developed a relationship over the years. Her name is Sarah Dawson. When the time comes and you need a secure safehouse, which you will, I suggest that you seek her out."

"Can't they tell if it's been removed?" I asked.

"Not if it is still on my person; if anyone were to actually run a search as long as the chip were somewhere on my body the user would be unable to tell that it had been removed. As you know, and as we were able to find you twenty years ago, these chips not only broadcast your physical location, but also transmit your voice and your conversation with anyone, depending upon their voice decibel level, within an approximate two-meter radius. Each chip is unique, and transmits on a different frequency from every other chip."

"Can't they hear us? Why aren't they here?"

"Oh, make no mistake, they're looking for us, well, they're looking for me, as I and my chip's locator signal have 'disappeared', but they can't hear us. Several years ago I had the inclination to test the chips limits, and I fashioned and tested this vial of sorts. It has been lined with led and a thick wadding which absorbs any sound," and he set the vial containing the chip on the table in front of me. "I got the idea, initially, from you and the foil from that wine bottle, actually."

"Pretty clever," I said.

"Whatever you do, Dr. Stattler, *never* open it unless you want the other agents to find you. When you do they will find you, and then they will kill you."

"How do you tell each chip's signal apart?" I asked.

"As I have already previously explained to you, Dr. Stattler, each agent within our organization has a number. This number not coincidentally corresponds with the frequency that their chip transmits. All agents transmit a signal in a millahertz bandwidth, however when we refer to each other verbally it is not by the whole number but by the hundredth. For example, my whole designation and the frequency my chip broadcasts is one thousand one, however, when other agents correspond with me they do so by simply 'number one.' It becomes tedious and tiresome very quickly to speak to one another using the whole agent code and including the thousandth."

"Interesting," I said. "But why do agents have the chips, I thought the implants were only for the purposes of tracking the abductees for future acquisition."

"The purpose of implanting us is two-fold. The first reason all agents are implanted at birth is so that if any agent were ever in any trouble, that agent could be located virtually instantaneously and support sent in to capture and terminate the persons responsible. As you are well aware from your experiences with Dr. Gottlieb, all chips still transmit a locator signal even if the host is deceased."

"And the second reason?" I asked.

"The second purpose of implanting us is how, shall we say, what brings us here today. If any agent were to attempt to reveal the truth to anyone, even a spouse if they had one, the agency would know, and the subject and their family would be eliminated, or as you experienced, taken for anatomical study and experimentation of further gene sequencing. The same follows true, of course, if any agent were to attempt to have their chip removed. As the chip broadcasts the voice patterns of each host, the agency would discover it and the subject would again be eliminated. Loyalty, and as I have already explained *information,* in our business is the greatest of commodities. Strict observance of our prime directives is essential to maintaining social order. Deviation from these directives in any manner results in immediate termination of the agent."

"How were you able to communicate to this 'Sarah Dawson'? How were you able to explain what exactly the chip was, where it was located, and how to remove it without exposing yourself?"

"You can accomplish quite a bit, Dr. Stattler, if you have the patience, ink pen, a lot of paper, and sign language."

"That's very convenient, and quite an undertaking," I said with a deliberate doubtful tone. There was something in the manner of his expression that betrayed him, as though he was hiding something—something he was hesitant to reveal and which he seemed to be protecting.

"I can see you don't quite understand, Dr. Stattler. You see," he paused and then reluctantly continued. "She's my daughter."

CHAPTER TEN

Gottlieb's Capture

I couldn't sleep that night. I kept going over and over in my mind the events of the day and what Gottlieb had said. *He couldn't remember.* But why? The more and more I thought about it the more I thought my instinct was right from the very beginning—he was hiding something. Something traumatic had happened in the past that was so horrible it had wiped his conscious memory clean. Somewhere in the depths of his subconscious lurked the answer. The answer to whether this whole bizarre conspiracy he imagined was real, or simply that, something he imagined. I *had* to know. I had to find the answer. Not just for his sanity but for mine. There were too many coincidences. Too many truths in what Gottlieb had said.

I wanted to believe and yet I desperately didn't. I needed to find a way to convince Frank to let me regress him. I needed to find some leverage I could use to help me persuade Frank to let me perform hypnosis on the Doctor. It was the only way to concretely find the path to the truth. The answer was there, in the dark recesses of his mind where even he dared not go. And that was saying something. For all of Gottlieb's uncanny brilliance I found it hard to believe he would purposefully deny himself of his memory, even at a subconscious level.

No, it was there. I knew it. I had to find it; I would find it. But how? I didn't know. But one thing was certain, the path to the truth of Gottlieb was through Director Frank Sikes, and I decided to speak to him privately the next morning after the staff meeting.

"You want to what?" he said, staring at me as though I had just declared that I wanted to strip and run down the halls naked. "What would be the point? He's here for *life*, Evan, for life. Do you know what that means? It means irrespective of what you do or what becomes of this, he's not going anywhere. Even if this hypnotherapy could somehow help him the most you can possibly hope for is in time to get his status reduced to Class 2. I just can't believe this of you."

"You haven't seen him, Frank. You don't know him," I said, standing my ground.

"No, and I don't want to. This is exactly as I had feared. You have been waiting and waiting for the big chance to present itself, and as soon as it does you start reading too much into it. It is as I have feared all along. You've become too close with this one Evan. The man's a psychotic murderer—fact. He killed two federal agents—fact."

"And what do we *really* know about that, Frank?" I interrupted him. "Only what he tells us because the men he killed were classified operatives, so instead of telling us anything the Federal Government kindly dumps him in our lap and says, 'here have at it, he's psychotic, he's yours now, and by the way we really can't tell you why.' Doesn't that seem a little strange to you?"

"First of all, the Federal Government didn't 'dump him on us' as you so eloquently suggested, the Phillips Institute in Wichita Falls, Texas, did. And secondly, even if events did transpire in the manner you have suggested there's not a God-damned thing I can do about it. What would you have me do, Evan? March right down to the NSA and kindly ask them to tell me the details of why this patient is here? They'd put me right in here with him and you know it."

I sighed audibly, letting him know of my displeasure at being ridiculed. "Of course not."

"Then what would you have me do?"

"Let me regress Gottlieb."

This time it was Director Sikes who sighed audibly as he leaned back in his chair as though attempting to recede from the room. I had to admit I was pleased with myself at how I was able to turn things around to my favor.

"I needn't tell you the dangers of what it is you are proposing. A patient of this sort, whom we *know* to be a violent offender with a history of violence he is unable to remember, can only bring about violence. Violence only begets violence, and I don't want it in my hospital."

"Frank, I'm close on this. I can feel it."

"That's what I'm afraid of. Look, isn't there something else you can do."

"What would you have me do, Frank? Beat it out of him? He quite simply can't remember. What would you suggest?"

"Send him back to Phillips," Frank said dourly. "And yes, I'm kidding."

"If we staged it properly, safely, say, in the observation room, monitored with his vital stats, with Sampson and several orderlies there would be no way he could surprise us. Besides, Frank, the guy's fifty-two years old. I don't suspect he's going to be able to put one over on four men nearly half his age." I could tell by his sour expression that I was beginning to wear on him and he was close to relenting.

"If I agree to this procedure, which I'm not sure I will, I'm going to insist that I oversee the whole operation and if something should happen and I tell you to call it to a halt you will do so. I'm not willing to risk another fiasco like the one that injured Doctor Stimple. I got my ass chewed royally by the state board and have to endure Howard gloating every time I see him, which is pain unto itself. Is that understood?"

"Yes, sir," I said. "How is Dr. Stimple, anyway?"

"He's fairing well, Kathryn tells me. She hasn't talked to you about him?"

"Let's just say when we leave Grove Haven, John Stimple is not the first conversation that comes to mind over dinner."

Frank smiled at this and snickered somewhat. "No, of course not. In any case, she tells me he is getting on, should be back within twelve weeks or so. I've placed him on Administrative Leave until then so he can recover. I think he's gone to Mexico, or something. Not a bad deal, huh? Get stabbed in the throat and get four months off in paradise with pay. Sometimes I wish I could trade places with him. Christ, what am I agreeing to here?"

"You're agreeing to help your patient, Doctor," I said. "There's no shame in that."

"For you maybe. You don't have to face the board if something goes wrong. I needn't tell you they'll have my head if you screw this up." He huffed and threw his Mont Blanc on the yellow legal pad in front of him. "All right, Doctor, you may proceed at your leisure. But I don't agree to anything unless you get Gottlieb's whole-hearted permission before proceeding. Is that understood?"

"Of course, I think that goes without saying. I'll let you know what he decides," I said, gathering my things off the board room table. I headed for the door, eager to confront Dr. Gottlieb with the proposal, when Frank diverted my attention.

"And, Doctor, no funny business. If I say shut it down, we shut it down. Clear?"

"Clear," I said, hastening myself out the boardroom door and down the corridor to the Class 3 detention area.

"Your library appears to have all the classics, Doctor," Gottlieb said as I rounded the corner next to his cell. He was, as usual, lying on his cot, his face buried beneath pages of whatever it was he was reading, and did not look up as I stood there in front of him. I looked at the title, Julius Caesar. He continued to speak without looking up at me.

"Shylock's lust for revenge against those who wronged him, Macbeth's ambition and subdued melancholy, Hamlet's crazed desire for justice and acknowledgment, Lear's deliverance into chaos at the cost of his self and his family, and Caesar's betrayal. Put them all together and it would make quite the novel," he said, finally looking at me and physically acknowledging my presence for the first time.

"Quite," I said pointedly. He smiled at this and folded the play shut and rested it on his chest.

"What's on the agenda for today, Doctor, or are you merely wooing me with your presence this morning?" he said as though suspecting something.

"I've been giving some thought to your problem and I may have a solution."

"Problem?" he said somewhat surprised, as though I had struck him. "What problem is that?"

"Are you forgetting where we left off last time? Your inability to remember the events of the night that inevitably brought you to be here with us?"

"Oh, that," he said, and began to flip through the pages of his play again. "I thought you meant something more dire or serious; perhaps something more important. For a moment there I thought that you were going to tell me my physical with Kathryn yesterday led you to believe I had contracted hepatitis or something."

I laughed at this. "No, I would let her tell you that. Besides, why don't you feel it's important?"

"Why should I, it won't change anything. It's not ever going to let me out of this cell. It's not ever going to allow me to walk through the meadow, hear the birds chirping or feel the grass beneath my feet," he said, and once again resumed reading, attempting to ignore me.

"I was under the impression you thought the search for the truth was more important than anything else. Why then all these plays, hmmm? Did you not say when we first met they contained *universal truths?* Why bother to go to such lengths to spell out for me paradoxes between them and your life? Why bother at all? You did say it is the nature of truth to reveal itself, didn't you?"

I had him and he knew it, and he once again set down the book and looked up at me begrudgingly, as though he wished he hadn't spoken to me at all, ever.

"Yes," he said, rolling his eyes and making believe this was nothing else if not a painful admission.

"How'd you like to take a little field trip today?" I asked, smiling at him.

"A *field trip*! Oh, boy, Oh, boy! Maybe Santa will even bring me some gifts this year," he said, clearly amused with himself. "Where to?"

"I've spoken to Dr. Sikes about it and he's agreed …"

He interrupted me. "Dr. Sikes?" he said rising off his cot, a look of concern washing over his face. He approached the bars and looked from side to side, as though he might have been hiding from his field of vision when he was recessed within his cell. "Do not trust Dr. Sikes, Doctor. He knows more than he is telling you about me. He's in league with them."

"In league with *who*, Doctor?"

He sighed and, stepping back from the bars, flapped his hands at his sides in apparent frustration. "No one. Everyone. Lawyers. Doctors. Scientists," he said, and then audibly humphed. "Archaeologists. Everyone that knows and has something to gain, or at the very least maintain, and everything to lose by their admission or suspicion."

I wondered what he meant by this. Was he saying there were people in everyday society, not just in the higher, classified levels of government but people in normal life, in positions of authority, who were in essence *protecting* this elaborate conspiracy he imagined? I couldn't be sure.

"Where are we going?" he asked.

"To the observation room, where with your permission I was going to attempt hypnotherapy."

"*Hypnotherapy!*" he said, as though I had struck him again.

"Yes, why are you so concerned Doctor?"

He began to slowly pace around his cell while idly twiddling his thumbs behind his back, clearly in a state of deliberation. After about thirty-seconds of this he finally answered, still walking slowly to and fro in the confines of his cell.

"Actually, Doctor, I have given a great deal of thought as to the reasons I am unable to recall the events of that particular evening, neither of which is very agreeable. The first, I am unable to remember because of the sheer horror of my actions in slaying those men, and my subconscious has repressed those events to spare what is left of my sanity, or, I was taken somehow, and they have found a way to block my memories. It is therefore with great trepidation that I am reluctant to accept your proposal. There is also something else I have to consider, Doctor. Trust."

"Trust?" I repeated, not understanding the relevance.

"Yes, trust, Doctor. You see, Caesar's trust was misplaced in his advisors and especially that of his 'honorable' friend, Marcus Brutus. It was Brutus more than anyone who killed Caesar, not because his blade penetrated deeper than any of the other conspirators, but because of the betrayal of his confidence. I feel we have come far, you and I, Dr. Stattler. Further than I have come or even dared to venture with any other physician in more than twenty years. It would destroy me to relive those moments and find that the trust, the confidence we have shared regarding these forces that have plotted against me, to be lost, because of them.

"Now do you understand what it is I am saying to you, Doctor? Now do you comprehend the reason why I am hesitant to do as you propose? I do not want you to share the same fate as Brutus, running yourself on your sword to save your career, and I do not wish to share the same fate as Caesar, not that it can get much worse," he said, somewhat humorously, and gestured to the cold, cement walls and bars around him.

His gaze, even in humor, was penetrating, and it cut me to the bone. Although I knew we had to continue his treatment, especially in light that really none had ever begun in his twenty plus years of incarceration, I wasn't sure I was going to be able to commit to what it was he was asking of me. There were too many things to consider, too many possible variables of what the outcome of his hypnosis might be, to say nothing of the conflicts of interest with my career and duty as a psychologist.

In short, what he was asking was impossible, and I knew it. Yet, I also knew he was my patient, and my first duty was to him and uncovering the truth, no matter how terrible or horrifying that may be. It was truly a terrible predicament, and one I had not been placed in before, but I decided the risks were worth the gains, and I placated him. "All right," I said, looking at him and returning his steady gaze.

"I could be well moved," he said, "if I were as you." And his eyes stared at me beseechingly. "If I could pray to move, prayers would move me. But I am constant as the northern star, of whose true fixed resting quality there is no fellow in the firmament. The skies are painted with unnumbered sparks. They are all fire, and every one doth shine. But there is but one in all doth hold his place. So in the world: 'tis furnished well with men, and men are flesh and blood and apprehensive. Yet in the number I do know but one that unassailable holds on his rank, unshaken of motion; and that I am he, let me a little show it, even in this—thank you, Doctor, for your candor, and for reminding me of my purpose. And this afternoon, you and I shall reveal it."

I returned to his cell at noon accompanied by Sampson, and two other orderlies on the day shift carrying restraints. When we reached Gottlieb's cell and stood in front of it Frank buzzed it open from Sampson's normal position at the gate. Once it was opened, Dr. Gottlieb put his hands behind his head and stepped back to the middle of the room and the two orderlies carrying the restraints entered. Dr. Gottlieb was very cooperative and polite while they shackled him. Once his restraints had been properly fitted Sampson gave me the thumbs up sign. We walked down the corridor of the cell block very slowly, as Dr. Gottlieb could only move at a child's pace with the restraints bound fast around his ankles. When we got to the man-trap, Dr. Sikes buzzed us through and together the five of us walked the long hall by the infirmary, out through the courtyard and made our way across toward the 'A' block entrance, which housed the observation room.

Dr. Gottlieb shielded his eyes from the brightness while simultaneously looking up at the heavens above us. "It has been so long since I have seen the sun," he said, and appeared to marvel at the brilliance of the clear blue sky above us. "They only move me at night, you know," he added, smiling and winking simultaneously at Frank. He returned his gaze to the earth as we approached the door to the cell block. Frank gave me a sidelong glance at this, as the two orderlies ahead of us opened the door.

We made our way through the corridor and through the door to the observation room where John Stimple had the pencil thrust into his larynx. Per my instructions the table and chair usually in the center of the room had been removed in lieu of the stereotypical psychiatrist's lounge. A small night table sat next to it, which held on its top a machine similar to an EKG, a *sphygmomanometer*, only instead of monitoring heart functions it recorded and transmitted pulse, blood pressure, and body temperature to a monitor on the observation deck. The orderlies unbuckled Gottlieb's restraints while I wrapped a blood pressure cuff to his forearm.

"Try not to be nervous," I said. "Just relax and open your mind."

"My mind is continually open, Doctor, it is the minds of others that are closed" he quipped while sinking into the lounge and staring directly at the mirrored glass of the observation booth.

I gave the thumbs up sign to Frank in the observatory and heard the intercom system click on overhead.

"All right, Doctor, I want you to relax and close your eyes," I said.

Doctor Gottlieb shifted in the lounge chair, which we had brought into the observatory until he was comfortable. Once he stopped shifting and his eyes closed I began. Frank, who was in the observation booth, dimmed the recessed lighting until the room had the incandescence of an evening at twilight. Sampson was standing ready behind me in case anything should happen and I began.

"I am going to slowly count to five. When I reach the number five you will be in a state of deep hypnosis. One, your eyes are beginning to get heavy now, and you're becoming more relaxed, your body is becoming lucid and you can feel your muscles starting to go limp. Two, your eyes are very heavy now, and you can feel the beginning of your subconscious begin to open. Three, your pulse rate and autonomic functions are slowing to a state of deep relaxation. Four, I want you to imagine and feel this relaxation moving through your body. Five, you are now in a state of deep hypnosis, and you can remember with perfect clarity any event I ask of you. How are you feeling?"

"I feel good," he said calmly.

"Now, Doctor, I want you to go back in time to the night you first saw the men in your apartment in New Haven, on the evening of November 28, 1963. What are you doing?"

"I'm unpacking; my valise is on the bed. I had just returned from Nasca late that afternoon, and I am looking for my notes for the conference I am to give at the Repertory Theater concerning my findings to the faculty of the Department of Anthropology in the morning."

"What stops you?"

"There is a board in the hall that creaks when you step on it, and I realize I am not alone."

"Who is there with you?" I asked.

"I don't know." he said, clearly becoming agitated, and I realized I needed to reassure him.

"I want you to relax, Doctor, that person can't harm you. You're just remembering what transpired." I waited until his breathing was normal before I continued. "Do you know who is there?"

"No."

"Has this person seen you yet?"

"No."

"What do you do?"

"I hide behind the door of my bedroom. I can hear him coming down the hall, slowly."

"How do you know it's a man?"

"The creak of the board was loud, as though from someone heavy."

"What do you see?"

"I see through the crack in the door between the hinges that he has a pistol drawn."

"What do you do?"

"I grab my rock hammer. I am scared. I am oh so scared," he began to whimper and shuffle in the lounge, and he held his arms to his chest as though he were holding something.

"It's all right, Doctor, he can't harm you. What is happening?"

"He's walking in my room, slowly, the pistol out in front of him. I wait until he has cleared the door."

"What do you do?"

He trembled before answering angrily, deliberately. "I strike him with the pointed end of my hammer as hard as I can in the back of his skull. He gasps, drops the gun which makes a loud clatter on the wood floor and his body collapses, twitching in front of me. I hear a voice call from down the hall, out in the living room, 'Number four?' The voice only calls once. I pick up the pistol and hide again behind the door. I hear footsteps coming toward me," he said shaking.

I turned and faced the one-way mirror, behind which Frank and several other orderlies were observing the situation. "Frank, how's his BP?" I asked, trying to keep my voice down so as not to disturb Dr. Gottlieb.

"Try to bring him down a little," was the response from the intercom panel on the wall.

"It's all right, Doctor," I said, trying to soothe him. He was clearly agitated and his breathing was irregular. "I want you to relax, you're still here, you're safe, but I'd like you to continue."

"I can't," he said, sounding terrified of the events.

"Doctor, I think that's enough for today," Frank's voice said from the intercom.

I ignored Frank and continued. "What is happening, Doctor?"

"He's coming," he said. "He's coming close now. He's walking slowly, methodically down the hall. I hear the board creak, which I know is about six feet from where I am standing behind the wall. I wait."

"And then what happens?"

Dr. Gottlieb began to whimper. "I shot him. I SHOT HIM!" he said. His breast was beginning to heave from breathing and he was sobbing as he said this. "I shot him through the wall. I shot every bullet in the gun. I shot it so many times I didn't even hear his body drop on the other side of the wall."

"It's all right, Doctor. You're fine," I said, and waited a few moments before continuing. Once he was calm and stopped sobbing I continued. "What are you doing now?"

"I figured they were here for me, that somehow, they knew what I was doing. They were here for the chips I had and my research! They must know, somehow, intercepted the telegram … I don't know. I am scared, I am oh, so scared, what if there are more of them? They must be here to kill me!" he said, crying and raising his voice.

"It's alright, Doctor, I'm here with you. They can't harm you. Now tell me, what are you doing?"

"I am kneeling over the first man I had killed, the one the other referred to as 'Number Four.' It occurred to me that the number might mean something. It might mean something connected with the chip. I went to the kitchen for a pairing knife, and made an incision where I found the others in the fossils I had collected, from his right ear down to his chin, and peeled back his face."

"What did you see?"

He voice was calm now, and the agitation and distress, which he exhibited earlier, were absent. "There it was, just above the parotid gland, precisely as I predicted, and I knew then for certain there was a connection, but what that connection was, exactly, I did not know. I removed the chip from the other man in the same manner, took his weapon and gathered my things. I knew someone had discovered I planned to go public with what I had found, but just who that someone was I could not say. What I did know was whoever it was felt that the fossil, and other evidence I had, was worth killing for."

"What did you do then?"

"I am leaving the house when I am struck from behind. I have no more memory of this event."

"What do you remember next?"

"I am coming to, and my head is swollen and there is a large scar where someone had struck me."

* * *

"You talk in your sleep." a voice said to me from the blackness of the room.

My vision was still foggy and I looked around my surroundings. I couldn't see where he was, there was a light shining in my eyes from what seemed like high above. My head hurt and throbbed with ache. Whoever it was in the room with me must have hit me, knocked me unconscious after I killed those men. I continued to look around to see who was there, but my vision was still blurred. I was on some sort of strange metallic table. It looked and felt like the same metal as the chip, but in my present state I could not tell. I tried to get up when I realized my legs and arms were bound somehow to the table. Gradually my vision cleared and I saw a man sitting in a chair to my left studying me. He appeared to be dressed in the same type of suit that the men who came to kill me wore, dark black, with a black silk tie with a white shirt and sunglasses, which he wore even though the room was dark. He was smoking, looking at me with a fixed stare. I didn't like the way he was smiling. It made me uncomfortable. It was almost maniacal, evil.

"How long I have been here?" I asked.

"Three days," he said casually. "We've kept you sedated until we could put your affairs in order."

"What do you mean *put my affairs in order?*"

"You were getting close, Dr. Gottlieb. *Too* close to us, to discovering us, too close to detecting us. Too close to unveiling *their* presence. I can not allow that," he said, rising from his chair, walking toward me.

"How can you know what I've been studying?"

"Let's just say we've been monitoring you. Monitoring your progress. Monitoring your discoveries. We've been aware of what you've been doing since 1950, since Swartkrans."

"… when I found the first chip," I said out loud, more to myself than him. I decided to question his intentions. "If you've known all this time why didn't you try and stop me before?"

"Because you posed no threat before, now you do."

"Who were those men in my house? Those men I killed. They had guns; they were there to kill me."

"I know. I sent them there."

My soul filled with dread as he said this and I felt helpless to this man, this 'Mr. Black' as he stood over me. My heart began to race and nervous sweat beaded on my brow.

"Those men were agents of our association."

"What association is that?" I asked, gasping at the thought that the United States government could sanction such an organization, and all my worst fears were true.

"The association that is ours," he said. "They were sent to kill you, Dr. Gottlieb. They were sent to kill you and confiscate all of your research. The latter has been completed, the former, has not."

I began to cry then, and tears streamed down my face, not for my life which was now hanging in jeopardy, but for the countless hours I had spent, all the diligence and time for which I had so long labored. It was all for nothing and now this man, Mr. Black was going to kill me for it.

He continued, "And those were not just *any* agents you disposed of that evening, Dr. Gottlieb." A snarl began to creep onto his face as he leaned down towards me, bound and powerless on the table. "Those agents also happened to be two of my brothers, so you'll forgive me if I have a particular aversion to your presence," he said sneering malevolently.

"What do you mean, *your brothers*? Who are you?" I asked. And stepping back he removed his sunglasses so that I could see the empty blackness of his eyes. Eyes that were without an iris, eyes that were simply black and white. It terrified me to look into them, and he seemed to know this as he continued.

"I am no one, and I am everyone. I am the sum of all your hopes and fears. I am what you will become in four hundred years. I am your newborn son and what will bring your soul to tears. I am your future. I am your past. I am your nemesis, I am your nightmare! I am the Capos that raped you when you were nine. I am the SS guard when you stand in that line." he said glaring at me, bits of spittle flying from his mouth, rage upon rage scoured his face, and then he continued, "All these things we see and *more*, that is what *nightmares* are for.," at this his snarl began to turn into a smile, and he chuckled to himself.

I was panting, searching for some sort of clue as to what he was going to do next. Was he going to slaughter me on that table, shoot me in cold blood? The sweat poured down my brow as I pondered the possibilities of my life ending in the middle of that forgotten room. But he merely stepped back, put back on his sunglasses, and straightened his suit coat, and spoke, his voice returning to normal.

"Normally I would kill you, Dr. Gottlieb. In fact, that is what I was originally ordered to do," he said casually. "But it would seem, much to my dismay I might add, that is not your immediate destiny after all. You see, whether you know it or not, Dr. Gottlieb, you are to play a part in this great, little, conspiracy of ours."

I didn't like the way this sounded as he seemed intent on making me suffer for what I had done to him.

"You see, Doctor, for reasons not even *they* can fully see or understand, it has been decided that your death should be *postponed*, and that it is very important you live. Unfortunately though, these reasons that I speak of, even if I knew them whole-heartedly, I could not tell you. But, before you take your leave of us this evening and venture to your new home, I have some friends here who'd like to make your acquaintance," he said, smiling menacingly again.

I then heard a strange swooshing sound, which sounded like a door opening, and then what sounded like a troupe of tiny footsteps, like those of a group of excited school children, coming toward me on the table.

* * *

"AHHHHHH!" Gottlieb screamed, and he rose from the chair with a wild and desperate fury in his eyes I have never seen before or since. He continued to scream and howl, making his way towards the door.

I heard Frank's voice over the intercom. "Sampson, take him, now!"

I rose out of my chair after him and Sampson and I circled Dr. Gottlieb. I tried to talk him down. "It's okay Doctor, we're not going to hurt you, calm down and come back to the chair."

"GET OUT OF MY MIND!" he screamed, and he clasped his arms to his ears as though trying to block some voice that was evidently speaking to him. At first I thought it was mine, but he continued even though neither of us was saying anything, and we both watched in horror as he continued screaming and ranting.

"GET AWAY FROM ME! GET AWAY FROM ME!" he howled, dancing and darting and dashing from people who weren't there.

"Sampson," I said. "Back off for a moment."

Sampson and I both stepped away from him.

He continued screaming as though we were not there at all, as if he wasn't he wasn't even aware of our presence.

"NOOOOO! DON'T TOUCH ME!" he screamed. "DON'T TOUCH ME!" his voice was pleading, desperate to whatever manner of creature that was besieging him.

I heard Frank's voice once again over the intercom. "Doctor, bring him out of it, now!"

"Doctor Gottlieb, you are under hypnosis in the Grove Haven Federal Institution for the mentally insane. These voices are not real. These beings are not real. When I count to three you will come back to reality. One. Two. Three," I said sternly and with authority, trying to penetrate whatever it was he was witnessing. But my efforts fell on deaf ears, as he still had his hands over them.

"GET AWAY! GET AWAY! GET OUT OF MY MIND!" he shouted, still wavering frantically between Sampson and me.

Frank came over the intercom once again. "Doctor, do something! NOW!"

I decided that he was trapped wherever he was, and we would have to use force to bring him back.

"Sampson," I said, and I didn't have to say more, for he nodded a silent assent and we both moved with our hands outreached towards Gottlieb to try and subdue him. This did nothing to help matters, as he continued to scream and howl when he saw us and reacted more violently in trying to keep us from coming toward him, flailing his limbs about in the air whenever one of us approached. When we finally got close enough to grab him he suddenly and without warning gasped, and with both hands grabbed the base of his neck just below his right ear, collapsed on the floor and began to sob.

Sampson and I both audibly sighed in relief and I kneeled down next to Dr. Gottlieb, who was curled in a fetal position on the floor and grabbing at his neck, crying as though he was an infant that had never cried before.

"Doctor, can you hear me?" I said tenderly, kneeling down on the floor next to him, trying to comfort him. "It's Dr. Stattler. Do you know where you are?" Dr. Gottlieb just continued to sob and shudder and cry on the floor. "It's all right Doctor, you're safe now. No one's going to harm you."

"It's too late, Dr. Stattler," he said between sobs, and I was glad to hear he recognized me and had come out of hypnosis. "It's too late," he repeated again. "They put one in me. THEY PUT ONE IN ME!" he wailed, with tears streaming out of his eyes and down his chin. Before I could respond he wrapped his arms around me and wept into my shoulder, howling with muffled gasps and sobs. I stared at him, curled and weeping desperately next to me on the floor of the examination room, having seen and bared witness once again to the faces of those who now, it would seem, indeed contrived and plotted this conspiracy against him.

It was in that moment I was reminded of *Caesar*, and I, like Marcus Brutus, had my own decision to make: do I sacrifice him to save my own career, or should I dare to believe in him? I did not know, and all I could do was sit there in wonder and hold him while he cried.

CHAPTER ELEVEN

Surgery

"What happened back there yesterday, Doctor?" I heard Frank's voice ask as I came through the door to his office.

I hadn't seen or spoken to him since what happened, and giving him my report was not something I had been looking forward to. He was sitting at his desk, glasses drooping down the front of his nose, and was wearing his lab coat with his usual dour expression, which left me unsettled. I had been attempting to put the pieces together of everything I had seen and heard from Dr. Gottlieb, trying desperately to draw some other, alternate conclusion to the events he described and I had been witness to, but to my great chagrin I could find none.

I still had to make a decision about what to do, despite further evidence Kathryn and I discovered after what had happened in the Observatory yesterday afternoon. I was torn; everything in me that longed for a successful career was being undermined by my conscience to help Dr. Gottlieb and to the preservation of the truth. It left my mind swimming and I felt utterly useless, as though I was drowning in everything I said or did since yesterday afternoon.

"Doctor?" Frank said again. "Yesterday?"

"Sure," I said, coming to my senses, wishing above all else that I could click my heels three times and disappear.

"What happened back there, Doctor?" he asked as I slunk into the red leather chair with large brass rivulets sitting opposite his desk. I did not wish to have a confrontation with him, but judging from his harsh demeanor and the tone of his voice that seemed to be the path down which we were headed.

185

"You were there, Frank," I said somewhat defiantly, preparing to stand my ground and not be steamrolled by him which everyone else on the staff usually let happen. "What do you think happened to him?"

"That's not what I asked," he said. "I want to know why you proceeded to push Gottlieb to continue against my specific instructions and against his will. I can not and will not tolerate behavior from a physician on my staff that jeopardizes the well-being of a patient."

"Don't feed me that bullshit, Frank. It would have eventually happened and you know it. You saw what he was up against, what he was witnessing, what they did to him."

"What *who* did to him, Doctor?" All I saw was a patient in hypnosis under duress."

"You son of a bitch," I blurted out without thinking. "Gottlieb was right about you. He said you knew more than you were letting on, and that you would betray me."

"Betray you? How, Doctor? In what way have I fed you to the proverbial wolves as you have so dramatically suggested?"

"You knew. You knew this would happen and you just went ahead and let it, with no concern to myself or Gottlieb. And now that it has you don't intend to do a damn thing about it."

"I tried to stop you, Doctor, but you insisted that regressive therapy be performed on the Doctor. It was your ego, not mine, that you were feeding when you pushed us into this situation, and what did it get you? A delusional patient, an incensed Facilities Director, and some difficult choices to make. Now I don't need to tell you what will happen to your career if you champion this patient, Doctor, so I suggest you take some time off to re-evaluate what it is that is most important to you."

"Are you putting me on leave, Frank?"

He sighed audibly before responding. "I'm asking you to look at your career objectively. There is nothing that you and I can do to help Dr. Gottlieb. He has his own demons and he buried them long ago. That is, until you charged in with your pick ax and shovel and dug them up. This hospital needs good physicians and, though I've never said it, you are a good physician Evan, and I can't afford to lose you. Not now, especially with what happened to Stimple."

He had me, and I knew he was right. What was I going to do, really anyway? I sat there silently, looking out Frank's office window to the courtyard below, where Sampson and some of the other orderlies were exercising some of the Class 2 patients. They were walking around the large fountain in the center of the courtyard, which though astonishing and beautiful, seemed out of place with the character of this establishment. It measured about twenty feet across, and had large baroque cherubs, pouring water out of urns, sitting and careening around a large statue of a woman, presumably Venus, or Mother Earth, or perhaps a rendition of the Virgin, who had her hands open in a gesture suggesting longing, or helplessness, while her eyes looked towards the heavens. I think there was a plaque somewhere near the bottom which carefully illustrated the scene and its purpose here at Grove Haven, but I don't believe I ever read it, or if I did, did not recall doing so or its meaning. But I felt it now.

For a moment, I too looked out the window towards the heavens in the hope that someone would listen and help me, but no one did. I was jolted to my senses by Sampson, who must have inadvertently looked up to the window and seen me looking out at the scene below. He smiled and waved, and it took me a few seconds to register that he was waving at me until I finally waved back.

I turned to look at Frank, who was still wearing the same sour, glum expression he had when I walked through the door to his office, and I realized then that I didn't think I had *ever* seen him smile. He was too absorbed in the complexities and intricacies of his profession, I think, to let the simple enjoyments and stuff of life in. Though there was no question in my mind he was good at what he did, I couldn't help wondering what he was like outside of Grove Haven, if he had a life. Did he have friends? Did he go out at night and socialize? Was he seeing anyone? And the more I thought about it the more I couldn't imagine it. I could only imagine the dour face in front of me, devoid of happiness and courtesy, where everything was not good enough and nearly everyone else was inferior. But I was procrastinating, in this whimsical musing, and I knew it. I was diverting my attention elsewhere rather than to the task at hand, and it was not a task that I was looking forward to.

"That's not all," I said, breaking the silence.

"What do you *mean*, 'that's not all'?"

I sighed heavily before replying; the burden I was carrying was too much to bear. "I had Kathryn order a CAT scan yesterday after what happened in the Observatory, to the right side of Dr. Gottlieb's head which he had grabbed as Sampson and I closed in on him."

"And?"

"There appears to be a large mass, about the size of a quarter, resting just below the parotid gland," I said, handing him the CAT scan from Gottlieb's file which I brought with me.

Frank leaned back in his chair and held it up to the light to examine it. He studied it for a few seconds before responding. "That could be anything," he said. "Probably a pleomorphic adenoma of some kind, a benign mixed tumor of some sort."

I didn't answer and waited for him to read my expression.

"There's more?" he asked hesitantly. I'm sure he really wished there wasn't, and that he didn't have to ask. "Let me guess," he said despondently. "When the results of the scan came back as being inconclusive, you ordered an aspiration."

A fine needle aspiration was a new technique in the early eighties whereby a physician inserted a needle into an afflicted are, such as in this case what appeared to be a tumor, and would attempt to remove cells to determine whether or not the tumor was benign or malignant.

"She couldn't penetrate it," I said glumly. "Possibly calcified."

Many times in cases with tumors, as often happens to the kidneys, minerals probably ingested through tap water form crystals of calcium carbonate deposits, just as you find at the bottom of a tea kettle.

"So basically you're telling me you don't know what the hell this thing is. Christ!" he said, throwing the CAT scan onto the table, and it was clear he was extremely irritated with this news, and much as I enjoyed upstaging Frank, I did not enjoy the effects it produced. "It's gotta be a coincidence. It has to be."

"That's not what your conscience tells you, Frank," I said.

He leaned forward on his desk, his hands together, and began to tap his forehead with the tips of his index fingers. Finally he seemed to get a hold of himself and take stock of the situation.

"Ok, when Dr. Bailey returns from St. Mary's next Tuesday I'll have him remove the tumor. If there's nothing else you're dismissed, Doctor."

"What?" I said loudly, more as a statement of objection rather than a question. "Kathryn is an ENT, and has more experience with conditions of this sort than that of Dr. Bailey, he's a general practitioner for Christ's sake. Frank, you know this, that's why you hired her. She's the most qualified."

"I'm aware of that, Doctor!" he snapped.

"Then why isn't she performing the procedure?" I responded, raising my voice to equal his.

"Conflict of Interests, Doctor. You're too close to this patient and I don't intend to allow you or your wife to further jeopardize his well being."

"You bastard!" I said. "You know that what this man is carrying inside his head is evidence that Extra-Terrestrials exist, and by Gottlieb's own account were here before us, to say nothing of the fact that it maintains his innocence and defends his sanity, and you intend on just letting that evidence slip away into some dark abyss just so you don't have to be inconvenienced by the truth!"

Frank rose out of his chair practically screaming his words at me. "I intend on safeguarding the lives of my physicians and patients, Doctor!"

I stood up and stared straight into his eyes so there would be no mistaking my intent or meaning. "I don't know why I ever looked up to you, Frank; you're nothing but a God-damned coward!"

"You're officially on leave, Doctor!" he screamed at me red-faced, particles of spittle flying in the air. "And I don't want to see your face anywhere near this hospital for the rest of the week, do you hear me?"

"Yeah, I hear you," I said, nodding my head, my voice returning to normal. "I guess it must be true, right? That's the first time I've seen you lose your cool," and slamming the door to his office behind me, I embraced the cool air of the corridor.

I waited until that evening to tell Kate what had happened that afternoon with Frank. Rather than risk waiting around until six when she usually finished her shift in the infirmary I told Kate I was taking the rest of the afternoon off and would pick her up later. It was over dinner while I was attempting to feed David a mixture of mashed bananas and Cheerios that I finally mustered the courage to tell her what had transpired.

"You did what?!!" she gasped. "Honestly Evan I just can't believe you sometimes."

"What do you mean?" I said trying to feign ignorance.

"Don't you ever think about anyone but yourself?

"But Kate," I said half stammering. "I can't believe you, you sound just like Frank."

"Well come on, listen to yourself, Evan! Regardless of the consequences to you, me, and David Malcolm you just grabbed your torch and ran with it, and didn't even bother to consider what might happen to the rest of us. You're just so desperate to believe in Gottlieb that you turn all matters of practicality aside."

"Jesus, Kathryn! You listen to yourself!" I continued. "This man has been locked away, held prisoner for over twenty years, twenty years, Kate. And the only thing he has to show for his experience is the tumor in his head, at the core of which may be a device of extra-terrestrial origin."

"You don't know that," she contested bitterly.

"I believe that!" I said raising my voice. "Why else would he have grabbed that specific spot behind his ear in the examination room? Why else would he have cut open those men's faces in exactly the same place? Why else would he have found strange metallic substances near the skulls of fossils millions of years old?"

"He could have been making it up Evan. I think it's clear he seems taken with you for some reason. He could have been contriving this whole thing just to mess with your head, since everywhere he's been, people mess with his. How many hospitals has he been in? Nine? Haven't you even considered the possibility that he was faking the whole ordeal in the examination room just to give more credence to his story?"

"All right, all right. I'll admit the possibility," I confessed begrudgingly. "But the only way to find out for sure is for us to go in and remove this thing and cut it open, and of course perform a biopsy on the tissue to be certain it isn't malignant."

"That's what this whole discussion is about isn't it? You want me to perform the surgery."

"Kathryn, if you don't whatever this thing Gottlieb described is in his head will disappear and you know it. It's the only way to prove whether or not he has been telling the truth, and if he has, than God have mercy on us. Think of it, Kate, something this huge, verifiable proof of an extra-terrestrial presence here on this planet, is the discovery not only of the century but of all humanity's existence!"

Kathryn exhaled loudly and stared daggers at me from across the table. I pressed on hoping I was making a dent in her seemingly inflexible shield.

"If Dr. Bailey performs the surgery he'll remove the tumor and send it to St. Mary's where it will go end up God knows where, and what do you expect the results will be? They'll come back and say, 'Congratulations, you are the proud owner of a vintage 1963 alien implant'? Come on Kathryn, be reasonable," I pleaded.

"You're asking me to not only risk my job but my career, one that I have worked very hard to establish, not to mention go against the expressed wishes of the hospital Director, and if you're right and this thing is inside of Gottlieb's head, stir up a hornet's nest the likes of which this hospital, not to mention this planet, has ever seen!"

"So you'll do it?" I said, grinning mischievously at her.

"Honestly Evan, I can't believe you sometimes!" she said laughingly while simultaneously tossing her napkin in my face where it fell onto my plate and into my mashed potatoes and gravy.

My attention was diverted momentarily to David Malcolm, who was sitting in his high chair making a mess of his Cheerios, and gurbling at me with an anxious tone.

"What's the matter, David?" I said.

My son's eyes slowly darted back and forth between Kate and I and I knew he was clearly distressed at witnessing us argue. He then picked up a handful of his Cheerios and, mimicking Kate, tossed them in my direction as they scattered across the table and dining room floor.

"Hey no fair!" I said. "Two against one!"

My son's face beamed with pride and he laughed while rubbing his infant hands covered in banana and Cheerio particles over his face.

Kate leaned over with a towel to wipe him while I continued the discussion.

"All right," I said. "If I'm right and this thing is not simply a benign tumor of the parotid gland, then Frank will have no choice to approach the board for an inquiry. He'll have too many witnesses and the evidence against him. We will not only have verifiable proof that what Gottlieb said is true, but proof of the greatest conspiracy ever known to mankind. It will be right there for him to see in full view. If I'm wrong, what's the worst thing that can happen?"

"You can lose your job, for one," she said, looking at me disapprovingly.

"Never happen," I said confidently. "We're too short staffed and Frank knows it. Why do you think he suspended me for only the rest of the week? That's one and a half days. I'll be assuming some of Stimple's case load when I return on Monday."

"I can't believe you're asking this of me," she fumed.

"Well come on, Kathryn, even if you forget the circumstances, irrespective of what it is you know, this tumor has got to come out. If you leave it in much longer eventually it could interfere with the functioning of the facial nerve, and some of it would have to be removed. And then, on top of everything else you'll have a patient with no motor control of the right side of his face, and you'll have that on your conscience as well."

"I doubt anything of that magnitude is going to happen between now and when Dr. Bailey performs the procedure on Tuesday."

I sighed heavily, audibly venting my frustration and leaned back in my chair, running my fingers through my hair and trying to pull some argument from my brain which could convince her.

"Kathryn, I know this man. I've interviewed a lot of patients under Howard and none of them is as cognizant and aware of themselves and their surroundings as he is. It is my belief that it is very possible he is innocent and telling the truth. If he is and we do nothing you'll have to live with it on your conscience for the rest of your life, and every time you look at another patient you're going to wonder and ask yourself whether or not it was possible that you made a mistake by not helping him. I can't live with that Kathryn. I won't."

I was wearing on her and I knew it. She had seemed suddenly a little withdrawn after this last argument and her expression had changed from one of diffidence to one hinting at genuine concern. This time it was she who released a begrudging sigh and looked at me with that beautiful, little pout expression I have come to adore in her. "What is it you propose?" she asked.

"Well, I've been thinking. Our facility doesn't have a proper laboratory on the premises to diagnose this thing, whatever it is. If we perform the procedure and send it to St. Mary's as usual, we'll be no better off than if Dr. Bailey performs the operation, because that's exactly what he would do. If they can't diagnose it, it gets sent somewhere, who knows. I'm not up to speed on where undiagnosed tumors get sent and what the protocol is, exactly."

"Right," she said, while nodding in agreement.

"Therefore, one of us needs to take this thing personally to a facility where it can be properly diagnosed and most importantly, monitor the process to be certain that if anything stellar, if you pardon the pun, is found."

"And how are we going to manage that?" she asked, somewhat exasperated.

"I've been thinking of Jeff."

"You mean Jeff & Melissa?"

"Yes. Last time I heard from him he was Director of the lab at Highland Park. I was thinking we remove it Friday night after Frank leaves, and I would leave with it packed on ice in a cooler soon after the surgery, drive all night, if necessary, and stay with Jeff and his wife Saturday night, and be back by Sunday evening. Once I get there and rest a bit, Jeff and I will cut this thing open and perform the biopsy and interior dissection."

"What if he's not there or on vacation or something?" she said cautiously.

"Oh, he will be," I said smiling at her with what I'm sure was a devilish sort of grin. "I called him this afternoon when I got home and arranged the whole thing."

A knowing, bitter scowl slowly crept across Kathryn's face.

"You mean you'd already arranged this whole thing without even consulting me, before I agreed to do it? Honestly, Evan, I don't know why I put up with you!" she said while simultaneously slinging a glop of potatoes at me with her fork, which I deftly caught in her napkin which was still lying on my plate.

David Malcolm then shrieked and giggled and threw some mashed banana at me, which clung to my forehead.

"It must be because you love me," I said with a wicked grin, wiping the banana from my face.

"It must be," she said, trying to conceal her laughter. "You're not still hot after Melissa are you?"

"Jesus, Kate, are you ever going to get over that? We had one date and that was before I even met you!" Melissa was a roommate of our mutual friend, Jonah, who went to school at RISD. Jeff, Jonah, and I were best friends in high-school and we gathered once a year during Spring Break to visit Jonah up in Providence. I tried to make a play for her the first time I went up there but the sparks didn't fly between us. Apparently they did for Jeff, as he ended up marrying her three years later.

"I know, I know," she said. "Still, you can't blame me for being just a little jealous."

We made love that night as if we both somehow instinctively knew it would be the last time, and as I held her in my arms afterwards she finally asked the question I had been both dreading and waiting for, and for which I had prepared myself earlier but found myself unready to answer now.

"Evan," she asked. "What if it is true? What if you discover there is some sort of alien implant inside this thing? What will you do?"

I stared at the ceiling trying to gather my thoughts.

"I'm not sure," I said. "I haven't really quite gotten that far. I only know this is something I *have* to do."

"But why?" she said pleadingly. "Can't you just do as Frank suggested and let Dr. Bailey perform the surgery? I've just got a really bad feeling about this."

"I can't Kate," I said, turning to look at her. She had propped herself up on her elbow and was curling her fingers around my chest hair. "I only know it's something I must do, something that I feel I was *meant* to do. I know it's strange, but I can't help it. I just feel, for lack of a better word, compelled by some force or something greater than I can understand. I feel it is as though it is my purpose for being here, on this earth, and that everything I have done or accomplished has been leading up to this moment. Haven't you ever felt that way?"

"No," she said flatly. "And I don't want to. Come on, let's get some sleep."

I nodded in agreement and put my arms around her, and it would be the last time that I would ever hold my beloved wife next to me.

We waited in the parking lot Friday evening until we saw Frank's Datsun Ladybird 240Z pull out of the gate. It was painted British racing green, and had mirrors on side mounts over the two front tire wells, and was imported from Japan, which meant, among other things, that the steering column was on the right side, and the odometer accounted for kilometers rather than MPH. He let me drive it around a few times when we would go out for lunch. It was a real eye-catcher, a 'ladies car' and I secretly wondered if it was the car that attracted Joan to him.

As he peeled off and left the gates of Grove Haven and rounded the corner, Kate and I exited our car, passed through the entrance and descended into the depths of the hospital. On our way to the Ward 3 checkpoint, we stopped by the infirmary for a gurney, and its wheels rattled and clattered and echoed off the hard tile corridor. All of the weekly staff had left early, as they tend to do on Friday's. Everyone that is, except for Sampson, who must have been pulling some overtime and he smiled at us as we approached the gate.

"I thought you were on leave, Doctor?" he said as he buzzed the first door to the man-trap open and we stepped in.

I looked down at my watch before responding.

"My leave ended at six o' clock. It is now six o' seven."

Sampson laughed while nodding. "Understood, Doc. Understood."

"Has everyone been fed yet?" I asked, hoping that we had not arrived too late. It would not be possible to operate if Dr. Gottlieb had eaten and had a full stomach.

"No. Vera should be up here shortly. She usually runs a bit behind on Friday's as she works her other job, but you didn't hear that from me. She'll whip me blue with that damned fly swatter of hers if she heard I'd told you that."

"Actually, Sampson, that's perfect, and if it should come up, tell her from now on I'd rather she be late on Friday's." I said jokingly, knowing full well what Sampson meant. Vera was a tough old lady and I certainly wouldn't want to be around when she was angry. Sampson buzzed the other gate open once the door behind us closed and we exited into the Class 3 cell block.

"Hold the door," I said. "We'll be back in a minute." I pushed the clattering gurney down the hall until we stood opposite Dr. Gottlieb's cell. "You can open her up now, Sampson." I shouted down the corridor.

"You don't want the straps?" he responded, sounding surprised.

I looked at Gottlieb who was looking at me blankly from his cot, clearly taken aback by what was going on.

"I don't think that will be necessary." I called.

"Dr. Sikes wouldn't like this, Doctor Stattler."

"Dr. Sikes isn't here now Sampson. Please open the door," I repeated.

Dr. Gottlieb smiled and looked up at me quizzically. "Another field trip, Doctor?" he asked, somewhat bemused by all this fuss.

"Something like that," I said smiling back. "We're going to take you down to the infirmary and have a look at that thing in your head."

"Oh, now I am intrigued. Do I get a treat if I've been a good little boy?" he said whimsically.

"*Only* if you've been a good little boy," I said winking at him.

Sampson buzzed the door to his cell and I pulled it open. Kate stood back behind me and eyed him suspiciously.

"Don't worry, Doctor," he said while rising from his cot. "I wouldn't want to miss out on my lollipop."

"Step right up, Doctor," I said smacking the center of the gurney. "And I don't even need to tell you, no funny business."

"Frankly, I'm insulted by the accusation, Doctor," he responded while climbing on. "Sampson informed me over dinner yesterday evening that you were on leave until Monday. I can only assume I was somehow the cause and that you're being here now makes our field trip a clandestine operation, of sorts ... no pun intended I assure you."

"I would have to say that you've hit the proverbial nail on the head, Doctor. Let's get going," I said. "Time is short."

He smiled and lay silent as we rolled the gurney down the hall of the cellblock. As we entered the mantrap I turned to Sampson. "If it's all right Sampson I'd like to call on you later, we may need some help getting him back into his cell."

"No problem, Doctor, I'll be here. Pulling a double today, need to pay off some of them Christmas presents."

"I hear you. I hear you," I said. "And Sampson, I'd appreciate your discretion in this matter."

"Dr. Stattler, I didn't hear or see nothin.' I was in the kitchen with Vera because she was laggin' behind."

"Thank you Sampson," I said, and he buzzed us through the gate once again.

We wheeled him down the corridor towards the infirmary and as we approached the door I decided to quiz our patient on his past medical history.

"Doctor, have you ever had an allergic reaction to Sodium Pentathol or any other anesthetic?"

"I don't know," he said, clearly concentrating. "I don't think I've ever been put under, except of course after they inserted the chip. They put some sort of oddly shaped mask over my face and then all went black."

"Then I'll take that as a 'no,'" I said, pushing the door open with the rear of the gurney.

"Get the EKG ready," Kathryn said, wasting no time as we entered the room.

"Right," I said. "Doctor, I'm going to unbuckle you now, can you still be a good boy and take off your shirt?"

"Of course," he said smiling. He removed his orange Grove Haven jumper top and lay back on the cot. Kathryn wheeled over the EKG and began to affix the sticky tabs onto his chest.

"They're not too cold, are they?" she asked, leaning over him while smiling.

"Mrs. Stattler, you amaze me," he said. "Here I've been consigned to cold dank cells at nine hospitals for twenty years and you're concerning yourself with my momentary discomfort."

"Just trying to perfect my warm bedside manner, Doctor," she said, smiling back at him. She looked at me and sighed. "Are we ready?"

"I'm loading the drip now," I said, adjusting the anesthetic and clearing the line of bubbles. "Here, you're the expert," I said, and wheeled it over to her. "I'll let you do the honors."

Kathryn prepared the syringe and needle to be inserted into Dr. Gottlieb's forearm.

"EKG looks good, all vitals are stable, BP one-twenty over eight-two. All right we're ready. Doctor, I'm going to count backwards from ten. I just want you to relax. Breathe in through your nose and out through your mouth."

He did as she had asked and said to her, "This facility is more impressive than I imagined, having such a fine staff and a lab on the premises."

"There is no lab, Doctor," I said. "I'll be personally delivering and escorting your tumor to a suburb of Chicago. An old friend of mine oversees the lab at Highland Park Hospital and I trust him."

He looked at me and his eyes widened in as though panic while simultaneously beginning to glaze. "Doctor, you must not ..." He didn't finish his sentence. He was under.

"All right, Doctor," Kate said looking at me. "No turning back now. Let's go to work."

The operation went smoothly. Kathryn was a real pro and from a clinical point of view it was a pleasure to see her work. She didn't ever let anything unexpected ruffle her cool demeanor, and I hardly recognized her from the feisty woman who had thrown mashed potatoes at me the evening before, and who screamed and twisted when we made love with the ferocity of a freight train. It was little wonder to me, then, as now, why I had married her.

"There you are," she said and I peered over her shoulder at the lump she was referring to. "Hand me that container there, will you?" she said, motioning with her elbow towards an elongated stainless steel bowl which sat on a tray next to her. I handed it to her and she removed the mass with a small pair of clamps and placed it neatly into the bowl.

"Interesting," she said.

"What's that?" I asked.

"It was hardly connected to any of the surrounding tissue. With the exception of a few threads it seemed to be just floating around in there."

I put the specimen in a plastic container I had brought with me and placed it in the Igloo thermos I had packed with ice before we left the house. It was amorphous in shape and multicolored in different shades of dark reds and browns and looked quite repugnant, and I was not sure how Kathryn could be so well detached from the whole procedure. I was always just a little bit squeamish when it came to this sort of thing, and I loathed dissecting cadavers at med-school, which I'm sure is why I was led to the field of psychology rather than internal medicine.

"Ok, I'm going to need your help now," Kathryn said as I finished stowing Gottlieb's tumor into the thermos. "Hold this drainage bulb and don't move it while I close him up."

I looked at the heart shaped bulb in my hand which had a tube leading from it which I held in place just in the back of his neck just below the right ear.

"Will he have to wear this long?" I asked. "It'll be a dead give away if anyone sees it."

"A few days. It should be able to come out by Monday morning. I'll have Sampson help me and check on him over the weekend while you're gone."

After about ten minutes of this she finally said, "Ok we're done here. You can take him off the drip while I get cleaned up." She let me release the drainage bulb which was firmly sutured into his neck and dangled next to the still unconscious Dr. Gottlieb.

"Thank you, Kathryn," I said looking at her adoringly.

"What do you mean?" she asked. "I'm your wife. You'd do it for me."

"That's not what I meant," I said. "My arm was killing me."

"Well, you know, Doctor, this is not how I'm accustomed to spending a Friday night either. You'll get no sympathy from me."

"I know," I said. "I'll make it up to you, I promise. Next year in Santorini."

"Santorini!" she exclaimed excitedly. "You know I've always wanted to go there. All right, I'll let you off the hook for now."

We waited around a bit for Gottlieb to regain consciousness before attempting to move him. I wanted to be certain he was all right before I left, and I needed Sampson's help anyway to get him back in his cell. He started to awake and moaned but his eyes were still shut, and he mumbled something in German which was barely audible.

"*Bewegt es night! Er wird es sehen! Er wird kommen! Er kann uns hören!*" He said, and he again seemed to slip into unconsciousness.

"What did he say?" I asked Kathryn who had a few years of German under her belt as an undergrad.

"Something about 'He will see it,'" she said unsure of herself. "Maybe 'He will come.' I'm not quite sure really, it's been a long time since I heard or studied it. I wouldn't worry about it though, when I had my appendix removed in my early twenties and was coming out of anesthesia, the Doctor who performed the procedure asked me to describe my father so that he could find him in the waiting room. Well, apparently I told him he was the 'man with the mustache.' Evan, my father hadn't had a mustache since I was nine years old! So I sent this poor man on a desperate search throughout the hospital until one of the nurses found him. Don't worry about it, he'll be fine. Why don't you call for Sampson and let's get him back to his cell. The sooner you're on your way the sooner you'll come back to me. I'll sit with him outside his cell until he fully recovers."

We wheeled Gottlieb, who continued to drift in and out of consciousness, down the corridor. Sampson was at the gate with Vera going over procedure on how to operate the man-trap.

"How'd it go?" he asked as we approached.

"Smooth as a baby's bottom," I said. "Are we ready?"

"Sure thing, Doc, Vera can handle it, can't you darlin'?"

"Don't you 'darlin'' me Mistah Sampson Brown!" Vera said defensively, shaking her head with her hands on her hips with one palm around the fly swatter she always carried. "Or I'll put your black ass over my knee and give you a whuppin' you won't soon forget."

Vera was a feisty old woman of African American descent who was well into her sixties and came in on weekends to prepare meals for the inmates. She was a tiny little woman, maybe four foot ten at the most, and full of vigor; but what she lacked in height she made up for in ferocity. She grew up in Alabama during the height of all the evils of Jim Crow and the civil-rights riots, and quite rightly had an enormous chip on her shoulder she let everyone else know about. I had only seen and spoken with her a few times as I too, would usually try to leave early on Friday, but as far as I could tell all of the hospital staff, even Frank, tiptoed around her, not only out of genuine respect, but for fear of her forked tongue and flyswatter which would strike out at you as soon look at you.

The thought of poor little ninety pound Vera putting Sampson, who was probably near three hundred pounds, over her knee and swatting him made all of us laugh, most probably because of the seriousness with which she said it.

When he stopped laughing Sampson said, "I think that's a 'yes', Doctor."

I smiled at her as we entered the man-trap and she glared at us coldly with the whites of her eyes as though her buzzing us through the gate was the greatest inconvenience one could think of or possibly imagine. She thumbed the controls of the gate slowly, but steady and deliberate, and as it buzzed open we wheeled Dr. Gottlieb down to the entrance to his cell.

"9A, Vera!" Sampson shouted down the corridor, and again came the familiar buzz of the door.

"Ok, let's prop him up a little," said Kate as she piled up extra pillows which she had taken from the infirmary at the head of his cot.

"Ok, Sampson, you take the front and I'll take the back."

"Sounds just fine, you just say when, Doc," he said.

"Ok, on three. One, two ..." and we groaned as we lifted him from the gurney and lowered him down onto his bed. I pushed the gurney out and the three of us exited his cell. Kathryn unfolded the chair that was resting against the wall that I usually used and sat in it.

"I'll wait here until he fully recovers. You go on to Chicago," she said.

I strode over and leaned down to kiss her, feeling her soft supple lips beneath mine.

"Be careful, Evan," she said.

"Don't worry, I will. I'll be back before you know it."

"9A, Vera," Sampson shouted down the corridor again as Vera from the booth electronically locked his cell. Sampson tested the door, and when he was satisfied it was secure and she had completed the process properly he turned to me.

"After you, Doc," he said, motioning for me to precede him.

As Vera checked us once more through the gate she exited the operators booth and with her flyswatter started whacking Sampson.

"Do you think I'm so auld an' stupid that I cain't member one '9A' from da odda?" she said while continuing to strike him with the swatter.

"I was just makin' sure, Vera! I just wanted to be sure you get it right, that's all," said Sampson, while attempting to block her whacking.

"Well, I'll getchu right!" she said, swatting him again.

For safety's sake I decided to stay out of it.

"Sampson, I'll see you Monday."

"Yes, sir, Doctor Stattler, Monday," he said while stepping up into the booth with Vera still hot on his heels.

"Would you get away from me woman with that damn swatter?" he said, half laughing and half annoyed.

Vera turned and angrily glared at me, her eyes widening. "God-damn people don sho' any respeck no mo,'" she said.

CHAPTER 12

Sarah Dawson

"Your daughter?" I said incredulously. "How is that possible?"

"You're a physician Doctor; I would suspect that you are more familiar with the intricacies of human reproduction than I, despite my training and upbringing."

I frowned at him showing my displeasure at stating the obvious.

"You *know* what I meant."

He smiled at my annoyance and feigned ignorance.

"How old is she? When did it happen? Was it part of some genetic experiment like you were or do you actually have a human soul?" I asked with a smirk, quite pleased at myself for my quick retort.

He suddenly became very serious and while leaning forward said almost in a whisper, "It is *imperative*, Doctor, that *they* do not discover her presence. If they discover her existence they will use her as they did me. I can not abide that. Just who she is and where she came from *must* remain a secret."

I nodded silently, as if I was going to expose myself and her anyway.

"I met her mother on September 23rd 1961, in the town of Whitefield, New Hampshire. I was there on assignment for an *Initial Contact* encounter that took place several days earlier on the evening of the 19th."

"What was your assignment?"

"On September 21st our organization was contacted from officials at Pease Air Force Base and the National Investigations Committee on Aerial Phenomena, or NICAP for short, who had apparently documented stories from an interracial couple who claimed they were abducted and subjected to experiments by extra-terrestrials. As you can well imagine this raised many eyebrows and it was essential an investigation be dispatched to determine what ramifications this might have towards maintaining secrecy. It was determined that an operative with, how should I put it, *expertise* with this sort of thing be dispatched, and that I would head this investigation and therefore was sent to the scene."

"What were your orders?"

"If at all possible, whenever an IC takes place an agent is sent to the site after the encounter to make certain no evidence or Gray technology gets left behind at the landing site. A precise map of the coordinates is provided to us and we are sent to ascertain whether anything of relevance was left. It is in this way that we 'police' each other. The other reason we are sent is surveillance of the abductees, and if necessary, extermination. My assignment was determining just that, if extermination in the case of Barney and Betty Hill was warranted."

"Barney and Betty Hill," I said, again thinking out loud. "That was the UFO Incident; I saw the film with James Earl Jones."

"The very same," he said nodding as though in agreement.

"You know I have to say it's been interesting hearing about all these loose threads in history being connected to you. I can't help but partially wonder whether you're making it all up. It seems rather convenient you know."

"I'm sure, Doctor that I needn't remind you of the past twenty plus years you've experienced. Surely you don't need me to connect the dots," he said, grimacing somewhat before continuing. "It was my diagnosis that, as they had already contacted two officials at separate organizations, a low profile be maintained until more evidence could be gathered on their intentions. Within several days after their encounter the Hills contacted a Dr. Benjamin Simon, a Boston psychiatrist who specialized in treating personality disorders and amnesia through hypnotherapy."

"What did you do? I mean, I know you didn't kill them, as I understand it Barney Hill died of a stroke sometime later."

"After much debate I decided that extermination, although effective, was not necessarily warranted in this case, and having someone with expertise discredit their story would suffice in the eye of the public. I met with Dr. Simon before he released his findings to the Hill's, and we had a *conversation*."

"You mean a bribe," I said.

"As it turned out no bribe or convincing argument was needed at all. As a psychiatrist yourself, and having been through the experience with Dr.

Gottlieb, I'm sure you realize the potential and danger to your professional reputation to support their story, at least in 1961. Had the Hill's account happened today you would have a line of psychiatrists willing to accept their claim, and in fact in some cases you do."

"Interesting, and I must admit I'm enjoying hearing the answers to pieces of history that have been shrouded in myth and secrecy, but what does this have to do with your daughter and your wife?"

"Quite right, Dr. Stattler, we do digress, but I assure you Sarah Dawson's mother was not my wife. We only had intercourse once. She worked as an overnight desk clerk in the town of Whitefield's only spot of accommodations, *The West Bend Motor Lodge*, located off of U.S. Highway 3 at the Whitefield Regional Airport Exit. It was in the office behind the desk that our encounter took place."

"It wasn't so much the specific place that your coupling took place I was chiefly interested in," I said wryly.

He seemed to ignore this comment and then continued, and what amazed me most was that the man who had hounded me for over twenty years, who was at one time, I believed, going to kill me, whose soul I was certain was as black and devoid of compassion as the eyes on his face, seemed to be idly reminiscing. He was clearly moved as he spoke, and he seemed to enjoy remembering the woman who at one time bore his child.

"She was a fragile creature, and she made me feel for the first time that I *was* human. All my life I had detested these beings I was protecting, these things called humans, which I never considered myself to be apart of. Being raised by them, fashioned by them, trained to destroy humans who might be a threat to them, and containing more of their DNA than any human on the planet, I thought of myself as what you call a Gray, unencumbered by emotion, ruthless, methodical, full of drive and purpose for existence. She touched something I did not believe I had, or could ever possess."

"What do you mean?" I asked hesitantly.

"She made me feel flawed, and I never thought that being flawed, could *feel* good. She was beautiful, with long black hair that stopped just below her waist, full red lips, a Reubanesque and tempting figure, and an intent, deliberate, and *wanting* gaze that stirred in me something I had never experienced before, and have not experienced since. She is the only woman I have ever loved, physically, mentally," he stopped for a moment and then continued almost whispering. "Emotionally."

"Whatever happened to her?" I asked.

"After that night I never saw her again," he said. "I could not allow myself to experience these feelings that she had unleashed. It's quite funny, actually, they were *alien* to me," and he laughed at this before continuing. "They were considered, beneath us, 'inappropriate' by my superiors. And more importantly, I could not further risk her detection by them. I could not allow her to fall into danger. I did keep tabs on her, however."

"Where is she now?"

"She is dead. She was killed six years after delivering the baby, by a drunken truck driver on Highway 3 while walking to her car. The baby, Sarah, was taken to live with her grand-parents in Coronado, just across the bay from San Diego."

"I'm sorry," I said empathetically, and what surprised me in that instant was that I meant it. I couldn't help wondering what a complex man Mr. Black was. On one hand, he was an assassin. He killed without pity, remorse, or want; it was a job to him, purely subjective. Yet at the same time, I could tell he genuinely loved the woman that was her mother, and I believed that he would do anything to protect the life of his child—anything which now included betraying the ones who made him.

"After her twenty-first birthday she entered a graduate program in the Biomedical Sciences Genetics division at the University of California, San Diego. It was after a lecture in her first semester that I introduced myself to her by handing her an envelope, in which I had asked her to meet me in a Mexican restaurant in the gas-light district. Also enclosed within the note I explained who I was, accompanied by my DNA profile, and that strict silence was of the utmost importance in order to maintain her and my safety. As I could not speak to her lest I reveal her presence our first meeting was difficult, and she was doubtful to say the least. She did not believe me, undoubtedly thought I was crazy, but that was only until she cross-checked my genetic analysis with hers at the university. The first few times we met was painstaking, as everything of course had to be written and passed between us, and then later destroyed.

"There was also the danger of arousing suspicion from my colleagues and superiors in accepting too many assignments to Southern California. It was she who actually came up with the idea of learning to speak sign language and we developed a Morse code of sorts using touch tones on public phones. Needless to say, when I was finally able to explain just who and *what* she was descended from she became," he stopped for a moment, quite obviously carefully considering his choice of words, "*distressed*. She wanted to know why I had sought her out, why I had told her the truth, and these questions I was not able to answer with any convincing argument as I did not know the answers myself. She would not see me, ignored my letters, and for the first time in my life I felt injured, not just because I had placed her at risk but because I hurt her."

"What happened then?"

"We did not speak for many years, and I tried to understand her reasons and give her the space she required and requested. It was too dangerous already, too many lives were at stake, and I did not wish for hers to be among them. It was not until two weeks ago, actually, when I knew what it was that I had to do, when I knew for certain the future I had seen so long ago was about to unfold, that we spoke together for the first time, unhindered, unmonitored, and uninhibited."

"When she removed the chip!" I said excitedly. The pieces of the puzzle were finally beginning to fall into place, and for the first time, though I knew it impossible, I felt as though the second sight *was* real, and I was experiencing it.

"Yes," he said in affirmation, barely moving his body or his lips. "You see, Dr. Stattler, like you, I am now 'on the lam', as they say. When Sarah removed the chip and I placed it into this vial my transmission was silenced. I was MIA, and they will be looking for me. In time, they will find me."

"How will they find you without the chip? For all they know you could be in China by now."

"They have ways, many ways of finding where I am. It is only a matter of time. There are satellites at our disposal, Dr. Stattler, which can photograph you taking a shower through the roof of your home. They will be watching, they will be looking."

I shuddered at this and wondered how I could possibly overcome the forces I was up against. He must have read my mind just then, because his next statement reminded me of one of the things that kept me going, that gave me strength and hope while I was running from him.

"Don't worry, Doctor, as someone very dear to me once said, 'It is the nature of truth to reveal itself.'

CHAPTER THIRTEEN

The Chase

The drive to Mount Prospect, a suburb north of Chicago, was long and tedious and I tried to pass the time by counting cars or road signs, or simply wishing Kate were here to that we could play 'pdiddle' and pull off somewhere every once in awhile, but I couldn't stay focused and my mind would invariably turn to the object in the cooler in the passenger seat next to me and what it might mean. What was it that Gottlieb tried to say when he first awakened? '*Er wird's sehen.*' *He will see.* What did it mean? I couldn't be sure, and I began to grow somewhat nervous and agitated as though some driven, malevolent force were pursuing me. *Hounding me,* like dogs on a scent.

Every once in awhile when the headlights behind me seemed to linger for too long I would pull off the road into a rest-stop or McDonalds, anything that was a public place, not that it would help anyway at that time of night, but they never seemed to follow. And the question also remained, who was *he,* anyway? Was *he* the man that Gottlieb described when he was under hypnosis? Was *he* the SS prison guard and, like Kate had suggested, a memory that spiraled out of his subconscious because of the anesthesia? It all seemed so surreal, and I think what led me on initially was the thought that it couldn't possibly ever be real. It was a hallucination or the acting out of some grand delusion.

But here I was, in the car, on my way to verify his claim. And I realized as I drove that long night for the first time that I was not only undertaking this clandestine operation to prove Gottlieb right—I was doing it to prove him wrong. For in proving him right, I would have no grasp on what reality had now become. I could not and did not even want to begin to fathom the lives and the burdens I would be undertaking if he was, in fact, telling the truth, and it was therefore essential to my sanity, everything I have come to believe in and everyone else's, that I prove him wrong. But there was also the moral complication of sacrificing his sanity for my own, and I had to ask the question, 'What makes the lives and sanity of everyone else greater than his? By what right do they have to exist, if his does not?' It made my head swoon. I realized for the first time in that long drive that I did not have all the answers. I didn't pretend to and the only thing I could rely on was my sense of duty as a physician and my conscience to protect the both of us. It was all I had. And what, in fact, would amount from this exercise I had no idea. But for the meantime, it seemed, contrary to my fears and agitation, I was not being pursued.

I longed to reach the safety of Jeff's house so that I could at last sleep and let the trials of the day, the operation, and the past week wash over my brain and subconscious. I knew I needed to awake in the morning focused, objective, refreshed, and with a clear strength of purpose I seemed to be lacking.

About six hours after leaving Grove Haven I finally reached the out-skirts of Mount Prospect where my friend Jeff Gould and his wife, Melissa, resided, and I found myself reminiscing about old times and was excited to see my friend. Jeff, Jonah, and I were the best of friends in high-school and we made it a point to get together at least once a year in Providence, as it was sort of central. Jeff was attending the University of Peoria in Illinois for his undergrad, while I attended Johns Hopkins in Baltimore for both my undergrad and post graduate studies. Every spring break Jeff and I would converge with Jonah at RISD and take Providence by storm. They were carefree days where we were in the prime of our lives, had no responsibilities or families to care for, and the future was limitless as was sometimes our intake of alcohol, and we were friends for many years.

Jonah was the first to fall from the group, to get married, start a career and have children. Both Jeff and I tried keeping up with him but I got the feeling that the lifestyle we represented, young, single, still pursuing our MD's and accustomed to reckless partying, was no longer what he wanted in his life. I can't say I blame him really. He married in July of 1976, right out of college, and I stopped trying to contact him once I met Kathryn, which was a shame as there were and are still times I miss him and think of our past friendship.

Fortunately, for Jeff and me, although we were in two completely differ-ent fields, we went through the latter half of med-school together so we had more in common in our adult lives than we did with Jonah. It is a shame, really, when friends grow apart as inevitably some always do, by the trivial banalities of life. Eventually we come to forget why we were friends in the first place, as though somehow we never were, and when we have at last forgotten why, we shrug off that time spent as wasted and without purpose.

I often think of and miss my friend, as I was never able to succumb to this simple truth of life that possessed him, and as I drove towards Jeff's house I found my thoughts turned again to that dear time the three of us would spend together in Providence. I wished we were all together again, if only for a brief moment, to celebrate and revel in the past, and maybe, if we happened to be drunk and inclined, to roll bowling balls down the bus tunnels of College Hill.

I had not been to their new house, which they purchased shortly after relocating to the Chicago area, and it took me about thirty minutes to find the place in the dark, fumbling through my directions and slowing down trying to read the road signs. When they purchased the property five years ago it was extremely run down and in serious disrepair. It was originally constructed in 1910, and in its hey-day was no doubt one of the most majestic homes in Mount Prospect. Melissa received her degrees both in architecture and art history while attending Rhode Island School of Design, so apparently after they purchased the property she went wild restoring the place.

In little more than three years she restored the property to its former glory; even chiseling out paint chips off the siding so that she could match paint samples to the original colors. It was quite stately, and had just enough Victorian flourish to give it some character. It had a turret that rose with circular bay windows on the east side of the house, with a white wrap around porch whose lattice work matched the honeycomb in the eaves. I remember I was loathe to show Kate pictures of it as I knew it would make our two-story rambler seem abysmal by comparison. But with Jeff's salary they could easily afford such elaborate renovations and they could probably buy our property seven times over.

I had to give Jeff credit though. He worked hard, extremely hard, averaging twelve to fourteen hour days five days a week. He was usually in the lab at five in the morning, as apparently that's when all the samples from the previous day were ready to be cut and prepared for testing, and often times he would not leave until six or seven in the evening. I knew this must have put some strain on he and Melissa's relationship, but she seemed to content herself by spending her days finding new ways to restore and improve the house, or on minor architectural projects. Jeff wrote to me that there were days he would come home and the entire color scheme for the first floor would have changed, though I'm sure he must have been exaggerating to some degree.

When I finally pulled into their driveway it was almost 3a.m. I had been on the road for nearly six hours and was awake for nearly twenty-four, so I was pretty exhausted. I knocked on the door and Jeff answered, unshaven and in his undershirt.

"Hey," he said sleepily, opening the door to let me in, and without further word plodded up the stairs and back to bed.

"Where should I put my things?" I yelled after him in a loud whisper.

"Second door, right," he said and kept going without turning around or stopping.

I didn't bother to ask him whether or not I could use the phone, and I fumbled my way in the dark to the kitchen so that I could call Kathryn and tell her I made it there safely. While I was there I cleared some room on the top shelf of the refrigerator and put the cooler inside. Hopefully, Melissa wouldn't open it as it might ruin her appetite for breakfast. After I called Kathryn who hung up with a sleepy 'I love you, honey', I got my bag and clambered up the stairs and into the room Jeff had indicated, threw off my clothes and climbed under the warm down bedding and quickly surrendered to my body's longing for sleep.

I did not wake up until nearly half-past noon, and though I was appreciative that they did not get me up, I rather wished I had gotten up a little earlier to get a start on the day. After I shaved and got cleaned up with fresh clothes I made my way down the antique staircase, which due to the hour and my grogginess I did not take the time to notice when I first arrived. It looked to be made entirely of rosewood, with the exception of walnut spindles and a mahogany banister, and there were little triangular plaques on the outside face of each step and polished brass dust catchers in the corners. Ordinarily I would think that the different contrasts of wood and everything else might be a little overkill, but here the pattern flowed quite nicely. As I came to the bottom of the staircase I noticed Melissa sipping coffee and reading the paper by the light of the bay window.

"Is that rosewood?" I asked, and she looked from her paper at me for the first time.

"Evan, darling, how are you!" she squealed, and came over to give me a hug. At this moment Jeff emerged from the kitchen carrying a coffee pot.

"You still trying to steal my wife?" he asked jokingly.

"I'm not trying to steal her, just borrow her for a little bit," I said and then turned to Melissa who had just released me from her arms. "So you're sleeping in my room tonight?" I asked mischievously.

"You guys!" she said smacking my chest. "Honestly Evan, you'll never change, that's what I like about you."

"So why didn't you go out with me instead of this clown?" I said winking at Jeff.

"Must be his size fourteens," she said, snuggling down into her chair and nuzzling Jeff who had come over beside her and kissed her while refilling her coffee.

"So what brings you to Chicago, Evan? Jeff says it's 'hush hush' and won't tell me anymore."

"Something like that," I said calmly, while coming over to shake Jeff's hand.

"How are you old friend?" I asked, and he reached out his arms to hug me, still carrying the coffee pot.

"It's good to see you," he said. "Have you heard anything from Jonah?"

"No. I got a Christmas card, I think, five years ago or something like that.

"Shame that. We sure had some times together, didn't we?"

"We sure did," I added laughing, attempting to suppress some of the ludicrous memories that came into my head.

"I see that you've brought us something for lunch. Where's it from?" he asked inquisitively.

"The parotid gland of one of my patients."

"Ahhh, yes, the parotid gland," he said thinking out loud. "I had it pegged as being from the lymph nodes, you typically see that sort of size and discoloration. I was hoping you wouldn't mind if a snatched an early peek."

"Not at all," I said. "That's why I'm here. Is the hospital far?"

"'Bout ten minutes. Don't you want to sit down, grab something to eat? You must be hungry?" he asked, motioning toward the table and empty chairs next to Melissa. "So we can all catch up?"

"Let's catch up at dinner," I said. "I'd feel better relaxing once we got this over with. I'll snack on a bagel or something on the way."

"Fair enough. Just give me a second to grab my coat."

"Anything special you two want for dinner?" asked Melissa, who was looking up at me with a beautiful pair of baby blues.

"Believe me when I tell you, Melissa, there isn't anything of yours I wouldn't eat," I said trying to suppress my laughter.

Melissa just rolled her eyes while blushing and Jeff looked on and laughed while his wife turned three shades of red.

The lab at Highland Park Hospital where Jeff worked as Director was on the main floor and as it was mid-afternoon on a Saturday was mostly empty except for a few staffers coming in now and again to check and return samples to the vault. I set the cooler containing the lump of tissue from Dr. Gottlieb down on the counter and took in my surroundings. In addition to the vault, which held all the slides of patients by case number, there were several large machines, the names and purposes of which I had not seen since med-school.

"Let's get started, shall we?" Jeff said, and he opened the cooler and removed the plastic container that held the tumor Kate had so expertly removed the evening before. He continued, educating me through the process of what it was he was about to do. "Now normally, this procedure would run somewhat different than the route we're going to take, but since we're pressed for time, we're going to perform the expedited version."

"Different, how so?" I asked curiously, trying to suppress the feeling of apprehension that washed over me as soon as I set foot in the lab.

"Well, in most cases before a tumor is removed from the body the acting physician knows full well whether or not it is malignant or benign, either through the use of a CAT scan or a fine needle aspiration."

"Yes, well, whether it is malignant or benign is really secondary to why I'm here, but, I'll get to that later. Kate tried an aspiration and couldn't penetrate it. The CAT results were inconclusive."

Jeff nodded and continued. "In some cases, such as yours, the test to determine malignancy or what in fact this is can not be performed until after the specimen has been removed, thus we find ourselves here today, but I'll get to that in a minute. Normally we would take the specimen and put it in this machine here, which replaces water within the cells with paraffin so that we can have a durable, solid mass in order to cut a slide. This process takes twenty-four hours, after which time we'll take the sample and place it in this machine here, called a microtome, which takes a very thin slice of it, approximately five microns or one one-thousandth of a millimeter thick to be exact." He lead me over to the device, which had what looked like a large, very thin razor blade on the top and several black knobs protruding from the base.

"After this is completed, we would deparffinize the sample and stain it to further isolate and identify the proteins and nucleic acids. Here," he said, and motioned towards a microscope. He then removed several slides from the vault which was really nothing more than a large metal storage cabinet with many sets of drawers, sort of like a dresser for medicinal specimens. He placed one under the microscope, looked into it and focused it, and then motioned for me to have a look. "The pink stains in the samples are Eocins, the purple are nucleic acids," he said over my shoulder as I studied the specimens.

"Interesting," I said, and then continued. "Now since we're not going the long route, what exactly is it that we're going to be doing."

"Yes," he said. "Let's say that, as in your case, a diagnosis of the material was not possible, you're in the OR and need immediate results." Jeff led me over to the opposite end of the room and removed the tumor from the container and set it on a plastic board and took a scalpel from a sterilized set of instruments. My heart began to tremor as he prepared to dissect it, and I felt my pulse quicken and perspiration begin to bead my forehead.

"First, you bread-loaf it," he said, while making a slow incision down the middle of the tumor. "Tough little bugger," he said again.

"What is it? What do you mean?" I said hastily.

"Calm down, calm down," he said. "It's nothing serious. Under the attached tissue here there seems to be a calcite formation of some kind. It's not uncommon and happens over time. Lipids and calcite from the blood-stream begin to clot and stick to the tumor, which can give it a hard shell. I've seen it before. To determine malignancy, what we'll do is take a sample of tissue and put it in the cryostat over there, which freezes it and there is a microtome inside the cryostat, which cuts and prepares the slide. It may take a little while to get to the center of this thing, but we can have an analysis of the tissue within minutes. Malignant cells are invasive and usually have a pattern that can easily be recognized. As for this calcite formation," he said, having completed circumnavigating the outside tissue and removed a round, greenish-white mass about the size of a nickel which he held in the air with a small pair of clamps.

"I'll prepare an acid bath which you can monitor while I prepare the sample in the cryostat." He then took a steel bowl from underneath the counter where he initially sliced open the tumor, filled it with hydrochloric acid, and immersed the calcified deposit into it. It began to bubble and hiss like a cauldron, and I couldn't help but to be reminded of Dr. Gottlieb acting out his strange scenario with the witches, while cackling, 'tis true! Tis true!' I heard his voice echoing inside my head, and I prayed the mystery of Dr. Gottlieb would be solved, here and now, as a paranoid-delusional schizophrenic with psychotic tendencies, a monstrous murderer with a keen intellect and gross imagination.

After about fifteen minutes Jeff had finished preparing the slide and was observing it under the microscope. "Well, it's not malignant," he said, sauntering over, trying to lift my spirits. "Bit of good news, anyway?"

"Well, I'm sure that Dr. Gottlieb will be happy to hear that," I said dourly, my mind still distracted by what might lay in the bottom of that steel bowl on the counter.

"Evan, I don't mean to pry, but what's got you so spooked anyway? Ever since you set foot in the lab you've been behaving, well, apprehensive, sort of withdrawn. You've hardly said a word. Is everything all right?"

"I don't know," I said.

"Come on; let's have a look at that calcite formation." Jeff picked up the clamps which lay on the counter and dipped them into the bowl which had stopped bubbling and was murky with residue. He pulled them out slowly and tapped them on the edge of the bowl, so as not to drip acid on the counter or floor.

When he turned around his face was ashen, as though he had seen a ghost. Clasped in between the delicate tweezers was a small, gray little ball approximately the size of a pea.

"No. Everything is not all right," I said.

"I know," he said nodding. "We can't talk here. It's not safe."

We drove in silence to McKinley Park, and my mind raced and wondered at what would happen, now that the proverbial genie was out of the bottle. What was I going to do? I had carefully planned all the possibilities and ramifications leading up to this point, but as for preparing myself for the contingency that what Dr. Gottlieb was telling me in all of our sessions was now turning out to be real I had no answers. I didn't believe it. I didn't want to believe it. Yet, at the same time, my conviction and faith in him was strong enough to risk my career. 'Why did I not plan for this?' I kept asking myself. He had told me, questioned me, and he knew from the very beginning that he was going to tell me. Undoubtedly that was why he had drilled me so much about religion that first day—he knew a religious mind was a closed mind.

A religious mind was a mind whose faith could not be shaken or stirred even when confronted with evidence to contrary. It would never believe, could never believe, and would never accept the possibility that the truth, no matter how glaring or blatant, what Dr. Gottlieb had seen and experienced and eventually would unveil to me, was real. Gottlieb knew the secret he had been keeping for over twenty years was of such a magnitude it could subvert everything humanity in the last two-thousand years has come to believe in, and that required an open mind, a mind that would consider what he was relating was, at the very least, a possibility.

Indeed, had I never met with him and Dr. Stimple never had the unfortunate mishap he did with James Grant and the end of a pencil, he would probably have never told his story at all. He would have sighed and performed the status quo of a psychotic paranoid schizophrenic, much as he probably had done in the other eight hospitals he had been to, while at the same time mentally frustrating his physicians as much as they frustrated him with their questions and theories concerning his behavior.

As I pulled the car into a parking place and we walked towards a bench that stood next to an exercise path, behind which was a clearing and a small group of trees, my mind turned the events over and over, searching for some clues as to the course I should next pursue. We sat down and let several minutes and joggers and cyclists pass before I worked up the courage to ask Jeff what I had seen in his face and suspected back at the laboratory as he held the strange gray object which I now had in a plastic vial in my coat pocket.

"You've seen this thing before," I said, more as a statement than a question.

"Yes," he said. "The first time was nearly five years ago. Back in seventy-eight. It was during my internship at the lab. I was working under Dr. Perry then, who was the Director," he continued, leaning back with his face up towards the sun.

It was a beautiful day. One of those rare May days where the temperature by noon had reached above seventy, the sky was a clear blue and nearly cloudless and full of warmth; everyone was out reveling in the spring and the bulbs were beginning to burst forth from their cocoons in a celebration of life.

"I was about to begin a diagnosis on a tumor that had just been removed from the operating room and was sent down to the lab for immediate testing in the cryostat. As I had finished slicing it open and was selecting a sample to put in the machine and the microtome, something odd caught my eye. A strange glimmer or twinkle of some sort reflected off the overhead fluorescent lights from *inside* the tumor. Its dimensions and configurations matched exactly the object which you now possess."

I removed the chip in its container from my pocket and looked at it. After we cleaned it in the acid bath, its surface was smooth and unblemished and it reflected the sun brightly through the plastic vial in which I now beheld it, and I had to catch my breath and consciously calm down my nerves as the premise finally began to take root that the object I now held was manufactured by extra-terrestrials, *aliens* from another world.

"Where was it from?" I asked.

"Your guess is as good as mine," Jeff replied.

"No," I said. "I mean the tumor, what part of the body was it from?"

"One of the lymph nodes I think. I don't rightly recall; I'm not sure. I do remember, though that it was taken from a small boy, maybe twelve. Being new I asked Dr. Perry if he had ever seen anything like it, and he simply took it and said that it didn't matter, and that he would send it out for further analysis. Since then I've come across maybe a dozen of them, in men and women, all ages, all races. There doesn't seem to be any discrimination in the hosts of these things, whatever they are, at least none that I can see."

I exhaled a deep sigh before pressing on, the heart of my fears being more and more exposed the further we dug and the further we went.

"You said that Dr. Perry took it and sent out for further analysis, that you have also discovered more of these things. What did you do with them? Where do you send them?"

A young female jogger approached obviously enjoying the day, her ripe, firm breasts bouncing in tune with each of her steps as she trotted briskly along, and we both watched and waited for her to pass before going any further with our discussion. After she had passed, Jeff continued.

"Any time any hospital or lab in this country can't identify something, either in the lab, through experience of the acting physicians, or through textbooks, whether it's one of those things," he said motioning toward the chip in the plastic vial in my hand, "or some incongruous or inconclusive tissue sample, the procedure is that it usually gets sent off to the AFI."

My heart quickened and shuddered as I asked with trepidation the next inevitable question. "And what, exactly, is the AFI?"

"The Armed Forces Institute of Pathology, of course. Anything and everything that is found that can't be readily identified through pathologists at every hospital in this country and at U.S. military bases around gets sent there. It's the largest repository for medicinal knowledge in the world. Nearly every doctor or pathologist knows that."

"Jesus Christ," I said, leaning my face over into my hands. "It's true. Of course it's true. It all makes sense now. They're in on it too. They know. They've known all along. They know *everything*."

"Christ, Evan, what is it? What's got you so spooked?" Jeff asked, clearly concerned about my bizarre behavior.

"Don't you see Jeff, if these things are sent to the military then that means they know that they have a record of everyone who's been abducted and had their implants removed? They know if you've been taken," I said, realizing for the first time the horror and thoroughness of the enemy I now found myself up against.

"Taken by whom?" Jeff asked, obviously completely unaware of the ramifications of our discourse. "I always assumed they were part of some secret military operation or testing vehicle of some sort, perhaps for new pathogens or antibodies. I mean, that's where we were sending them after all."

"Why didn't you say anything?" I said desperately and began to shake him. "Why didn't you come forward?"

"Come forward to what?" he said, pushing me away. "And even if I had reason to come forward I wouldn't for the same reason that no one else would, Evan. It's a career killer! I didn't bust my butt to go through med-school and get this far in my life only to blow the whistle on some military operation I know nothing about, and which very well could be intent on saving lives. And besides, just who could I tell and what would I tell them? That I found strange metallic spheres inside the bodies of U.S. citizens? It could be anything, Evan, some strange deposit from years of drinking tainted water or who knows what," he said defensively.

"I know what," I said somberly, and as he looked at me for the first time since we sat down I now detected the slight glimmer of fear in his eyes.

"What do you mean, you know what?" he asked. "Does this have something to do with why you're here? Do you know what these things are?" he said, his voice clearly becoming agitated.

"They're implants, Jeff," I said.

"Well, I gathered that from your discussion," he said, his voice patterns now clearly stressed.

"They're implants, put there by extra-terrestrials. *Aliens*, Jeff."

"And who told you that? This *patient* of yours? Jesus, Evan, maybe you're the one that needs to see a shrink," he said, turning away from me, clearly in denial as I once thought I was.

"He was an archaeologist, Jeff. And he found them; found devices similar to these in or near fossils of many early hominids as well as excavated caves and villages all over the world. He believes, and I am now forced to agree, that they are put in humans to serve as tracking devices of some sort."

"Tracking devices?" he turned and looked at me, clearly anxious and worried. "For what?"

Before I could answer I heard a strange, 'swooshing' type sound, and Jeff fell face forward from the bench and onto the paved foot path in front of us, his body convulsing and going into spasms.

"Jeff!" I screamed, and as I rushed down to turn him over I felt the familiar wet stickiness of blood between my fingers. I rolled him over so that I could begin CPR, but there was only a large, semi-circular exit wound where his face used to be. I gasped and recoiled as I could see *inside* of his head, and into his jaw, and bits of his nose and head spurted blood into the air and some hung from strands of sinew still attached to his face.

"JEFF!" I screamed again, and I heard the sound of bullets ricocheting and saw cement chips flying from the right concrete post that supported the wood of the bench, opposite of which was my head. Instinctively I ducked, and through the trees in the clearing behind the bench I saw two men in dark suits and sunglasses, weapons drawn and running directly toward me. Judging by the length of their guns and the fact that I heard no report either from the bullet that killed Jeff or the other shots I gathered there to be silencers attached to the end of their pistols. I did not wait for the two men to get any closer. I ran for cover, having no choice but to leave Jeff, still twitching on the ground behind me in the last throes of death.

I dodged in front of other bikers, runners, and people exercising on the path as I headed toward the parking lot. I hated to use them as human shields but didn't have time to much care. By now I could hear their footsteps plodding heavily in the distance behind me, as they had undoubtedly reached the hard, asphalt surface of the path. I heard screams from behind me, mostly from women, and I ran as fast as my legs could carry me toward the parking lot, and once I reached my car, threw the door open and launched myself inside.

The two men, who were still in pursuit, must have stopped to fire off a couple of shots once I reached the car, as I heard and saw the sound of metal being struck by several multiple projectiles on the door to my left which was still open. I reached out, slammed the door, and kept my head down as I started the engine, threw the car into full reverse, not even looking to see who or what was behind me. As I sped out of the parking lot, through the rearview mirror I could see the two men with their pistols, straight-armed and firing at my vehicle. Several bullets whizzed passed me, and I heard the crash of the rear windshield come flying into the passenger cabin in a barrage of little bits.

Only once I was clear and on the highway back to Jeff's house was I able to gather my senses about what just happened, where I should go and what I should do next. 'Think dammit!' I said out loud to myself. I knew I had to get off the highway. I knew those men would be pursuing me. I knew that a pock-marked seventy-three Buick with no rear wind-screen looked at the very least suspicious. I had to get to Jeff and Melissa's. I had to take their car. But where? Those men had somehow tracked me.

And then it occurred to me. Tracked me, no doubt, through Gottlieb's chip in my jacket pocket! I was trapped. It was the only piece of evidence besides a convicted psychotic killer's testimony that I had, and it was also the very thing that alerted and drew these forces that had just killed Jeff to me. If I abandoned it or threw it out the window I might very well escape them for now, but when the authorities came, as eventually they would, to question me about what had happened to Jeff, not only would I not have the chip, but those two men who were undoubtedly working for the government in some fashion would find me anyway. There had to be a way; a way I could retain the evidence and escape with my life intact.

I drove frantically to Jeff's house, trying to think of something, anything that I could hastily make or fashion to somehow prevent or mask the chip from transmitting its locator signal. Finally, I pulled in front of the house and raced up the steps and pounded on the wooden and stained glass door. "Please let her be here!" I shouted at the house as I continued to hammer on the door. "MELISSA!" I screamed. Finally the door opened and Melissa had a somewhat agitated and annoyed look on her face until she saw that it was me.

"Evan, honey, what's wrong?" she said, "Where's Jeff?"

I said nothing, but merely held up my hands still covered in Jeff's blood.

"You're bleeding!" she screamed hysterically and then retreated to the kitchen with me trailing behind her.

"Melissa, wait!" I called after her, and she turned around to face me after grabbing a roll of paper towels from the counter.

"I'm fine," I said, trying to calm the situation which I knew was to be a bad one.

"Ok," She said. "Where's Jeff? Where's my husband?" she demanded, this time angrily.

I could barely get the words, "Melissa, I'm so sorry," out of my mouth before she read my expression and knew that he was gone.

"WHAT HAPPENED?" she screamed hysterically. "WHERE IS HE?"

"He's gone, Melissa," I said flatly. "We were in McKinley park when from a clearing of trees behind us two men shot him. I tried to give him CPR, but he was gone Melissa, it was a head wound. There was nothing I could do. I had to get out of there before they killed me too."

"NOOOOOO!" she screamed. "This can't be happening. This can't be HAPPENING! I had just gotten back from the store," she said sobbing. "I was just about to make dinner. I even got a great bottle of wine, Bordeaux, Jeff's favorite," she said, as tears trickled down her face and onto the kitchen counter below her.

I looked into the dining room where I saw the solitary bottle she had mentioned sitting on a coaster in the middle of an elaborately dressed table. 'The wine. The wine.' I said to myself. "That's it!" I cried aloud, remembering my chemistry just then and it probably saved my life.

I ran over to the table and, with a butter knife I took from one of the place settings, frantically began to peel off the led foil covering the top of the bottle.

"WHAT ARE YOU DOING?!" Melissa screamed at me hysterically. "We need to call someone, we need to ..."

"STOP IT, Melissa!" I interrupted her, trying to calm her down. "You don't understand what those two men were after. They were after this!" I said, removing the plastic vial from my coat pocket and shaking it in front of her. "There's no time to explain, but if I'm correct, the led foil from this wine bottle should block its signal."

"What are you talking about!" she screamed again. "WHERE IS MY HUSBAND???"

I didn't answer her as there was literally no time to lose or spend wasting in a discussion. Those men would be here soon and when they found us they would kill us both and take the chip. I opened the container and wrapped the chip in the foil I removed from the 1976 Pichon LaLalande until it tightly covered it in a mashed, mold-covered black led-ball. I put it back into the plastic vial and sealed it, returning it to my pocket. I walked resolutely over to Melissa, who by this time was curled in a ball and sobbing on the floor. I knelt down and tried to console her while holding her firmly.

"Melissa," I said. "Jeff's car keys. Where are they?"

She didn't answer.

"WHERE ARE THEY?" I said, shaking her and raising my voice, trying to penetrate her grief and bring her to her senses but she still didn't answer.

"Every moment that you don't answer is a moment that those men draw closer!" I shouted at her. "And when they get here, they will kill us both. Is that what you want? His car keys, WHERE ARE THEY?" I demanded.

"On the dresser, in our room." she said, sputtering her words between tears and sobs.

I ran up the gilded rosewood staircase to their room and looked about for the dresser. They were, just as she said, in a large green-glass ashtray filled with foreign coins, cufflinks, and other small curios sitting on top of his bureau. I looked around and grabbed her purse, which was sitting on a chair next to their bed and returned downstairs. Melissa was still sitting in the middle of the kitchen floor, dazed and staring. I knelt down next to her and gently touched her shoulder.

"Melissa, honey," I said. "I need you to listen to me now. I need you to get out of this house. Those men could be here any minute. They must know I am here. I need you to drive to a safe place," I said, and placed her purse down on the floor next to her. "I need you to go to the police, a friend's house, the movie theater, somewhere, anywhere but here. You've got to leave now!" I said, practically shouting at her. But she just sat there, as though in a trance, and I knew I couldn't wait for her to come out of it. I rose from the floor next to her and headed for the front door and was about to open it when I saw a black, Crown Victoria pull up in the driveway in front of the house through the stained glass of the door. I ran back to Melissa, still on the floor.

"Melissa! They're coming!" I screamed. But she didn't respond, just slowly rocked herself to and fro, her arms wrapped about her knees, sobbing and trembling. I heard someone began to fumble at the door knob which I had locked once I saw their car. I then heard a swift kick, and then another pounding at the door and I did not linger to see the faces of my attackers. I went out through the kitchen door as fast as my legs would carry me, as I heard the wood from the frame splinter and the front door burst open behind me in the hall.

I ran across the back of their yard to the garage house, opened the door and turned on the light. There were two cars inside, a Mercury station wagon, which was still warm and crackling from Melissa's trip to the store, and what looked to be a restored 1967 Jaguar coupe convertible, painted jet black with chrome mirrors and fixtures. Little doubt of which was Jeff's car, and as the reality of my situation struck me I wished it was Melissa's keys I had taken and not Jeff's, as her car was much less apt to draw attention than his. A single shot that echoed across the yard from inside the house helped remind me of the perilous ness of my predicament, and I opened the garage door, got inside, started the Jaguar, and peeled off their property as fast as I was able.

CHAPTER FOURTEEN

Caught

I drove non-stop for three hours desperately trying to sort out the events of that afternoon out in my head, but in vain. He was gone, my longtime and dear friend Jeff, and his wife, Melissa too. Gone because of me. Killed and murdered before my eyes in cold blood because of me and my stubbornness, my insolence, my pride in what I thought was the truth. But the truth of it was, it didn't matter what the truth actually was, it was only what we wanted to believe. I never imagined, not even in my wildest musings first inspired by Dr. Gottlieb, that this would be happening to me now, and as I pondered the future as to what my Fate would be, it looked severely grim.

There were forces now pursuing me. Hunting me. Intent on killing me. Government forces they must be, to kill so brazenly in the broad daylight of a public place no less, they obviously feared no reprisals or consequences. They were, quite clearly, above them. Only an agency that feared no one or no thing could be responsible, and that smelled and reeked of the secret government forces Dr. Gottlieb hinted at. I could only hope that my wrapping the chip in the led foil from the wine bottle was enough to shield it from whatever it was that somehow transmitted my whereabouts, and would hopefully buy me some time.

If what Gottlieb said were true, which it now appeared it was, then this thing was, in fact, sending a signal that alerted this agency. My taking it out of Gottlieb's skull at Grove Haven and driving it across state lines must have alerted whoever was now chasing me that it was either no longer inside Dr. Gottlieb, or that he had somehow escaped and was on the run. I thought about this for a few moments before the dark truth dawned upon me. And if that were true, then undoubtedly that would also lead them back to

Grove Haven and my Kate. I was jolted upright in my seat at this realization. I had to pull off. I had to call her. I had to warn her, if it wasn't already too late. I had to tell her to take the baby and get out of the house, that these men, whoever they were, would be coming. Oh, Katherine? What had I done?

I pulled off the highway at the next exit and into the first place I could find, *Bo's Biker Bar*, read the sign, and the parking lot was replete with Harley's of all makes and models and rusting jacked-up pickups with oversized tires, ultra-absorbent shocks which could be seen clearly from the wheel wells and gun-racks complete with rifles and confederate flags. It was undoubtedly a rough place, but I placated myself to enter with the notion that at least if those two men who were chasing me had the foolishness to draw their weapons in here, they'd be in for one hell of a brawl.

I put the Jag in neutral, pulled the emergency break on and made sure to lock the doors, as judging from the look of their vehicles and the characters who might be in here, I needed to make certain my ride was here when I got back.

I opened the door and was greeted by the smell of sweat, wafting stale cigarette smoke, cheap beer, and bad country music blaring out from a jukebox in the corner of the bar. There were several pool tables to my right, where evidently a contest of significance of some sort must have been going on, as a brood of broad, large, hairy men wearing T-shirts and leather vests were hootin' and hollerin' and carrying on about something or another. The bar was decorated in brightly lit neon signs for several of the local tasteless beers, as well as a few other national brands. A TV sat on a ledge above the bar, and a group of men and women in tight jeans and cowboy hats were gathered around watching a NASCAR race of some sort.

I looked around for the bartender to ask him if I could use the phone. He was pouring pitchers of *Budweiser* from a tall brass tap, and wearing blue jeans, a red bandanna around his head, and a T-shirt stretched so tight on his protruding beer gut that it barely covered his belly button, upon which was depicted the skeleton of a confederate soldier with the caption, 'The South will Rise again.' Upon seeing this I immediately felt like an out-of-place guest star on *The Dukes of Hazzard* with my *Izod* and *Members Only* jacket. His bottom lip was partially extended, and he appeared to be either dipping or chewing tobacco.

I made my way through the jumble and disarray of cocktail tables and vinyl chairs, and stood at the bar patiently waiting for him to acknowledge me. I stood there for what must have been several minutes while he ignored me, carrying on a conversation about motorcycle carburetors with the man perched on a stool next to me.

After several minutes I decided I could wait no longer as Kathryn's life might potentially be in danger, and I had to be sure she was all right.

"Excuse me!" I said with a raised voice, trying to talk over the jukebox, and the barman looked at me with a stare that read something akin to, 'Just what the hell do you want?' "I'm sorry to interrupt," I said. "But I need to use your phone!"

The bartender looked at me, and he reached around behind him for a paper cup, into which he spit a large brown wad. "S'in the back," he said, with a somewhat muffled voice while pointing with the cup of spittle in his hand to a dimly lit hall to the left of the bar. "By the res'room."

I padded my pockets and they were empty. I reached into my wallet and pulled out a dollar bill. "Do you have any change?" I asked.

He sat there and looked me with an irritated expression on his face, as though my interrupting his conversation concerning motorcycle carbure-tors was the greatest of all calamities. He looked at me up and down and finally smirked, laughing at my attire undoubtedly. "Yah, I got change," he said, and he reached in the register behind him and handed four quarters to me. I took the change, thanked him and went down the hall he had indi-cated.

It reeked of smoke and fetid urine, and judging by the stains and smell in the corner next to the phone, I quite quickly deduced that some of the patrons here must not have been able to wait in line to use the facilities. I nudged the receiver between my ear and shoulder, put in my change and dialed home. I had to leave my other hand free to plug my ear because the music and noise from the television at the bar were so loud I could barely hear the dial tone. Finally after a few minutes the phone on the other end of the line began to ring.

"Pick up Kate!" I said aloud. It rang again. And again. "Come on dammit!" I said bitterly after it rang a fourth time. Finally on the fifth ring I heard her pick up and was filled with relief as I heard her voice utter a shaky, 'Hello?' I thanked God. It was her, and she was all right. They hadn't found her yet. There was still time.

"Kate!" I said, practically shouting into the phone, partially because fear and anxiousness swept through me once again as I knew I had to tell her the fateful events of just a few hours ago, and partially so I could hear myself speak. "Kate! It's Evan. Listen to me. You're in danger. You've got to get out of there. Take David Malcolm and get out of the house. There are men after us. They've already killed Jeff and Melissa. Kathryn, do you hear me?" I said, as her voice though usually quick to respond was silent on the other end of the phone.

"Evan." I heard her say, but I continued.

"They'll undoubtedly come for you next; you've got to get out. Get to your parents house, or the police, or ..."

"Evan!" I heard her shout at me through the receiver and I stopped so I could hear her. "There's someone here who wants to speak with you."

At that moment an ominous dread began to spread through me, and I knew then that I had lost her too, and my heart sank as I also knew I had lost David Malcolm. She sounded as though she had been crying, and was fighting back tears just to even speak with me. A chill spread over me, as though Death himself had exhaled his breath upon my body, and I felt it's clinging, bitter bite right down to the marrow of my bones. I tried to compose myself, which was useless as I stuttered, "Put him on." A silence passed while the receiver was exchanged on the other end, until I heard his voice that from then on would be forever etched into the fabric of my memory.

"Good evening, Dr. Stattler. We've been expecting you, haven't we Kate?" I heard a smug voice say.

"What have you done to her?" I demanded angrily. "What do you want with us?"

"I think you know what I want, Dr. Stattler, and as to what I have done to her, I assure you it was nothing that wasn't worth doing."

"You son of a bitch!" I said. "If you've hurt one hair on her head ..."

"Dr. Stattler ..."he interrupted. "I'd rather not get into this sort of name-calling, it defeats and deters us from our purpose here, and besides, I don't think you are yet fully aware of the severity of your position. Now, bring me what I want, and we may yet forgive this whole adventure."

"Bullshit!" I said. "You expect me to believe that if I bring you the chip you're going to just let us go after killing Jeff and Melissa? They weren't even involved."

"They were involved enough, and besides, I didn't kill them. You did," the voice said with a cold, detached certainty. "Bring me the chip."

"Who are you?" I demanded. "Who are you working for?"

"Who I am is not important ... that I have your family is. Bring me the chip," he said again, and I could tell by the way he slowly repeated himself and by his tone that his patience was wearing thin. "What do you *really* have anyway, Dr. Stattler? No one's going to believe you. No one wants to believe you. No one would more believe you than the ravings of a mad-man like Dr. Gottlieb."

"I believed him," I said.

"Then that shall be your undoing. Bring me the chip, and come home if you ever wish to see your family alive." He paused and then continued, "Where are you?"

I was about to respond when out of the corner of my eye I saw something familiar. It was my faculty photo from Grove Haven on the television! I un-plugged my ear and let go of the receiver so I could hear what it was they were saying about me. A female news-anchor wearing a blue suit began to speak.

"... This just in ... Chicago Metropolitan police are looking again for this man, Dr. Evan Michael Stattler, in connection with today's shooting and double homicide of Dr. Jeff Gould in Mckinley Park, and his wife Melissa Gould in their Mount Prospect home. Suspect should be considered armed and extremely dangerous. Police advise to not attempt apprehension of any kind and ask the public if you see him to please call the number at the bottom of your screen. Suspect is reported to be driving a black 1967 Jaguar, and was last seen en route on portions of Interstate 90 West, and may possibly be attempting to return to his home in St. Paul."

"Jesus ..." I said out loud. I was trapped. The led foil I had used must have worked, only too well. Since they could no longer track my movements or whereabouts, they now turned the whole world against me. I did not have long to think about my predicament, and my attention was then diverted to the man who was sitting on the stool next to me when I first approached the bar.

"Hey, Vinny!" he shouted across the bar. "Ain't that that fella jes' come in here?"

The severity of my situation instantly became apparent—a murderer who had killed in broad daylight and in cold blood an innocent Doctor and his wife, and who was now trapped in a biker bar chock full of rowdy, drunk, and boisterous individuals, each of whom was probably seeking to make a name for himself. I did not bother to wait for a response from the bartender, as I dove into the men's bathroom next to me and prayed that there was a window I could escape through. It would turn out that wasn't the only piece of luck I would have.

I stood on the toilet tank and squeezed and wriggled myself out of it, and fell to the ground on top of some broken down boxes and empty beer kegs next to what I took to be the rear kitchen door. I scrambled towards Jeff's car, limping slightly, as I had bruised my ribs on one of the kegs when I landed. I opened the door and started the engine. When I looked up from the steering wheel I saw that the bartender had emerged with several people from the bar through the front door, and was carrying a shot gun which was now aimed at the rear of my vehicle. I did not wait for him to fire, and threw the Jag into gear and floored it, spraying a cloud of dust and gravel into the air and in their faces as I skidded back on the exit to the interstate.

Even though I had escaped I knew that I was trapped. Where could I go? What could I do? The world was now against me, the manhunt was on, and they, whoever these forces were, had my wife and child. Perhaps, I thought, I should give this strange man what he wanted. He may yet keep his word. He may yet let us live. But who was I kidding? These were murderers. Professionals, apparently, with a great and unrestricted license to accomplish their objective. If I didn't turn myself in to them it was likely they would hunt me down to the ends of the earth. But despite all this my mind would inevitably turn to the question: who, exactly, were *they*? What, exactly, was I dealing with? There was only one man who could know, who had seen them, who knew who they were, and who had been with them directly. Dr. Gottlieb. He was the answer. Only he could tell me who these men were and what I should do. The only question was, would they catch me before I reached him?

As I began to draw closer to the outskirts and suburbs of St. Paul an ominous dread began to take hold over me, as though I were heading into the jungles of Joseph Conrad's *Heart of Darkness*, and I feared that whatever fate I was inextricably headed towards would consume me whole, as an anaconda might an antelope, digesting even the most coarsest of bone. And my Kate, my beloved Kathryn and David. What of them? I couldn't just leave them in the hands of this assassin, who had no doubt ordered the deaths of Jeff and Melissa, this man, this killer, whose cold and soulless voice I had just spoken to. No. I couldn't leave them there, but at the moment what choice did I have?

Despite what the news said I did not have a gun. I had never owned a gun, and even if I did, I had never in my life done anything to prepare myself for the task of killing a man. And this 'man', whoever he was, was certainly not alone. He was clearly not acting on his own volition, he had help, and I had clearly seen that back in Chicago. No. The answer was still with Gottlieb. I had to get back to him before they reached me, or suspected that I might try to reach him before coming home, and in order to do that I had to throw them off my trail and douse any suspicion of my intent.

I pulled over to a gas station and used what was left of the change the bartender gave me at Bo's Biker Bar to call home. It rang several times before someone picked up on the fourth ring.

"Honey, is that you?" I heard a familiar voice say, but it was not Kathryn who said it. "We're still waiting for you," he continued with a gloating viciousness to his words.

"I'm coming in. I've seen the news. There's nowhere for me to run," I said. "Just don't hurt them."

"Very good," he said again in a mocking voice. "When can we expect you darling?" I heard David Malcolm crying in the background and what sounded like Kathryn trying to shush and comfort him.

"Cut the crap!" I demanded angrily. "And let me speak to Kathryn. Let me know she's ok."

"No," the voice said calmly.

"And why not?" I insisted.

"Because you wish it," he answered, and then continued. "When can we expect you?" he asked again, this time without the cold humor, but in a much sterner voice.

"I'll be home in two hours," I said and hung up the phone before I could let him reply.

I drove as fast as I could while still obeying the speed limit to the gates of Grove Haven. It was about nine o' clock now, and the stars that guided me to St. Paul were now beginning to cloud over in what looked like would be rain in a few hours. Once I pulled into Grove Haven I hid the car behind the dumpsters of the service and delivery entrance, so if any of these men suspected this move and drove by they wouldn't see it. Nervous and chilled with the coming cold front, I fumbled outside the service door with my keys, trying desperately to remember which one would unlock the door. Once inside I sprinted as fast as I could to the Level 3 checkpoint. My heart was relieved by the familiar sight of Sampson in the operator's booth, who was reading a magazine while slowly rocking back and forth on the rear two legs of his chair.

"Sampson!" I shouted out, and I must have surprised him as he fumbled in the air with his hands, dropping the magazine, groping for the desk and nearly falling over.

"Doctor Stattler, oh it's good to see you. Mr. Gottlieb, well, he's been right out of sorts since you left, and especially when those men come."

"What men?" I demanded sternly of him.

"They came this morning, 'round ten or so, when Miss Kate was here to look in on him." He said, motioning his head in the direction of Gottlieb's cell.

"How did they get in here? How did they know she was here?" I asked.

Sampson looked at me wearily, clearly afraid of the news he was about to bestow upon me and what I might do or say when I heard it.

"Doctor Sikes, uh, he must have let them in, cuz they were with him. He came in from home. Don't know why, he never comes in on Saturdays, least not that I've ever seen," he said, while looking pitifully at me. "Thought you must have known about it, I mean, why else would Ms. Kate go with them. She left with Dr. Sikes and those men, though I can't say that she wanted to go."

"Frank," I said out loud at this revelation. "I should have known."

Sampson then became agitated and responded hastily, "I wouldn't go blaming Doctor Sikes. He looked as though he was quite spooked himself. There was one of 'em, don't know who he was, but he put a chill in my bones that I ain't felt since my daddy died, when I saw his ghost one night rocking in his favorite chair, right there on the front porch, and that's the truth!"

"Was there a struggle? Why wasn't the police notified? Why didn't you do anything Sampson?" I said, beginning to raise my voice at him.

"No, no struggle, none at all. He just said something to her and she went with them. Don't know why. Mr. Gottlieb though, he ain't been right since. He's been screaming and carrying on about something or another. I had to have Vernon help me sedate him a bit this morning. We was afraid he might injure himself, but he's been quiet since."

"Thank you Sampson. I'm sorry," I said. "I didn't mean to get mad at you."

Sampson looked at me with deep, understanding eyes and said, "It's all right Doctor Stattler. I'd be worried too."

I stepped into the man-trap. "You'd better buzz me through now."

Sampson merely nodded and I heard the gate buzz as it slid open on its track in front of me. Though I was still in a somewhat panicked race to get here and finally confront Dr. Gottlieb, having now known with absolute certainty he was telling the truth from the very beginning, I found myself in the corridor of the Class III wing terrified to approach his cell, and the fear gnawed at me more and more like a dog chewing and salivating over a juicy bone. When I finally stood opposite his cell, he looked up from his reading and smiled at me.

"Good evening, Doctor," he said. "We've been expecting you."

"We, Doctor?" I questioned him, and in answer he held up the cover of the book he was reading so I could see.

"Richard and I," he said, and I saw the title read *William Shakespeare's Richard III.*

"Talk to me, Doctor," I said imploringly.

"And what shall we talk about, Doctor, shall we amuse ourselves on the subject of the death of Kings?"

"No more riddles, Doctor. They have her. They have my Kathryn. They have my baby, and only you can tell me who they are. Please, I beg you," I said beseeching him, grasping the bars between us with my hands until my nails drove into the depths of my palms. "Tell me who this man is who's pursuing me and has taken my family hostage."

He studied me and reflected for a moment before responding, clearly trying to suppress his emotion concerning the events. "Your family isn't being held hostage," he answered. "Your family is dead."

"NO MORE GAMES!" I shouted at him. "That's not true!"

"Yes," he said, while looking at me calmly. "It is."

"WHO IS HE?" I demanded again. "He's MURDERED two of my friends!"

"What is done can not now be amended," he said and continued. "Men shall deal unadvisedly sometimes, which after hours give leisure to repent." He began to sob after he said this and leaned over and put his face into his hands. "Forgive me, Doctor! It was not my intention to drag you and your family into my suffering, to grant you a part in this play, this *farce* which I have for twenty years found myself in." He rose up off his cot swiftly to face me, while tossing the play aside, the drainage bulb from Friday evening's operation swung and was still hanging from the tube at the base of his right ear. "Forgive me," he said weeping as he staggered towards the bars between us. "Forgive me."

"Who is this man, Doctor?" I pressed on. "What really happened at your trial? TELL ME!" I shouted at him.

He wiped his tears on the sleeve of his shirt before responding bitterly, "There was no *trial*, Doctor," he hissed back at me. "And as for the man I have come to call 'Mr. Black', who now lives only in my thoughts and fears and dreams, I know no more than you. After I saw those beings with my own eyes, those *creatures* who put that thing in my body, the next thing I remember was waking up in a sealed, padded room, poked and prodded, doped and besotted, and studied by men, men like you, who have the audacity to call themselves 'physicians.' After some time I came to realize that I had been tucked away in a federal institution somewhere, the name of which now escapes me, as I have been in so many.

"It was *him* who put me there, Doctor. It was *him* who saw to it that I be put here. It was *him,* who out of rage for the deaths of his brethren and for reasons I can only contemplate, would rather see me suffer the rest of my days on this earth as a raving *madman,* of whom no one would ever believe or listen to, my theories, my research and work, destroyed! Everything I had ever wanted and hoped to achieve lay in forgotten relics, the enlightenment I wished to bring mankind about his fate and existence on this earth irrevocably lost, and for this wish, this desire to uncover the truth about our beginnings and the beings responsible, for this I am here, now, standing before you! An empty shell of a man, with all I ever hoped or dreamed for in ruins! And this, this is now my penance. This is now my suffering. *This ...* " he said, looking around the cell that caged him, raising his arms in the air to accentuate his point. "*This* is all I have left in the world. But to answer your question, the man you ask after is the best and worst in men; he is all men, and none. For the longest time I waited, feigning what I gathered to be psychotic and schizophrenic episodes and tendencies, waiting for the right person, someone who might *dare* to believe in me."

"For years I gave up these hopes and began to wonder whether everything in my past, everything that I had seen, witnessed, and been privy to, was, in fact, a product of my mind. Between all the drugs you physicians gave me, and the horrors of being incarcerated for so long, I began to doubt my own sanity, and almost began to believe that everything I had experienced, the death camps, Ain Ghazal, Nasca, was all a lie. And then, as *providence* would have it, I met you, Doctor, and I had to know. I had to know if my whole life was a dream, and if so, were the pursuits of which I dreamt real, or a machination of my own mind. I had to know.

"But I fear it was at you and your family's expense, and as Richard himself would say, 'I am now so far in blood that sin will pluck on sin, foes to my rest and my sweet sleep's disturbers are they that I would have thee deal upon.' What I said to you earlier is true, Doctor. If your family isn't now dead they soon will be, and that you are yet still alive brings me hope, the hope that the truth about these beings and their sinister protectors within levels of our government will one day be unveiled, and I pray you live long enough to tell someone who is in a position to listen, my friend."

I studied him thoughtfully at this confession, and though I wished to lament my own grief I found that I could not, and felt it important to share some information with him before I took my leave. "I may have found a way to stop them, to stop them from tracking me at least," I said, and I removed the lead foil ball from my pocket to show him. "This lead foil apparently has the ability to mask the chips locator signal. I spoke with the man you call, 'Mr. Black', who now has my family. He gave no indication that he knew my whereabouts."

Dr. Gottlieb's eyes widened when he saw it. "Then there is still time," he whispered, "but there is something else that I haven't told you, something else there is that I fear, that this device will not be mimed, as it also allows those listening to *hear.*"

As the thunder from the approaching storm shook the building and the lightening flashed through the barred windows in the cell-block hall, he began to become agitated and nervous. He had, suddenly, a wild, crazed look in his eyes, and they were bloodshot with both fatigue, no doubt from his surgery, and adrenaline, the cause of which I would soon come to know.

I reached my hands through the bars and began to shake him. "What is it? What are you saying?" I shouted at him. "What do you mean?" He began to laugh as I shook him, as though he had now just understood something lost to him, and he looked up at the ceiling as though someone, somewhere above us were watching. "Tell me what you're saying?" I said, still shaking him. He still gazed upward and his laughter now turned to that maniacal one I first heard with Frank when he impersonated the witches of Macbeth. Then all at once he stopped and stared blankly at me, as the thunder clamored and boomed outside.

"Is there a murderer here?" he asked, his face contorted in deep thoughtfulness and what appeared to be a suffering regret.

"No. No," I said.

"Yes I am," He said. "Lest I revenge."

"Revenge?" I said. "How? Doctor, we don't have time for this, I mean to take you with me. I ... ."

He interrupted me. "I am a villain," he said, and stared at me through the bars between us. "I have destroyed your career and your family to satisfy my sanity, no, my ego, much like you have sacrificed yours by believing in me. I am a villain, yet I lie, I am not." And as he continued I realized he was telling me something, something from Shakespeare, something from Richard III. "Fool of thy self, speak well, fool do not flatter, my conscience hath a thousand tongues, and every tongue brings in a several tale, and every tale condemns me for a villain. Perjury! Perjury in the highest degree!" he shouted and continued. "Murder, murder stern murder in the direst degree. All several sins, all used in each degree! Throng now to the bar," and he shook the cage between his fists. "Crying all, Guilty!" he stared at me transfixed as though in a trance. "Guilty," he repeated, whispering this last word. "You must leave now Doctor," he said, returning and composing himself. "You must leave now and never come back, or he will find you, and suffer my fate or worse you will."

A tear began to trickle down his cheek, and as much as I wanted to blame him for everything that had happened to me, the loss of everything I had worked so hard for, my career, my wife, my child, my beloved Kathryn, I could not. For the blame that he heaped upon himself was more than he could bear. "I'm sorry, Doctor," he said, and he leaned his head forward onto the bars he still gripped between his hands. "Forgive me."

"There's nothing to forgive," I said. "You once asked to shake my hand, and I rebuked you for reasons I now know were petty and selfish. I can not begin to imagine all you have had to endure these many years, wondering desperately whether or not everything you had come to know was either illusion or real. It must have been like waking from a nightmare in a strange place, literally, not knowing where you are, only the worst part was, the dream didn't end."

I stuck my hand through the bars and he stared at it, as though he could not believe what it was he was witnessing. But in an instant he pulled his hands away from the bars between us, grasped my hand and wept upon it. When he looked up at me, his tears glistening in the overhead fluorescent light he said, "Doctor, away! You must fly! Fly now, while there's none else by!"

I was about to respond when the loud 'whack' of the thundercloud outside once again shook the room. He immediately let go of my hand and looked frantically about the walls of his cell.

"In a sieve I'll thither sail, and like a rat without a tail! And the very ports they blow, all the quarters that they know. Hang upon his penthouse lid; *He* shall live a man *forbid!*" he said, creaking and cackling in his witch's voice. "A drum. A drum. Herr Black doth come!"

I was about to respond when I heard the clang and the familiar buzz of the man-trap down the cell-block hall beginning to open, and my attention was diverted from the maniacal Dr. Gottlieb dancing in nervous apprehension about his cell, to the men that emerged. Slowly, and deliberately, they walked towards us. There were four of them, three dressed in dark suits, ties, and sunglasses despite the storm outside, accompanied by Dr. Sikes, who was carrying a straight jacket in one arm and a bundle of folders in the other. He did not face or look up at me as they approached.

"Where are Kathryn and my baby? What did you do with them?" I demanded angrily of the man in front, whom I assumed to be *Mr. Black*, and the man I spoke to on the phone. He did not answer until they all stopped directly in front of me.

"And why should I tell you? Hmmm? Especially when you have forced this confrontation from a private to a public setting by not returning home as you agreed. Pity. Dear Kathryn was so very entertaining." he said, his voice intonation cool and resolute, unrevealing as much as his attire.

"You son of a bitch!" I shouted, as I lunged toward him, and the two other men, who were presumably his associates, moved quickly from behind him, grabbed me and wrestled with me until I eventually relented. Surprisingly, they released me after I stopped struggling. I straightened my clothes which had been ruffled by the struggle and which were uncomfortable before addressing him again.

"If I could I would kill you for what you've done!" I spat at him angrily. They all laughed at this except for Dr. Sikes, who stood there wearily with his head down like a beaten dog who has been up to no good and patiently awaiting judgment.

"Yes, I'm sure you would," Mr. Black answered, still snickering somewhat from my outburst. "Doctor. Evan. Michael. Stattler." His words were carefully chosen, and he pronounced each of them slow and precise, drawing out every syllable with a despondent, detached tone. "Born, September fifteenth, nineteen-fifty-one to Karen Ann and David Malcolm Stattler. Graduated Grover Cleveland High School in Witchitaw Kansas, June twelfth, nineteen-sixty-eight. Accepted to John's Hopkins University in Baltimore, April, nineteen-sixty-eight, Bachelor of Science degree attained May seventh, nineteen-seventy-two, received MD's in spring nineteen-seventy-five and Ph.D. Psychology, nineteen-seventy-eight. Married Kathryn Jane Helgenstein, May fifteen, nineteen-eighty-one. Interned at St. Mary's Hospital in downtown St. Paul until January nineteen-eighty-two. Hired to the faculty of physicians and psychologists at Grove Haven Institute for the criminally insane, and father of David Malcolm Stattler, born July thirty, nineteen-eighty-two."

I looked at the man who now stood before me. I could see my reflection quite clearly in his silver sunglasses, and he smiled at me once he finally stopped in front of me with what I could only call an almost fanatical grimace. His hair was greased and slicked back. It was as dark and shiny as the polished shoes he was wearing, and as coal black as everything he wore except his shirt, a white oxford button down with a shiny silk black tie.

"It's nice to finally make your acquaintance, Dr. Stattler. I've been looking forward to meeting you."

"I haven't," I said frankly.

The three men in black all laughed at this as though it was some last ditch-effort at humor on my part, though I was completely serious.

"Though, suffice it to say Doctor, the truth is you aren't in a place to make any such threats or demands. Even if you could kill me, you can never undo what I've accomplished, and you could only kill me once."

"Then consider that a regret. I would make you pay for the lives of those people you killed, you murdered! The Gould's didn't know anything about this, they weren't even involved."

"Were, Dr. Stattler. Were. Were being the opportune word here. And besides, I didn't kill them, *you* did. You did it by involving them and meddling into affairs that do not concern you."

I lunged for him again but the other two men who were with him were obviously ready and trained for this response, and though they did not seek to restrain me, they nonetheless blocked me from reaching him and throttling his throat with my bare hands, which was what I had in mind.

Suddenly from behind me, I heard Dr. Gottlieb scream, "A HORSE! A HORSE! MY FREEDOM FOR A HORSE!"

Mr. Black turned and faced Dr. Gottlieb for the first time, who was angrily clutching the cage of his cell, his knuckles nearly bursting from the inflamed veins that filled them.

"I regret, Doctor, that freedom is something that is not on your agenda either this evening or for the rest of your life," Mr. Black said quite coolly, his calm demeanor unchanged and unruffled, his eyes staring straight ahead through the mirrored sunglasses he wore in the dark of the cell block, and I wondered if this was some shrewd attempt at humor on his part. He then turned to face me, still impeded by the men who kept me from lunging at him and tearing out his throat and entrails with my bare hands.

"Tell me, Doctor," he said. "Do you not see at last that this patient, this *prisoner* of yours, is quite clearly *insane*? He needs to be protected from himself, for his own sake, and others. Surely you realize this? Look at him," he said, glancing over at Dr. Gottlieb who was now curled in a ball at the foot of his cell and pulling out small tufts of hair from his head.

I stopped struggling with the two other agents in front of me, stepped back, and slapped down their outstretched arms in a final fury of disgust.

"I realize nothing!" I said. "Except that you would kill, incarcerate, or torture whoever you wished to suppress the truth of what he claims! That the Grays are *REAL!*" I shouted. "That they are here now amongst us, and working in conjunction with you and members of the U.S. government to whatever foul, evil, and sinister end that is their goal, and that you would do anything, nothing short of murder to protect them!"

Mr. Black then began to clap slowly, methodically, as if he were giving an appraisal for a dead pan performance without meaning or luster.

"Wonderful," he said sarcastically. "Just wonderful. I see that Dr. Gottlieb here has been keeping you well practiced, versed, and over-embellished as he often is in the repeated, pedantic, and over dramatized motifs of Shakespeare."

He then turned and faced Gottlieb, who was grimacing with the foulest countenance I had yet seen in our many sessions together on his face.

"I would think after all this time you would have tried some other theme to seduce your jailers into believing you."

"The truth is the truth," Gottlieb countered from the dark depths of his cell.

"AND WHAT WOULD YOU KNOW OF IT?" Mr. Black shouted back to him in his first show of abrasive defiance and anger. "All my life I have been defending this nation, this country, this world, you, Dr. Stattler," he said, pointing a long, thin and white bony index finger at me. "From narrow minded and overzealous beings such as yourself. Beings that would bring this earth and society to the edge of destruction! And am I ever rewarded for this duty? Am I ever once thanked? Does the President ever call me on the phone and am I ever once congratulated? I am *saving lives, Doctors! Many lives! So many lives that can not be counted!*" he shouted, and then continued, his voice now returning to normal while staring directly at me. "When you go home at night Dr. Stattler, to your nice white house on Brittania street, tend your garden, play with your child and sleep with your wife under the blanket of security that I provide, don't you dare question or patronize me with the manner that I provide it! It is because of *me* you *have* those things. It is because of *me* that those things exist! It is because of *me* that you are *alive*."

I was about to let him continue when something odd he said struck me, something that didn't quite fit, yet I knew not why.

"What did you mean, 'beings like you'? Do you mean to propose that as sure as you are standing here, you are *not* human? Do you mean to propose that you are, in fact, a creation of these 'benefactors' of yours whom you are sworn to protect and kill for? You sound crazier than he does!" I said, motioning to Gottlieb, who was watching the whole exchange in a quiet, rapt attention.

He then faced me with the most unpredictably calmest countenance and said, "Yes, Doctor. That is exactly what I meant to propose. I can see why you chose him, Dr. Gottlieb. He's not like the others. Very intuitive. Pity the Grays never took him as a child, with his genes he might have been a candidate for future human development. There's always his child though."

I ignored this last comment as I knew Mr. Black was saying it just to provoke and get a rise out of me. I wasn't going to let him.

"What do you mean, *not like the others*? What others?" I asked, turning to Dr. Gottlieb, as I was beginning to realize for the first time that there were many pieces of the puzzle Gottlieb had possibly omitted in his discussions.

"No, he isn't," Gottlieb answered. "And therein lies the pity, because he was on the verge of tearing down you and all you stand for."

It then finally began to dawn on me what he was saying, and I turned once again to Dr. Gottlieb blank faced.

"You lied to me. You *had* told others before. I was *not* the only one!" I screamed in outrage, demanding an answer from him.

"But you were the only one to come so close," he whispered, trying to beckon me again into his knowing confidence. "You were the only one who dared to risk his life and family and sacrifice his friends by *believing*. By believing the truth which has for so long been hidden from mankind. I do not mock you, Doctor. I applaud you. You were the first among my keepers to show compassion, the first to show humility, the first to show true wisdom in braving and potentially sacrificing your life and the lives of others for mine," he paused and then continued. "The first to have this removed," he said, winking at me, while tapping the side of his cheek where the drainage bulb still dangled. "And that is a debt that I can never repay. Never."

"A futile endeavor at best," Mr. Black spat at him. "We'll correct that again soon enough."

Dr. Gottlieb ignored him and continued pleadingly, "The only reason I did not tell you was because I knew how much you longed to find out the truth for yourself, and that I assure you was my only deception."

"You see," Mr. Black said, pointing at him. "He is a liar. A self-admitted liar and what's to separate this lie from another? *Nothing.* Don't listen to him Doctor, lest he drag you down with him. Indeed, how *would* Shakespeare describe him, hmmm? Perhaps as nothing less than a *mis-believer, a cut-throat-dog! A lying, usurious Jew.* Isn't that right, Gottlieb? *Gottlieb,* God's Love? As if any such thing even existed."

"To be sure you wouldn't know," Gottlieb countered him. "You see, Doctor Stattler, he is evil. Evil incarnate. The worst of man's trappings spun and wound in a Petri dish in some laboratory for the soul purpose to serve his dark masters. He is truly, in every sense of the word, a *monster.*"

I suddenly became incensed and filled with rage at what had now become puerile banter between the two of them and their using me to juxtaposition their causes.

"Enough!" I shouted. "Shut up, the two of you! You both equally disgust me with your self-serving rhetoric, and I will be a part of it no longer!"

"No longer, Doctor?" said Mr. Black, his face withdrawn with a look of feigned surprise. "Well, I'm afraid that's not possible. But you're right, we do digress with this pointless bickering, and our business here is not concluded. Dr. Sikes, may I have the file please," he said, and he outstretched his hand to Frank, who was still standing with his head down meagerly to his right. Frank handed him the file saying nothing.

"Dr. Sikes, here, has kindly under my advice, supervision, and with permission from the state board, drafted a proposal which will bring about a happy end for all parties involved in this little repartee of ours. Plainly speaking, it is a transfer request for our guest here, Dr. Jacob Francis Gottlieb, to the new federal institution of Greenmont Hospital and Mental facility in Dallas, Texas, where he will be cared for under the scrutiny of the finest physicians using everything new technology has to offer. Now, as Dr. Sikes is Director of this facility, he can of course authorize this transfer himself, but, as I would like to include within his records a current patient psychological profile to the Directors of Greenmont, I will need the signature of his acting psychologist, which would be you, Dr. Stattler."

Mr. Black opened the file and the two other agents who separated us stood aside so I could see it. I stepped forward, looking at his face, scanning for something, anything in his expression I could determine might help me, but all I saw was his smug expression and the silver lenses of his sunglasses staring back at me. I looked down at the pages he separated and with my finger quickly went over the file to find the patient analysis.

Transfer Request Order,
State of Minnesota, Grove Haven Hospital #54902—
Dr. Jacob Francis Gottlieb, white male, German descent, aged 53

Patient Statistics: Convicted of Capital Murder, November 30, 1963, for the execution style homicide and mutilation of two Federal Agents (for reasons of national security involving current on-going assignments related to their deaths, their names have been omitted from this document but may be obtained by court order through the Federal Bureau of Investigation Registrars Office reference#673165b).

Patient Profile as related to DSM-IV reference specifics:
Patient displays the following signs of advanced paranoid schizophrenia with wild mood swings and behavioral disorders, possible dementia, and/or antisocial personality disorder with specifics to the following conditions and/or symptoms.

Preoccupation with one or more systematized delusions or with frequent auditory hallucinations related to a single theme, specifically in the case of Dr. Jacob Francis Gottlieb, that of influence from 'Extra-terrestrials.'

None of the following behavior has been observed: incoherence, marked loosening of associations, flat or grossly inappropriate affect, catatonic behavior, grossly disorganized behavior, and thus has been labeled "Stable" for Paranoid Schizophrenia.

Impairment in functioning has been weakened to due the advanced stages of the disease and the extreme duration that it went undetected and undiagnosed. Patient additionally displays the following dysfunctional behaviors (e.g., polydipsia, mannerisms) which are frequently observed in chronically institutionalized schizophrenics of this type.

Patient has tested with results of over 67% on a confirmed MMPI Over-Controlled Hostility (Oh) scale, which for the record has been especially useful in predicting uncommonly violent acts at this facility.

Patient Synopsis Class III, Axis V: GAF = 33

Patient Psychopathy involves:
superficial charm and "good" intelligence
absence of delusions and other signs of irrationality
unreliability (does not seem able to keep time)
untruthfulness and insincerity (pathological lying)
lack of remorse or shame concerning his victims
antisocial behavior (whim or caprice)
poor judgment and failure to learn from experience
pathological egocentricity and incapacity for love
general poverty in major affective reactions
unresponsiveness in interpersonal relations
fantastic behavior (appearing intoxicated at times)

Additionally, Dr. Gottlieb seems attracted to danger and authority, and craves the excitement and the power that comes with these responsibilities. It should be noted that while being held as a child at the German concentration camp of Bergen-Belsen, it is very likely that Dr. Gottlieb suffered extensive sexual and physical abuse which may have increased the likelihood of his condition (synop. page 6), as recent discoveries by the Daystrum Institute reveal that the brain chemistry of victims of violent crime can change as a result of having lived through such traumas.

From preliminary testing, we have been able to determine that the patient has substantial elevated dopamine levels and the contin-ued use of dopamine inhibitors is highly recommended and war-ranted due to the extreme nature of this case (a full list of current patient medicines and dosages is attached on page 4 of this dossier).

EXTREME caution is recommended at ALL TIMES when dealing with Dr. Gottlieb, as he is prone to wild, erratic, and often violent anti-social behavior. A full report and statistical analysis of these behaviors as well as patient notes follows.

Summary:

After many thorough and successive interviews with Dr. Gottlieb it has been determined by myself, Dr. Evan Michael Stattler, PhD and Director Franklin Woodrow Sikes PhD of the Grove Haven Institution for the Mentally Insane, at the above address 6113 Baker Street, St. Paul MN, that the aforementioned patient and his needs supersede those that Grove Haven can effectively provide, as Grove Haven lacks the laboratories and additional medicinal facilities we believe are needed to determine a proper course of treatment. As is the case in many patients, chromosome anomalies are responsible for a significant proportion of patients with mental retardation, and congenital anomalies. Development of new molecular cytogenetic techniques has provided a powerful tool for detection of patients with subtle chromosome abnormalities. Particularly, investigation of the gene-rich subtelomeric regions has generated interest regarding the implications and prevalence of cryptic chromosomal rearrangements. As your facility is more modern and equipped with a subtelomeric FISH probe, the Director and physicians of this facility believe it is in the best interest of this patient to be administered and transferred to yours with due haste so that a comprehensive analysis can be completed.

Dr. Franklin Woodrow Sikes, Ph.D, Director, Grove Haven Institute
Dr. Evan Michael Stattler, Ph.D, Grove Haven Psychology

I looked at him incredulously, as he stood there staring at me, like the cat who had cornered the canary and was about to engulf him in a single swoop of the tongue.

"I'm not signing that, or anything else you put in front of me," I said resolutely. "While I agree there are many truths that are evident concerning Dr. Gottlieb's behavior, they have been conveniently twisted to exercise your intentions. It's you who belong behind bars being tested and fingered and probed for the rest of your days, not *him*."

"I wouldn't be too hasty, Dr. Stattler, as I don't think you'd find the alternative to your liking."

"Sign it, Doctor," I heard the voice from Gottlieb's cell whisper. "Sign it. At least you can go back to your old life. At least you will still be *alive*."

"To say nothing of your wife and child," Mr. Black said, interrupting him, sneering malevolently at me. "Would you endanger their lives too? Hmmm? How many lives would it take to convince you, Dr. Stattler, besides your own? How many people must suffer and continue to suffer because of your impertinence and stubbornness for what is only an abstract ideal. You know, I could even see to it that the charges for murder in the deaths of Jeff and Melissa Gould were dropped. You would be a free man, you would have a normal life again, and all this could be put behind you, by simply signing this piece of paper."

"Aren't you afraid I'll talk?" I asked.

"And who would you tell, and what would you tell them? Hmmm? Do you think I believe you'd risk your career, your reputation, everything that you've worked for, or the ability to provide for your family with no evidence but conjecture?"

"Sign it, Doctor," I heard Gottlieb say again from behind me. "It's the only way. My life is lost, but you still have a chance at yours. Forget about me. It is all a lie anyway. No one will believe you."

"I know you're just saying that Dr. Gottlieb because you care about me and don't want to see me harmed, but you forget, I've lived it. I've experienced it, and I've been through it, and I now know what you know is real."

"So let's have it, Dr. Stattler. I am going to waste no more time with you," Mr. Black said, and with a mock impatience, he handed me the transfer order and a pen from his coat pocket.

I held it in my palms and looked at it, reading it one more time. What I thought was strange was how well Frank had interpreted everything I had told him. Though of course, I am certain he had help from Mr. Black who, evidently from years of experience and monitoring him, knew Gottlieb quite well. Everything that was said in the report *could* be real and not just a concocted lie to suppress one man's version of the truth, just as easily as Dr. Gottlieb's story could have been a delusion spun from the dense fabric of his mind.

"Sign it," Mr. Black demanded of me again. "Sign it now. I won't ask again."

I don't know what filled me just then because my head began to swoon with anger and rage and fury at the pointlessness of it all.

"No," I said blankly, and shoved the file with the stack of papers into his chest. "I won't. I will not allow Jeff, Melissa or Gottlieb's life to be sacrificed in vain."

"What about your own, or your wife's or David Malcolm's? I thought you a smarter man than that?"

"I am," I said defiantly.

"Doctor, *please*, you don't know what you're *doing*! This man will kill you!" I heard Gottlieb plead again from behind me.

I turned to face him, standing between Mr. Black and the entrance to Gottlieb's cell.

"But I do know what I'm doing, Doctor," I said. "I do. You once said that this man was *evil*? Perhaps he is."

Mr. Black just stood there, his face bereft of emotion, as though I might somehow change my mind and accept their mutual demands and sign that paper. And as I stood there watching Mr. Black, gloating over his own authority, over me and my helplessness, and on the other side of me Dr. Gottlieb whose face was twisted with remorseful rage, I was filled with revulsion for both of them.

"Do you want me to tell you what *true* evil is, Doctor?" I asked abrasively.

Dr. Gottlieb stepped back and released the menacing and concerned grip he had on the bars of his cell, while Mr. Black's expression changed to one of a sudden vague curiosity. I then felt elated, as though the hand of God himself were on my shoulder and whispering in my ear, and knew then as I know now that what He said rang true.

"True evil, Doctor, is to submit to you, the two of you!" I said, staring bitterly and coldly at both of them. "It is when we sacrifice our freedom and self-determination and what's even more so important, the *truth*, and allow them to be destroyed and manipulated by the hands of greedy and usurious men, who while claiming justice as their ally are always inextricably linked to tyranny." I turned to Mr. Black to further emphasize just who it was I was speaking of.

"I came here to Grove Haven, I signed my life on in this industry and have devoted it in it's entirety to the cause and to helping others find it when I can, and when I sign that piece of paper, *IT IS ALL A LIE!*" I shouted at them both from the barrels of my lungs. "*A FARCE!*" I shouted, this time turning to Dr. Gottlieb. "*A MEANINGLESS PLAY WITHOUT WANT OR PURPOSE!*" and turning again to face Mr. Black I continued. "And I will *NOT* live out the rest of my existence knowing what I know and carrying on about my profession as though this and nothing ever took place? *THAT*, gentlemen, is what *true* evil is," I said, my voice returning to normal. "And I will not allow my death, my wife's, or my children's, or the sacrifice of Jeff and Melissa Gould, to go unnoticed or recognized in the annals of history, even if they are not discovered for another thousand years."

I then looked boldly, defiantly, at Mr. Black, so he would see there was no further convincing me otherwise of my decision and repeated again, "I will not sign that transfer order, or any other piece of paper that will wash away what I know to be the truth!"

Mr. Black stared at me emotionless through his silver-mirrored sun glasses, clearly trying to establish that he was unimpressed with what I said.

"Then you and your family will die," he said plainly.

To this day I don't know whether it was God, bravery, righteousness, or madness that filled me when I answered, I only know that I was unafraid. I stepped forward, slowly, methodically, deliberately, as I had seen him walk down the corridor when he first arrived.

"If that is the will of the universe," I said. "Than so it shall be!"

As I watched him closely, his expression began to change, from a look of wonder to a look of anger and then to a subdued, melancholy fury. His jaw began to tighten and the muscles round his neck began to bulge. The breathing through his nose increased and quickened dramatically, the veins began to become visible on his forehead, and finally he began clenching his fists around the file he carried in a show of deposed bravado. I literally thought his face would explode when he shouted, though facing me obviously he was speaking to other men who were still no doubt with Sampson in the gate outside the cell block.

"*AGENTS!!!*" he shouted, and I heard the door to the man-trap buzz open and the clack of polished shoes treading down the hall which were accompanied by a two men dressed identically to Mr. Black. When they arrived Mr. Black held me tightly by the right arm and began searching my pockets until he found the chip which was still wrapped in the led foil from the wine bottle I had taken back at the Gould's.

"Agents 203 and 307," he addressed them politely and courteously. "Take Dr. Stattler here to the cars and wait for me to return. We'll be going to the safehouse. Be sure you have all the necessities in the trunk."

He then turned and faced the other two men who originally accompanied him down the hall and had been previously restraining me from attempting to injure Mr. Black.

"276 and 569, take Dr. Gottlieb here to our headquarters in Washington, and advise our friends to be ready for surgery when he arrives," he said looking at the chip which he held in his hand. "Dr. Sikes, the straight-jacket if you please, I promise it will be returned." Dr. Sikes meekly offered the straight-jacket to the two men, and he stepped back abruptly as one of the men with a sneer and a powerful thrust removed it from his hands. As they approached the entrance to Gottlieb's cell Mr. Black shouted over his shoulder.

"9a, Sampson."

I once again heard the familiar buzz to Gottlieb's cell open for what I knew would be the last time, and the two agents stepped forward in front of the entrance, the straight jacket between them outstretched to block any hint of escape. As they were about to enter, Mr. Black addressed them one more time in a manner that suggested tediousness with the whole affair.

"And this time, gentlemen, when you arrive, *please* be sure to tell our friends to place this in a spot where no one will *ever* find it," he said, gripping the chip between his thumb and his index finger, while he cackled with a maniacal giddiness.

I turned to look at Gottlieb, who had recessed to the back corner of his cell; a look of panic filled his eyes, and terror was outstretched upon his face as the two men entered his cell and progressed towards him. As they drew closer and were about to surround him he shouted at the top of his lungs, "CRY HAVOC!!! AND LET SLIP THE DOGS OF WAR!" while lunging at them with all the brute strength his meager five foot five, fifty-three year old body could muster.

I stood there watching him as he grappled with them, and for a man of his age, size, and infirmity due to years of exposure to Haldol and other anti-psychotics, I was genuinely impressed with the vigorous tenacity with which he attacked those two men. He lunged and would extend his jaws at their arms as they came in any proximity to his face, and at one point he clamped down onto the palm of one of the agents, and blood began to trickle down from the man's hand onto Dr. Gottlieb's neck. I have to give the agent credit, as he merely grimaced in a show of detached annoyance and while bleeding, his hand crushed between Gottlieb's jaws, the other agent saw the opportunity to at last wiggle the last of the straight-jacket on.

"NO! NO!" he shouted, wriggling on the floor between them once it was fastened, and the two men simply picked him up by each shoulder and dragged him out of his cell, his feet dangling and sliding on the floor behind him. As they passed Frank, who was *still* standing helpless in the center of the cellblock hall, Dr. Gottlieb again shouted, this time in the voice that I encountered during our first meeting, as the *Jew, Shylock*.

"He hath disgraced me, and I will have my bond! I have sworn an oath that I will have my bond! Thou call'est me dog before thou hadst a cause, but since I am a dog, beware my fangs! A Daniel! yea, a Daniel! A Daniel come to judgment!" he said, and as the two men dragged him into the man-trap and around the corner I could still hear his screams echoing off down the corridor of the Class III ward. "A Daniel come to judgment!"

CHAPTER FIFTEEN

Divine Providence

As I heard Gottlieb's screams echoing down the corridor I looked over at Mr. Black who was still grinning at me with a morose and evil smile.

"I'm afraid that it's going to take more than a signature to save you now, Dr. Stattler," he said looking at the unsigned document he still held in his hands. "It's going to take nothing short of divine intervention, if you're foolish enough to believe in that sort of thing—it's going to take *Providence.*" He sauntered towards me, relishing the moment of my helplessness stuck between the two men who held me.

I glared at him, wondering how he knew I that I would come to Grove Haven before going home. I had been so careful, so meticulous. I had wrapped the chip in lead from which surely no radiation, or whatever it was the thing transmitted, could escape. What was it that I had overlooked? By what means did he find me and take my poor Katherine and David Malcolm. I was filled with rage; rage at having believed Gottlieb and rage at myself for allowing me to be manipulated by mere ideals. I had made the decision to give some of what Gottlieb told me the benefit of the doubt that it was worth the risk, and look now where it had gotten me! In not signing the transfer order I had called his bluff, and there was no way to take it back. I was engulfed in fury at both the man who now stood in front me and myself. I spit at him and a large hunk of my phlegm hung precariously from his sunglasses.

"Now that wasn't very respectable, Dr. Stattler, especially on our first date, and don't forget Doctor, *you* made the choice of things to come, not I," he said, and removed a handkerchief from the inside of his jacket pocket and wiped the front of his mirrored spectacles without removing them from his face. "I can see we're going to have to teach you, along with your wife, a lesson in manners. Take him to the cars with the others."

I struggled as the two men forcibly led me down the cell block hall, and as we began to pass Frank I looked at him pleadingly, begging him with my eyes to intervene, but he did not even return my gaze, and instead held his head in shame to the floor.

"Cheer up, Dr. Sikes," Mr. Black said as we passed him and he stood to face him. "At least we're lightening your case load a little." And with that, Mr. Black patted him on the back, handed him the transfer order, and led us out of the cell block.

I heard the cage of the man-trap open and the sound of two sets of footsteps emerging from the corridor on the opposite side of the operator's booth. There was a man pointing a gun at Sampson, who smiled at me, and then quite abruptly whacked him on the head with the butt of his revolver rendering him unconscious on the floor of the operator's booth. I tried to struggle, but the men holding my arms clamped down tighter with their grip and their thumbs burned into my muscle as I flailed about. They took me outside and threw me face first into a black sedan, by the look of it a Crown Victoria. One of the men pulled out some handcuffs from his coat pocket and clasped it around my right wrist while I recovered from the impact of being thrown against the car.

I was somehow able to wrench my arm free and bashed the man who had put the cuff on my arm and he howled and covered his face. The man on my left, seeing his comrade's distress, grabbed me by my hair and thrust my face onto the roof of the car several times. After that I decided struggling with my captors was pointless, and I lay against the vehicles, blood streaming down my face from my nose. The man whose face I had hit then smacked my head against the car again for good measure and put a hood over my head once my hands had been shackled. They stuffed me in the vehicle and I heard the car doors slam shut.

We were driving for what seemed like hours. I was seated in the back of the car, handcuffed, my arms behind my back between the two men, presumably the ones who were holding me earlier and who I had grappled with in the parking lot. The cloth they had put over my head was stifling and breathing was becoming laborsome. I had tried to distract myself from the misery of my situation by attempting to figure out which direction we were headed but the driver had taken so many turns that I couldn't tell anymore. I could only imagine what Kathryn and the baby were going through. I could only assume we had taken two vehicles to wherever it was we were going but I couldn't be sure, though I was certain that I heard more than four sets of doors shutting when we were led in to the cars.

No one had said a word since we left. I thought I might hear someone over the radio, a dispatcher of sorts giving these men instructions but there was nothing but the sound of the windshield wipers shlushing off the rain. Other than that there was just pure silence, as though the silence itself had some deliberate purpose and whose meaning escaped me. The heat of the hood was beginning to make me dizzy. I decided I could take it no longer and was the first to speak.

"Can't you take this God-damned hood off? I feel like I'm going to pass out." I demanded.

It was *the man*, Mr. Black who seemed to be orchestrating this whole macabre affair, who responded from what sounded like the front passenger seat.

"I assure you, Dr. Stattler, you're in no position to ask for anything, but if it makes you feel any better we've almost reached our destination."

We drove for about another five minutes before the car came to a halt on what sounded like a gravel driveway. When the engine was turned off I could hear another car pulling in, which I was hoping would be Kathryn and the baby. The men on either side of me each opened their doors. It was the man to my right that led me out.

"Take them inside," the man said.

I could hear several sets of footprints behind me shuffling on what sounded like loose gravel. I could also hear poor David Malcolm beginning to cry at all this hustle and bustle. He was clearly unhappy and was making sure everyone knew it.

At that moment I honestly didn't care what happened to me, but only that my son would be all right. I had no idea what these men were planning on doing with us but after the chase, my refusal to sign the transfer, and hitting one of them in the face, I was certain it wasn't going to be anything remotely pleasant.

I could then hear a door opening and we were led inside what sounded like a cement corridor with high ceilings as I could hear our steps echoing off the walls. We walked for about two minutes and were led into what I thought was a large room. Behind me I could hear Kathryn sobbing, which wasn't doing anything to comfort the baby.

"Remove the hoods," said the man, after which a hand from behind me took the cover off my head.

We were in a large room of what appeared to be an abandoned factory. There was still some old machinery lying around as well as empty cans, food containers, and broken beer and cheap wine bottles. The windows were black, stained with age and soot, and some of them were broken. The only light that came in was through their openings, which wasn't much due to the rain outside. There was a single wooden chair in the middle of the room.

"Sit down," he said.

I looked around and saw seven men, all dressed identically, all dressed in black suits with white starched shirts and black pressed ties. They wore shiny, black, patent leather shoes which reflected even the dim light strewn in from the windows, and despite the rain were still all wearing sunglasses. It was the one who I had come to identify as Mr. Black, and then later *the man*, who spoke first.

"Agents 307, 276, 569, and 203. Secure the perimeter of the building and bring in the equipment from the vehicles."

Four of the men filed out of the room, leaving only Mr. Black, the man holding Kathryn, and another man holding David Malcolm.

"Where are we?" I asked hesitantly.

"Every city in this country, Dr. Stattler, has a place we use as a safe-house, an execution center we agents use to carry out our clandestine operations. You have now become just such an operation Dr. Stattler, and because you were foolish enough to involve the ones you love in it, so has your family."

I spoke immediately, trying to salvage the lives of my wife and child, "Please, do whatever you want to me, but spare their lives. They know nothing."

"Though the pleasure of hearing you beg for mercy fills me with unbridled passion Doctor, I'm afraid my orders in this matter are quite specific and there is no resolution other than your death. You had your chance to save their lives. You didn't take it."

I began to weep then, blubbering like a two-year old in that hard chair, in that cold room.

"You'd have been wise to listen more carefully to your patient, Dr. Jacob Gottlieb, Dr. Stattler," said Mr. Black, carefully pronouncing the first name 'ya-cub' in Dr. Gottlieb's native German tongue.

"Why is that?" I asked defiantly.

"You gave a good chase, quite frankly one of the most entertaining I have ever had. It was very clever of you to conceal the chip with this piece of lead foil ..." he paused and looked at the chip, wrapped in the foil from the 1976 Pichon Lallande I had taken from the wine bottle at Jeff and Melissa's, seeming to admire my ingenuity, and from where I was sitting I could see it reflected in his sunglasses. "But you made one critical error, and it was that error that led us to you."

Two of the four men returned carrying a chainsaw, several bags of pre-mix concrete, two wooden boxes, duct tape, and a large blue plastic tarp. When I saw this I began to feel ill, and Kathryn began to become hysterical.

"What do you want!" she screamed, the baby crying in the background.

"203," Mr. Black said to one of his subordinates who had just returned with the supplies, "Silence that!"

One of the men set down his equipment and came toward Kate with the duct tape outstretched between his hands, while he slowly ripped a piece off. Kathryn attempted to free herself from the grasp of the man who held her and made it as difficult as possible for the agent carrying the duct tape to paste it over her mouth.

"You son-of-a-bitch!" I screamed at Mr. Black, who was standing in front of me calmly smoking.

He turned and pointed his pistol at me and cocked it in front of me.

"What was that, Dr. Stattler?" he asked.

I said nothing and grimaced as I watched in silence as the agent grappling with Kathryn grabbed her by her hair, forcing her face forward. The man Mr. Black referred to as '203' then placed the tape over her lips, and I could only watch as my poor Kate protested this abuse with muffled groans beneath the tape.

"I'm sorry, I didn't hear you." Mr. Black said, taunting me again. When he could see I was not going to protest any further he reholstered the pistol under his jacket. He then addressed the agent who had gagged Kathryn. "Thank you, 203. Please join the others and prep the vehicles." The two men nodded, saying nothing, and walked out of the room leaving just the six of us again.

"As I was saying, Dr. Stattler, before you so rudely interrupted me, it would have been prudent to give more credence to the confessions of your patients. Dr. Gottlieb was the only person ever implanted to realize the truth of what he was carrying—the truth of which drove him mad."

"What do you mean?" I asked.

"That's how we found you, Dr. Stattler," he said, unwrapping the foil from the chip, and continuing as though he were speaking to it. "We were listening." He then held out the chip at arms length in front of me. "*They* are listening, right now, right here, as I speak these words, this chip is broadcasting not only our position, but our entire conversation, Dr. Stattler. Though the lead foil was able to conceal the locator beacon within the chip, it failed to conceal voices, which operate on a carrier wave relative to the signal we can triangulate within ten city blocks. However, this proved not to be necessary. We could still hear everything you said, everywhere you were, every place you went, every conversation you had, and it is *that* Dr. Stattler, which eventually lead us to you. That's how we followed you to McKinley Park, that's how we followed you afterwards. That's how we knew you were with Gottlieb when you didn't come home at the appointed hour. That's how we knew all along, everything that he was telling you."

I sat there, in mute silence, going over in my head all the places I had been and hidden while carrying the chip, Bo's Biker Bar, the rest stop, and it finally began to dawn on me the truth of it all. I was dumbfounded, unbelieving that I could have been so careless as to not realize just *who* Dr. Gottlieb was talking to in our sessions. He *was* performing a play for an audience, because he *knew*, at the very least on a subconscious level, that they could hear him. He was telling me the *truth* the entire time, and I was too full of disbelief and conjecture to know it. He *knew* about the chip and its purpose. He *knew* they were listening. He *knew* the chip was relaying our conversations. He *knew* everything; he must have seen it before. I began to understand that it was Mr. Black he was talking to, in the voices of Shylock, Macbeth, Caesar, and Lear, and the aliens themselves, if for nothing else but to mock them from afar. As if to say, 'You have not yet beaten me, and I defy you.' He tried to tell me but I was so sure of myself, so over-confident of my position and authority, that it didn't even occur to me to entertain the notion that what he was saying and the purpose of the plays was *real*.

I sat there in silence, absorbing the truth and my failure and reluctance to believe it, and see it. If I did, it might have saved my life, I thought. But I also knew in truth, how could I have? And after a few moments of deliberation I came to the conclusion that despite my inability to foresee these events unfold, by not believing in Dr. Gottlieb I had failed to protect my family. It was not just mine but their deaths on my conscience. It was they who were going to suffer because of me. It was they who might die because of me. Everything that had proceeded and everything that I had thought and believed since I met Dr. Gottlieb was a failure; my failure. I decided in that moment I could take no more and my failure was in essence 'complete', and I wanted this charade and my life, if it was to end here and now, to be over as quickly as possible.

"Can we just get this over with please?" I asked. Kathryn moaned in protest but if I was going to die I didn't see much point in belaboring the process.

Mr. Black smiled at this, clearly amused at my effrontery amidst the situation. "You're a brave man, Dr. Stattler, braver than most would be at the prospect of being killed in front of your wife and child," he said, pacing around my chair as he spoke. "But before I do kill you, and you'll have to forgive me for indulging in the cliché', I'm going to gloat over you and your helpless position and inform you just why you are to die."

Kate moaned what sounded like a "No!" beneath her gag. I looked at her pleadingly, as if to say, "I love you, but please don't make this harder than it already is."

"Do whatever you want with me, but *please* leave my family out of it. They're innocent. They know nothing. It's me you want, it's me who took the chip, it's me who knows, not them. Please let them go."

He leaned over towards my left ear and hissed, "And just what is it do you *think* you know, Dr. Stattler? Hmm?"

I said nothing and let him continue his monologue.

"And as for their *innocence,* that is a make believe word. *Innocence* is something that exists only in the minds of madmen. You are born in this universe and you *die* in it. When galaxies collide and millions of worlds and civilizations are destroyed, they are not *innocent.* They are casualties of existence. No one is *innocent.* It is a word only invented by poets to describe an ideal, and ideals do not exist. As you have just found out, only *truth* exists, Dr. Stattler. And the *truth* of the matter is you have stumbled upon a conspiracy that is far greater and more encompassing than your feeble, albeit genetically enhanced, Cro-Magnon brain can ever begin to imagine."

"I don't understand," I said.

"Of course you don't, and as much as I would love to tell you everything I know before you die, it would take months, years perhaps, and I just simply don't have the time."

"I thought you said you were going to tell me why you were going to kill me." I stuttered, partially out of want to delay what now seemed inevitable, and partially so that I could look at Kate one last time.

"I have every intention to, Dr. Stattler. You see, much like the Roman Empire, ours is a nation that has been consumed by excess. Excess in the food we eat, the alcohol we drink, the cigarettes we smoke, the drugs we take, the clothes we wear, the cars we drive, the homes we build. Nowhere else on the face of the earth will you find such broadcasting, such boasting, if not bragging, of such excesses. The prosperity, security, and, more importantly, the rise of technology we have enjoyed in the last sixty years has been partially due to influence of those beings you would expose, and in turn this prosperity has produced envy from other nations and many enemies abroad.

"Indeed, while the rest of the world waits eagerly, salivating at the thought of America's downfall and destruction so that in the chaos they may pillage and plunder the wealth and prosperity of this great nation of yours, I defend it. It is my job to keep people like you from making that happen, Dr. Stattler. It is my job to keep people like you from exposing information, information that can lead to the truth we have just spoke of. And that, Dr. Stattler, is the reason you are to die."

He came toward me then, unwavering, so resolute in purpose and duty that it began to overwhelm me, like some machine devoid of compassion or soul. I tried to mentally prepare myself for what was about to happen but I found I could not, I could only stare blankly as he came toward me. He stopped about five feet from me and opened his jacket and again revealed the large stainless steel caliber weapon at his side. I could hear Kate moaning and sobbing in the background and I could only imagine what she must be going through having to witness the death of her husband, right in front of her eyes. She struggled meekly in the arms of the man holding her but her efforts were useless.

I looked up at Mr. Black, trying to see some glimpse of mercy but all I could see was myself, sweating and trembling in his mirrored sunglasses.

"It's been a pleasure, Dr. Stattler, but I'm afraid the pleasure is now over."

He unbuttoned his holster once more and placed his hand upon the gun inside it. I cringed and closed my eyes, bracing myself against the hard back of the wooden chair for the impact, and I imagined my insides being strewn about the floor behind me as he unloaded his weapon into me. I sat there, waiting, in silence for what seemed to me to be an eternity, but in reality was no more than several seconds. Finally unable to endure anymore I opened my eyes. Mr. Black stood before me, motionless, his hand on his weapon still holstered on his hip. His gaze was impenetrable, and seemed to be focusing on something, but because of his glasses I could not tell which direction his eyes were facing. Finally, after what seemed to me to be about a minute the man holding Kathryn spoke.

"Number One," he said. "Is there a problem?"

Mr. Black straightened and said, "No." He then turned to face the one who addressed him. "Just thought I saw something is all."

He then removed the gun from his holster, slid back the bolt cocking it, and addressed the two men who were holding Kathryn and my son. "Take them to the Groom Lake facility for interrogation. Agents 203 and 307, have the car ready in fifteen minutes." He then looked at me and cocked his weapon. "I'll finish up here."

At that moment I heard Kate scream a muffled, "No!" under her gag, and she tried desperately to escape but this was useless against the overpowering strength of the agent who held her, and she began to sob as the man in black quite literally dragged her out of the room. My poor little boy, my David Malcolm, began to shriek when he heard the muffled cries of his mother and I could hear his screams echoing down the hall as they left and shut the door, and the sober realization struck me that it was to be the last time I was to see either of them again.

Once we were alone Mr. Black strode toward me and stopped about five feet in front of me. He stood there, blankly staring at me for a moment beneath his sunglasses, as if deliberating on the choice that lay before him, or more so, as if he was waiting for something, but whatever it was that something did not happen. Without saying a word he raised his weapon and pointed it directly between my eyes. I shut them almost wincing, and I could feel sweat begin to stream down my brow and I felt myself beginning to hyperventilate. I tried to mentally prepare myself for death and attempted to imagine what I would say to God. How would I tell him that it was my pride and arrogance that destroyed my family? How could I justify my actions against their lives? What right did I have to put my righteousness before them? I did not know, and was filled with such self-loathing I actually *wanted* my life to end. I waited there for what seemed an eternity for the bullet to blast open my skull and surely send me to the Gates of Hell itself. It was in that moment when I thought life was over that I heard a crash from behind me, which sounded like an empty bottle breaking on the floor.

I opened my eyes and looked at Mr. Black, who still had his weapon raised, and someone with a slurred voice began to speak.

"Please don't kill me!" the voice said pleadingly.

With his lips curling, a look of surprised rage spread across Mr. Black's face and he screamed, "Fool!" He then ran toward the back corner of the room where the voice came from.

"No!" said the voice, which was followed by the loud report of Mr. Black's gun. *Blam. Blam. Blam*, which reverberated throughout the factory, out the broken, blackened windows and seemed to ring off the old machinery still lying in ruins about the room. Then all was silent. I tried to turn the chair I was sitting in around so I could see what was happening, but that proved to be futile as my hands were still handcuffed behind me. I stood up and turned around to look at what was sure to be a grisly scene behind me.

Mr. Black stood there silently over the body of what looked to be a vagrant or homeless man. He was dressed in raggedy navy jeans, and a tattered black overcoat. There was a pool of blood collecting beneath his head from his wounds. His body was still twitching and Mr. Black unloaded another round into his skull. Finally the body was still and the room silent except for my breathing, which was still heavy and Mr. Black turned to look at me. His face was an ashen gray, and looked damp from a cold sweat, as though he had just seen a ghost. We stared at each other for a few moments, neither of us saying a word, the only sound my breathing. It was then, after staring at each other blankly, that he did the most peculiar and unexpected thing: he smiled. He smiled at me with such a smile that bordered on what I would call pure joy, or as though he had experienced a revelation, and in every sense of the word and with every fiber of my being as a professional psychiatrist I thought him truly insane, not that I didn't to some extent before, but now I was certain of it. And as I stood there watching him with this curious expression I was certain at any moment it would end abruptly and he would unload the rest of his gun into my body, but he did not.

He holstered his gun, looked down at the body, and began to undress it. It was while taking off the poor dead man's shoes that he started to speak for the first time since the other agents left the room with Kathryn. "Now do you see what your ideals have cost you Dr. Stattler? Now do you understand the *real* meaning of truth? Are you now finally aware of what happens when you meddle in affairs that do not concern you?"

I stood there trembling, not sure or even just how I should respond to his inquiries. He gathered the dead man's clothes into a bundle and came toward me with a deliberate swiftness. He then thrust the bundle into my chest and since my hands were still cuffed behind my back they fell to a floor in a heap. He put his finger to his lips, signaling me to be silent. When he lowered his finger he looked directly into my eyes and said as if in response to himself, "Of course you do, Dr. Stattler, you're dead."

I stared at him blankly, still not fully aware of *what* he was saying. He pointed his gun at me, not in a threatening gesture but more so as if it was an extension of his hand and he waved it in front of me, back and forth as if to say, "Shoo," while motioning toward a pile of cardboard boxes in the back corner of the room that the poor homeless devil he killed must have been hiding under. I looked at him puzzled and his stare was cold and life-less. Clearly he meant for me to hide before the other agents returned but I was unsure as to why he had given me the dead man's clothes. I flapped my arms about to remind him of the cuffs I still was wearing so we could pro-ceed with whatever he had intended.

He holstered his gun and with a smirk walked behind me and spoke as though I was not there, or, more precisely, I was there and dead. "Dr. Stattler, if there's one thing I detest it is a corpse that can't cooperate.

He unlocked the handcuffs which were still behind my back and when he was finished began to tug at my jacket. I got the point and began to undress. As there was obviously no heat in a dilapidated abandoned factory it began to get chilly very quickly. When I was finished undressing he gath-ered up my things. I tried to retrieve my wallet from my jeans but he pushed my hand away and glared at me. He then took everything to the center of the room where the other agents had laid the equipment and put it in a pile. Inside one of the boxes they brought in he pulled out a small one gallon can of gasoline which he began to pour over my clothes.

When he was finished, he removed a silver Zippo lighter from his inside pocket and a package of Marlboro Red cigarettes. He began to thump the bottom of the pack while simultaneously removing a cigarette which he placed between his lips. He flicked the lighter between his thumb and index finger and lit the cigarette, then took several drags, and after a deliberately strong exhale threw it on the pile of clothes. It ignited with a loud "Pfwhump!" and burned in a cool blue green haze which was no doubt from the dye in my pants and jacket. I watched my belongings and my very identity go up in smoke and become ashes and for the first time my thoughts were turned away from Kathryn and the baby and I began to wonder what this Mr. Black had in store for me next.

My teeth began to chatter, which reminded me that before I went or did anything I was still standing there in the middle of the cold, wet floor in only my underwear. I leaned over and picked up the dead man's clothes which reeked of cheap booze and human waste. I made my way over to the pile of boxes and started to dress.

As I stuck my foot into the trousers I realized it was not just residual waste but physical waste that I smelled, and I couldn't helping gasping as my toes were now emerged in human feces. I came rapidly to the conclusion that the man in his last death throws had undoubtedly shit himself. Mr. Black looked up at me with an annoyed look and once again put his finger to his lips signaling me to be quiet, and I couldn't help but look at him reproachfully as I slid one leg then the other into the dead man's trousers. It felt like I was bathing in excrement.

He then tapped his watch, which I inferred to mean time was running out, and if I wanted to remain alive I had best get my legs, feces and all, out of sight and under those boxes. I put on the tattered black overcoat and plunged myself under the crates which were in front of me. From my vantage point I really couldn't see much of the room or what Mr. Black was doing, and this was probably a blessing. I was able to tell though, that it had stopped raining and a full moon was shining in through the broken windows. Although I couldn't see much from where I was lying I could, however, hear practically everything, as the cold, hard, concrete floor of the factory and the high ceilings made every noise echo throughout the room.

I heard what sounded like plastic being unrolled, and I assumed this to be the rolled blue tarp the other agents had brought in earlier. I then heard Mr. Black's footsteps move toward the body lying next to me, which he began dragging across the floor and, from the sound of the rufflings, onto the tarp. It grew quiet for a few moments, but this silence was quickly broken by the unmistakable sound of the chainsaw attempting to be started. After about the fourth time it finally caught, I heard it rev, and winced when I heard the blade make contact with its target as it undoubtedly ground the dead man's flesh in to manageable pieces.

This lasted for only a few minutes. When the saw stopped I heard the dull thud of what must have been human body parts being put in the wooden boxes and the sound of the cement bags being torn and their contents spilled into the waiting containers. The smell of the dead man's clothes was filling my nostrils and I felt as though I was going to retch when a group of footsteps echoed in the outer corridor. I heard the hinges of the great metal door we had entered through creak and one of the men came in the room. His footsteps were not evenly spaced, and seemed to be slowed as though carrying something heavy. I heard two objects being set on the floor and the sound of water splashing and figured he must have been carrying several pails of water with which to set the cement.

"Bring in the others," the man said, and the agent who brought in the water left and I heard the old metal of the door once again creak and slam shut into it's frame. It was silent and then the unmistakable click of the Zippo and Mr. Black exhaling filled my ears.

He stood there by the boxes in silence, smoking, until the other men arrived to retrieve their grisly parcels, now hardening with cement around the poor man's body parts. I was still trembling, wondering if the ruse was going to succeed, and this fear began to worsen once the other agents returned to collect the remains. I assumed that it did, as one by one of the men left the room, huffing under the weight of the body parts and wet rock until only Mr. Black remained.

"I'll clear the building," he said as the last agent puffed through the door carrying his load. He then strolled, almost casually toward my position, his very footsteps seeming to enjoy and relish the moment of the success of his ruse. He stopped, inches from where I was lying and I could see the moonlight glimmering off the shine in his shoe. I wondered what he was doing there. Though the stench from my clothes was horrific, I was still terrified by the events that had transpired in less than a quarter of an hour. I couldn't help but wonder if he was pondering whether or not to change his mind and kill me anyway.

Though I was no longer handcuffed I was quite helpless and even if I was on my feet I had nowhere to run anyway. These thoughts were dismissed, however, when I saw what appeared to be a silver money clip bounce on the floor directly in front of my face. He then dropped his cigarette, snubbed it out with his toe and walked across the room to the heavy metal door. I heard it swing open on its rusting hinges again, and I laid there, still petrified of this monster who had found me and taken my family in the night, wondering what would happen to my poor Katherine and baby David. I did not have to think long before the realization took hold of me that I would never see them again. As I heard the door slam shut and his footsteps echo off down the corridor, I somehow knew this wasn't the last I would see of Mr. Black, somehow I knew our lives were intertwined in what I feared was nothing less but a great downward spiral. It was in that moment I knew my life would never be the same again.

I heard the sound of car doors shutting and their engines being started outside, followed by the grating of their tires on wet, loose gravel. I waited several minutes to be sure they had all left before I emerged from hiding. I dusted myself off from all the pieces of cardboard which had stuck to the jacket due to the blood of the dead man, not that it made much difference anyway considering the state of my clothes.

I leaned over and picked up the money clip. It was a clear and shining polished silver, on which was engraved the letters 'SD', and I wondered what it stood for. Judging by the wad of hundreds it appeared to contain several thousand dollars. I flipped it over to count it and take stake of exactly what my options at this point were.

On the first bill underneath was something written in black ink, which I surmised he wrote while he was standing in front of me after the others had left. I opened it to read it and what I found froze my soul even more than what I had been through that evening. It read:

If you ever let me find you again, I will kill you.
—the Man in Black

CHAPTER SIXTEEN

Back to the Present

"I still have it," I said while reaching behind me and pulling out my wallet. I removed the bill which I kept in the flap with a clear plastic insert, where one would normally keep a drivers license or I.D. and held it out in front of me between us. The hundred dollar note was tattered and wrinkled with age, but the ink with which Mr. Black wrote his last message to me was still clearly visible.

"Why didn't you spend it, surely there must have been times in your twenty-year exile from society when you would have needed it?" he asked calmly.

"Oh, there were, and I came close several times," I said thoughtfully. "After you found my place of work in New Orleans I ended up sleeping in cemeteries for several weeks until I could work enough odd jobs to gather up bus fare."

He smiled at this.

"It's kind of silly really," I said. "Over the years I somehow came to think that if I spent it you would find me, and my life would be over. I thought it was an omen and that once I spent it you would find me one night and just leave me there, or worse." I said, remembering the homeless man who had inadvertently saved my life.

"Maybe it was," he answered. "So what are you going to do with it now that I *have* found you?"

I looked at him for a few seconds before responding, trying to gauge if there was yet another, hidden message in his words, if he had had another vision and my fate was at hand. "Is that another attempt at humor, or have you *seen* something I should know about?"

He leaned back and chuckled at this before answering, "And remember I *did* find you, I just didn't kill you. You know, Dr. Stattler, the sight isn't something one can simply summon and have all the intricate pieces of the universal puzzle unfold and fall into place—it is a test of one's abilities, completely random, like deja-vu only it happens *before* the event itself. You experience it only when *it* wishes you to, and the test is to determine whether or not you can figure out what *will* transpire *before* it comes to pass."

I thought for a moment before responding. "I've been giving this some thought, and I'm not quite sure I buy it. Let's say you're right, and the future has, in fact, already happened. And let's also say that the second sight allows you to see glimpses of the manner in which the universe will unfold. If that's true, what's to keep you or anyone else from altering it?"

Mr. Black stared at me blankly, mashing his cigarette in the ashtray. "To answer to your question, Gray Science tried to answer that mystery many times and all with disastrous consequences when they first began interstellar space travel. Each and every time they thought they were on the verge of manipulating future events contradictory to the visions they witnessed with the second sight, their actions in some manner always served to facilitate the future they were attempting to avoid. Though humans have not yet discovered this fact, it is just as impossible to alter the future as it is the past, they are, essentially, no different, they *have* already transpired."

"Attempting to alter the future is just as futile as trying to alter or change the force of gravity. Time, like gravity, is a constant in the universe; even when you approach the speed of light you experience time just as you normally would, it is only everywhere else that it *seems* to pass more quickly, and to everyone else time has passed in much the same manner it normally does. So how is this possible? Surely there is a paradox here, *unless* these events *have* already happened. It is, truly, a terrible thing to consider, knowing that the second sight allows you glimpses of the future, yet you are unable and powerless to do anything about it."

"In the first test cases in humans with the Grays second sight gene, it eventually drove them to madness and suicide, as they eventually saw and were able to comprehend their own deaths. They were unable to mentally grasp and control this very awesome power. This is why humanity is continually and meticulously experimented with by the Grays before new DNA installments, which grants humans these abilities, are, in effect, put into place. A more precise way of putting it might be, 'turned on.' The consequences for not testing these abilities could literally create genocide of the species."

I studied him intensely while he lit another cigarette and began to pon-
der the meaning of what it was he was trying to tell me. He was right, as in
so many of the experiences I have had with him he continually surprised me
as to what I *thought* would happen and what *did* happen. I wasn't sure if
having the sight was an ability I wanted to possess, much like people don't
want to live in a world with the Grays in it.

He looked at me closely. "Do you miss them?" he asked, as though he
was incapable of experiencing an emotion so basic.

"Every day of my life," I said. "Their memory is all I have to hold on to;
it's all I have to keep me going, to keep me on the run, to keep me in hiding
from you." I slipped then and remembered my dear Kathryn, her flowing
hair, her quirkiness, her love, her shapely hips.

"I'm sorry," he said, and I believed he meant it. "There was little I could
do, saving you was the only miracle I could perform that day, which it truly
was Dr. Stattler. I had every intention of killing you. I had my orders, I had
obeyed them before, but the sight took hold of me, and then that man crept
out from under those boxes. My men had just surveyed that building, Dr.
Stattler. They had walked through it before we found you and took you
there. There was no one under those boxes. It was, shall we say, no pun
intended, or perhaps maybe a little, *Providence.*"

I smiled at this as did he, remembering just where we were, and we
shared a moment of silence together, each of us remembering that terrible
evening and realizing that after over twenty years there was still some good
that came out of it: my life.

It was he who spoke first, and brought us back to the present time and
the seemingly impossible task ahead of us. "In addition to the chip there's
something else you will need to have. It is what allowed us to detect and
monitor you once you had the chip concealed." He then removed a small,
polished, stainless steel box from his pocket. It had what appeared to be a
small LCD display, probably three and a half to four inches on each side,
about a total of twelve square inches, and a keypad below it. "This is a
position locator and monitoring device which will detect anyone carrying a
chip. It has been manufactured to run on the power of your typical nickel-
cadmium battery." He flipped it over to reveal a sliding insert and removed
it. "On a full charge you can use the device continuously for seventy-two
hours, after which time you will need to re-charge it."

He then reached in to his coat pocket and produced what looked like a
cellular phone charger. "With this device you can find and locate any chip

on the surface of the planet. I told you before that all agents operate on a millahertz bandwidth, all persons that have been abducted and are carrying chips are on a decahertz frequency, so you will always know the difference between an agent, and someone who has simply been taken and implanted. You can tune to a specific frequency by using these indicators." He then pointed to a keypad with two up and down arrows. "Once you have located the frequency of the chip you wish to monitor, you can listen to the subject with a simple ear piece," he said while removing a small ear plug with a long black cord from his jacket pocket.

"How do you know how to locate a specific frequency?" I asked

"Unfortunately, you will not be able to know just who a specific frequency belongs to. This information is only available on an index at our bases of operation. For example, let's say your name is John Doe, and you've been abducted and are transmitting a frequency of say, two-hundred-five decahertz, then you can find them using this device. Watch." He tuned the device until the numbers 205 were in bright red on the indicator. He put in the ear piece and handed it to me.

I looked at him surprised, and somewhat baffled, and took the instrument and put the cord containing the plug into my ear. I listened for a few seconds and was able to determine the person talking was speaking another language which I recognized. "They're speaking German," I said, and handed the device back to him.

"Not all abductees are taken from this country, Dr. Stattler. It is imperative to the Grays 'research', I'll call it, that the modifications to our DNA they are implementing take place on a global level. But, in answer to your inquiry, if you happened to be scanning and found this person, you would have no way of knowing their name was John Doe, and they had been assigned to this chip number, you would only know where they were located and what they were saying, though it's very likely while monitoring conversations that you will in time be able to determine a subjects name."

"Gotcha," I said. "I can't begin to imagine the wealth of information you can discover using one of these ... I'm not so sure I'm ready for this."

"The device is more so not for you to monitor conversations but to be able to protect yourself from the proximity of other agents."

"How do you use the locator?"

"The locator works sort of like a touch-screen, and it has a database that contains maps, street names and addresses. Sort of like a self-contained 'Map-Quest.' When you first turn it on it shows a map of the globe." He pushed a small red button on the keypad and the screen lit up depicting a green line-drawing of the earth. He then touched the North American Continent, which enlarged that section, and then again on the United States. He then pushed a button on the keypad that said "Emit." On the screen appeared what looked like thousands of little red dots. "These are all the chips broadcasting in the decahertz bandwidth in the continental U.S."

"You mean these are all people who have been abducted?"

"Precisely. You can further narrow the search by clicking on a state," and he demonstrated this simultaneously while speaking as he clicked on Rhode Island.

"Then by touching a city, this enlarges a map of the city, then a portion of a city, and then a location." A street map of Providence emerged on the screen and there were several red dots remaining. He narrowed the search to further isolate one of the dots, and I realized by the address readout at the bottom it was in the very building we were sitting.

"Listen," he said, and handed the device back to me.

I couldn't believe the power of this instrument and what I was actually witnessing. I held the locator in the palm of my hand and again put in the ear piece and listened. The voice was female, and she seemed to be going on about problems with her boyfriend. In the background I could hear noises I recognized, plates clattering, glasses clinking, fuzzy conversations, and I realized it was because I was hearing them not just out of the speaker in my ear; I was hearing them simultaneously and I realized the voice was coming from a woman sitting at the bar.

"The red dress," Mr. Black said.

I looked up, and indeed there was a woman with a red dress with long dark hair talking to who appeared to be a girlfriend or co-worker. I concentrated and listened, and indeed, the voices matched. She then turned slightly and looked me over as one tends to do in a bar. She had a knowing, striking expression, as if she somehow knew I was listening. Her stare was captivating, and her dark, hazel eyes stirred in me feelings I had denied myself for so long. For obvious reasons, I knew it was neither the time nor place for such thoughts, and decided therefore to break the tension and turned back toward Mr. Black.

"Incredible!" I said, still in shock of the sheer power of the small piece of machinery I held in my hand. I took the ear-piece out and handed it back to him with the instrument, but he held his hand up in protest.

"It's yours now," he said.

I put what I would later christen the 'super-palm-pilot' in the inside of my coat pocket with the ear piece.

"And the chip," he said, while pointing at the little black vial on the table.

"How did you know who it was?" I asked incredulously while putting the chip and the adapter in my coat pocket with the super palm pilot.

"After a while you'll begin to develop a knack for it," he said.

He then looked at me sternly and became very serious.

"You must understand, Doctor, the forces that will pursue you once discovered will be unrelenting and full of more intent on finding you than ever I was; more than you can begin to imagine. I am giving you this device so that you may yet prevail and avoid them. It is *imperative* they never find out you possess it, or they will use it against you, and you *will* be discovered."

I looked at him gravely, still unsure of whether exposing the truth, now that I actually knew it, was something I wanted, and if I was doubting it, what right did I have to reveal it to everyone else? The gravity of the situation now began to dawn on me and I slowly realized I was trapped. I could no longer live out the rest of my existence in hiding, and yet, if I chose to take on the under-government and all the power and resources they possessed I thought a victory was moot at best. Half my life I had been running from the man, Mr. Black, because I believed what he wrote on that hundred dollar bill. I believed he would kill me. I believed he was an evil, sinister man with some evil, sinister plan.

But now I had come to discover he was in essence saving me, keeping me from being discovered, hiding the truth of my existence for a greater purpose, some parts of which he had already seen unfold. But where would I go? Who would I turn to? What source could I rely on that wasn't in on the take, that couldn't be corrupted, or wouldn't betray me? The power given to me was a tremendous burden, more than I thought I could bear, and I wished I had finished out the day prepping pizzas and washing dishes at Fillini's. I ran my hands through my hair and opened my eyes, stretching them while expressing a huge sigh.

"It's a lot to grasp in one afternoon," he said, studying me, trying to offer me comfort.

"You can say that again," I said. "I don't even know where to begin."

"You can begin with my daughter; she *knows* what is at stake, what lives are on the line, and where you can run."

I remembered the name, Sarah Dawson, in San Diego. I pulled out the money clip which he had given me all those years ago from my pocket and once again looked at the initials which had become all too familiar to me: S.D. "S.D., Sarah Dawson," I said, putting the pieces together. "Did she give this to you?"

"I had it made," he said. "For her."

"But why give it to me?"

He smiled, and leaned back, the cigarette smoke wafting up out of the ashtray between us. "Because I knew I would see it again."

I handed the clip to him and he rubbed it curiously, with the tenderness and emotion that one might a beloved pet, upon being reunited after a long absence.

He then put it in the right pocket of his suit jacket, seemingly still locked in reminiscence.

We had been in that booth for hours and the bar was beginning to fill up again. It was nearing five o'clock and the happy hour crowd was beginning to stream in from work. Jake was starting his shift on the piano and he began to tickle the keys in a familiar, reassuring melody. Despite all I had learned that afternoon I was beginning to feel optimistic about the future; that somehow my role in it would be a good one and that the world would be secure with the knowledge of aliens in it.

This jovial feeling did not last long, however. I looked back at Mr. Black and he sat there, frozen, unwavering, like a statue, his face looking away from me at something in the distance, but the likes of which wasn't really there. It was exactly like the scene I had witnessed that night in that abandoned building so many years ago, when he had his hand on his holster, ready to draw the gun and burst my insides all over the factory floor. I realized with an unprecedented and monotonous dread what was happening. It was the second sight. The universe was unfolding around us, precisely as he had seen, and was now witnessing again, like some siege engine battering at the gates, pounding at the door, desperately trying to enter the present, and no force anywhere, short of divine intervention, if it even existed, could stop it.

My heart pounded and my brow began to dampen and bead with sweat. It was as though I was there, sitting on that chair, my hands cuffed behind me and helpless all over again. The reality of Fate began to set in, and it filled me with both elation and horror. After what seemed like days, but in reality was probably no more than ten seconds, he came out of his eerie trance and looked at me.

"We haven't much time," he said. "They're coming."

CHAPTER SEVENTEEN

The Men in Black

I reached into my coat and pulled out the small instrument he had given me and tuned it into the millahertz bandwidth. The map of Providence was still on the screen where he had left it. There appeared seven bright red dots converging on our position at Magiano's address. I looked up at him terrified.

"You had best leave now, Dr. Stattler, if you wish to ensure your survival," he said calmly, with only the slightest hint of urgency.

"Where will I go?" I asked.

"Behind this restaurant, across the alley and behind the bookstore you will find a white Ford Taurus, license number XJ7-1016 with Rhode Island plates. Here is the key," he said, and reached into his jacket pocket and handed it to me. "In the glove compartment you will find a vehicle registration, a firearm, ammunition, funds, and a driver's license with your picture on it and a passport."

"How did you?" I stopped, thinking better of it when I saw his expression at this. "Nevermind," I said, remembering that the agents were going to be knocking down the door any minute.

"The name on the I.D. is Bill Jacobson and the social security number is printed below it. Remember it if you are asked any questions. The DOB on the license is the same as yours."

I was about to get up to leave and then stopped, as there was still a question he had not answered that I felt needed to be.

"There's one thing I still don't understand." I said.

"And what might that be, Dr. Stattler?"

"Why keep me on the run all these years? Why keep me in hiding and never let me hold down a job?"

"It's very simple really, you see Dr. Stattler. If I could find you, then *they* could find you, and they would know for certain I disobeyed orders that night, and did not kill you. As for having you laid off from your various places of employ, it was simply my way of telling you that."

"I owe you my life; I guess I should thank you," I said.

"Nonsense," he said, waving hand in a mock gesture. "Who knows, maybe I was preparing you for the task that lies ahead."

"Maybe, you were." I said, forcing a smile, while nodding my head. "It's been an interesting journey Mr. Black, but you'll have to forgive me when I say it's not one I care to repeat."

"The journey isn't over yet Dr. Stattler, not for you anyway."

"Goodbye, Mr. Black," I said, extending my hand.

He shook it firmly in silence and smiled.

I rose to leave and put on my jacket, taking care not to drop any of the precious items that he had bestowed upon me when a thought occurred.

"You know, Black," I said. "There's one thing in universal plan that seems to have escaped you."

Mr. Black looked somewhat offended at this.

"And that is?"

"Maybe there *is* something outside the universe. Maybe everything *is* happening for a reason, maybe it's God himself in the 4th dimension, outside the universe, and the only way to reach him is by actually breaking the light-speed barrier, or through death."

He paused at this, carefully considering what I had said. "I had not considered that," he said, and seemed to be mulling in his head for something to say. "But if for some reason that *should* that be the case, then I will not say goodbye, but rather 'until next time.'"

I smiled and turned to leave when two men approached me wearing the all too familiar attire I have come to loathe and fear when I see it.

"What is your business with this man?" the first man addressed me sharply.

"I was just leaving," I said, and looked around me. The happy hour crowd was deep at the bar and most of the tables around it where we and Mr. Black was sitting were now full. It was Mr. Black who spoke next.

"203," he said. "How nice to see you again."

"I wish I could say the same," one of the men said. "We've been looking for you." The agent then looked me up and down and as I looked at him I not only remembered his number, '203', but his face. He was there that night over twenty years ago. He was the one that bashed my face into the roof of the car outside of Grove Haven, and I prayed he did not recognize me.

"I'm not surprised. You're early. I was expecting you a little later," Mr. Black said, with a face full of dire seriousness at the man I had just spoken to.

I was wondering what exactly he meant by this when the other agent looked at me and said, "You'll be coming with me."

"Let this man go 405," Mr. Black said. "He knows nothing."

"I think you know, number one, that we'll be the judge of that," the man who Mr. Black addressed as '405' said, eyeing me up and down as though he were surveying a commodity. "You know the rules. Why don't you two come with us. Now," he said, putting emphasis on this last word.

I turned to look at Mr. Black, who was still sitting in the booth, for some sign of what to do, but he sat there motionless, staring at the man placidly, when to my great surprise he did something I was not expecting.

"MR. FIORENTINO!" he shouted. The whole room including Mickey looked over and after a few moments grew silent, even Jake had stopped playing in the middle of "Piano Man" to witness this strange spectacle.

I stepped away from the agent who had approached me and turned to look at Mr. Black, wondering just what his intentions were.

Mr. Black looked across the bar to Mickey and said in a calm, cool mannered voice as though he were simply about to order a drink, "I'm afraid you're going to have a mess to clean up."

Before I could realize what was happening, he pulled the gun from the table top and squeezed off three rounds into the man called '405' who had just spoken to me. His body stood limply for a moment and then crashed on to a round cocktail table behind him, smashing the table sideways and then rolled onto the floor with a loud thud. The other agent, 203, completely taken aback attempted to draw his pistol, but Mr. Black was already ready for him and unloaded several rounds into his face. Screams filled the air along with the sounds of glasses breaking from people either ducking for cover under tables, jumping across the bar or fleeing out the door, which was difficult as the other agents who heard the shots from outside were now desperately trying to get in. I looked down at the man who had just spoken to me, who now had a large hole in his face where his left eye should be. Blood was spattered everywhere behind him and I could see bits of blood and flesh clinging to some of the glasses that were not turned over at the bar.

"Run, Doctor, now!" Mr. Black said as he stood up from the booth and began to take aim at what appeared to be three agents struggling at the door to get inside against the throng of patrons trying to escape. One of the agents emerged from the pile with his weapon raised and pointed at Mr. Black.

Dashing across the bar room floor, crunching bits of broken glass beneath my shoes, I flew into the kitchen door. I heard gun shots in the background. Once I reached the safety of the kitchen I crouched behind the door. I saw Mr. Black's arm raise and his weapon fire again at the agent closest to him. The bullet pierced his neck and blood and bits of spinal tissue sprayed into the faces of the agents emerging behind him. He grasped his throat and fell to the floor making a sickening guttural noise as he thrashed about on the ceramic tile next to the cocktail tables.

By this time one of the other agents was able to draw his weapon and fired several rounds, which struck Mr. Black directly in the chest. Mr. Black was thrown backwards into the table where we were sitting and he clasped the edge of it, catching his balance. He then smiled menacingly at the agent who had shot him and started to walk toward him raising his arm to fire. The other agents then unloaded a barrage of bullets into his sternum and he fell backward onto the table by the sheer force of the impact. He lay there for several seconds, very still, and all was quiet except for the sound of bits of glass still crackling about the room. I knew he was still wearing the Kevlar vest he had pointed out to me earlier, so I suspected he was either faking it or was knocked unconscious. The other two agents crept forward cautiously, their weapons raised and balanced with both hands, and I could hear the glass fragments crunching with each step beneath their black leather shoes.

Mr. Black lay motionless, spread eagled on his back across the table, the ten millimeter pistol still in his right hand which was dangling over the edge. My limbs and hands were shaking from the grisly scene that I beheld and bared witness to, and though I was terrified I might be discovered, I thought that I should do something to try and save him if he were still alive. I looked around my feet for something, anything I could create a distraction with, and found a large metal spoon that must have been dropped in the mayhem by one of the kitchen staff. I grasped the spoon tightly between my fingers and tossed it out into the room where it resonated with a large clatter. The agents momentarily looked away from Mr. Black and it was in this instant his head rose off the table and he squeezed several shots into men in dark suits in front of him. They fell to the ground almost simultaneously and blood began to coalesce on the bar-room floor from their head wounds.

Mr. Black slowly rose from the table, looked toward my position and repeated again, this time with even greater urgency, "Run, Doctor. Now!"

I was turning to leave when I heard a single shot come from the direction of the front door. I saw Mr. Black look towards me. A bullet had pierced the dead center of his forehead, and a single strand of blood dripped and trickled down his brow and off his nose. The expression on his face, though at first surprise, turned into somewhat of a smile, and he began to chuckle to himself, at first what was nothing more than a snicker, until it grew and grew and finally developed into a full bellied laugh. After a few seconds, he abruptly stopped, as his soul slipped from him, until finally he fell backward on the table once more. This time I knew he wasn't going to get back up.

I made my way, running half-blind through the kitchen, stumbling over trays and pots the staff had dropped in the ensuing confusion. Fortunately, I had closed the place down with Mickey several times and knew where the employee entrance was. I wondered what had happened to Mickey and hoped he was all right and not injured or shot in the melee.

Once out in the back alley, I started to run as fast as my legs could carry me. 'What was it that Mr. Black said to me?' I thought, and then I remembered the white Ford Taurus, across the alley behind the bookstore. I rounded the corner and I saw it parked next to a blue mini-van. I reached into my pocket, desperately, afraid I might have dropped the key in my flight to and from the kitchen, but was reassured when I felt the cool metal pressed against my fingers. I unlocked the door, and was about to sit down, when I saw there was something resembling a large, black ledger or something that resembled an ancient tomb resting on the driver's seat. It's cover bared no markings except a few signs of age; it's pages were turning yellow, and although the front cover was obviously leather, it had the look of something that was somewhat old, though, obviously, lovingly cared for. The binding and leafs of the book were polished, and by the look of it, was recently shined. It had a bright, satin gloss, and although the pages within it were yellow and frayed, the cover, although showing signs of age, seemed to be in exquisite, if not, exceptional condition. I took the book and put it in the passenger's seat so that I could sit down.

There didn't seem to be anyone following me, in fact, there didn't seem to be anyone around at all. Everyone had undoubtedly gone to the street to gawk and find out what happened at Magiano's. I heard sirens beginning to wail and knew the police would be there in moments.

I remembered the super-palm pilot, pulled it out of my coat pocket, plugged in the ear piece and put it on. If Mr. Black or any of the other agents were still alive I would be able to hear what was happening. I put the piece in my ear, desperately tuning it to try and find the frequency of the men who had entered the bar, when I remembered something Mr. Black said. It didn't matter whether they were still alive, the chip still broadcasts even after you're dead, so it would be able to pick up voices within a 2 meter radius. I tuned the device to 1203 millahertz, the number of the agent Mr. Black had shot right there in front of me and listened.

"Nice shooting 509. Are you injured?" a voice said.

"No. I'll check his person," said another voice, judging by the volume a little more distant than the first.

I heard the sounds of what appeared to be someone rummaging, mixed with crackles of what sounded like shoes grinding glass fragments on the bar-room floor, and then several moments of silence.

"Did you find anything?" the first voice asked.

"No"

"Was he with anyone?"

"Before I killed him he spoke to someone. Someone he referred to as 'Doctor.' Any ideas?"

"No. We'll have to check the database."

"Don't worry 509, we'll find him. Whoever he is, we will find him."

My heart froze and sank simultaneously as I again heard the number of the agent who had killed Mr. Black, and I was filled with an unequivocal sense of horror. It was a number Mr. Black had mentioned earlier that afternoon, one I would never forget, and one that had been consigned to my memory since I reached over the table and grabbed Mr. Black by the tie— the number was that of my son.

Epilogue

As to whatever happened to Dr. Gottlieb I do not know. Often times I will see or imagine him taunting me with some clever Shakespearean witticism, or I envision him in the back corner of my mind, torturing some poor psychologist, some *chrisssssstian* in some institution, in some forgotten corner of the country like Dr. Stimple. Actually, I have it on good authority that Dr. Stimple would eventually assume Frank's position as Director of Grove Haven, while Dr. Sikes went on to become chairman of the state board. As for me, you now know what happened. And as for *The Grays*, now you know the smallest inkling of the truth. Who knows what more Mr. Black could have divulged to me if the universe had not played itself out so precisely as it was supposed to.

As for my 'official' analysis of the patient, Dr. Jacob Francis Gottlieb, although I have obviously not filed any formal documents as a psychologist in over twenty years, I would say that my conclusions concerning his character and state of psychosis is this: He *is*, quite clearly and irrevocably, insane. Not because he was born with a condition of schizophrenia, though his life experiences may have, in fact, pre-disposed him to a condition of this sort. It is my opinion, and I believe, that it was we, his society, who failed him. We failed him because of his inability to reveal the truth to us without fear of reprisal, and it was also in our inability to listen and believe that drove him to depths of madness of which he now finds himself a prisoner.

I often wonder why I put pen to paper to tell this horrible tale, despite the insidious forces of the United States government that now pursue me and all others with knowledge of *them*, without conscience, remorse, or empathy. Eventually I came to realize that if I could bring about an enlight-

274

enment concerning *the Grays*, and in doing so, our minuscule existence, that I might stand a chance of surviving. We are so self-important, so fragile, and our lifetimes so finite. What is the purpose or logic in wasting what precious time we have fighting amongst ourselves over trivial ideological and religious differences, especially when we consider the true awesomeness and enormity of time itself, and our short brief flicker within it?

Finally, in my years of silence, I concluded that if I could help answer the question where we possibly came from and to truly define 'what it means to be human', and pardon the cliché, if I were able to salvage one soul from the abyss of ignorance and oblivion, then I would have been successful. One soul can, and has, made a difference. I guess I must have figured my own soul was lost. It has been lost for a very long time and as Fate would have it, I have been given a second chance by the very man whom I thought took my first.

I don't quite know what to make of everything Mr. Black told me concerning 'universal time' and 'the fourth dimension.' I do know the future is inevitable, and if we believe in a past that is written, as Gottlieb found in stone and Mr. Black confirmed, then it follows the future is written as well. For what is the future, really, anyway, but a set of events and variables that we have *not yet* experienced? Perhaps we are not ready, either physically or psychologically, to accept the consequences of this discourse and it is *The Grays* who are guiding us, somehow, through this troubling and difficult stage of enlightenment. I truly hope it is so, but my conscience for some reason tells me otherwise, as the parallels Gottlieb illustrated to the practices of Nazi Germany are all too familiar and eerily real.

I wish I could see what my future holds, but all I see is darkness. How I long and spend hours wondering whether I will, in fact ever again encounter my son. My boy. My beloved David Malcolm; or whether I will in fact truly be able to shape the course of human history and bring humanity out of what I have concluded is *the second dark age* and help us attain cognizance of our true origins. I also wonder whether I will succeed or fail in this quest to reveal the truth I so desperately cling to, and yet also seems forever to elude me.

I wish I could see these things, but I cannot. Unlike *The Grays* and Mr. Black, I do not have the benefits of *the second sight*, and even if I did, have neither the experiences nor mental capacity to interpret it. I can only wait and play my own small part, in someone else's cosmic Shakespearean-like drama, and content myself to allow the universe to unfold as it should. The future hangs in the balance, as they say, and as to what happens, what *has* happened, and what *will* happen, that is another story.

Afterword

When I first began writing *The Gray Conspiracy* I wanted to bring to the forum a discussion concerning aliens that had never been attempted before. I wanted to bring something *real*, something tangible, something that when read would shed credibility on their existence and their repeated interference in ours. It is for this reason I chose what I believed to be key archaeological finds that in and of themselves were not that consequential but when cast in comparison with each other opened a whole new field of expedition.

I also thought it pertinent to ask one's self the questions: 1) Are *the Grays* in fact real, and 2) If they are, what evidence of this could be found, and 3) what professions in the private sector might be privy to this knowledge, that is to say, not in direct control or working for secret services or intelligence's of the United States government?

The answer, I found, was if we accept the first premise, i.e. that the Grays *are* real, than it stands to reason that there *must* be evidence of their activities, which leads to the direct conclusion that there are those among us who have knowledge of this information. So I asked myself which professions in every day society might come across evidence of extra-terrestrial origin.

The answer, I found was two fold: Archaeologists, and Cellular Pathologists. Archaeologists for the simple reason that assuming they are not biodegradable or corrode over time, any implants or devices aliens placed in humans theoretically should still exist, even after thousands of years, and therefore should have the ability to be found. The argument against this of course, is why haven't they? My answer to that is, 'Who is to say they haven't'? Much as we would like our nation's institutions and museums to blatantly

276

advertise this information if they were found I think we all know this to be an unlikely scenario. And more important, who would risk their career and reputation by attempting to do so? This is one of the most prestigious arguments that this novel attempts to make—that our society is so desperate in clinging to the notion that the Grays and extra-terrestrials do *not* exist, we are willing to believe and entertain the most ludicrous of ideas in order to write off the possibility that they do.

The second profession, I decided, that stood a great chance of coming into contact with alien implants was that of Cellular Pathology. For, it is not surgeons themselves who in removing things from the body see these devices. It is those who actually see what's inside and carve up tumors and other lesions and gross formations removed from the human body; it is the job of the lab pathologist. One of the most interesting and chilling things I found in my pursuit of this novel was that there is, in fact, a procedure that nearly all cellular pathologists follow when they find something either in a tumor or other object that is removed from the body that they can't readily identify. It gets sent to the *AFI*, the *Armed Forces Institute of Pathology* at the following address:

> *ATTN: Receiving and Accessions Division (AFIP-RRS)*
> *Room G-071, Building #54*
> *6825 16th Street, N.W*
> *Washington, DC 20306-6000*

Though this was mentioned in this text, *this is not a fiction*, and one is forced to wonder then, if our service professionals in the medicinal industry are blindly turning their eyes and handing over to our government evidence to a possible horror of unprecedented magnitude. It is my sincere hope then that after reading this novel, *someone* will take a chance and step forward with this evidence that I believe exists.

Another thing I thought pertinent to investigate was whether or not any government agency addresses the practice of domestic terrorism against its citizens in matters concerning national security. I was not surprised to find the following on the National Security Agency's frequently asked questions web page at http://www.nsa.gov/:

> *"I've seen NSA/CSS in movies and on TV. Do you assassinate people? Do you secretly perform experiments on us?"*

Their answer:

> *Because we work with highly sensitive information, we are*
> *frequently the subject of speculation—and highly imaginative*
> *and creative fictitious pieces in the media. However, it is*
> *important to distinguish fact from fiction. The fact is that the*
> *Executive Order 12333 (EO 12333) strictly prohibits any*
> *intelligence agency from conducting these unethical activities,*
> *and we strictly abide by that Order.*

What I think we need to ask ourselves is *why* the National Security Agency is even addressing this question, and secondly, would they honestly admit to engaging in such activities? Further, it is important to note that the prohibition of engaging in 'unethical activities' that Executive Order 12333 mentions is a purely a farcical statement, as it may be and no doubt probably is, perfectly ethical to kidnap and murder someone who may have evidence of Extra Terrestrials and as such is a threat to National Security and deemed 'a terrorist'.

The quest for the truth can often be a dangerous and deadly pursuit. In publishing a treatise which stated that the earth rotated around the sun and not vice versa, Copernicus violated Canon rule and quite effectively made himself an outlaw. Truth, is often the enemy of Faith, because of the established social pillars it often serves to undermine. The parallels between 'Canon law' and 'National Security' are one and the same. Our elected officials who are aware of the truth wish to conceal it for many reasons. First, and this is especially true for Republicans, whose political base relies upon constituents of whom many are radical conservative Christians, they fear that the revelation of this truth would undermine their power. Second, they fear the economic upheaval which serves to consolidate their power. Third, they fear the public chaos which would ensue and of their inability to maintain public order.

If we can learn anything from history, it is that public denial can exist for only so long. Like Copernicus with his telescope, with the advent of new inventions and technologies, humanity at some point is going to be able to circumvent efforts by the state to suppress the truth concerning Extra-Terrestrials. Someone, somewhere with a picture phone or the latest gadget is going to change history. Unfortunately, in matters of potential crisis, as was aptly demonstrated with 9/11 and hurricane Katrina, Washington doesn't believe the public can handle the truth. The policy of Washington concerning the release of sensitive information has always been reactive vs. proactive, which in every instance will always serve to make matters worse.

In this *Afterword*, I also wanted to discuss some aspects concerning the text of the novel. All of the discoveries, and in most cases the discoverer's, that the character Dr. Jacob Francis Gottlieb discusses in the text are real with the exception of the chips, the alien implants he supposedly finds amidst the skulls and fossils of our forbears. These are indeed fictions and completely created from the fabric of my mind, however, I believe the possibility of the unearthing of such devices, as I have indicated previously, exists. The rest of the discoveries he discusses, are not. The only fiction among them is Dr. Gottlieb himself and his 'interactions' and discussions with these real scientists and archeologists.

The theories he puts forward concerning the statues of Ain Ghazal and the skulls and peoples of Nasca are that of my own, which I believe as the text demonstrates have some credence and should further be investigated. Further, all the dates concerning the archaeological finds he discusses are to the best of my knowledge, correct, with exception of the statues found at Ain Ghazal. In the text it was necessary to place their discovery before Gottlieb's incarceration by Mr. Black in the early 1960's. The statues were not actually discovered until 1985. With the exception of Dr. Ibin Hammas, Gottlieb's 'former student' who is also a fiction, the people he discusses surrounding the project are real individuals who studied, restored, and worked with the statues, specifically, the senior conservator of the Smithsonian project at the time, Carol Grissom.

Just a minor footnote I personally found interesting while composing this novel and for copyright reasons feel it necessary to point out, the references to the statues themselves and the skulls and dig sites of *Cahuachi*, were literally cut and pasted from the actual excavation notes. There was no fictionalizing these discoveries and their accounts of any kind. What you are reading in Dr. Gottlieb's descriptions are *literally* the text from which this information was taken, in many cases as I previously stated, simply copied, and these texts can be found via links attached in the *Sources* of this book. The only fiction was conforming it to the discussion in the novel.

To further the case so that I do not misrepresent myself, Dr. Gottlieb and all his conversations and interactions with those actual persons who either were alive or are still alive, in all the scenarios that I constructed to aid in furthering this story, are completely fictitious. I would like to think that the events discussed in the story, while they obviously are *not* true, they, in essence *could* be true based on the archaeological evidence, and someone else's experience.

Lastly, I feel it important to reveal one of the most major sources of inspiration for this novel. Although there were many, as I have been carrying the idea for this story around in the back of my mind for over ten years, one of the things that helped aid, concrete, and cement the possibilities and idea for me more than any other was the discussions that Carl Sagan makes in his award winning tribute to humanity's evolution and discovery of itself, *Cosmos*.

Indeed, in many cases in the discussions of Dr. Gottlieb, I borrowed Dr. Sagan's arguments, because they were so compelling. Ann Druyan, who worked with Dr. Sagan on the project, I believe, sums it best, when she states on the new DVD introduction, "Even after twenty of the most eventful years in the history of science, *Cosmos*, requires few revisions, and is indeed rich in prophecy."

Cosmos, for me was truly an inspiration, and it led me to truths most of us dare not dream or imagine in our lifetime, lest they disturb our own self-created illusions and sense of reality. And *that*, I feel, is what this novel *really* is about.

—*J. S. Hunsaker*
June 23, 2004

Sources

Books/Articles

The Riverside Shakespeare, Houghton Mifflin Company, Boston. Copyright 1974. *Richard III, Merchant of Venice, Caesar, King Lear, Hamlet, Macbeth, &* Pages 1249-1254.

Shakespeare: The Invention of the Human, Harold Bloom. Riverhead Books, New York. Copyright 1998. Pages 476-515.

Fire in the Sky: The Walton Experience, Travis Walton. Marlowe & Company, New York. Copyright 1979. Pages 88-96.

Diagnosis Schizophrenia: A Comprehensive Resource, Rachel Miller & Susan E Mason. Columbia University Press, New York. Copyright 2002. Chapters 2, 5, 8.

Beyond Roswell: The Alien Autopsy Film, Area 51, & the U.S. Government Coverup of UFOs, Michael Hesemann & Philip Mantle. Marlowe & Company, New York. Copyright 1997.

Man's Search For Meaning, Viktor E. Frankl. Pocket Books, a division of Simon & Schuster, Inc, New York. Copyright 1959. Part One: Experiences in a Concentration Camp, pages 19-116.

Psychoanalytic Case Formulation, Nancy Mc Williams. Guilford Press, New York. Copyright 1999. Introduction, Chapters 1-3.

Fundamentals of Anatomy & Physiology, fifth edition. Frederic H. Martini, Ph.D. Prentice Hall, New Jersey. Copyright 2001. Chapters 6, 10, 12, 14.

Psychology, second edition. David G. Myers. Worth Publishers, Inc., New York. Copyright 1986. Chapters 10, 15, 16.

Spark Notes: King Lear, Brian Phillips & Stephanie Stallings. Spark Publishing, New York. Copyright 2002.

Gray's Anatomy, Henry Gray F.R.S., Bounty Books, New York. Copyright 1977, Crown Publishers. Pages 639-810.

The Washington Post: Staring Across 9,000 years at the Sackler, Otherwordly Statues from a lost people of Jordan, Paul Richard, Washington Post Staff Writer, July 28, 1996, Page G1.

The Washington Post: Visitors From Another Time, Hank Burchard, Washington Post Staff Writer, August 2, 1996, Page N47.

National Lampoon, May, 1976. *Foreighners Around the World*, by P.J. O'Rourke.

Television/Video

Cosmos, by Carl Sagan, Cosmos Studios, Copyright 2000.

Good Eats, by Alton Brown, History of the Carrot, The Food Channel

The Matrix, Matrix Reloaded, Matrix Revolutions, the Wachowski Brothers. Copyright 1999, 2003, 2004.

The Silence of the Lambs, Directed by Jonathan Demme, based upon the novel by Thomas Harris. Copyright 1991.

Star Trek: The Next Generation, The First Duty, Skin of Evil, Qwho, DejaQ. Copyright 1987-1994.

Star Trek: Deep Space Nine, Duet. Copyright 1996?

K-Pax, Directed by Iain Softley. Copyright 2001.

Interview with the Vampire: The Vampire Chronicles, Directed by Neil Jordan, based on the novel by Anne Rice. Copyright 1994.

THE UFO INCIDENT, Directed by Richard A Colla, 1975 Universal Studios TV-Movie.

UFOs: THEN AND NOW, History Channel Documentary, A & E Television Networks. Copyright 2001.

The Nasca Lines, The Travel Channel Documentary, Written and Directed by Bob Strange. Copyright 2001?

The Terminator, Directed by James Cameron, Copyright 1984.

A Beautiful Mind, Directed by Ron Howard, Copyright 2001. Based on the story of John Nash.

The X-Files, Directed by Chris Carter. Fox TV Network.

Men In Black, Directed by Barry Sonnenfeld. Copyright 1997.

Internet/Web Pages

Schizophrenia and Miscellaneous

http://www.healthyplace.com/Communities/Thought_Disorders/site/
paranoid_schizophrenia.asp#signs

http://www.healthyplace.com/Communities/Thought_Disorders/schizo/
medications/index.asp

http://www.healthyplace.com/Communities/Thought_Disorders/schizo/
medications/side_effects.asp

http://www.ncbi.nlm.nih.gov/entrez/
query.fcgi?cmd=Retrieve&db=PubMed&list_uids=14708108&dopt=Abstract

http://www.ncbi.nlm.nih.gov/entrez/
query.fcgi?cmd=Retrieve&db=pubmed&dopt=Abstract&list_uids=1457389

http://web.ukonline.co.uk/sanelink/SCHIZOPHRENIA.htm

http://strangerbox.topcities.com/killers2.html#schizophrenics

http://faculty.ncwc.edu/toconnor/301/301lect06.htm

http://www.newtimes-slo.com/archives/cov_stories_2000/cov_05042000.html

http://ufocasebook.com/moon.html

http://www.francedirect.net/leseyzies.htm

Ain Ghazal

http://www.goldenageproject.org.uk/43jericho.html

http://www.goldenageproject.org.uk/294jericho.html

http://campus.northpark.edu/history/WebChron/Prehistory/Jericho.html

http://campus.northpark.edu/history/WebChron/World/HumanEv.html

http://www.ju.edu.jo/

http://inic.utexas.edu/menic/ghazal/

http://link.lanic.utexas.edu/menic/ghazal/ChapVI/dsb.html

http://link.lanic.utexas.edu/menic/ghazal/intro/int.html

http://www.ucl.ac.uk/archaeology/frontpage/tubb.htm

http://www.asia.si.edu/jordan/html/discov.htm

http://www.asiatour.com/jordan/e-03amma/ej-amm10.htm

http://t3.preservice.org/T0211549/asia.htm

http://www.relst.uiuc.edu/Courses/106/index.html

http://www.stedwards.edu/bss/aflorek/neo.htm

http://www.ancientanatolia.com/historical/chalcolithic.htm

http://www.ancientanatolia.com/historical/chronology.htm

http://catal.arch.cam.ac.uk/catal/catal.html

http://catal.arch.cam.ac.uk/catal/Archive_rep00/farid00.html

Nasca

http://www.discovery-kids.co.uk/mystery_hunters/episodes16.htm

http://www.bbc.co.uk/science/horizon/1999/nasca_script.shtml

http://www.oneworld.org/ips2/june98/19_10_075.html

http://target.untd.com/
ATAG?Site=WEBHOSTING&Loc=RIGHT&Size=BUTTONTWO&W=
120&H=60&brand=NZ&MPV=F&MNUM=null&p=27&rnd=15107119344308756

http://www.htw-dresden.de/~nazca/gis/nazca.html

http://www.crystalinks.com/nazca.html

http://www.geocities.com/tasosmit2001/geoglyphs.htm

http://www.talecatcher.com/books/events/workshop.html#slides

http://xfacts.com/old/

http://www.marsearthconnection.com/ancientart.html

http://www.ufoarea.com/encounters_hill_astronomy.html

LaVergne, TN USA
24 August 2009
155703LV00001B/48/P